For
Cherry, Jaybird,
Tenacious B, & Honey

Madness Heart Press
2006 Idlewilde Run Dr.
Austin, Texas 78744

Second Edition
ISBN: 978-1-967517-03-9
www.madnessheart.press

PINS

JESSICA MCHUGH

A Madness Heart Press Publication

CHAPTER ONE

There's nothing quite so liberating as tossing a training manual out the window as you speed away from a new job, never to return.

That's the first thought that raced through my mind as the telemarketing documents blanketed the road leading back to Cumberland. The second was the declaration I'd made before storming out of the new employee orientation that afternoon. It was the third, fourth, and fifth too, over and over, spurring my exit like a slow-mo march from an exploding building, but the thought lost fire with each mile in my rear-view. After the red dust of my tantrum had settled, "Fuck it, I'll just work at the strip club," didn't feel like the paragon of practicality it was in the orientation.

But I couldn't abide the idea of making another bullshit sales call or carrying another tray of greasy pizza, which was all the surrounding towns had to offer a college dropout with a proclivity for weed. It felt like a drunk-under-midnight-stars sort of decision, scarier than I preferred, but compelling enough to make me reason with my anxiety instead of giving into it. There wasn't any harm in checking out the club's vibe, was there? I didn't have to stay if I didn't like it, and throwing a g-string out the window was probably just as satisfying as pitching a training manual.

Just over the state line in Ridgeley, West Virginia, the strip club called "Pins" was like none I'd seen before. It was fully nude like most of the others, but it had the added allure of being a bowling alley as well as a strip club. Considering the combo, the club's name made sense, but I wondered how many hillbillies would understand that the word "pins" was British slang for "legs." I supposed it didn't matter to them as long as they got a good look between some splitting pins.

I knew the bowling side didn't negate the sleaze of the stripping side, but the notion that customers could toss a ball down the lane instead of tossing off in a private dance room made me feel safer. A ludicrous thought, but one I fully embraced. The golden justifications of desperate shitheads really were the most intriguing and least appreciated of art forms, and I was feeling artistic as hell.

Scott had called my cell phone twice since I walked out on orientation, like he already knew I'd done something "wrong." I felt his scowl in Cumberland, all the way from Westminster, chillier than any mountain breeze.

What a doll he was. What a ragged haughty doll I could never seem to toss aside, never seem to pack away with the rest of my childish things. Granted, at twenty-one years old, I still regarded myself as a kid. That was one of our biggest issues. Scowlin' Scott figured it was time for me to grow up and accept responsibility. I figured it was time for Scott to get a clue and accept me as I was. Neither of us could win. I'd wanted to ditch his annoying ass for a while, but I could never muster up the courage. Annoying I could handle. Alone was a different story.

Fidelio was already meowing at full volume as I started up the stairs to my apartment. He barreled at me the moment I opened the door, winding around my legs like a serpentine collie herding sheep to his food bowl. A minuscule portion of the bottom was exposed, the rest of the kibble piled around the empty spot. He yowled as he did a little dance of desperation around the kitchen, the kind of annoying that didn't actually annoy me.

"What?" I sang dopily. "What do you *want?"*

His response sounded like something between a mew and the puff of a glaucoma test. I picked him up and kissed each whiskered cheek until I couldn't stand the stench of his breath anymore. Setting him down, I shook his food level, and he pranced over in purring gratitude.

I had three new voicemails and a pretty good idea who they were from. After packing a sticky bud into my pipe, I sparked up and listened to my one-day supervisor from Spherion berate me for wasting his time. The second and third messages were from Scott, wondering why I wasn't answering my phone. Where was I? Was I hiding something? What kind of dumb wasteful selfish reason could I possibly have for ignoring him?

Thank fuck I still had weed. Spicy smoke rolled over my tongue and left a fruity aftertaste that curled my mouth until the voicemails ran out, taking Scott's judgmental tone with them. His words remained, though; calling me lazy, calling me a leech, then telling me to call him back. He wasn't wrong, but I wasn't about to let him know it. I was fortunate my mom had agreed to pay my rent and utilities as long as I stayed in college, and as long as the college didn't inform her that I was no longer attending, I was going to milk it as long as possible. I felt a little guilty, but I would've felt worse if I had to move back home and admit yet another higher education failure. After a few bad semesters at the community college near home, I'd decided Allegany would be a perfect change: close enough to visit and do laundry but far enough to dodge the constant pressure from my ex-beauty queen mother.

Too bad "dodge" didn't mean "destroy."

In front of the mirror, beholding the beauty I'd never be, her vise-like expectations squeezed and prodded every part that couldn't compare with her perfect Pilates body. I patted my bare belly, softly at first, then harder to hear the deep slap I synonymized with F-A-T. I was an average weight for my height, not overly fleshy, but thanks to the near-constant teasing and diet advice from my mom and older sister, Hollie, I rarely saw a pretty girl in my reflection, let alone someone sexy enough to be a stripper. I pulled off my top and slid my jeans to my ankles, popping one knee forward and pouting my lips.

I looked like a constipated duck with rickets.

Crossing my arms over my stomach, I ran my hands up my sides, across my tits, and up into my hair, where they promptly became tangled. I squealed as I pulled them free, and Fidelio bounded in to mimic me with a series of mews. He took the opportunity to nestle into the crotch of my jeans, kneading the denim with eyes closed.

"Sorry, buddy." I shooed him out, pulled up my pants, tossed on my shirt, and gave another look.

Never pretty. Never sexy. Never confident enough in myself to make my mother's dream of having two pageant queen daughters come true. How in the hell was I supposed to get naked and shake my ass for strangers?

Wine.

Wine would help.

One large water glass of pinot grigio later, I pushed myself toward Pins for the first time. I was jittery with excitement, and slightly tipsy, but once I saw the sign exhibiting a tapered neon leg crisscrossed with a glowing bowling pin, my stomach flip-flopped like it was trying to make a getaway. Butterfly wings turned to sticky spider legs trying to walk me in the opposite direction, but I was too desperate and curious to retreat now.

Stepping from the tranquil day into the flashing florescent jungle was a bombardment of mind and body. The thunder of the alley and the lightning of the stage tossed me into the heart of a storm, from the shuddering clouds of which a seraph named Lady Gaga beckoned. Her robotic siren song was personified by a buxom brunette who appeared to have a purple landing strip on her pelvis. It took a hard squint to recognize it as a tattoo, which prompted a chorus of lusty snickers from the customers who saw me peering at the dancer's pussy. Red-faced, I scampered from the stage.

The club side of Pins was glitzier than the alley side, but the alley was festooned in its fair share of retro bling. The decor was less intense than the Rock-n-Bowl of my childhood, but the clientele made up for it with their own brand of redneck intensity. While I waited to ask the club-side bartender if I could speak to the manager, one such creeper sidled up and flashed a shit-eating grin, or so I assumed by the shade of his teeth.

I expected a cheesy, if not disgusting, line to follow. Instead, he croaked, "You might be in for a long wait while he's talking to his girlfriend. I was your age when I sat down."

"Was it time well spent?" I asked.

He chuckled, but the deep crease between his brows suggested he was deeply pondering the answer.

"Can I help you?" The bartender's focus was still glued to a girl with electric blue eyeshadow, shimmying the sparkly fringe on her skirt as she counted a stack of ones.

"I'd like to speak to the manager."

He finally looked at me. Raking his gaze up and down my body, he bounced his eyebrows and glinted an incisor before pointing out a thick, ebony man housing a BLT in the bowling alley.

Multicolored lights bounced off the manager's shiny bald head and rippling muscles, making him look smooth as a marble statue and just as solid. At only five feet tall, his head barely crested the sticky caramel bar when he approached to throw away his trash.

"Hey Cecil, this chick wants you."

The manager's eyes widened, then sweetened, and I shook my head "no" before shaking it "yes."

I could hardly hear my own voice when I said I was looking for a job, so God knows what kind of "job" he thought I came for when he began escorting me to his office. Cecil's handshake felt like he was challenging me to a tug-of-war, and he sped through a twenty-word introduction in two seconds, during which I only heard every other word over Miley Cyrus's latest banger. He walked like Danny Kaye danced, with swift, exaggerated strides and splayed fingers, but I was the bigger spectacle as I struggled to keep up with him. Bowlers fondled their balls as we rushed past the lanes, their faces flushed with the wisdom of knowing what a trip to Cecil's office usually produced.

Fresh meat, pungent with possibility.

The office was tiny, almost stifling. A dim tomb that blocked out nearly all the chaos of the club. As I sat, I surmised that was the appeal. But as accommodating as he seemed during the interview, he didn't seem very happy to be in it. He rushed through questions and answers as if my desire for the job would fade the longer we spent in negotiations.

"What's your name?"

"Eva Finch, but everyone calls me Birdie."

"That gonna be your stage name?"

"Oh, I don't know. Sure, I guess."

"You ever dance before?"

"I took ballet and tap for almost six years."

"Fascinating, but not what I meant. You ever done this kind of dancing?"

"Oh no, nothing like this."

"So why now?"

"I need money."

He laughed more riotously than required. "That's what I like to hear. Someone who wants to work for a living!"

I was suddenly hyperaware that I reeked of weed.

"Can you start tomorrow?"

"Just like that?"

"Just like that."

My voice creaked. "I have a few questions first."

"Go ahead."

I felt ridiculous being so nervous. All day every day, this guy saw snatch—bubblegum-pink and rose-brown, smooth, wrinkled, open flowers and tangled forests, springtime-wet and sickday-warm, innies, outies, a coven of sacred circles and Bermuda Triangles, yawning like stray Sphinxes in the sunshine with answers to the universe's deepest mysteries in their teeth—and I had to steady myself before asking snatch-related questions.

"What's the policy on shaving?"

"Shaving?"

"I heard some places don't allow the dancers to be fully shaved. Like, bald."

"Bald is fine. What else?"

"What about during 'that time of the month?' What do the girls do?"

He twiddled his fingers nervously. "Oh. You'd have to ask them about that sort of lady business."

"How many dancers do you have?"

"Sixteen…I think. An average of twelve girls work Friday and Saturday nights. The rest of the week has about six, depending."

"Depending on what?"

"Whether they show up. Lots of times, it's not. I hope you won't be one of those types."

"Me too."

"Sometimes our dancers double as alley side waitresses. They do pretty well, but it's a tough gig. You done any waitressing?"

I wasn't about to add any more nuggets to that particular dung pile of experience. "Sorry, no. I can still make money only dancing though, right?"

"It depends how hard you work. Aside from what you make on the main stage, there are table dances and private dances to make quick cash, and we open up the side stages on weekends. You have more than enough opportunity to walk out with close to five hundred bucks on a Saturday night."

"Wow. Really?"

"Like I said, it depends on how much effort you put in, but a few of our girls make a very healthy living."

Healthy wasn't the word I would've chosen, but at that point, I couldn't judge. It was only my second time setting foot in a strip club, and this was my first glimpse at the nitty gritty. Except for a few stares that cut down to the uterus, it wasn't very nitty or gritty. I could abide all of that better than I could abide another serving job.

A grin stretched Cecil's face. "Is that it? Are you ready?"

"For what?"

"Your audition."

"Oh. That makes sense. You probably need to make sure I don't have any disfiguring scars or hideous hairy growths."

"Neither of those would be a deal-breaker, but... yes."

He stared, silent.

"Right now? I didn't bring any strippery clothes."

"The ones you have on are fine."

A million thoughts charged through my brain as

I approached the stage for the first time. For one, I couldn't remember the last time I'd shaved my legs. My bikini area was recently shaved, but I was sure I'd missed a patch or two. What if the stage lights magnified the strays, transforming them into coarse black insect hairs that caused the customers to point and shout, "Brundlefly! Brundlefly!" as I struggled to peel my jeans over my pubic spikes and fleshy thighs? I imagined the indentations in my skin looking like tire tracks onstage, a clear sign my clothes were too small for someone of my girth, and unable to force my pants past my sneakers while maintaining my balance, I assumed I'd fall flat on my back, legs splayed and flashing a shriveled tampon string, stained pink from hours of neglect.

In reality, I was a little shaky at first, and I didn't take off my underwear, but everything else went smoothly. No one was sitting at the stage when I started, but by the end of Guns N' Roses' *Used to Love Her*, three wide-eyed gentlemen had moved from the bar to the stage. When the song was over, I picked up my clothes, clamped them against my chest, and started down the stairs.

One of the guys pointed a dirty fingernail at my faded blue panties. "You didn't finish."

"It was just an audition," I said, and beneath the blaring beginning of *Cotton Eye Joe*, I heard him whisper to his friend, "I can't wait for the real thing."

The bartender's girlfriend, an adorable redhead named Heaven, directed me to the dressing room before jumping onstage and slapping her ass to the beat. I didn't understand if she was supposed to be the cowboy or the horse, but it started a stampede of singles regardless.

Upon entering the dressing room, I stuttered a step at the sight of four naked chicks chatting like they were enjoying a casual day at the zoo. I felt like the one on display when they faced me, staring in curious awe like I was a rare species of woman that hadn't evolved to a state of full nudity yet. The room reeked of cigarettes, but beneath the oppressive smell, I detected something sweeter. I could've probably sniffed out both pot and piece within minutes, but my future coworkers were looking at me strangely enough already.

I pulled on my pants and squatted to tie my shoes, but a voice with a decidedly Cumberland flare interrupted me.

"You shouldn't crouch like that. Crouching causes stomach rolls." The emaciated blonde with black roots popped a hip and twiddled her long black acrylics at the couch. "You can sit there."

I wondered which scientific journal taught her that factoid as I moved to the brown floral sofa in the corner, but another girl screamed, "STOP!" before I made contact. As the skinny blonde snickered behind her hand, a lovely young woman glided toward me with every feminine wile cranked to eleven. She wasn't wearing heels but fooled me completely. She walked like a ballerina, crossing one foot over the other with hips swaying and a demure expression that sent a surprising tingle south. She was sublime: slender but curvy, lean but strong. Her breasts were small and perky, topped with light pink nipples that looked like mint-nonpareils.

My face flushed, and my tongue felt like a massive slab of ham. Not many women had affected me like this—Angelina Jolie, for sure, and Halle Berry, and the girl with the opal medusa piercing and a penchant for bralessness at the college cafe—so I didn't have a lot of experience handling it with grace.

"Don't sit on that couch," she said. "A girl got crabs from that couch."

I shrieked as I scooted away, frantically brushing at my clothes despite having made no contact.

"I think you'll survive," she said. "I'm Honey, by the way."

"Birdie," I said, still searching my jeans for bugs as the blonde cackled at me from the corner.

After a quick round of introductions, Honey asked me, "When do you start?"

"Tomorrow."

"Cool. I work tomorrow too."

"Cool. So I'll see you tomorrow?"

She crinkled her nose, possibly in pity. "Uh, yeah." I tried not to stare as she covered herself with lotion. It boosted the vibrance of her tan, making her skin glow and muscles pop. It did little to improve the faded angel tattoo catty-corner to her pussy but still invited the notion that Honey's pie was a little slice of heaven.

Sweet.

Hot.

Honey.

I lowered my voice. "Can I ask you something?"

She laughed, tossing her chestnut tresses. "There are no whispers here, sweetie. No secrets either. After all, where would we hide them?" she said, slapping her naked body all over.

A dwarfish girl named Faith chimed from the corner. "You're forgetting the God-given pocket."

"You're forgetting two, actually," added Ginger, combing her black roots with glitter-encrusted fingers.

"Maybe you are," Faith replied, then coughed, "Ass-freak."

Ginger slapped Faith's butt, leaving a bright red handprint on her sienna skin. I expected a full-out brawl to erupt, but Faith just laughed and chased Ginger across the dressing room, trying to give her a matching red mark.

"What's the question?" Honey asked.

"Oh, the thing is...I have my period."

"Overshare," Ginger hollered.

"Shut up, chowder clam," Honey snapped. She wrapped an arm around me, which would've been a sisterly gesture if I could stop ogling her hills and valleys. "If you're wondering what to do with the string, it's no biggie. You just have to cut it, then tuck it in your God-given pocket."

"The first one!" Faith chirped.

"Yeah, but make sure you tuck it up good, cuz that shit *will* show up in blacklight."

"Holy shit, I didn't even think about that." It made me wonder what else I hadn't considered.

"You got a boyfriend?"

There it was.

"Yeeaaah...I do."

"Is he okay with you dancing?"

"I haven't told him yet."

"Ha!" Ginger trumpeted. "Then you don't know if you still have a boyfriend or not."

"Forget her, Birdie. Do you have any other questions."

"Nah, I should get home. I'll see you tomorrow?"

She rolled her eyes with a chuckle. "Yeah, tomorrow."

I came on too strong. She probably thought I was a total weirdo. A weirdo on her period.

I exited the dressing room stairs in time to witness two splits: one in the bowling alley and one on the stage. The latter was much more interesting. On Honey's heels, the dancer working the pole captivated my eye with ease. Her legs went on for so long that where I had a belly button, she had a leap year. Autumn, winter, and spring passed before my gaze finally summered in her eyes, which she batted at me with her tongue curling sensuously across her lips.

I fanned my flushed face as I headed for the exit.

"Have a good gay," the bouncer said, and I whirled around.

"What was that?"

"Bi-Bi."
"Oh. Thanks."
Tomorrow, I'd skip the pinot grigio.

CHAPTER TWO

Scott never interrogated me right away. He always made sure to fuck me first in case we broke up later. I expected a brawl when I arrived in Westminster that night, and I knew it would be a doozy because he didn't even grumble over me having to remove my tampon. It was even more evident when our usual routine became a fight in itself. Kisses turned to bites, and caresses became gropes that might've left bloody tracks down my back if I hadn't remembered my new line of work before he dug in too deep. A tinge of confusion crossed his face when I pulled away, but I climbed on top and obliterated his suspicion with the arch of my back.

Collapsing on the bed, wet with satisfaction, each slowing breath carried us closer to confrontation. I felt it like a UTI, a subtle burning as he contemplated how he'd start incinerating me at the stake. I didn't give him the chance, though. I rolled out of bed, cupping my snatch as the goo began leaking out, and scooted to the bathroom to pee.

I was wiping when I heard the floor creak outside the door. He was already on his feet, ready for a fight.

"Was your phone dead?"

"I can't hear you, I'm peeing."

"It doesn't sound like you're peeing."

"That's because my lips are stuck together and it's dribbling in a weird direction."

"Eww." He raised his voice. "I was asking about your phone."

I flushed and fixed my hair before opening the door.

"What about my phone?"

"Was it dead when I called earlier?"

"No."

"Yeah, I figured, since it didn't go to voicemail."

I swerved around him to collect my clothes from the bedroom. "So why did you ask?"

"I wanted to see if you'd tell me the truth."

"I have no reason to lie. It wouldn't make any difference anyway. The truth makes you just as mad." I pulled on a tee-shirt and underwear, and removed my stash from my overnight bag. Cross-legged on his bed, I carefully broke up the sticky bud and packed it in my pipe.

"How did the orientation go?"

"Fine," I said, my voice muffled by a hit.

He stared at me, eyes narrowed, then crossed his arms over his chest. "You didn't stay, did you?"

I blasted smoke from my lungs. "Nope."

"Birdie, if you walked out on another good job—"

"*Good* job?"

"Any job is a good job right now."

"That's not true," I said, then added, mumbling, "and I bet you won't think so in a few minutes."

"You could've given it a chance."

"I literally did."

"What, a whole hour?"

"Three. I left at the lunch break."

He tossed a towel at me, and I threw it back.

"It's for the bed. I don't want to sleep in the wet spot again."

"Some guys would kill to have a girl who cums like this. Show some appreciation."

"I'm the one who gave you the orgasm. Maybe you should show *me* some appreciation."

"I think we both know it was picturing Ewan McGregor banging Christian Bale in *Velvet Goldmine* that gave me the orgasm," I said, laying the towel across the splash zone.

"Look, I'm not trying to get on your case, but if you ever want to move in with me, you need a job."

"I have a job."

"Where?"

"Pins. I got hired today, I start tomorrow."

"PINS? The strip club?!"

I waved my finger like a magic wand. "*And* the bowling alley."

"So you're going to be a pin monkey?"

"Not exactly."

He grabbed my bowl, spilling the ashy crown on his sheets. With an indignant fling of his bedroom door, he pointed down the hall. "Get out."

"Come on, Scott."

"I'm serious. Get out."

"It's not a big deal. You don't have to freak out."

"I'm not freaking out. I'm having the same reaction as any other normal person who finds out his girlfriend is a stripper."

"You're blowing this way out of proportion."

"Am I? So you won't be flashing your pussy to a bunch of strangers?"

I shrugged.

"That's what I thought. You can leave now."

"We can talk about this."

"Okay, Birdie. Let's talk," he said, his voice jagged as a steak knife. "How's school?"

I knew this line of questioning wasn't going to end well, so I started searching for my sweatpants.

"What did you learn in sociology today?"

I pulled them on and tightened the drawstring. "Normal stuff."

"Ah yes, normal Sociology stuff. I know all about

that." He reached into the drawer of his bedside table. "I've had plenty of opportunity to learn since you left your textbook here two weeks ago." He tossed it onto the damp towel, and I winced.

"You got me; I'm probably never going to be a sociologist."

"So you're going to be a stripper instead?"

"For a little bit, sure."

"This is insane."

"No, being in this relationship is insane. All you do is judge every decision I make. If it's not my job, it's school. If it's not school, it's weed."

"You do smoke too much weed."

I huffed. "See? I can't win with you."

"You can't win if you stop trying."

"Why do we have to try at all? Why can't we just… be?"

"Spoken like a true stoner." His voice was harsh, but his hand moved softly as he brushed the hair out of my eyes. "You didn't used to be like this."

"I used to be sixteen."

"You used to have so much energy, so much drive. Why the sudden change?"

"It isn't sudden. It only seems that way because you're finally paying attention." I slung my bag over my shoulder. "Anyway, how do you know I'm not those things when you're not around?"

"So it's my fault you're a complete waste of space? Jesus Christ, Birdie, there are other ways to make money!"

"I've tried them. I hate them."

"All people hate their jobs. You're not unique."

It was surprisingly hurtful, and he knew it. When I grabbed my keys, he stood in my way.

"I really thought you were one of the good ones," he whispered.

"We've been dating for almost five years, Scott.

You've never had one of the bad ones. You've never had one of the mediocre ones."

"I have now."

My foot flew of its own accord, and I commended it for doing so when it made contact with his shin.

He howled and rubbed his leg as he rolled onto the bed. "Jesus Christ, Birdie, I don't get it. I still love you like crazy, but it seems like all you want to do is hurt me. You're like a mean little kid."

"I'm twenty-one, Scott. I *am* a kid."

"Twenty-one isn't a kid."

"Maybe to people who know what they want, but I don't know what I want yet."

"Not *me*, obviously."

"I just need to figure some shit out. I'd like to do that with you, but if you can't handle my new job, I don't know how to make you feel better."

He shrugged. "You can get out of my house."

"No problem." I dashed around the room, picking up socks and underwear and other random garments I shouldn't have left there in the first place, stuffing them into my purse. "I'm sorry it had to end this way."

"Me too, Birdie. Because you know what?" He drew so close I could smell my pussy on his breath. "If you work at that club, you're going to regret it."

"It's my body, Scott. I should be able to do whatever I want with it."

"You certainly can now."

"Yes, I can."

I swiped the wet towel from the bed and launched it at his face. "Sorry about the blood."

It marked the third time we'd broken up that year, and it was only April. Did I think we'd get back together? It was possible, but I sure as hell wasn't going to be the one to apologize first. He'd taken the step I'd been too afraid to take. Whether I was afraid of loneliness or freedom, I didn't know, but when I slammed his front door, I heard a big brass band playing my liberation tune. "Fuck Him" was the song that flooded my Tercel, composed and performed by Eva "Birdie" Finch, second soprano. The lyrics were amateurish and the melody inconsistent, but the message was universal.

"Fuck him, fuck him, fuck him hard. Fuck the pickup trucks in his front yard. Fuck his dumb bachelors degree and fuck how awesomely he fucked me. Fuck his face, fuck his place. Fuck his dick, ass, and shins. Fuck his balls. Fuck it alls. Here's to motherfucking Pins."

A two-hour drive, five bong hits, and one extended Fidelio snuggle session later, I was exactly where I wanted to be. I fell asleep during a *Project Runway* marathon and had wild dreams about trying to seduce Tim Gunn. He was having none of it, but he did teach me that mermaid silhouettes were not for me. It wasn't surprising, but the fact that he was a secret vampire was a shock. Sometime after he bit me, while calling me matronly via telepathy, a whirlwind of fear and anger swept away the fashion and sucked me into a place of choking darkness. It knocked me back and forth and up and down so that ten hours of sleep felt like two. I didn't remember any details, but I awoke with a gasp that turned Fidelio into a puffball. I scritched his whiskers, and with a squeaky yawn that propelled a gust of fishy breath in my face, his fluff deflated. I groaned as I stretched my back and flopped over onto my stomach, but Fidelio wouldn't be ignored. He walked up my back and plopped his fifteen-pound body across my shoulders.

"Okay, I get it. Big ups." I tipped him off my back and grudgingly crawled out of bed.

I dawdled in the shower and took way too long styling my hair, and by the time I felt sufficiently shaved and moisturized in all the right places, I realized I was due at work in less than three hours, and I had no clothes that could pass for stripperwear, except maybe the little black dress I wore to my grandfather's funeral. But I had barely any money either, so I made my way to Gabriel's, a discount department store that sold irregulars and lightly damaged designer apparel.

Panic and desperation took the wheel. I flew through the store, grabbing anything with sequins and tassels. Pleather and animal prints spilled out of my cart as I ran in and out of the dressing room to refresh the eight-item maximum. Nothing fit quite right, and I wouldn't be caught dead in any of my acquisitions in public, but I kept reminding myself I wouldn't be wearing them long enough to be caught dead *or* alive.

I arrived home with fifty-five minutes to spare, too many of which I spent staring at myself in panic. Swathed in fringed pleather and tarnished sequins, I looked like a discount cowgirl at her first rave.

To be fair, it wasn't far off.

I did a few spins and awkward body rolls in front of the mirror and instantly wanted to trash the whole idea. I assumed a couple of hits would help my confidence, and if not, they'd make the room too smoky for me to see my shittiness.

Too bad my bag was empty. A bit of kief remained in the corner, but it would go up in smoke before I had the chance to inhale. And I'd recently scraped my bowl, leaving me little resin left to burn.

Fidelio crawled onto my lap and mewed as he pawed at the empty bag.

"I can't play now, babe."

He nipped at the bag until I lifted it out of his reach. Then he attacked my newly exposed necklace instead. I tucked it under my shirt and grabbed his nearest toy, Catnip Carl. With a squeeze that crackled the ancient catnip hidden in his belly, the memory of my last dry spell returned. Without a dime to spend on weed, I'd researched legal highs online and stumbled upon catnip as a potential alternative. I'd found half an old joint in my drawer before I got around to testing catnip for myself, but I didn't anticipate the same luck happening twice. As I squished the mouse, Fidelio looked at me with eager eyes. His head bounced on his brawny shoulders as he followed Carl's every tilt and dip.

His expression screamed: "Throw the goddamn toy!"

I would, but Catnip Carl needed surgery first.

Along with smoking an ounce of weed in less than eight hours, catnip extraction turned out to be a natural talent of mine. Smoking said catnip didn't work, of course, but it also served as a burning reminder of my desperation, which was a fun little bonus. Luckily, the kief helped more than I'd thought, and after tearing out Catnip Carl's eye, Fidelio was in heaven. He was on his back when I left, purring and pawing at…nothing, which was exactly what I felt like, heading out to my new sexy job.

CHAPTER THREE

As soon as I entered the club, a burly bouncer with a stiffly gelled crewcut grabbed my wrist. "Hi. Stu. Come with me." The club became a cacophonous neon blur accented with faces that might've been just as distorted at a normal pace.

"Ginger didn't show. There hasn't been a girl on stage since five."

"I'm the only one here?"

"So far."

"What about Honey?"

"Late. They're all late." At the dressing room, he glanced at his watch, then sneered at me. "I guess you aren't any different."

"By a minute maybe."

He shook his head as he towed me up the stairs. "Excuses. Always excuses." Shoving me inside, he said, "Hurry up," and slammed the door.

Hurrying was the last thing I could do. For the next couple minutes, my eyes were the only moving objects in the room. They slid over the Crab Couch, the rusted racks of tacky gowns, the open suitcases with shiny boots hanging over the sides, makeup-stained Caboodles, and the most terrifying: panel after mirrored panel of myself. I shrank from my reflections, which were somehow taller than me, buffer too. They were also prettier, so of course they knew better when they spoke in chorus: "Oh Birdie, you are so fucked."

"Birdie, come on!" I barely saw Cecil's mahogany melon dip into the room, but his staccato voice stayed, echoing me into agitation when the door shut again.

I ripped off my clothes and stood naked before the army of me's. My hair and makeup were as good as they'd get. My biggest concern was my tampon. Honey's instructions seemed straightforward enough, but once I was squatted with scissors in hand, I couldn't help but imagine every horrible scenario associated with putting scissors that close to my vulva. I tried pinning my lips open, but they were too dry to stick. Holding the tampon string taut, I lifted the scissors. My hand trembled as I closed the distance between blades and string, my thoughts unable to shake the image of a sloppy snip begetting a fount of blood spewing from my massacred labia, cascading off my palm and flooding the dressing room.

With a crisp slice, the string slackened in my fingers. And since I remained drier than my mom's microwave meatloaf, I assumed I hadn't accidentally snipped my lips. With a sigh of relief, I tucked up the string, whispered a prayer to find it, and faced the nest of Birdies again.

I inspected my body from tits to taint, checking to see if anything was out of sorts. There were a few spiky hairs along my bikini line, hopefully not enough to incite chants of "Brundlefly." After triple checking my tampon string, I was prepared, though not ready, to go onstage.

I was the very model of a redneck hooker. Several customers hooted when I clomped out of the dressing room in my chunky black sandals. I stood for a moment in silence, fidgeting with my stone-washed skirt until Stu ran up to the stage and informed me that the DJ wouldn't arrive until 8. In other words, the music wouldn't play until I played it. With all of the strobing neon, I hadn't even noticed the jukebox beside the stage.

On the other side of Pins, an exuberant bowler got a Turkey that drew several patrons' attention. I was glad for the distraction, considering the state of the jukebox catalog. When I saw a song by Florence and the Machine, I was instantly tempted to select it, but I wasn't certain if the clientele would appreciate it. I wanted the customers to think I was cool, and since I assumed our definitions of "cool" varied a bit, I decided to play it safe. For my first song, I chose Def Leppard's "Pour Some Sugar on Me." Classic, raucous, a perfect song for panty-dropping. For the second, my finger hovered over two versions of "Light my Fire" with no discernible difference, so I made a random choice and clomped back to the stage.

A few men were seated along the edge, but I was too nervous to see them as anything but one middle-aged balding blur. As the music started and I began my spinning sashay along the mirrored wall, I couldn't bring myself to look at them. I could hardly bear to look at myself. My fake smile trembled the entire time, and it felt like every wild rotation would fling me off the stage. It had been a while since I'd done any real dancing, and my nerves didn't help, causing me to move spastically, repeatedly slamming my knees and spine against the floor, spreading my legs wider than I ever had for Scott. I did every sexy move I could think of, most of which I assumed looked comically unsexy from someone gyrating like an uneven lump of clay on a potter's wheel.

Then something magical happened. I didn't recognize myself in the mirror. I just saw a girl, a woman, a fucking beauty queen taking flight in the whirling light. Like a dancing flame, I spun and twisted and reached out only to shy away. Sweat poured down my body like boiling oil by the time "Light my Fire" started, and my tortured knees slid across the floor as I crawled to the pole. I'd avoided it like the Crab Couch until then, but I dared myself to do a mini twirl, which might've looked hot if my clammy palms hadn't immediately slipped off the pole. I stumbled a bit and caught the communal chuckle from the audience, but adrenaline-laced terror nudged up my zeal. I clicked my heels together like Dorothy Gale and discovered I had the power to make my ass clap all along. I bent over in front of a customer with my thighs spread wide, and hanging my head between them, I opened my eyes. Courage shone brilliantly in my grin, but the customer's face quickly chased my verve away. The beard, the receding hair line, even the blue polo shirt: the man sitting between my legs looked just like my dad. It had been more than a few years since I'd seen my father, but the guy could've been his stunt double. And there I was: bent over, staring into his eyes, stroking my pussy.

I felt like I was either going to puke or shit, and neither would've been profitable.

At least, I hoped not.

Blood rushed from my head as I flipped it right side up, and I dizzily pulled out my garter for his contribution. He slid a bill up my thigh and I snapped the garter. Five bucks. He must have liked me. *Daddy's Little Girl.*

Once I'd collected money from everyone at the stage, I didn't know what else to do. I was exhausted, my knees and hips screamed with every twist and bend, but the song kept on going. Four minutes, five minutes, six. Apparently, I'd chosen the extended version. By the time it faded out in minute seven, I was panting through the pain and slick from head to toe. My hair had degraded from a high ponytail of romantic curls into a wet rat's nest of frizz. But I whipped it one more time, collected my clothes, and trotted backstage.

I collapsed limp into a chair, dropping my clothes on the floor. There was no way I was pulling them over my sticky flesh anyway. My mascara was running and my foundation had melted into patches across my chin and cheeks, but at that moment, I couldn't have cared less.

Cecil stabbed his head into the room. "What are you doing, Birdie? Get back on stage!"

"I was just on stage," I wheezed.

"None of the other girls are here yet. You gotta cover till they get here."

I stared at him in disbelief. "You've got to be fuckin' kidding me."

"I can't have an empty stage."

The door slammed, and I rocked off the chair, marveling at my sweaty ass-print before cleaning the seat with a wet wipe. I stood in front of the fan, rotating until I felt dry enough to put on my clothes so I could take them off again.

I dallied at the jukebox, causing Cecil's fingers to rap against the bar in increasing frustration until I made my selection. I walked to the stage as gracefully as possible, but all vestiges of Dorothy Gale had melted away, and the Tin-Man had taken her place. I clunked back to the stage drenched in grease that would never lubricate my joints, terrified about how I was going to bust out another six minutes of dancing when I felt like curling up in the walk-in freezer at one of my former restaurant jobs.

Then it happened again. The magic. Once the music began and my cheap-ass heels hit that stage, I felt in all ways sublime. I kicked up my legs to "Santeria" and spun elegantly to "Rocketman," and once I beheld the men's bleary eyes gone glazy, I barely felt the pain anymore. During Tori Amos's "Leather," I pinched my nipples and smirked coyly as I stood naked before them, asking if they wanted more than my sex. From the reactions, the stage was a draw: half the men wanted my sex and only my sex. It didn't offend me as much as it would've if I were anywhere else. Something about knowing I looked like trash and they desired me anyway, and they would continue giving me money for as long as I demanded it, made me shine with power I'd never felt before. But even though I was a glittering goddess making decent money as the only girl, I was tired and hungry and really had to pee.

When Honey finally arrived, I didn't know whether to hug her or punch her. Then she flashed me a sonnet of a smile, and I forgot why I was mad. Ginger showed up next, giving me a sour grin as she marched past the stage, followed soon after by two more girls I hadn't met. When the set was through, I went backstage to demand answers from the truants, but all that came out was a timid, "You guys were late."

"Sorry," Honey said. "It's tradition."

"What is?"

"Torturing the new girl," Ginger replied. "C'mere, wouldya?"

I pulled on a dress and stood where she instructed. Then, she sat down and planted her leg in my hands. Her thigh-high stiletto nearly nailed me in the face when she shoved her foot at me.

"Lace them tight, willya?"

"You want me to lace your boots?"

"Uh, yeah," she replied so matter-of-factly, I was surprised she didn't follow it with "Duh."

Ginger's laces had to be fed through more than twenty holes, and as I started, I found the threading far more difficult than it looked. The patent leather was slick and rigid and the holes were almost too small for the thick laces. As I worked, Ginger traced her eyes with thick, black liner, increasing her trashiness with each forceful swipe.

Whispers drew my attention. I looked over my shoulder to see the other girls clustered, looking at me sadly. Honey was even shaking her head in...what? Disgust? Disappointment? Whatever it was, it made me feel worse than if I'd refused Ginger's order. I continued to lace, but I became mindful of when the pencil was against Ginger's eyelid, especially as I neared the top of her boot. I looped the last laces together, and as she put the finishing touches on her right eye, I tugged them violently, jerking her foot forward and causing the eyeliner to jump from lid to brow and up into her hairline.

She shrieked. "Look what you did!" Trying to rub it away only made it worse, and she grabbed a pack of makeup wipes.

"Clumsy me," I trilled. "Maybe boot-work just isn't my forte."

"Oh, so you think you're smart or sumthin'?'"

"Only comparatively."

Ginger continued to growl at me, cleaning her forehead as I headed out the door. But Honey grabbed my hand.

"Nice work," she said, and I thanked her, aglow as I descended the stairs.

The compliment made me consider what I'd actually done. I'd never had balls like that before, unless I was supremely drunk. I'd always been a bit of a doormat, but I stood up to Ginger just like I stood up to Scott, just like I'd stood up on stage and stripped off my clothes in front of strangers.

Maybe Pins was a step in the right direction after all.

"Where's the bathroom?" I asked a rail of a dancer named CJ, who pointed me at the door marked "Ladies."

"Isn't that for customers?"

"It's ours too."

That didn't make sense. What if a customer was in there when I farted, or God forbid, had to take an unexpected shit? Whoever was in the stall next to me would be able to recognize me by my shoes. The next time I took the stage, the person present at my defecation could point me out to her friends. She could describe the sounds and smells of my ass while I shook it around the stage. If anything, you'd want to think the girl spreading her cheeks in your face didn't shit at all.

Luckily, there was no one in the bathroom…that time. When I returned to the dressing room, Honey handed me a pack of baby wipes. I pulled one out and started wiping off my hands.

"It's for your vag. You don't want any pussy pearls showing up on stage."

"I'm sorry, pussy pearls?"

"The toilet paper pieces you get from wiping. The last thing you want is to get out there and see a piece of toilet paper glowing in your snatch. Blacklight is a hasty girl's worst enemy."

I felt strange about wiping myself in front of other girls until Honey bent over in front of the mirror and started scrutinizing her own undercarriage. Joining the chorus line of girls with their backs to the mirror, they checked each crevice, every fold, every TP-trap in every wrinkle of their assholes.

When Honey's inspection was done, she said, "So… your first set. How do you feel?"

"Like I got beat half to death."

She shrugged. "That's why they call it a club." She suddenly chirped and fetched a little glass pipe and a prescription bottle that smelled like blueberries. "Want a hit?"

My heart fluttered. "Is this a trick question?"

Her brow furrowed. "I don't think so."

"Then yeah totally," I said, a nerd too desperate for the cool kid's approval. "I guess you don't care if you get caught smoking in here?"

"All I care about is peace, love, and ear."

"Huh?"

"Peace…love…and…"

She took a hit. With the smoke trapped in her lungs,

she handed me the pipe and said "here," but it sounded like "ear."

I liked Honey, and as more girls joined our smoke circle, I realized that most of the dancers were pretty cool. They were all unique individuals who shared a common trait: they wanted money, whether for the essentials, for school, or for fun. As the rest of the Saturday night lineup filed in, Honey introduced me to each dancer. I assumed it would take time to learn their intricate quirks, but a lot of their personalities shone right on the surface. They had to. Personality was the nature of the business. Having nice titties was great, but it was the shimmy that got the green, and every Pins girl shimmied in her own way.

One of the easiest girls to know was Heaven. A cute chick with zero shame, she flashed her deepest desires as she danced, along with her tattooed snatch and rampant bisexuality, usually while staring at her bartender boyfriend, who had a thing for tattooed snatch and rampant bisexuality.

"She's a great girl to do doubles with," Honey said as we watched Heaven hump the pole. "She's a fan of lesbian shit, so if you're willing to play along, you're in for a huge payday. Good luck to anyone who wants a drink though."

I didn't understand what Honey meant until I saw Heaven's sapphic set in action. She and Ebony worked the stage like foreplay: fondling, pinching, and even lightly kissing each other as they crossed paths. But if Jason was bartending, it was impossible to get a drink during her doubles; all he saw was the shining gates of Heaven opening just for him.

"They're a cute couple and all, but I feel like she thinks someone's gonna steal him away if she's not always showing off their relationship. She needs a have a little faith," Honey said. As an impish girl in a sparkly bikini came backstage, she whispered, "Speaking of which…"

Faith was a butter-face. Actually, she was a bit of a butter body, depending on your type. Four feet of stacked muscle unevenly stained in fake tan, she looked like a bodybuilder that shrank in a hot wash with an orange sock. She was also the laziest dancer in the group. She clearly had the energy and drive to maintain her muscular physique, and she could probably climb the damn pole like a spider monkey, but she barely touched it. In fact, she had one move: a hands-over-the-head hip swish followed by the same wiggle from behind. But she had regulars and made enough money that she didn't feel the need to bump up her showmanship, so I respected her for that. Faith also had a unique way of speaking. Several years before, her husband had fallen out of love with his stripper wife and fell in love with a Professor of Philosophy at Frostburg State University. Since then, Faith tried to be the philosophical sort while still being the stripping sort. Every so often, her particular brand of wisdom slid out and made shallow people think, "Damn that chick is deep." That's what she hoped for anyway. I was giving a table dance to a newlywed when I heard one of her gems for the first time, as she propositioned some nearby clientele.

"That's not much of a stage," the customer said, and Faith's giggle flexed dozens of previously hidden muscles.

"One woman's stage is another woman's factory floor," she said. "Here at Pins we manufacture only the finest wet dreams."

Maybe it wasn't enough to earn a philosophy degree or win back her husband, but it was enough to make her one of the good ones.

Unlike Ginger. Ginger was a straight-up bitch and it didn't take long to deduce why. At twenty-eight, she was the second oldest dancer at Pins. The oldest was a middle-aged piece of tanned leather named Cookie. She had fake hair, fake tits, and a smile she was trying to manipulate with huge chrome braces. Cookie was also a thief, so being lumped in with her didn't put Ginger in the best of moods. And that was before listing off her other mood-ruiners. She had a five-year-old sugar-addicted son, a convict ex-husband, and she still lived with her parents in a rundown house barely clinging to a hill in Cumberland. She hauled her own personal cloud of cigarette smoke wherever she went, which was quite a triumph in a club as smoky as Pins. Ginger was as dumb as a bag of white trash, but looking the part somehow made her feel chic. It didn't matter if her black roots reached her ears or her heavy eyeliner was smudged halfway down her cheeks. As long as she was a skinny blonde in makeup, she was classy shit. Sometimes she was okay to be around, but no one knew when she was about to flip the bitch switch. It was safer to have a doubles partner selected before arriving at work, so you didn't accidentally end up onstage with her. She was a good dancer and she brought men to the stage, but she also had no doubles courtesy. If she was on the far end of the stage and saw a guy flashing higher than a five, she'd zero in on him whether her partner was spread eagle in front of the cash or not. She wanted that money. She "deserved" that money.

"What is she using it for?" I asked. "Not to keep up her dye job, that's for sure."

"The kid, probably," Honey said. "Daycare fees. Her ex forgets to pick up their kid from daycare all the time and Ginger gets stuck with the fees. It's no excuse for being a dick to us though."

I smirked. "You should probably just kick her ass."

"I probably could." She shrugged slyly. "But we wouldn't want an old hag like her breaking a hip. Speaking of which, pass the Tiger Balm. My back is killing me."

I would've paid top dollar to see a Honey versus Ginger cage match. Both were thin but strong, and both seemed to have an inherent catfight instinct, as did many of the others. While I avoided confrontation, they thrived on it.

Luckily, I had Jade as a subdued partner in crime. Starting at Pins only a few days after me, she was a dancer in Baltimore before moving to Frostburg. I thought she'd get the new girl treatment too, but as a seasoned dancer she knew the game and refused to play right off the bat. She enjoyed other games though. Her favorite consisted of slapping the other girls' asses as hard as she could so they'd have to go onstage with a bright red, sometimes purple, hand print on their moneymakers. It did nothing to impede tips; if anything, it suggested certain sexy backstage antics that lubricated the wallet. But that didn't make her slaps sting any less. It was a dirty quirk for someone who looked so stylish. Jade had cropped black hair with bangs that always fell perfectly. The hairstyle made her look like a model, but her gangly arms and legs made her look like she'd rather be climbing trees. Her smile reminded me of the kids I'd been young with: friends that favored nature's jungle gyms to manmade ones. It was a smile I could picture with a few temporary holes caused by reckless bike rides and bold leaps from swing sets. But she didn't only enjoy leaps; she enjoyed running. She would sometimes disappear for weeks at a time. She attributed it to never wanting to settle into a routine, but I had a feeling she enjoyed making people wonder where she was. We bonded over our mutual love of weed and classic movies, and it wasn't long before she was hanging out at my apartment on our days off. It was extremely beneficial as she also sold weed. It was during one of her drop off / hangouts that I discovered how much she enjoyed being naked. Anywhere.

While I grabbed drinks from the kitchen, she hollered from the living room, asking if she could take off her shirt. Thinking she meant her top layer, wondering why she felt the need to ask, I said it was fine. When I walked out of the kitchen, Jade was sitting on the couch watching *Barefoot in the Park* bare-chested in my living room. I saw her nude three nights a week for six to eight hours at a time, but seeing her tits in my apartment shocked the hell out of me. She probably thought I was the strange one for not following suit, but if so, she didn't show it. Jade was cool like that: a go-with-the-flow chick who'd rather smoke a joint than deal with dancer drama, of which there was plenty.

The most current war was between Honey and Ebony who'd done doubles together since Honey's first day at Pins. A fight ended their two-year partnership after Ebony hit on Honey's new boyfriend, James, while high on ecstasy. The thing was, Ebony was usually rolling at work, and extremely flirty while doing so, so it must've been pretty bad to end their partnership. Along with her happy hardcore habit, she was also the owner of the most gorgeous skin I'd ever seen. A supple onyx color with a glistening terra-cotta sheen, her immaculate body made cheap gold-plated jewelry from Gabriel's look like Bulgari. Something about the way she glistened, the way she twisted, the way her pupils never constricted, the way she ran her neon pink nails over her body during the techno remix of "Build Me Up, Buttercup" made me want to lick the girl from toes to tits. And if she was on the upside of a roll, she probably wouldn't have minded.

But Honey would've. After taking me under her wing, she resented when I said more than a few words to Ebony.

"Are you sure she wasn't just being her overly-friendly faced-as-fuck self?" I asked over a bowl of cookie dough one night.

"You weren't there, Birdie. She's been after him for as long as I have. She couldn't accept that James chose me over her. Even after I told her James and I were dating, she kept grinding on him during table dances."

"Wait a minute. Your boyfriend was a *customer*? Isn't that a little..." I wanted to soften it, but I couldn't think of a gentler word. "...gross?"

"Talk to me in a few months. Situationships happen more often than you'd think around here."

"I don't think you'd be so pissed at Ebony if you considered it a situationship."

She blushed and took a sizable lick of the spoon.

She was right about dancers and customers though. A quick survey of the other girls concluded that 60% had fraternized with a customer outside of the club, and a whopping 20% of those had ended up charging for their time. One of the chicks who didn't fall into either percentage had the distinction of being one of two eighteen-year-old college girls at the club. They were the absolute antithesis of each other.

First was Diamond, who had the face of an angel and the biggest pair of natural knockers I'd ever seen. They were as perky as they could be for their heft and I often found myself ogling them, mystified by the wacky biology that pasted such monsters onto an otherwise petite frame. She was also American as apple pie, the kind of wholesome and hardworking that all Appalachian daddies hoped their daughters would be. And seeing as she did her job with the same gusto and professionalism as any other, the fact that she was spreading her cunt and asshole for drunkards didn't bother her in the slightest. Which was the kind of wholesome and hardworking that all Appalachian daughters were.

The other eighteen-year-old was a girl named Destiny who could've passed as Diamond's twin if twins included the placenta. She usually worked the alley side, but Cecil conscripted her for the club side when dancers were lacking. She was a chunky girl, but it had no bearing on her likeability. The prickly attitude did that. The smell too, like clam chowder topped with corn chips and chaw, was strongest when she was angry, yet seemingly emitted from the greasy tangled forest between her pimpled thighs. While every other girl was determined to be neatly groomed, Destiny left her body up to fate, and fate had a hairy sense of humor. But every dog had its day, and every near-sighted, tobacco-encrusted trucker needed someone to adore, even if for a night.

I knew extremely little about one of Pins' coolest dancers. In fact, what the girls knew collectively about the woman, who called herself Pantera, might've filled one page in the book of her life. A lean, heavy-metal chick who fully embodied her stage name, she had so dry-ratted and bleach-stripped her blonde hair it tended to look gray under the lights. She served it, though, and wouldn't have given a shit someone told her otherwise. She had kitchen tattoos and body modifications literally out the twat. More of a performer than a dancer, she had no qualms about leaving the stage if someone pissed her off, which she did nearly as often as she flashed her metallic poontang. With two studs glittering in her clitoral hood and four rings to rule each labium, she once mentioned she pierced her pussy as a deterrent. A suggestion of vagina-dentata, so to speak. But as it turned out, a lot of Pins customers had a thing for metallic poontang. As the resident "bad girl," she had a sizable following of young punks, and middle-aged men secretly into nut-crushing. She was more easygoing offstage, but you wouldn't want to cross her wherever she was. She once kicked Cookie in the stomach for stealing her favorite heels, and while I wouldn't say Cookie didn't deserve payback, it was a pretty scary scene to witness. The kick knocked Cookie off the lineup for nearly two weeks and earned Pantera a week suspension. But when she returned to the stage, her fans were waiting with wallets open for the iron maiden of mystery. She came in, rocked the house, collected her cash, and left. And she did it all with an unexpected grace I admired.

In some small way, I admired them all, but before the first night was over, I felt like I knew Honey the best. She eventually confessed she showed me so much attention partly to make Ebony jealous.

"Partly? What was the other reason?"

She didn't give me a definitive answer. Instead, a dimple appeared in her right cheek, followed by a toothy smile, like a secret treasure I'd uncovered by accident. The dimple disappeared quickly, but it made me strive to bring out that smile as much as possible.

CHAPTER FOUR

After cashing Honey's bowl, the rest of my body matched my rubbery legs. I would've been content to stay in that spot for the rest of my first night, watching glitzy dancers pass me in sweaty smears as I dissolved into the floor, but my new boss had other plans. His voice alone propelled the door open, and Honey tucked the bowl behind her leg.

"Empty stage, empty floor." Cecil's noggin popped around the doorframe like someone was waving it around on a stick. It bobbled and swooped—I was also incredibly high—until the puppeteer jabbed at me with a bark. "Let's go!"

I jumped to my feet, and Ginger snickered. But the stick shoved the Cecil head at her next.

"You girls could learn a thing or two from Birdie here. She made all of the money you shoulda been making. I even heard Petey say she's his new favorite. He was one of your regulars, wasn't he, Ginger?"

She snorted. "She can have him. That guy's a freak anyway."

Cecil's shoulders finally appeared when he shrugged, which was comforting in regard to knowing my boss hadn't turned into a lollipop, but discomforting in regards to my state of inebriation.

"Still...easy money, guaranteed money, every single night...that must've been nice. Oh well. Enjoy the freak,

Birdie."

He closed the door, and Ginger shot me a dagger glare before storming out.

"Don't worry about her," Honey said. "Have you been to the alley side yet?"

"I haven't really been anywhere yet."

"Then allow me to give you the grand tour."

She waved her arm elegantly, allowing me to precede her down the stairs. But when the customers lit up with excitement, I knew I wasn't the one inspiring it.

Honey was clearly the house favorite. Even when the money was good, dancers often embellished how much they made, but Honey downplayed her profits. She was a fantastic dancer, full of energy, full of passion, and she worked hard when she wanted to, but most of the time, she was just being Honey. It was instinctual for her; she came into womanhood knowing how to walk, talk, and dance her way into fistfuls of cash without breaking a sweat. But she enjoyed it more when she did. And luckily for me, she was in the market for a new doubles partner.

We toured the club side first. Flanking the main stage were smaller, elevated side stages. On Friday and Saturday nights, there would be two girls on the main stage and one girl on each of the two side stages. It was a good way to squeeze some bills out of customers who were too shy to go to the main stage. But as the side stages were no more than 8 by 8 cubes with clusters of lights, no one except Honey made much money there— unless Destiny had driven a large group of customers in that direction. Passing them, we rounded the DJ booth, and landed at a bank of Megatouch machines.

"If you're going to play the Megatouch, play the Photo Hunt with pictures of naked chicks. You're more likely to get drinks that way," she said.

"I don't know if I should drink and dance. I can go overboard pretty quickly."

"Drink them or don't, but you do want guys to buy them. You get a dollar for each alcoholic drink someone buys you."

I twiddled my fingers with a facetious giggle. "Ooh...a dollar."

She scrunched her nose at me, then leaned against the bar with a sigh. "Man, I could really use a drink."

A cluster of customers immediately snapped to life and signaled for the bartender, who poured every drink and collected payment before offering them to Honey. After choosing one Vodka and Red Bull, she said "thank you anyway," to the other kind strangers, then collected five dollars from the bartender.

Tucking it in her garter, she shimmied at a group of boys that hooted at her as we crossed into the alley. "You probably won't find yourself over here too much, but it's good to know the layout. If it's busier over here than in the club, you might wanna come fishing for people to sit at the stage. You can also do table dances and try to sell private dances."

"Table dance, private dance. Which one is a lap dance?"

Honey laughed like I was an idiot, then suddenly became pensive. She tapped her chin. "Well, a table dance can turn into a lap dance, and a lap dance is typically expected during a private dance, but it's not required to touch their laps at all. And sometimes the private dance rooms have little tables in them..." She sipped her drink and licked her lips. "How's this: lap dances are the ones that make the most money. A little..." She shook her ass. "...on the lap, a little..." She swiveled her hips. "...on the leg, and you can double your table dance tips."

The thought made me sick to my stomach. Then again, money bought weed. And weed always took away my nausea. But when I remembered the first "father-daughter" dance of my life that night, my brain fell back into sickness. As if able to see my green face under the swirling neon lights, Honey handed me a cup of water.

"Stay hydrated," she said. "You're going to sweat a lot here."

I gulped the water and sighed loudly. Again, she laughed, but I detected no condescension that time.

"Private dance rooms are in the middle," she said, pointing at a sparkly purple door between the club and the alley. "It's fifty bucks for a two-song private dance, and you get twenty of that. Not too bad. I've gotten better and I've gotten worse."

"How many clubs have you worked in?"

"If you count auditions, pretty much every club in West Virginia."

"You mean you auditioned somewhere that didn't hire you?"

She snorted. "Nah, they always want to hire me. The Golden Lariat has been after me for years, but I like it here. The customers are pretty harmless on average. Cecil's a dick, but at least he doesn't make you fuck him. And there's no other place quite like Pins. I like the setup: the split-ness."

"Duality," I said.

She rolled her eyes. "You're a college kid, right?"

"I was supposed to be. I was going to Allegany College, but...I don't know. I wasn't feeling it."

"And you're feeling this?"

"I've only been at it for a few hours."

"And you're already a big bright shining star. You'll do fine."

I couldn't help staring at her. If I was shining, she was the cause. I'd never seen someone so effortlessly beautiful in my whole life. With bedroom eyes and soft rosy lips plumped by a smirk that made me quiver everywhere that counted. I knew what was coming. She'd peeled me down pink until I was quivering under her questions, staring at her cool loveliness. I had no choice but to admit the truth.

I started to speak. "You're really prett—" Thank fuck she interrupted me.

"This is your first club, right?"

My voice cracked. "Does it show?"

"You do seem a little nervous. But you shouldn't be. You're really cute."

The quivering turned to quaking. "No, I am not."

"You are!"

"Thanks, but I'm really not."

"You're never going to make money with an attitude like that. But I get it. Even the hottest chicks on earth have off-days."

"You do?" I said it jokingly, not realizing how flirty it sounded until the words were out.

I was sure Honey was going to think I was a freak, but it wasn't disgust that appeared on her face. It was the dimple I cherished so, like a shooting star, gone in an instant but the source of all my wishes.

"Fake it till you make it, as they say. Plus, men dig a new girl. Especially one that looks like you."

My blush was hot and heavy and I wanted to slap it off my face. It was a first, for sure, but it blended in with so many other firsts that night.

Pantera was giving a lap dance to a bowler on lane six while his friends waited impatiently. They heckled him to take his turn, but he was blissfully ignorant. To me, the scene was amusing, but Honey instantly saw the profit in it.

"You take the guy in the hat. I'll get the other one." She strutted over to the bunch with a wave. "Hey, darlin'. You want a dance?"

"We're in the middle of a game."

"Looks like your buddy is in the middle of Pantera. If you have to wait on him, you might as well wait with me, right?"

The rube didn't stand a chance.

"How much?"

"I tell you what: Give me $10 and Birdie will take care of your friend too."

The two men whispered to each other as if they had some choice in the matter, but it wasn't long before Honey had their money in hand. She handed $5 to me with a wink and went about her work. I approached the man in the hat slowly, even cautiously. It was my first time giving a table dance, and I wasn't sure what to do. Honey was balanced lightly on her customer's lap, straddling one of his knees while Pantera's legs were wrapped around her guy's waist, practically dry-humping him. I didn't feel comfortable with either proximity, and my customer's partially toothless grin shriveled my resolve until Honey's voice entered my mind.

"Fake it till you make it," I whispered in agreement, and I released my fear.

I released the notion that I wasn't as pretty as Honey or as badass as Pantera. I released feeling chunky and uncoordinated and way too sensitive for the situation I'd put myself in. I released all the anchors that held me down, and released my inner wild child as I leveled up. Smiling, I ran my hand down my chest and lowered myself until my crotch was barely touching his thigh.

"You look nervous," he said.

In a silky voice that made it sound like I was aching for him to deflower me, I said, "It's my first time."

It was almost too easy.

When the dance was done, Honey nodded in approval. I was surprised by how success spurred me to dance a little closer, a little bolder, and actually enjoy each evolution of my sex appeal. I improved with each dance, but the one thing that didn't change was my refusal to *see* the customer. Even when I made eye contact, I didn't see them. They were just a collection of standout features: missing teeth and glass eyes and fake tits in various denims and plaids. It was easier that way, keeping my mind at a distance when my body was too close for comfort.

The alley was okay for tips, but it was mostly occupied by men who wanted a free, albeit faraway, show. I decided to stick to the club side, but I eventually danced for everyone I could. To my right, a handicapped guy with American flag wheels gave Ginger a humpy ride. To my left, a frat boy with frosted tips set up the DJ booth and talked to Ebony as she casually changed her bikini top in front of him. And straight ahead, CJ squeezed her pancake titties and a drop of congealed milk oozed out of her nipples. Where was I supposed to look? What was I supposed to do?

"Come on," Pantera said, hooking her arm onto mine as she stomped backstage.

Like the club floor, the dressing room had come alive with activity. A bevy of smoke, powder, and pills circulated the room like old friends.

"Is this what it's always like?"

"This is what it always *is*—and it's not always pretty," she said, gesturing at Ginger blotting a drop of blood from her nostril. "It is sometimes, though. Almost too pretty, and the longer you look the quicker it turns to poison."

"That's kind of poetic," I said.

"Flattery will get you everywhere, baby beaver," she said and dropped a pill in my hand.

"What's this?"

"Vicodin. It'll cool you off and make you hotter."

"What do you mean?"

"It's obvious the guys like you. Girls too. But they'd like you even more if you danced slower, sexier. I don't know if you're aware, but you kinda dance like you're hopped up on something. Honey's too sweet to tell ya."

"But you're not."

"If you look too long, I turn to poison too." She closed my hand on the pill.

"I don't know. Maybe my nerves will go away on their own. Once I figure out what I'm doing."

"Bitch, if any of us had anything figured out, you think we'd be here?" Pantera popped a Vicodin of her own and chased it with a clear liquid that smelled like kerosene.

"And you're demented if you think a pill's gonna make this flappy bird a good dancer," Ginger said.

"It's only my first night. Plus, I did just break up with my boyfriend of five years, if you want to know."

A collective "oh" rose from the girls backstage. It wasn't sympathetic. It wasn't derisive. It was the "oh" of baggage revealing itself. Whether it led us to Pins, or Pins was just another piece of scenery on an aimless road, we shared the same key to an array of different worlds, broken in myriad ways, and conquered it. When we stripped, we were in control. When we got high, we were free. Some of us didn't have the wisdom to jump our respective fences yet, and some of us never would. Some of us were even okay with it.

But fuck if Pantera wasn't right. Vicodin did make me feel sexier. A slow thrum caught hold while I was onstage and melted my frantic shakes into sexy hip grinds, back and forth in gyration. Gwen Stefani's "Hey Baby" sounded like its so-so usual, but under the heavy whirl of the drug, it *felt* like a warrior dream. Like sultry butter in spiked heels, I leapt to the pole and slid my fingers over the steel skin. They promptly slipped and I stumbled away, right into the jumpy beginning of "Apache." Honey was sitting at the stage, but when we caught eyes, she stood and climbed up beside me.

"Try again."

"I'm too scared."

"Of what?"

"Falling mostly. And breaking my head open."

She chuckled. "You just need practice."

"Has anyone ever gotten hurt practicing?"

"Even the best fall sometimes. When I first started here, Barbie was the best pole dancer I'd ever seen."

"Who's Barbie?"

"She wonders that too now," Honey replied, her eyes far-cast. She giggled and did a little spin. "She fucked up an aerial invert when she opened her legs too wide during the drop. She plummeted to the floor and cracked her skull."

"Oh my God! She was okay though, right?"

"For the most part. She stopped dancing and settled down with a nice fella named Ken. At least, that's what she told me at the hospital two days after the accident."

"You're kidding."

"Am I?" She winked, then shouted over The Sugarhill Gang. "Heaven, can Birdie switch spots with you for the next dance? I wanna teach her the pole."

"Oh hell yes," Heaven replied, more enthusiastic than I would've liked.

"Now? In front of everyone?"

"Sure. Don't worry, we'll still get tips."

"That's not what I'm worried about."

Heaven ran over to the DJ booth, informed Brian of the change and ran back to me with a giddy smile that flipped my stomach.

A small man with wispy gray hair sniggered at me. "You going up next?"

"I guess so."

"You'll do fine. You *are* fine." He licked his thin lips so sloppily, a waterfall of drool cascaded to the floor.

"Up next we have Honey and Birdie," Brian said in a deep, soulful voice that surprised anyone looking at the stick-thin white kid with frosted tips.

Meatloaf crooned out an intro as Honey took to the pole with a grandiose sweep that made her airborne. She was cyclonic sex, effortlessly in control of every spin, flip, and subtle slide that moved hands to wallets. I watched her in awe, but when she spun away from the pole and gave me an "it's your turn" nod, every bit of grace fled my body. The audience watched me like they would watch a stunt driver: half cheering me on and half hoping to see blood. I started to bend my leg around the pole, but when my fingers started to slip, I unwrapped myself and backed away.

"I can't do it."

"It's not as hard as you're making it," Honey said. "Think of it this way: Who do you like? Celebrity-wise, who do you think is hot?"

"Alexander Skarsgard."

"Okay, so pretend the pole is Alexander Skarsgard. It's tall, thin, and if you can wrap your legs around him and hold on, you're in for one hell of a ride."

"Really?"

"But don't get too excited and rub your pussy on the pole. That's not cool," Heaven shouted from the sidelines.

As my favorite part in "I Would Do Anything for Love" started, I leaned into the waltzing whirl of Vicodin, I curled my hand around Alexander Skarsgard, and allowed the gritty sex in his voice to devour me, terror and titillation. Whispering yet forceful, his words were tinted with a subtle accent that made me want to be very, very uncool.

"Hold on tight, Birdie. It's time to fly."

With my left leg wrapped backwards around the pole, I pushed off and sailed through the air. The rush of flight cooled my sticky skin as I heard the steamy backup singer begging for holy water, and the crowd decorated the stage with ones. When I dismounted, I spun to the edge with surprising grace and realized they were cheering even though I'd neglected to remove any clothing.

After that, the pole was all I wanted. I wanted to learn

every move: ones that propelled me forward, dropped me backwards, flipped me upside down, anything that made me feel that light and free.

The rest of the night raced by. I didn't even realize how late it was until Cookie tapped me on the shoulder and said, "Last dance."

I wasn't sure what that meant, but when a techno version of "In the Hall of the Mountain King" summoned the dancers to the stage, I clustered behind them.

"What are we doing?"

The girls were too busy with the final squeeze to answer, but I caught on soon enough. We peeled off our clothes and went wild across the stage, dancing like witches of the wood gaining power from every falling leaf. By the time the song was fading, we'd stripped the audience several times over, but there was always a little green left to pluck. I followed the girls lowering to their knees and stomachs, unsure of why until a voice rang out: "Face down, ass up! That's the way we like to fuck!" The customers hooted as each dancer pounded her body against the pine and grasped for anything that fell from the last shake of the branch. I didn't know how long I was supposed to hump the stage, so I followed Honey's lead. She gravitated across the width: standing, kneeling, banging away at the floor and collecting a lot more money than the rest of us.

"This is fucking crazy," I said as she laid down next to me and did come-hither pedaling motions with her legs.

"You think this is nuts, just wait for a Saturday night. All of the girls strip down and do the 'Cha Cha Slide' at the end."

"What's the 'Cha Cha Slide?'"

Her only response was a sly smile that turned into a cheesy grin when a patron slipped a ten into her garter. The same guy gave me a dollar.

CHAPTER FIVE

"Got a second?"

Brian's DJ Booth smelled like Nautica and Baja Blast when I sidled up a few weeks later.

He said, "Not really," as he scrolled through his music database, but once he clamped his eyes onto my triple-coated, batting lashes, he softened. "What up, Birdie?"

"I made a mix," I said, holding up a thumb drive.

"A mix of what?

"There's a punk version of 'Rainbow Connection' and a song from *The Rocky Horror Picture Show*. Motley Crue, Tenacious D, and…Eminem."

"No Eminem, Birdie," he said. "You know how Cecil feels about rap music."

"It's so weird that Cecil won't let us play rap."

"Cuz he's black?" He scoffed. "That's racist."

"No, it's just weird. Unless, is it racist? Shit."

Brian shrugged. "Hey, Ebony, is it racist to assume Cecil should like rap because he's black?"

"About as racist as you assuming I know all the rules of racism because *I'm* black," she snapped, then resumed dancing for her customer. "But yes, ya'll are racist as hell. Cecil just has shitty taste in music."

"There you have it," Brian said. "I gotta skip the Eminem track."

"Fine." I was trudging away when he spoke again.

"Wait. Can I ask you something?'"

"Sure."

"What's your real name?"

I twitched my nose. "Do you know anyone else's real names?"

"Some of 'em."

"Did they tell you, or did you find out on your own?"

"On my own, I guess."

"I'd hate to be accused of breaking tradition." I flicked my teeth with my tongue.

He chuckled. "You seem shier than the other girls."

"What gave you that impression? The way I take off my clothes in front of people?"

He cocked his head, looking at me deeper than any other man in the club had.

"I don't know what it is. This just doesn't seem like your scene."

"You don't know that much about me, Brian. "

"I know this is your first time working at a place like this," he said as if the venue left a bitter taste on his tongue.

"You work here too, you know."

"I just handle the music. I hardly even notice the T and A anymore."

My eyes took a glittery tour of the club, bouncing from breasts to bills to every beautiful attribute between. But when they fell on Honey's gyrating ass, the tour came to an end. I still found it a little frightening that she was always the final destination, but she was so gorgeous, I couldn't imagine anyone her charms couldn't captivate.

"I hope I never reach that point," I said.

He shook his head. "Just be careful. I've seen this lifestyle turn lots of nice girls into something else. It changes people."

"Now you know what brought me here."

I knew he was watching me walk away, and I liked it. In spite of his frosted tips and southern yo-boy accent, there was something sweet about him. But I wasn't about to tell the guy. Juggling real attraction to a co-worker and fake attraction to customers seemed like a pond that would quickly become a hungry swamp. I never made my interest known, but his attraction to me was obvious enough, even if it wasn't obvious which version he wanted: the girl hiding behind the glitter or the one delighting in it, whipping her ponytail around like a good girl gone bad. It was true, even in hiding.

I was the same person I'd always been, but stepping on stage transformed me in dazzling ways with each shift. It wasn't long before I started craving it: the blinding lights, the perplexing scents, the ritual of preparing the cocoon I would shed again and again. Zipping my boots, lacing up my dress, buckling my metallic chaps, even spraying the hell out of my hair. Honey had mentored me well, and we were soon doing doubles regularly. I'd adopted a bit of her dancing style in the creation of my own, but my routine couldn't hold a candle to hers. She moved like the inside of a lava lamp: vibrant, hypnotic, and aglow with feminine fluidity. My scissor kicks would slow, and my gyrations would languish on all fours as I watched her dominate the stage, so enraptured I'd forget I was supposed to be working the customers. But some asshole would inevitably make a crude comment and I'd snap out of it. That particular night, it was Petey and his broken grin that halted my reverie. He studied my snatch too intently as he licked his hand and replastered three ropes of hair forming his comb-over. Then it was back to squinting at my crotch. It was pretty as far as pussies went, but it wasn't exactly a Georgia O'Keefe warranting special worship or scrutiny.

When I'd collected my clothes, Honey approached from behind, pressing her bare breasts against my back as she threw her arms around my neck. Several men cheered at the contact. I wanted to cheer too.

Until she sang in my ear: "My boyfriend is here."

"Here? At the club here?"

She bit her lip, nodding. "He just got back from a trip with his friend Josh, and I've been dying to see him."

"Who? Which one?"

She pointed to a guy with spiky hair, a dark goatee, and a black t-shirt that clung to his muscles like a second skin. She blew him a kiss, and he fired a finger-gun at her.

"Let's go sit with him after the set. Alexxxa is up next anyway."

Alexxxa Love, porn star, cam girl, part-time baker, and our Featured Dancer for the night, was well into her dirty thirties, but her tits defied age, along with gravity and good taste. The gargantuan implants were unnaturally round, stretching her skin taut over every painfully apparent cyst and vein. The triple Fs—not *her* triple Fs, mind you, because the alien spheres affixed to her chest didn't resemble the sort of biological material a human could possess—looked like cartoon eyeballs, bulging and widely-spaced, the kind that could spin and whirl around before hitting Triple 7s and spewing quarters out Alexxxa Love's slot. Before I knew what was happening, I reached out in morbid fascination and chirped, "Can I touch?"

"Of course!" Alexxxa arched her back as if I needed the extra inch.

I didn't know what to expect, but when my fingers were on her breast, I was neither mortified nor surprised. It felt like very thin latex stretched around a sack of... well, "otherworldly pudding" was the first descriptor that leapt to mind. But I smiled, and I nodded with my eyebrows raised like I was surprised, and potentially aroused, by how natural they felt.

"Come on, let's go sit with James."

When I hesitated, Honey slapped my ass so hard the pain buckled one knee, and I nearly sank to the floor.

Jade and Diamond roared with laughter, and when Honey tossed an arm out to help me, I reached around and smacked her thigh. She yowled and hopped on one foot as my scarlet signature throbbed beneath her fingers.

"Below the skirt, Birdie? At least I was nice enough to get you where no one can see it."

"Really? Cuz I have a feeling my ass might make an appearance sooner or later."

She laughed, but in the middle of a chuckle, she slapped my thigh and left her fingerprints behind.

"Okay, truce!" I screamed.

"Truce."

With flesh enflamed, we headed for the door, where she turned and added coyly, "For now."

Her boyfriend sat at a table near one of the vacant side-stages with two other guys, sipping brown liquor. She introduced me, her cheeks matching my marks on her thigh, and James extended his hand. I wasn't sure if he was trying to break my fingers, but his grip definitely suggested it. I pulled my hand free with a shaky smile and turned my attention to his two friends. All three guys were similar in coloring and stature; they even had similar button noses. But when it came to the eyes, one guy stood out. Sitting directly next to James was a guy named Landon, who had the greenest eyes I'd ever seen.

"You're a very nice dancer." It was James's other friend Josh who spoke, but I was too entranced by Landon to reply.

"You really are," Landon said, and I tossed away his compliment with a girlish shake of my head. "How about a dance right now?"

Honey rolled her eyes. "We're on a break, Landon."

"Maybe *you* are. I think Birdie wants to dance."

"No, I'm good. I just wanna chill for a minute."

"You sure? You looked like you were pretty eager

to get on my lap a few seconds ago. Come on, cowgirl. Mount up!" He licked his lips, and I withdrew every flirty flag I'd hung out for the guy.

"Hey, Landon, go throw some balls, why don't you?" Josh shoved a ten-dollar bill into his hand. Here, I'll buy your shoes."

Landon flashed him an icy glare but pocketed the money and headed for the alley.

"Thanks," I said to Josh, finally noticing how nicely-colored *his* eyes were. Chocolate, deep and rich.

Honey smacked James's arm. "Why did you bring that moron?"

"He was in the parking lot, babe. You know I don't usually hang out with dicks like him."

"So I guess that means *you're* not a dick?" I asked Josh.

"I try my damnedest not to be, but everyone has their bad days, right?"

Honey leaned against James as the stage lights changed for Alexxxa Love's show, and although I wouldn't have minded moving a little closer to Josh, he had switched his attention from me to Diamond. I listened to enough of their conversation to learn that he and Diamond had met a few months back at a nearby bar. I didn't know Josh, so I wasn't sure if I was jealous of the attention or the money she'd be able to glean from him, but every time he made her giggle, I felt a sickening pang.

All conversation suddenly stopped, and three spotlights shone upon the stage. Blue first, then white. The opening instrumental for "God Bless the USA" began pouring out of the speakers, and when Alexxxa walked onto the stage with an American flag draped around her naked body, the final spotlight turned her massive melons red. She lifted the flag over her head, fanning the front row a few times before laying it on the stage like a picnic blanket. Her mammoth tits heaved but didn't shake as she did a surprising split and spun onto all fours. With the flag beneath her, she crawled across the stage with a nimble grace that suggested she had legitimate dance training before allowing giant space-frogs to lay eggs in her chest. Despite my ambivalent patriotism, the song always made me cry, and Alexxxa danced with such passion that even the fish-white cannonballs on her chest couldn't stop my tears.

"Are you okay?" Josh craned to look at me. "Are you crying?"

I dabbed my eyes with my fingertips. "It's kind of smoky in here, you know? I think I'm going to head over to the alley side for a bit."

"Do you mind if I come with you?"

"If you're looking for a table dance—"

"Don't worry. I'm on a break too," he said warmly.

I didn't notice Josh's incredible height until he stood. He was a tall drink of water, and I was suddenly parched. I leaned against the alley bar and two men immediately offered to buy me a drink, but Josh slapped his money down first.

"Amaretto sour."

As Felix the barback mixed my drink, I noticed Josh looking me up and down. It was a normal occurrence at Pins, but I didn't feel the usual cringe that accompanied a stranger's gaze. Josh's eyes were preternaturally soft, like he'd been run through a dreamy filter, giving him a smile too sweet to give me the shivers. But I was still wary. I wore a different personality while at the club. Who was to say customers didn't do the same thing?

"Nice handprint."

"Thanks." I shimmied my hips. "It was a gift."

"From Honey I assume. Looks like her handiwork."

"Are you an admirer?"

He chuckled. "Of Honey? Isn't everyone?"

"Mmm hmm...What does your friend James think

about you ogling his girlfriend?"

"Ogling? No way, you've got me all wrong."

"Do I? You seem to know the girls here pretty well."

"Well, I come here a lot. And I'm a friendly guy."

"Uh huh..."

"I'm not going to lie and say I hate the company." A brief smile flashed across his lips, and a singular butterfly fluttered in my belly. "But I probably wouldn't hang around places like this if it weren't for James. It's not my fault he always wants to come see his girlfriend."

"The naked women are a nice bonus too, I'm sure."

"When they're as pretty as you, absolutely."

"Smooth," I cooed, trying to hide my grin behind my drink.

"You just started, right? Do you like it?"

I nibbled on the stirrer in my amaretto sour. "I like some things."

"Not the taking off your clothes part, I assume?"

"It has its moments, but...you assume correctly."

"You could be a server on the alley side instead."

I gasped in offense. "How dare you! I would never debase myself like that."

He laughed. "If it's any consolation, you're very good at taking your clothes off." Another few butterflies joined the first, but Josh groaned, and his body curled in on itself like a dead beetle. "That was so cringey, I'm sorry. Please forgive me, I take it back."

"It's okay. It's pretty much the pinnacle of compliments around here. Along with, 'You've got nice feet for a dancer' and 'Boy howdy your asshole is clean!'"

He snorted, and his drink caught in his throat. He dabbed his face with a napkin, chuckling. "I must say, I was also impressed with the cleanliness of your asshole."

"You're too sweet." I meant to whack his arm in a cutesy way, but thanks to repeated rounds of smack-ass backstage, I was used to leaving my signature behind.

I hit him entirely too hard, and his eyebrows jumped up his forehead. But when his shock cracked into amusement, the urge to fill my pockets with stones and walk into the Potomac receded like the acidic waters of the river's north branch.

As best I could, I massaged the embarrassment out of my face. "What do you do, Josh?"

"I'm a painter."

"Wow. Really?"

"A house painter. It's not quite as impressive, right?"

"I wouldn't say that."

"Because you're too nice to say that."

"Do you like it?"

"To be honest, I think I'd rather work in a place like this. I don't get much satisfaction out of stripping paint. Maybe stripping clothes would be more fulfilling."

"I've heard men make more money. I guess horny women are more generous."

"Speaking of horny women, I think Honey's looking for you," he said, pointing toward a table across the club, where Honey scanned the room like a meerkat.

"She probably wants to smoke a bowl." My breath froze in my throat. I shifted nervously and averted my gaze. "I'm sorry, I shouldn't have said that. I don't even know you."

"It's cool. I smoke too."

I exhaled. "Oh, thank God."

"Why 'thank God'?"

"My ex didn't smoke, and it was a nightmare for me."

Josh crinkled his nose. "Ah, so you're looking to make me an ex, are you?"

"No...I..." I sucked up the last of my amaretto sour and stood. "Sorry. I'm a little out of it today. I should go see what she wants."

"You sound just like James. I don't get it."

"Get what? I thought you liked Honey."

"I do. She's a cool chick." He shrugged. "I just don't understand why everyone needs to go running when she calls."

"I don't *need* to."

"Do you have a crush on her?"

I squeaked. "What?"

"It's fine if you do."

"We're friends. We're coworkers. She's showing me the ropes, and I'm grateful."

"It's perfectly understandable if you're attracted to her."

I laughed, a little too forcefully. "I'm not. Is she attractive? Obviously, but I'm not..." A rapid montage of all the gorgeous women I'd seen naked over the last month flashed and writhed and damp-humped my mind, and I couldn't find the right word to finish my sentence. "...I don't know what I am, and I'm not ready to label it yet, but I know I don't have a crush on Honey. I admire her is all."

"You don't have to label anything, and you don't have to convince me. Like I said, she's a cool chick."

"But you're not attracted to her."

"She's gorgeous. She's just not my type."

"Oh? What is your type?"

"I'm more into the fresh-faced girl-next-door type. The high pony, clean booty type." He winked. "Do you know any girls like that?"

I gave him a sassy flip of my ponytail. "Not a one. But I'll keep an eye out for you."

I started away, certain he was watching every sway, but when I tossed a cheeky look over my shoulder, he was already at the center of a stripper swarm. CJ and Diamond flanked him on both sides, and Ginger's hands were on his thighs. I could tell she was propositioning him, and he was into it, chuckling at one of her stupid jokes. Girl next door, my sparkling ass. When he pulled out a five-dollar bill, part of me felt like marching back over there, ripping Ginger off his lap, and impaling his pecker on my stiletto. The other part wanted to run into the bathroom and puke up every shitty little butterfly he'd hatched in me.

Honey leaned her chin on my shoulder. "Wanna smoke?"

"You're goddamn right I do."

I followed in a giddy sort of rage, but as we were passing the stage, someone grabbed my shoulder. My natural reaction was to violently shrug it away, but I'd been trying to soften my reactions since starting at Pins. So many hands reached out for me every night, and considering my frequent lack of attire, a touch on the shoulder should've been nothing.

But then Alexxxa Love spun me around with a pout that revealed her uneven filler, and she pulled me onstage.

I had no idea what was happening, but I'd worked at Pins long enough to recognize the howls and cheers that usually preceded an influx of cash, so I played along. She coaxed me onto my back, then stood above me, swiveling her hips and gyrating with feigned pleasure as she pinched her unresponsive areolas. I was wondering if she could feel them through the congealed tapioca sewn onto her chest when her spike heels landed on either side of my face, and the shadow of her ass began to cover my fake smile. Panic spurred my pulse when her pussy lowered, closer and closer, until she was squatting over my face. She tilted forward onto her hands and knees, and waggled her tongue as she crawled down the length of my body. The crowd cheered, and I felt people stuffing money in my garter, so I leaned into the act a little more. As Chappell Roan's casual vocal flips filled the club, I closed my eyes and curled the tip of my tongue at Alexxxa's cunt. It wasn't until what sounded like an old-timey prospector shouted, "Fuck yeah eat that pussy!" that I realized she was lowering herself onto my face again. My eyes popped open, and my tongue shrank into the back of my throat, half an inch away from licking someone else's lips. I tried to hold it together, focusing on the weight of ones in my garter instead of the pussy pumping up and down over my mouth so fast, it created its own weather system. Breezes and sprinkles I didn't want clarified cycloned around me with an increasing swelter that dotted my face with sweat.

Alexxa's simulated face-fuck doubled as a mind-fuck. Ten minutes ago, I was considering expanding the definitions of my sexuality. Now, I was desperately trying not to smell Alexxxa Love's pussy. However, the nearer her wrinkled vulva, the heavier my garter. If I'd been able to analyze tying my evolving sexuality to a profit, which increased the more uncomfortable I felt, I might've noticed all the ways I was setting myself up for future confusion, but I dropped out of college only two weeks into my Psych course.

Attracted to women or not, I certainly didn't expect to be an inch from a pornstar's pussy that night, and I prayed that my failed attempts to look sexy through panicked mouth-breathing disappeared between Alexxxa's thighs.

Someone hooted, and I peeked around the dancer's leg to see Honey clapping joyously between James and Josh, the latter of whom smiled when our eyes met. I licked my lips and arched my back, though I wasn't sure who for. But when the cash fluttered down and Honey screamed my name, I was distracted just enough to forget...not...to...

SNIFF!

I inhaled as deeply as I would any bouquet of fresh-cut flowers, and my panic roared like a secondhand lawnmower when the smell permeated the membranes of my nasal cavity.

It didn't smell bad. Similar to my own scent, especially after a night of dancing put the tang in "poontang." A natural musk with layers of salty sweetness, it was the aroma of strength, of sex, of new life, one we've all worn at one time or another, and I was recoiling like it was a music festival port-o-john. It wasn't a personal rejection; I was afraid it was a universal one. If the only other pussy I'd gotten close to smelled like my own and I still didn't like it, maybe I wasn't bisexual after all.

I left the stage a little richer but more perplexed than ever. Honey awaited me at the stairs, patted my back, and said, "Good show."

CHAPTER SIX

When I entered the dressing room, Pantera and Jade were seated in front of the Crab Couch in a cloud of smoke, but all I could smell was pussy. Had Alexxxa gotten closer than I thought? Was there a dot of Love juice on my nose, seeping into my skin, dooming me to smell nothing but the confusingly torturous scent of snatch for the rest of my life? It was so overwhelming I didn't even get the usual butterflies from seeing Honey change into her glittery red suspender-style bodysuit.

I sat across from Jade, who accidentally exhaled a thick stream of smoke into my face. She apologized, but I wafted it back at myself until green overwhelmed pink. She laughed as she passed me the bowl. I took a hit so deep it burned every membrane in my head and seared away the smell of confusion.

As I exhaled, Honey sat beside me and leaned her head against my shoulder. The butterflies fluttered back in abundance, but their wings weren't as big as before. There was no doubt Honey was a beautiful girl and a wonderful person. Smart, funny, even a bit weird. But I clearly wasn't cut out to be anything more to her than a friend.

"Girl on girl suits you," she said.

I flinched. "What makes you say that?"

"You usually tense up a bit when I lean on you. But you're so relaxed right now. It feels nice."

The shrunken wings tripled in an instant, and I hoped she didn't feel it. She looked up at me, her sapphire eyes sparkling like a goddamn My Little Pony.

I might not ever fuck this girl, but this girl had already fucked me.

"It's the weed," I said.

She hummed a little as she shook her head "Okay, sure. But a lot of girls don't make it this far. You're getting comfortable...settling in."

"That's dangerous," Pantera said, making the clouds she exhaled swirl in front of her face. "You should never settle into any place. Or any person."

"Cheerful," Jade coughed.

Ginger clambered backstage fanning her face. "Fuck me bloody, your boyfriend's friend is so cute, Honey. You think you could set me up?"

"After what happened last time, no way," She jumped up and checked for carpet marks on her ass.

"What happened last time?" I asked.

Ginger wiped black mascara out of the creases under her eyes. "None of your business."

"She punched my friend Mike in the face," Honey said as she rubbed lotion on a red indentation.

"He wanted me to strip for him!"

"You're a stripper, Ginger."

"Only when I'm here. Out there, I should be something else, *anything* else."

It was the first time I caught a glimpse of the real person inside, someone who would never be a stripper if she'd been born in any other place to any other family.

"Then why did you tell him it turned you on to strip for people?" Honey said, swiping some extra highlighter on her cheekbones.

"Because I got no idea how else to—" She squinted at the girls staring at her, then crouched at her suitcase to find a new top. "Forget it. I'll get the number myself."

I muttered "good luck" like an old-world curse

and focused on counting my tips from my stint with Alexxxa. I was inspecting a rolled up twenty-dollar bill of perplexing girth when Jade hooted in amusement.

"Hey hey! Birdie got a joint!"

"Huh?" I unrolled the bill to reveal the joint hidden inside, along with a message scrawled above "E Pluribus Unum":

Come to Honey's after work.
—Josh

"What's it say?" Ginger asked.

"I can't tell." I rolled the bill back into my stash and rubber banded it on my garter. "Probably some sexist shit. And the joint's probably laced with angel dust or something."

"Score," Pantera wheezed through smoke.

"Come on, ladies," Heaven said, loosening her halter. "Let's *Cha Cha Slide*."

With our knots slackened and buckles undone, we filed out of the dressing room and onto the stage for the group dance. I'd finally gotten the hang of the moves, but my first time was an utter disaster. Naked and nervous, I'd followed the instructions like "left foot, two stomps" and "cha cha now, ya'll"—but I stuck out like a sore cunt, tripping over my feet and stomping when I should have been hopping. It was a stupid little number, not at all sensual, but if one was into naked women stomping and hopping, regardless of synchronicity, I'm sure it got the job done.

With the dance ended and our sweaty bills collected, we set ourselves to packing our gear into suitcases and duffle bags and changing into more comfortable clothes. After only a month of having a thong as part of my professional attire, I couldn't stand wearing one off-hours. In time, I abhorred the restrictive feeling of underwear in general. Skin-tight gowns and two-piece halter sets were replaced by relaxed tank tops and loose drawstring sweatpants, in which I felt far sexier than any of my dancer wear. Looking like a put-upon single mother, I scrubbed my face, turned my high pony into a messy bun, and slipped on my glasses. I always had a casual style, but getting fitter made my hip bones pop just a bit more, making my lazy outfits look, dare I say, flirty.

"You look like a sexy librarian," Josh said as I jogged down the stairs. He leaned against the stage; even in his slouch, much taller than me.

"All librarians are sexy," I replied. "What are you still doing here?"

"Did you get my note?"

"I did. Thanks for the joint."

"No problem. There's plenty more where that came from." He grinned. "So, how about it? Are you coming to Honey's?"

"Can't. I have a date."

"At 2AM?"

"Yep. Goliath and Demona are waiting for me." I expected confusion to cross his face, but he smiled in recognition.

"Are you talking about Disney's *Gargoyles*? Like, from the 90s?"

"You've seen it?"

"Pretty much the entire series, but I haven't watched in years. It's streaming on Disney, right?"

I nodded.

"So you can watch it pretty much whenever you want."

I saw where this was going. I did want to continue the night with Josh, but I was too tired to do anything as strenuous as flirting. I just wanted to melt into my couch and let my turkey-filled belly hang out. If I went over to Honey's, I'd have to sit up straight and pretend that I wasn't just a slob in disguise.

"That's right. And I will be," I said coyly.

"Maybe another time? Tomorrow?"

"You're coming back tomorrow?"

"If you'll be here..."

James bellowed for Josh to hurry up, and Honey tugged on my arm. "You coming?"

"Birdie already has big plans," Josh said. "We'll have to persuade her to hang out another time."

"Okay, see you tomorrow," Honey said, giving me a quick hug before crashing back into James's arms. His hand immediately went to the back of her head, and he grabbed a fistful of her highlighted waves, giving it a firm tug. It shocked me at first. Then I imagined giving her hair the same little tug, and I blushed in secret camaraderie with James.

"Have a good night." Josh squeezed my arm gently, but I felt the roughness in him also. His hands, a painter's hands, could color me in all sorts of reds and pinks. Hell, I wasn't opposed to a few black-and-blues if the journey was worth it.

"Don't stay up too late watching cartoons," he said with a chuckle.

I snapped back to reality and began towing my suitcase to the exit. "Are you kidding? That and eating cookies for breakfast are the best things about being an adult."

"I can think of a few others."

I watched him walk away with a slight tilt of my head that drunk up every inch of his exit, but the pleasant sight was quickly killed by Landon's simpering smile as he hopped in front of me and waved goodbye.

I grumbled. "Yeah, yeah, bye."

Landon continued waving as he drunkenly marched backwards to his Uber, and the bouncer, Gary, closed the door behind me.

"Need an escort?"

"Nah, I'm right here."

"What are you getting into tonight?"

I pulled the joint out of my pocket.

"Nice. Want some company?"

I shook my head. "I've got all the company I need."

After a quick stop at Sheetz for a turkey sandwich and a pack of cigarettes, I headed home. My "company" was yowling as usual, pawing at the door, then at my leg once I was inside. After Fidelio was fed, I began my after-hours ritual: I checked my social media, queued up *Gargoyles*, and unfurled the thin silver wrapper destined to dissolve in the globs of mayo leaking from my sub. But where a freshly packed bowl usually sat was Josh's joint. I sparked it as Keith David's voice rumbled out of my speakers, gritty and gorgeous as I inhaled.

"One thousand years ago, superstition and the sword ruled..."

"You're goddamn right it did," I said, mouth full. "Preach it, Goliath.

I was asleep in under an hour, only vaguely aware that Fidelio was helping himself to my half-eaten turkey sandwich.

CHAPTER SEVEN

Josh's joint made a good appetizer when I woke up at noon. After setting up a plate of toast and eggs, I packed the remainder into a bowl. But, as if able to sense my proximity to happiness, my phone screen lit up with my mother's photo.

I set down the bowl and swiped to answer. "Hello?"

"Hey, Sweet Pea, what are you doing?" Her voice chimed cheerfully over the speakerphone.

"Hey. Nothing really. Just hanging out."

"At work?"

I kept forgetting my mom thought I worked at the park reservation place six days a week, instead of three or four at a strip club. Yes, at noon on Sunday, I would've been at work.

"I'm on my lunch break."

"So you can talk?"

"Yeah, I have a few minutes before I have to clock back in."

Clock back in. Genius. Now the genius just had to figure out how to balance the phone and smoke the bowl simultaneously without her mom hearing the lighter or the inhalation.

"So, what's up?"

"Oh, not much. I just felt like calling. We ran a new ad for pageant sign-ups and it made me think of you, so I thought I'd give you a call."

"An ad for something I never participated in made you think of me?"

"It's the last year you can compete, you know."

"Last year, first year..."

"You've done it before."

"Not voluntarily. I was just a little kid. I didn't know I wasn't..." I sighed. "Never mind."

"Eva, what? You didn't know you weren't what?"

"Beautiful. At least, the way you and Hollie are beautiful."

"Oh, Sweetie, how many times do I have to tell you? You're ten times more beautiful than I ever was."

"You have to say stuff like that. People with assface children say stuff like that."

"Oh please, I've seen women call their daughters prize heifers seconds before they're due onstage. I've seen jealous mothers shred pretty girls to confetti, and it disgusts me. But," she chirped, "I get it. I'm certainly jealous of your youth and beauty. It's so relaxed, like you're not even trying."

"Is that a compliment? I can't tell."

"Of course it is! I wish I had half of the natural radiance you and Hollie have." She cleared her throat. "Have you talked to her lately, by the way?"

I barely spoke to my sister for several reasons. Teasing aside, we didn't have anything in common. Three years older than me, she left the house right after high school and didn't contact any of us for more than a year. It caused my mother to latch onto me, pressuring me even harder to be something I felt I could never be. I had hoped time on her own would change Hollie into a nicer person, but when I received a friend request from her on Instagram a few years back, a quick look at her profile made me wary. Always a glutton for punishment, I approved the request anyway and invited in a new generation of insults disguised as concern. Nearly every picture received a comment about how I wasn't dressing to flatter my "unique body type," or how I needed to start sleeping on a silk pillowcase "to stop all that breakage." Luckily, she didn't visit my page often enough to notice when I deleted her comments. Our relationship existed solely online in disappearing virtual ink.

"I know she'd like to hear from you. Or you could just come to the tryouts. Hollie's helping me organize it this year."

"You two are the beauty queens and everyone knows it. And that's fine with me. I don't want to be a beauty queen."

"But Eva..."

"Did you call to berate me for sticking to my boundaries, Mom?"

A little gem from our failed attempts at family counseling when I was in middle school. It never failed to wound her.

"Not intentionally." The tone of her voice made me picture her with large, sad eyes and a bottom lip hanging halfway to the floor. It stung my heart a bit, but when she mumbled, "Boundaries? Or walls?" I nearly hung up the phone. "How's school?" she added quickly.

I sighed. "Schooly."

"How's work?"

"Worky."

"How's Scott?"

"Oh. I guess I didn't tell you yet."

"Please tell me you broke up."

"We broke up."

"Yes!" She caught herself and cleared her throat awkwardly. "I mean, I'm sorry, Sweet Pea."

"Yeah, I bet. It would've been more convincing if your cheer wasn't still echoing in the background."

"He was nice enough, just not for you."

"I'm aware of your opinion of Scott, Mom. It doesn't

matter now anyway. He's out of the picture."

"Completely?"

"I haven't seen or spoken to him in a month, so yes, completely."

"But you two have broken up before."

"This isn't like that. It's over. For good."

"So...what happened?"

"Irreconcilable differences," I said, packing the roach deeper into the bowl.

"Are you seeing anyone new?"

"Not...really."

She hummed in interest. "Is there a candidate?"

Since my dad had vacated the picture, my beauty queen mother had a lot of suitors, but she never seemed too interested in tying any of them down. So she put great care into following my relationships, which until recently had consisted of Scott and a boy who took me to mini-golf in 9th grade. The news of my break-up was just the kind of development she'd been waiting for.

"There's someone I'm a little interested in."

"That's wonderful, Sweetie."

"Yes, it is," I said as I fiddled with the resin-soaked paper from Josh's joint.

"Well, I should probably let you get back to work."

"Oh yeah."

"Are you sure you don't want me to send you an application for the pageant?" she said. "The deadline isn't until November, so you'll have plenty of time to mull it over."

"No, that's okay," I said, knowing full well she'd probably already filled one out on my behalf.

"Okay, Sweetie. Have a good day."

"Thanks, Mom. You too."

I ended the call, then hit my bowl. I hated having to repeatedly dash my mom's dreams of having a daughter whose beauty was rewarded by trophies. But trying would only end in disappointment for both of us, and I'd rather she be let down by my fear of failure than by the failure itself.

Besides, looking like I wasn't trying apparently suited me. I hoped it would continue to carry me through my shift that night.

I hated dancing on Sundays. The abundance of men in their "good" church clothes led me to believe they'd dumped every sin earlier in the day in the hopes of restocking at night. Afternoon, if brunch with the family ended early. Still plump and sticky from all you can eat pancakes, they waddled in with their wallets depleted after a guilt-induced donation to the collection plate. The only perk to working on Sunday was a slightly shorter shift, but it also meant a significantly lighter garter. After an hour, I began to regret my decision to pick up the shift, but when Josh walked in during my "Jessie's Girl" routine, I was glad for a slow night. He sat front and center at the stage, his first time watching me like this, a five-dollar bill at the ready. Even though he wasn't the next customer in my rotation, I spun over to him and got down on my knees. It felt so fun, so natural, that I forgot about the other men staring at my naked body; his wandering eyes were enough. He started to put his money in my garter, but before he could fold it over, I plucked the money from his fingers.

"Bite down," I said, holding the bill in front of his face.

Obediently, he clamped his teeth on the cash, and with a jiggling giggle, I pinched my nipples, pressed my tits together, and pulled the fiver out of his mouth. He laughed and clapped, and I took a trip around the pole to hide the excitement prickling my skin. When the song ended, Josh moved to a table and flashed me an inviting smile. But by the time I'd slipped back into my favorite purple gown, frizz sprayed, face dabbed, and makeup reapplied, Diamond and Ginger were hovering around him.

Brian waved from a nearby table, and I averted my eyes from the feeding frenzy at Josh's as I strutted over.

"What are you doing here? Are you DJing tonight?"

"No, just bored."

"So you came here? I figured you'd rather be anywhere else on your day off."

"Aren't you usually off today too?"

"I needed money. But it doesn't look like I'm going to get much."

"You sure it's about money? Or is it about the dude burning holes in your back?"

He nodded in Josh's direction, and I fought the impulse to turn my head. I didn't want to seem too desperate. Although, I did just have his face between my tits.

"He's looking right now?"

"He hasn't stopped looking all night."

"How would you know? Are you watching him?"

"I'm watching you. Watching *out* for you, I mean."

"I don't need you to watch out for me."

"Look, I know you haven't worked here long, so I'll tell you the truth: dating a customer is one of the worst moves you can make."

"I'm not dating him. I just met him."

"I've seen this shit go really wrong, Birdie." He tried to touch my hand, but I pulled away. "Just be careful."

"I appreciate your concern, but at this point, I have no intention of getting close to Josh outside of the club."

He squinted. "Josh? I'm not talking about Josh."

"Oh. Who are you talking about?"

"The dude in the corner who's been staring at you all night."

Brian pointed out two eyes flashing in the neon haze. When the voyeur caught me looking, his eyebrows jumped up his forehead, and he slipped out of his seat. He tried to slither out of the club, but I caught up with him at the private dance rooms.

"Scott?! What are you doing here?"

He stared at my hairline instead of my eyes. I'd never seen him so ashamed.

"I wanted to see you. I was curious, I guess." His gaze lost its grip on my forehead, briefly connecting with mine, before slipping over my body. "Have you lost weight?"

"I don't know. Probably?"

He still had trouble meeting my eyes, but he also seemed awkward looking anywhere else. His eyes moved to the girl on the stage and to the dancers strolling by.

"Scott? Answer me."

"When are you going to quit this place?"

"Why would I quit?"

"You're better than this."

"Thanks for the affirmation, but I need to get back to work."

"What about us, Birdie? You're really going to throw away everything we had?"

My frustration was so heavy, it nearly collapsed me. I wanted to kick him square in the nuts for asking such a stupid question, but I refused to give him the satisfaction of seeing him affect me. Instead, I took a deep breath and smiled.

"You're the one who ended it."

"Because I can't have my girlfriend working as a stripper."

"I guess it's a good thing I'm not your girlfriend."

I started away, and he grabbed my wrist, prompting Gary to rush over with a bloodthirsty growl.

"Hands off the girl, punk!"

He backed off, but he pointed at me, like he was trying not to lose any real proximity. "She's not *the girl*, she's *my girl*."

"Not anymore," I said, smacking his hand away. "It's over."

"What the hell is your problem? Has this place turned you into a complete bitch that fast?"

"Nah, you did that long before I started working here."

The confrontation drew a few stares from customers, but most of the witnesses were dancers, like members of the same wrestling team just waiting to be tagged in.

"Everything okay, Birdie?" Diamond cinched her ponytail and stood beside me.

Scott snapped, "This is a private conversation," and she chuckled like a child who knew he was about to drink poisoned tea.

"Then buy a private room."

"It's okay, Diamond. I'm fine."

"Your name's Diamond?" Scott snorted. "That's priceless. Actually, you probably *have* a price, don't you?"

"Not for a peasant like you."

Scott rolled his eyes, then approached me slowly. Gary got closer too, though I didn't think it was necessary. Scott wouldn't hurt me. He loved me. And I guess I still loved him too. We were in a relationship for five years and friends for even longer. As much as I wished I could expel him like clumpy uterine lining, it might take a few more months to slough off all these feelings.

"Birdie, don't let yourself turn into one of these people. You're smarter than this. You're better than this."

"Excuse me?" Diamond stepped forward, her spike heels leaving the ground as she leaned into him on tiptoes. "I have a 4.0 GPA."

He rolled his eyes. "Yeah? Why don't you get on all *fours* and spread your *point-O* so everyone can see how smart you are."

The sound of Diamond slapping Scott was a summoning spell for every male employee in Pins. Not that they were needed once the bodyguards had him. Never considered a tough guy by any means, Scott struggled futilely as they dragged him to the exit while I watched in a surreal sort of detachment.

Diamond shook her head beside me. "On the Lord's Day no less."

Josh ran up to us. "Are you okay? What's going on?"

"No biggie," she said. "Stu and Gary just took out the trash. Actually..." She peered after them, then excused herself to see if she could get close enough to spit on Scott. I thought it was a bit dramatic, but I wasn't about to stop her.

"What happened?" Josh asked. "Who was that guy?"

I grumbled. "My ex."

"Damn. I guess he isn't taking the breakup so well?"

"I guess not."

"Well, I can't blame him. I'd never forgive myself if I let someone like you go." Josh had a nice smile. Slightly crooked, a little yellowed from smoking, but nice enough to make me forget my tits were one girlish giggle from popping out. It also held my attention when someone who was very good at stealing it walked in the front door.

Honey was late, but even with Cecil watching the door, she sauntered in like she was early. James trailed behind with her suitcase, falling back even further when he spotted Josh.

"I thought you were staying in tonight," James said.

"I changed my mind," Josh replied, smirking in my direction.

Honey noticed instantly, giving my hip a knowing knock when she retrieved her suitcase from James. "Who was that guy with Stu and Gary outside?"

"That would be Birdie's crazy ex," Josh said.

"Oh my God, are you okay?"

"I'm fine, and he's not crazy," I said. "He's just a little..."

"Crazy?" Josh offered.

"If anything, I'm the crazy one. Working here is so out of character for me."

"Really? So this girl I've been talking to...she's all an act?"

"No, I think...maybe everything before was an act. But I didn't realize it."

Honey whispered, "Damn. That's heavy."

"No, no heavy. Everything light and bouncy," I said, twiddling my fingers in the air. "Like glittery titties."

Honey touched her heart. "Aww how poetic!"

"Well, whoever you are, I'm glad to know you. And I don't care what anyone does for a living," Josh said. "Especially when they're as good at it as you are on that stage."

Like generational trauma, Cecil was suddenly apparent, demanding we start selling table dances.

"Okay, okay, we're on our way," Honey said.

"Good. I wouldn't want to ban these gentlemen just to get your ass in gear."

"I don't know, maybe banning them is a good idea," she said. "It'll get all our asses in gear."

James snarled, turned on his heel and stomped away. Confused, I waved goodbye to Josh as Honey towed me backstage.

Something felt off the entire time she was getting ready. She started drinking her vodka and Red Bulls much earlier than usual, and when Ginger produced a vial of cocaine from her boot, she didn't even wait to be offered a line. She inserted herself into the rotation like Fidelio begging for chunks of my turkey sandwich.

"Sorry I didn't come over last night," I said as she checked her nostrils for white clumps. "I hope you're not pissed."

"I'm not. Not at you, anyway. No one came over."

"Not even James?"

"Nope." She hocked up her cocaine drip, swallowed

it with a wince, and took a sip of her drink. "I'm not sure I want to know where he was."

"You don't think he's cheating, do you?"

"Maybe I'm being paranoid."

"Probably. He hasn't cheated before, has he?"

She looked at me with an expression I'd never seen cross her face. It was anger, exasperation, and something desperate as well, as if she were still clinging to a small hope of his fidelity.

She cleared her throat. "What was your ex doing here?"

"Trying to convince me that I'm too good for this place."

"Too good for fun, friends, and cold hard cash? God forbid!"

As Ginger headed out to the floor, Ebony walked in with her sparkly blue dress slung over her shoulder and her panties balled up in her hand.

"Jesus, Honey, are you ready?" she snapped.

"I'm not dancing with you, Ebony."

"I just got off the stage, stupid. It's your turn."

Honey leapt from her chair and strutted over to Ebony with her hands clenched. They stood face to face and propelled insults at each other with vicious neck thrusts. I had a fleeting compulsion to jump in and stop them before they could start, but I didn't. I figured it was the closest I'd ever get to seeing a cockfight in person.

"Don't call me stupid, cuntshart."

"Don't call me cuntshart, smegslut."

"You're one to talk about being slutty. You were probably the one out with James last night, weren't you?"

"No, but I'm sure he wanted me to be."

There had been enough backstage brawls between Honey and Ebony in the past month for everyone to recognize this as the proclamation that would launch one toward the other. I had Honey covered, but unfortunately, the only other dancer backstage was Faith. Ebony easily evaded the dwarf, pushing her to the floor, then lunged at Honey. With Ebony loose, it didn't seem fair to hold Honey back, so I let go. They crashed into each other like rabid raccoons with acrylic claws, but when the backstage door flew open and Pantera marched in, it took one glare for the fight to dissolve.

With a huff, Honey headed for the stage, a defeated hunch ruining her usually perfect posture, but as soon as she stepped onto the stage and Prince purred, "You sexy motherfucker," her spine melted back to its concave cool.

I helped Faith up. "Are you okay?"

"Sure. You gotta love the excitement. One woman's Sunday mass is another woman's stripper brawl." She snapped her top back into place. "It's funny if you think about it. Us and the Churchies spend just as much time on our knees, but only one of us is losing money on the deal."

"You're not wrong. Anyway, time to get out there and rub our twats for the poor suckers," I said, genuinely tickled as I headed out to massage my twat for money.

There were plenty of customers willing to take me up on that offer, but I would have been much happier playing Monster Madness on the Megatouch. Unfortunately, Cecil was watching me like a stunted hawk, which meant I couldn't socialize with Josh either. There were fewer than twenty customers on the club side and only two at the stage. The alley side was a little busier, but none of the bowlers seemed keen on abandoning their games to drop money on what they could squint at for free.

Honey didn't mind the lack of customers. Without a designated path along the stage to follow, the dancers who actually prided themselves on their dancing abilities took the time to shine for something deeper than the Almighty Dollar. She worked the pole beautifully, as if she thought only of her own grace, her own pleasure.

I derived pleasure from dancing too. Although I'd never been a fan of my body, there was something about the way I looked in those mirrors. Perspiration actually added to my appeal; each salty river glittered in the lights and allowed my fingers to slip over my skin with sensual ease. If a customer noticed me getting hot, I made no hesitation in saying, "It's all you, baby. You have no idea how wet you make me." But I always had one eye on my reflection.

I knew Josh's eyes were following my search for willing customers because I was watching him just as hard.

"Here we go again," Brian sighed into his beer as I passed his table.

"What's that?"

"This is your job, not a meat market," he said.

"You wouldn't be saying that if I were eyeing up *your* meat."

"Maybe not," he said. "So, why aren't you?"

"I am," I replied, smirking.

Jade laughed as she danced by. I wanted to make her laugh more, so I stared deliberately at Brian's crotch. She laughed even harder when I started giving him a theatrically horny table dance.

"Stop it." He shoved me away, and Josh jumped to his feet to defend my honor.

I waved him back to his seat. "It's okay. We're just kidding around."

Brian hissed. "You think I'm just West Virginia trash, dontcha?"

"No. What's your problem?"

"My problem is that you Pins girls think you can do whatever you want."

"I don't."

"If you don't yet, you will," he said, took one more sip, and turned from the table.

"It isn't my fault you have a crush on me," I said as I stomped after him.

"So why do you keep on flirtin' with me?"

"I'm sorry if you got the wrong impression, Brian, but it's pretty much my job to flirt. I make money from customers' crushes."

"I'm not a customer."

"You are today," I said. "It's your day off, remember?"

"I'm still not a customer. I came here to—" He shook his head in exasperation. "Forget it."

"Go on, you came here to what?"

"To ask you something. But you know what? Forget it. You girls are all the same. You're not worth my time. Hell, you're not worth the air you breathe while you hump a goddamn pole."

"What the actual fuck. You fall out of love fast."

"Thanks for saving me the time upfront."

"Thanks for the preview of what you're like in a relationship. No wonder you're single."

His face reddened, his jaw tightened, and without another word, Brian stormed out of the club.

A tall drink of trouble was still watching me from across the room, and I was really starting to hate how thirsty this place made me. Once I verified Cecil had disappeared into his office, I danced toward Josh. But a sporty chick nearly bowled me over on the way, flying toward the stage where Honey danced to the 1975's *Girls*. I was surprised when Josh leapt up and intercepted her: something Honey noticed immediately. I couldn't hear what he and the girl were saying, but it was obviously an argument. She stuck her finger in his face and screamed out a stream of garbled obscenities before continuing her march toward the stage.

Honey had stopped dancing and stood naked,

glaring down at the girl with her teeth bared. I couldn't tell if they were speaking; it looked more like they were snarling at each other. Then, like a jungle cat, Honey pounced. She dove claws-first from the stage and tackled the girl with an explosion of fluttering money. The bouncers didn't waste any time reaching the two women, but there was a definite delay in their attempt to stop the fight. Everyone watched with varying degrees of awe. While several of the men looked on in lust, I was amazed by how viciously Honey attacked the girl. She had no concern for her nudity or the dozens of people crowded around her. Eventually, Stu and Gary shook off their stupors, already filling more than their quota for a Sunday. They ripped Honey away, but she flailed wildly as she tried to regain her grip on the other girl.

"Calm the fuck down, both of you!" Stu roared.

By the time the bodyguards released Honey, I'd already gathered up most of her money. She was molten rock glaring at the girl, but when I handed over the cash, she softened with gratitude. Then Josh slipped himself in front of her enemy, and she became scalding stone again.

"Where's James?" she growled.

"Fuck if I know. Last I saw he was with you."

"Do you know this bitch?"

"Yeah, we met right before I fucked your boyfriend," the girl warbled.

"Fuck you, whore!" Honey screamed.

"What did you call me?"

The girl tried to lunge, but Gary stopped her before she could make contact.

Honey looked to Josh for confirmation. "Is it true? Did James fuck her?"

The girl broke out in song again, "You bet your fat ass he did."

"What the fuck are you doing here, Marlene?" James strode over. "I told you to keep your raggedy ass away from me."

When Gary released the girl, she promptly spat at James and clawed at his face. He pushed her so hard, her feet left the floor and she landed hard on her tailbone. The bouncers tackled James as he was patting blood from the scratches on his face. Falling beside her, he roared like they were trying to wrench off his arms.

"She's a liar! Don't listen to her!"

"Gentlemen, get these boys out of my club;" Cecil said, appearing behind the Megatouch, making me wonder if he'd been there all along. "Birdie, Honey, get your asses backstage."

"Honey, I swear I didn't touch her!" James shouted as Stu pushed him and Josh over to the bar.

"Honey, backstage," Cecil repeated firmly.

"Did you fuck him?" she asked the girl.

Marlene stood slowly and wiped dirt off her leggings. "Three times. And that was just last night. And he went so much deeper than that." She caressed her belly. Her fingernails were dirty, her arms covered in welts.

I'd had enough. I stared in her eyes and asked, "Honestly?" and Marlene swallowed her smile. "I'm looking at Honey and I'm looking at you, and something's not adding up. So, either you just want to sleep with him, or you slept with him before he met the most beautiful woman in the world, and you're trying to get him back."

Her chin trembled. "It's her fault! We were about to go official when he met her."

"That was never going to happen!" James shouted as Gary pulled him outside.

"No! I broke all my rules for him. I wept for him! I bled for him!" The girl who had been so puffed up by bravado suddenly looked as small as a mouse. I briefly wondered if I should try to hook her up with Brian, but a shrill scream instantly emptied my mind. And I wasn't the only one.

Stu grumbled. "What the fuck is going on today? It's a goddamn Sunday."

The scream continued, followed by scores of frantic voices. The crowd became animated in shock and fearful curiosity, and I couldn't help but join them. Even Honey abandoned her rage, tossed on her dress, and joined the people rushing toward the source of the dissonant shrieking in the alley.

Drawing closer, I detected hidden sounds emerging from beneath the commotion. Whirring first, then a grinding squeal of malfunction, followed by a series of rapid off-tempo thumps. An abrupt squelch led to a prolonged scrape that changed into frenzied crackles and clicks. The auditory puzzle lured me forward, but when I reached the front of the crowd and the pieces fell into place, I backpedaled so hard I fell onto the neighboring lane. But I could still see the horrifying scene through the crowd's trembling legs. A thousand extra crimson markers were splattered across the floor, blooming into puddles surrounding the pinsetter. The machinery jerked up and down, slamming the butt of the pins against the pulpy remnants of a girl's face. Blood and meat erupted with each blow, and bits of bone and tooth tumbled across the lane like hapless dice.

"For God's sake, turn it off!" The crowd pleaded, but there was a palpable gasp of regret when the machine stopped, and the bludgeoning pins no longer obstructed our view of the girl. Many fled when the horrific spell broke. I would have joined them if my legs hadn't turned to jelly, leaving me paralyzed on the floor.

The damage was far worse in an inert form. Her forehead was caved in, with bits of gray matter seeping between the cracks. Her mouth, stretched to an unnatural degree by the base of the pin, gave her a permanent look of shock framed by shards of teeth in her flattened gums. Chunks of her face slid down the pins and dripped back into their obliterated origins, filling the silence with nauseating plops of postmortem percussion.

Even if her face had been identifiable, it wasn't necessary. Her massive sinew-spattered breasts might as well have been a nametag declaring: "Hello. My name is Diamond."

Burning revulsion inched up my throat. I was able to choke it back, but when Heaven hurled on Lane 5, the stench of blood and vomit was too much. Still tucked between the legs of gawking customers, I had no choice but to give my stomach the floor. The world blurred, and I wilted. Thankfully someone grabbed me before I collapsed into the amalgamating puddles of puke. They dragged my limp body across the lanes, my feet dipping in and out of gutters, until depositing me into a chair. It was probably gentle, but I felt like I was thrown into it.

A faraway voice broke through the haze in my brain. "Hey, you okay?"

I looked up woozily, expecting to see Josh's face— no, desperately wanting to see Josh's face. Instead, it was Petey looking down at me. He was touching me, holding me, his fingers moving up and down my arms, slick in sweat and...something else. Vomit. It was vomit. It was...

I caught the sickening surge at the tip of my tongue, slapped my hand over my mouth, and ran to the bathroom. Nearly bursting by the time I was in the stall, I curled myself over the toilet. As I emptied, the images that filled my head summoned everything my stomach had left, but my mind refused to follow suit with its contents. Diamond's mutilation swam in my brain. Her sweet, milky face now nothing more than a mashed motley of bone and meat. Then there were her breasts; those gigantic twins that led men like the Pied Piper were now just heavy sacks hanging off her ribcage like blood-spattered globs of mucus after a violent sneeze.

People vomited all around me. The stalls in the ladies room were full, but that didn't stop anyone. The sink overflowed with puke, which spilled onto the floor and seeped across the tile. When it pooled cold against my leg, I began gagging again. But with nothing left in my stomach, I alternated between dry-heaving and belching through my revulsion.

A tiny voice said my name from the neighboring stall. I didn't even recognize it as Honey's—usually so commanding, so confident—until she stuck her head under the wall. She trembled as she handed me a bottle of water.

I took a large gulp from her bottle and opened the stall door for her. I was quaking and glazed with the sweat, but when she wrapped her arms around me, I started to feel better.

"What happened to her?" I asked.

"I don't know. I didn't even know she was working tonight," Honey said. "Did you see her earlier?"

"Yeah, when Scott was here. They were arguing before Stu threw him out."

"Your crazy ex-boyfriend was fighting with Diamond?" She spat a sour loogie into the toilet. "Didn't you say something about him hating strippers?"

My mind swelled, but not as violently as my stomach. The sound of someone's lunch hitting the toilet bowl made me heave again, but to little result except blinding pain. When Honey held back my ponytail my heaves turned into moans, and tears streamed into the frothy water.

"Don't worry, Birdie. Everything will be okay," Honey said as she stroked my hair. "Maybe it was all a horrible accident."

"Unlikely." Ginger gave the door a little tug, and it swung open. Lighting a cigarette, she said, "Her throat was cut open."

"Oh my god, Ginger! Don't say that!" CJ squealed before dashing into an open stall.

"How do you know that?" Honey asked her.

"I used my super-duper powers of sight," she said facetiously. "I guess you missed it when you were balled up in puddles of barf."

"Have some goddamn courtesy, Ginger." Honey's voice cracked. "Our friend just died."

"Yeah? How many times did you hang out with her off the clock?" Ginger scoffed and folded her arms over her chest. "Some friends you are."

The bitch was right, but it didn't stop several girls from bursting into tears.

I wiped my face with scratchy toilet paper and stood. "I have to get out of here."

Ginger ashed her cigarette in a sink clogged with regurgitated bar food. "They're not letting anyone leave. The police want to question everyone. Oh, and I'd hide your stashes if I were you." Dropping the butt in the chunky brown lake, she marched out.

When Honey and I left the bathroom, the police were talking to Cookie, who had already lost her false eyelashes to tears and tissues. Even from my distance at the top of the stage stairs, I saw Diamond lying on Lane 5. There was a sheet draped over her, but the upper half was largely drenched in blood. I felt the urge to throw up again, but the backstage door flew open and Honey yanked me inside. She shoved my suitcase into my hands and threw my hoodie on top. Pantera frantically pressed her fingers to the makeup table and rubbed any residue powder onto her gums.

"What's going on?"

A whisper answered, "Hand me your bag."

Josh poked his head in from the broken emergency exit and gestured for my suitcase.

"Guys, we can't just leave. What about the police?"

"The police are why I'm leaving," Pantera said, then

slipped out the back door.

"Are you going?" I asked Heaven, and she shook her head.

"If Jason's staying, so am I."

"Come on, Birdie. You said you wanted to get out of here. We can go to my house," Honey said, tossing her bag at James. "Besides, what if the killer is still here?"

"Oh." Shivers climbed my spine, but I shook them away. "I'm sure the police will scare him—her—whoever away."

"Those idiots couldn't scare a hamster," James spat.

"They're scaring you pretty well."

James looked like he wanted to fire back, but Honey pushed him out the door. She reached for me, and I thought of what Ginger said about Diamond, how we were never really friends, and running away just seemed wrong.

"You were on the schedule tonight. When the police realize you left, they're going to come looking for you."

"Birdie, did you fill out an application to work here? Did you fill out any tax forms or emergency contact info?"

"Not that I remember." She was right. As far as the club was concerned, I might as well have been a ghost. Diamond certainly was now.

"Cecil doesn't know where I live," Honey said. "I'd be surprised if he remembers my last name."

"What *is* your last name?"

She bit her lip. "Potter."

"You're joking."

She chuckled. "I wish I was."

"Well, Miss Honey Potter, I want to go with you, but I don't feel right about it. Maybe I saw something that'll help them find whoever did this to Diamond."

"Are you sure?"

"Be careful getting out of here," I said.

"Be careful staying here," she replied, gave me a

hug, then leapt out the back door.

James was on her heels as she fled, but Josh didn't move. His eyes asked a dozen questions, but I wiggled my fingers and mouthed "goodbye" as I closed the door. Trying to occupy my brain with something normal, I wiped my face clean and changed into my street clothes. I was pulling down my ponytail when Cookie trudged into the dressing room, her makeup like runny pancake batter and wig noticeably askew.

"Hey Birdie, the cops wanna talk to you."

"Me specifically?"

I lost her to the mirror. She gasped in horror as she pawed at her face and tugged on her hair, a few zealous swipes away from matching Diamond's current makeup. Her sloppy face burned in my mind again, and my stomach turned as I left the dressing room. They were loading her onto a gurney, her hand hanging loose under the blood-soaked sheet.

"Your name?" I wasn't sure which officer was addressing me. They looked like one long blue blur as I struggled to generate enough saliva to speak. I felt so out of it, I wasn't sure if I said "Eva" or "Birdie;" I might not have responded at all. But I did speak eventually, my voice like a hollow drum pounding at the back of my brain. They asked a string of questions for which I had no answers and a lot of questions with answers that didn't seem relevant.

"Thank you for your time, Ms. Finch," said the blue fuzz. "You can head on home now. Get some rest."

Rest. Right.

"Have you seen Honey?" Cecil shuffled over, hands on his hips.

"Honey? Was she working tonight?" My voice trembled. It squeaked. It betrayed me at every syllable.

"You know she was. Remember the fight?"

"Oh yeah. There were so many."

He narrowed his eyes, then patted my shoulder

in consolation. "Don't worry about it. We'll be closed tomorrow. Probably the day after too."

"I'm not scheduled until Friday," I said blankly, feeling strange discussing the schedule with EMTs still wheeling Diamond's corpse through the club.

"Hopefully we'll be back open by then. Give a call that morning, though." He touched my shoulder again. "Get some rest."

That word again. Rest. Who the fuck could rest after seeing something so awful? What kind of person could do anything but curl into a ball and cry?

I pushed open the door to see Josh leaning against my car, smoking a cigarette like an oversexed cowboy on a romance novel cover, and when lust pulse between my legs, I knew exactly what kind of person could do something besides cry. A shitty person like me.

I half-expected him to say "Howdy, little lady" when I approached, but he gave me a sympathetic smile that made my eyes water.

"Are you okay?"

I sank against the carbeside him. "I feel like eight thousand people have asked me that in the past hour."

"It's because you're such a fragile little porcelain doll."

His voice was playful, and however inappropriate the timing, the fat clumsy ox I always saw myself as appreciated the compliment. In five years, Scott never made me feel as slight and pretty as Josh had in those few words. The way he touched me mirrored the sentiment, like holding me too tightly might shatter my delicate frame, and in turn, all the beauty in the world.

"I thought you were going with Honey and James."

"I wanted to wait for you. You shouldn't be alone."

"What a line."

He chuckled as he directed his eyes at the ground, but when he looked back up, he stared at me so intensely I didn't notice him take my bag out of my hand.

"Can we go to your place?" he asked. "I'll follow you."

"That's probably best. You don't wanna get stuck in my apartment in case I turn out to be the killer."

His eyebrows lifted. "I'm not sure that would be a dealbreaker."

"I don't think I'll be very good company, just so you know. My head is...everything's so muddled."

"I know what you mean." He stretched his neck until it cracked. "The truth is, I'm the one that doesn't want to be alone. I *can't* be alone. I'm not very good at dealing with death."

"It would be weird if you were."

"I guess that's true."

I raked my lip with my teeth. "Okay, you can follow me home if you want."

Affection felt strange on top of horror. Two kinds of nausea dwelt in my belly and I couldn't handle it. One had to go.

"But I don't want to talk about what happened tonight," I said. "If you come over, I don't want to get into some deep dark conversation about death, okay? I can't."

"I promise."

The horror didn't flee entirely, but it paled. I knew it could leap back up at any moment, but for the next few hours, I was resolved to think of life, not death.

As I drove, I couldn't stop my eyes from darting to the rear-view mirror to check if he was still on my tail. More than anything, I did not want to lose him. When I opened my apartment door for us, Fidelio went nuts. Maybe it was because of my visitor, or because he sensed that I needed a good snuggle. Either way, his bouncy vocal dance made Josh chuckle. When he scooped him up and booped his nose, Diamond was pushed even further out of mind. More and more, my thoughts moved to Josh.

"You have a nice place. Two bathrooms?" he asked.
"Yeah, but don't go in the far one, okay?"
"Why not?"
"It's going to make me sound really stupid." I flung the refrigerator door open. "Would you like a drink?"
"What do you have?"
"Light beer, box of Chablis, water, milk..."
"I'll take a beer."
"And I'll have a box."

I was amazed by how easily we fell into a comfortable dance. He made me laugh, blush, even feel beautiful. Anyone who could do that impressed me, especially after the night I just had.

I sipped my wine, smacking my lips discerningly. "You know, the cardboard really gives the wine something. A bouquet of thrift, if you will."

"Birdie, you're not getting out of telling the bathroom story."

I groaned. "Fine. I was trying to teach Fidelio how to use the toilet instead of the litter box; you know, *Meet the Parents*-style. I put the box in the toilet like I was supposed to, but I didn't get far before disaster struck. Not even a day, actually. When I was adjusting the box, I lost my grip and all the litter spilled into the toilet. Now it won't flush."

He snorted behind his hand. "I'd think not."

"So, technically, I have two bathrooms but only one useable toilet. And the floor in there is pretty littery, so you should probably avoid that room altogether."

"Don't worry. I won't go anywhere you don't want me to go," he said, keeping his eyes on me as he tilted back his beer.

"I think the living room is safe."

Sitting with a foot of sofa between us was awkward. After all, he'd already seen the goods. I decided to pack a bowl in the hopes it would numb my jitters.

"Your hands are shaking," he said.

"After what happened, can you blame me?" I dropped a few chunks of weed onto the carpet, and Josh picked them up.

"Let me." With nimble plucks and twists, he packed the bowl in under a minute. Watching his hands, my brain unfolded a fantasy in which my body received the same masterful treatment. He passed me the bowl but held onto the lighter as I inhaled.

The smoke clouded the room but cleared my head, and with a gulp of wine, I was able to force myself to focus on Josh again.

"Tell me about yourself," he said to me.

"That's a tall order," I said, gulping more wine.

"Okay, tell me *something* about yourself."

My brain screamed for me to say something cute, something enticing, something that would make him smile and scoot a little closer. Even something boring would've been better than what lumbered off my tongue, but like an idiot, I said, "My mother is also my cousin."

He coughed. "I thought you just worked in West Virginia. I didn't think you were one of *those* West Virginians."

"No, it's not like that. It's a very weird distant relation. My great great grandmother is the fourth cousin of my great great grandfather, or something like that. It's dumb. I don't know why I said it."

"Hey, if you're the result of inbreeding, you make a good case for it," he said, clinking his beer against my glass.

"What about you?".

"I don't think I have any double relations."

"I mean, it's your turn to tell me something."

Josh crinkled his nose. "I have a feeling you're way more interesting than me."

"You might be disappointed."

"I highly doubt that. Tell me something else about

you," he urged.

"I grew up in Carroll County, graduated from high school, took off some time before going to community college, and another community college, then I ended up here."

"You're only 21, right?" he asked, and I nodded. "Then you're not 'ending up.' And why Cumberland?"

"I was going to school."

"But you're not anymore?"

"I don't think school and I get along. I want to do well, I don't want to waste my mom's money, but I think I learn a lot better on my own."

"What's the last thing you learned?"

I wanted to say something cheesy like, "You're really easy to talk to," but I opted for something stupid instead. Luckily, when I blurted "Platypuses are poisonous!" he erupted into laughter.

"You're fucking adorable."

My face hurt from smiling and my legs hurt from squeezing them closed.

"Enough about me," I said. "Your turn."

"But I want to know more about poisonous platypuses."

"Too bad. Where'd you grow up?"

"Ohio. I moved here about four months ago."

I scrunched one eye. "So why Cumberland?

"A job opportunity. I was working for my dad for a while, but I couldn't take it anymore, so I left."

"You and your dad don't get along?"

"I don't get along with either of my parents. I never have."

"Do you have any brothers or sisters?"

"Yes, I—I mean, no."

He looked down at his beer. I didn't know if he was searching for the right words, or if his answer ended there. Then, he gave me a pursed smile, the kind that never looks real.

"I had a brother, but he died."

"Oh God, Josh, I'm sorry. I didn't mean to stir anything up. Especially after—no, we're not talking about it."

"Calm down, Birdie. I didn't think you were stirring anything up. You didn't know." He touched my hand reassuringly. "Anyway, it happened a while ago. Let's just say my brother needed help and our parents didn't care enough to give it to him." He swirled his bottle. "I don't like to talk that much about my family."

"I don't blame you. My family isn't perfect either. Well, except for my mom. She's gorgeous— beauty queen gorgeous. She was always on one side telling me to enter pageants, and my sister was on the other calling me a 'fatty flatty' in front of the whole school."

"What's a girl to do?" he warbled, and I shrugged.

"Become a stripper, apparently." I laughed as I rocked onto my feet. "I'm going to get another drink. Do you want one?"

"Absolutely."

I couldn't walk from the couch to the kitchen without looking back at him. He was so magnificently different from every other guy I'd liked. I'd always envisioned the tall, dark, and handsome type to be the kind of man who would break my heart, but Josh was so soft, so pretty, yet so deliciously commanding. When we stood opposite each other and he looked down from his heavens, I felt small and fragile, like if he took me in hand, what could I do but surrender to him? I'd lost myself in those thoughts so often since we met. When I danced, when I slept...when I accidentally dropped a wine glass.

I screeched, "Shit!" as it shattered at my feet.

Groaning, I collected the shards from the kitchen floor, dropped them in the trash, and turned to the cabinet for a plastic cup, but Josh had another wine glass ready. It was sweet, but as my gaze climbed to his entrancing eyes, I didn't want sweet. I wanted the needy intensity of his umber eyes to hypnotize me, to make yeses of all my nos, and convince me I could only feel warmth if he kindled it in me. And I *needed* him to kindle it, over and over, so I could stay ablaze. If only he would touch me...

His fingers lightly caressed my chest, my lips, my cheek, and his hand curled around the back of my neck, but he was barely touching me, and I was losing my goddamn mind.

With a growl, I grabbed his face and crushed it against mine. He moaned in gratitude, and every molecule in my body ignited in desire, even as he released me. I wanted him to push me against the refrigerator and grind my pelvic bone to lusty dust, but when I tried to kiss him again, he shook his head and backed me slowly against the wall.

"Tell me something else." He licked his lips, his fingers hovering above my left breast. "Something no one knows."

"Like what?"

"What do you jerk off to?"

"What?"

He brushed his thumb against my nipple and a swell of pleasure shot south.

"What do you jerk off to?" He danced the tip of his tongue up my throat and nipped at my flaming skin.

"I don't know," I whined, aching. "Stuff."

"What do you jerk off to?" He breathed the question against me, lowering, teasing me, his fingers creeping under my waistband, his pinky playing with my drawstring bow.

It felt like my clit might burst if he didn't touch me soon. He whispered his question again, his hand hovering inches from my throbbing body, and in desperation, I said,

"You."

I opened my mouth, prepared for the gasp that would follow his pressure, but the pressure didn't come, so neither did I.

He narrowed his eyes. "You're lying."

"Just tell me what you want me to say. Please."

"I want you to tell me something no one knows. I want to know what you jerk off to."

With a ravenous whisper of both desire and shame, I said, "Hentai."

It sounded terrible escaping my lips, but his face lit up, and one eyebrow crooked to the heavens. His fingers clamped against my clit and I moaned as he slammed his leg against his hand, pushing it harder against me. Shifting his thigh between my legs, he grasped my face and plunged his tongue into my mouth. I squeezed my thighs around him, rocking desperately as my pleasure built, my skin prickling hot and cold, the aching, the throbbing, the promise of release. I broke away from his hungry lips and released a grateful groan as his hands moved under my shirt and pinched my nipples.

He dove back into my kiss as he untied my drawstring. My sweatpants sagged on my hips but didn't fall. I tried to shimmy them down without releasing the sensual curves of his arms, but he took care of it when he stepped on a loose fold of fabric and stomped then down with one clean jerk.

He kissed me again, brushed the hair out of my eyes, then sank to his knees and kissed me deeper. I leaned my head back, ran my fingers through his hair, and enjoyed every delicious moment of his tongue giving its own sort of lap-dance. When he stood again, I figured it was my turn to kneel, but he stopped me.

"Not tonight," he whispered. "I want tonight to be about you, about your pleasure."

"It *would* give me pleasure," I said caressing the bulge beneath his zipper, hardening with each inch I dropped to the floor.

He had a nice cock. Sometimes male genitalia made me feel like a judge in the world's ugliest dog contest. I'd seen some shriveled shar-peis and patchy chorkies during my frequent breakups with Scott, but Josh's was damn near appetizing as far as dicks went. The harder he was, the better it looked, and the more I remembered why I hadn't questioned my sexuality too much before starting at Pins. There was just something about a hard cock that did it for me. Wet, even better.

I didn't consider myself especially skilled at blowjobs, but his hard wet cock didn't stay that way for long once I started. I barely had time to back off his dick so his cum didn't ping against the back of my throat and up into my Eustachian tubes...which had never happened, but with all the labyrinthine channels of the human head so tightly interwoven, I wasn't taking any risks.

He apologized profusely, but I chose to take it as a compliment—then surrender to his demands to let him "make it up to me."

I sighed in theatrical defeat as I pushed down his head. "If you insist..."

He enveloped me in cyclonic heat, our bodies driven together by the need to feel something beautiful on such an ugly night. Lost in our desperate lust, I hardly noticed our transition from the kitchen to my bed, where he threw me down, and I disappeared—mind, body, and soul—into dizzying scores of orgasms. Too foggy with bliss to do anything but obey, I grinded my slippery cunt against him, delighting in how my gratification dripped down his chin. We didn't need to speak, didn't need to think. We didn't even need his cock to have a good time.

All at once, sticky thoughts penetrated the fog, and I felt my body tense under his tongue. I thought of Honey. She wouldn't need a cock either. I thought of glittering girls and sweaty stages and the feeling of my fingers sliding over my pussy onstage, how it tickled my heart to get myself wet. And Diamond. I thought of how Diamond would never have another orgasm, never have another kiss. She would never again sparkle with affection for the people she loved. I didn't know anything about her except that she was a straight A student with perfect D tits. I hadn't even thought about whether she had a husband or a boyfriend or what her friends and family were like. I hadn't considered how unfair it was that she'd never again enjoy the liquor of life while I was enjoying three fingers of Josh on the night she died. It all seemed so very wrong all of a sudden. I scooted away with an apology and closed my legs.

"Is this totally inappropriate?" I whispered. "I mean, after what happened, should we be enjoying ourselves like this?"

"Maybe." When my head bowed, he touched my knee. "*But*, yes, I think we should enjoy ourselves. We should enjoy life. Bad things happen all the time."

"This night wasn't just 'bad things.' It was... something else."

"You're right, it was, and I'm sorry for being so cold about it. I just, after what I've seen in the past, with my brother, it's hard to remember the 'right' way to act. I'm just so happy you're safe. I'm happy I'm safe. I'm happy we're together," he said as he brushed away a curl that had attached itself to my lip. "I can wait for everything else, Birdie. We probably shouldn't go much further anyway. Not tonight. Not on a first date, if you would call it that."

His winking smile was adept at pushing away danger and welcoming back frolic. It caught the moonlight with a devil's promise.

"Was this a date? I thought dates were supposed to involve eating dinner or something."

He clicked his tongue. "Well, I did eat *something*."

"That was more dessert than dinner."

"It certainly was."

His warmth, his sympathy, his tenderness—they were all so intoxicatingly powerful, I was able to shove aside the horror long enough to enjoy another kiss.

"I like you, Josh," I said, surprising myself with the honesty.

He wrapped his arms around me and kissed the top of my head. "I like you too."

We didn't have sex that night, but we slept together, cuddled in the darkness with our hearts alight.

He fell asleep quickly, but sticky thoughts lit up in me like fireflies once the lights went out. I pictured Diamond dancing over me the way Alexxxa Love had, but unlike the featured dancer, her pussy didn't smell like mine. It smelled like burnt hair and tampon receptacles in gas station bathrooms. And she didn't wave it alluringly; she threatened me with it. On all fours, gurgling around broken teeth and a tongue like tenderized ribeye, Diamond slammed her putrid pussy downwards like a malfunctioning pin setter, just short of my nose at first, but incrementally closer with each stab of her rotten crotch, over and over, until her pelvic bone smashed against my skull and her slaughterhouse cunt exploded like watermelon at a Gallagher show, burying me in the reeking meat of her deceased crease.

CHAPTER EIGHT

It hadn't even been two months, and I was addicted to Josh. Hanging out, getting high, getting sweaty: it was all good. The latter became an issue when my air conditioning unit broke, but we soldiered through. We panted through blistering euphoria and usually came out victorious, but while I could survive playing that way, I could no longer survive sleeping that way.

My hair was wet, wrapped around my neck in sticky ropes that choked me with every frustrated flip. Summer had arrived with sauna strength, causing me to toss and turn and tear my hair free with angry grunts. And the angrier I got, the more Josh giggled.

"It's not funny. I'm so hot." I kicked the covers off of the bed and throttled the mattress with my heels.

"Did you talk to the maintenance people?"

"A bunch of times." When he raised his eyebrows dubiously, I twitched my nose. "Okay, no, I didn't, but they scare me."

"It's wacky that someone who does what you do is so skittish. Then again, I know you pretty well now, so it doesn't shock me anymore."

"You only think you know me."

"So what don't I know?"

I leaned into him with an eyebrow arched and my voice primed for a gritty growl.

"I'm Batman."

His eyes widened in theatrical shock. "I had no idea."

"I'm very good at keeping secrets."

"I can empathize because, you see..." He lowered his voice. "I'm Superman."

I groaned like a teenager forced to go to church on a Saturday night. "No! I hate Superman!"

"What?! How can you hate Superman? What did he ever do to you?"

"What did he ever do *for* me?" I flopped my fists against the bed. "It's too hot to argue."

"You just know you can't win." He chuckled and blew cool breath across my neck. "You know, my air conditioning works."

"Are you inviting me to your house? Am I going to meet your parents too?" I poked his side playfully, but he tossed me a loaded look. "Sorry, I forgot."

He blew another gust of air, then pulled me close with a forceful but passionate jerk that almost landed me on top of him. Although I immediately began to sweat, I couldn't be bothered to mind. I'd tried pushing him into discussing his family before, but every time I broached the subject, he kissed me or tickled me or gave me some other affectionate form of dismissal.

"What do you say? Stay with me until your AC is fixed?" He wiped a drop of sweat from my cheek. "Fidelio can come too."

"Moving in after less than two months? We must be crazy in love."

"Definitely crazy," he said. "But I don't care. I'm looking forward to playing house with you."

"If you think I'm going to parade around in an apron and nothing else, you're—"

His fingers found my obliging nature, and I hummed in supplication.

"Okay, maybe an apron wouldn't be so bad..."

It was nearly midnight by the time we decided, but I

was so eager to see Josh's sanctuary, I didn't care about the time. All I wanted to do was sleep in the cool comfort of air conditioning—and investigate his inner sanctum. I didn't think he was lying about anything, but I was determined to discover if he really was as perfect as he seemed. He lived just north of Frostburg in a house that was larger than I'd pictured. It was the sort of place that needed kids barreling through corridors and filling up the empty spaces with shrieking laughter. It was never more evident than when I released Fidelio from his carrier, and he ping-ponged around the cavernous house, warbling at every new discovery. Without itthat sort of energy, the building almost felt morose.

Then I felt the blast of central air. I threw open my arms and sighed as a frigid breeze rushed over me.

"Feeling better?"

"Much." I knocked Josh a kiss that pressed him against the wall. "You don't have roommates, right? We're alone?"

"God I hope so," he said as I unbuttoned his pants.

Josh had me perpetually turned on. I couldn't help myself when he was around, and I didn't want to. All I wanted was him. Against the wall, on the floor, hanging half off the bed, it didn't matter. Something that I didn't even know was sleeping was awakened when we met, and I was determined to keep it awake. Being well-sexed and happy made me more fun to be around, and it boosted my earnings at Pins, too. I didn't just slap my fingers against my pussy, wishing I were anywhere else. Honest euphoria magically turned ones into fives, which helped when the incident with Diamond obliterated my bank account. After over a week's closure for the ongoing murder investigation, the club's business had dropped dramatically. The alley side, conversely, was doing better than ever, thanks to the morbid curiosity of people with little else to do. I didn't blame them. If I hadn't gotten an eyeful, I probably would have paid to roll a game on the "Diamond Lane" too.

But I did get an eyeful, and I could still smell it. For weeks afterward, I felt like I was going to throw up every time I passed Lane Five. I forced myself to get over it because I needed the money, but it was the last straw for some of the girls. Ebony and Faith both quit, and Heaven cut back to working Saturday nights only, so Cecil was forced to move Destiny to the club side permanently, much to the chagrin of the remaining dancers. He also beefed up the security. Along with more lights in the parking lot, he added two more bouncers on weekdays and four more on weekends. Eventually, business got back on track, but none of the dancers felt any safer, not while Diamond's killer was still on the loose. It was almost enough to make me want to go back to waitressing.

Almost.

"You're miles away," Josh said, pressing me against the wall. "Where are you?"

"Ammparrmipa."

He chuckled. "What?"

I stopped kissing his neck and repeated. "Antarctica." I purred, eyes closed. "This is so nice. I'm so cool here."

"I'm sure you're cool wherever you are."

"You know what I mean, goofus. I don't ever want to go back to my apartment, and I definitely don't want to go to work tomorrow. But I never really do anymore. I'm still so freaked out."

"Do you really think the same killer would hit the same spot?"

"I don't know what a killer would do."

"Why would you?" He started at my collarbone and dotted a map of anxiety relief down my body before burying his face in my treasure.

I shivered in bliss. "Now I really feel cool."

He jokingly slurped on my clit, then smacked my ass

as he jumped to his feet.

"You hungry?"

"Always," I said, wiping spittle from my thighs.

"I'll make us some sandwiches. Turkey all right?"

"My favorite." I tried to open my email, but my phone wouldn't connect. "Hey, do you have a wifi password I can get? My signal's nonexistent."

"Wanna check your OnlyFans?"

"I want to check my *email*." I twitched my nose, adding quickly, "I checked OnlyFans before we left."

His eyes widened, and a slow smirk inched up his cheek. "I can't tell if you're kidding."

"See? You don't know me as well as you think." I covered the lower half of my face with an imaginary cape. "Batman needs to keep *some* secrets."

"I can't argue with that," he chuckled, then asked for my phone. He typed in his password, saved it for next time, then handed it back. "Voila! You can hang out in the bedroom, second door on the right. I'll bring your sandwich in when it's ready."

"You're too sweet."

"For you? Or for my own good?"

"For this dangerous dogshit world." I kissed his cheek and bounded into his bedroom for the first time.

Once I was alone, a subtle investigation began. I read into every un-puttied hole in the wall. Did it say something about his comfort with imperfection, or was it a subconscious expression of his fear of attachment? There weren't many pictures in the house, landscapes mostly, one that looked like an overexposed self-portrait. Nothing like my place, splashed with movie posters and treasured memories, but it didn't exactly surprise me. We had a lot in common, but our personalities differed in many ways. I was cruder and decidedly louder while his rowdiness was more subdued, simmering just beneath a calm surface that I splashed right through. He was guarded. A man like him, so confident, bordering on imposing, and one question about his past balled him up like a bashful hedgehog. It was sexy too though, a keen duality I craved enough to stave off curiosity a while longer.

I had one new email, but I didn't need Miracle-Gro for my dick, so I deleted it and moved on to tending my garden of notifications. I had a few messages from friends wondering if I was going to a party on Saturday, or going to the Wine Fest the following weekend, both of which I'd already declined due to work. Someone commented on a picture I posted of Josh and me with our tongues out. On one of Honey and me too. I had to be careful about what I posted to protect the tenuous web of lies I'd draped around my new profession, so I never posted any pictures taken in or around the club. But outside Sheetz at 3am lying on the hood of her Mazda sucking on Rocket Pops was completely acceptable. I was zooming in on Honey's off-kilter smile when my finger accidentally tapped the West Virginia location tag, generating a grid of recent posts.

The first image in the upper left corner was a screenshot of the headline: "West Virginia Killer Tweets Crime." The grid contained a few other images of the tweet in question, one of which was pasted over a fuzzy picture of Pins' exterior. I tapped it, and tears instantly filled my eyes.

Thirteen hours ago, someone with the username @Chastity_Bellows posted: "She bowled me over, so I pinned her. Now that Diamond is looking rough."

I screamed, and Josh ran in with a head of lettuce in his hand.

"What's wrong?"

"Whoever killed Diamond tweeted about it!"

"What? That has to be a joke," he said as he scrolled up and down the page.

"I don't think so."

He stared at the screen. "Does that mean the police

know who the killer is?"

"If they don't yet, they probably will soon."

"Good. Maybe there's a chance of catching this Chastity Bellows, huh? Maybe it was some chick who was jealous of Diamond," he said. "Where did you find it?"

"Instagram, but..." A quick Google search led me to an article from the Cumberland Times. "It's everywhere. Listen to this: 'Tweet about Slain Exotic Dancer has Town on Pins and Needles.'"

"Clever."

"And completely insulting to the poor exotic dancer. Diamond was a straight A student, but I don't see a single thing about that. She busted her ass to afford school, and now she's just some dead stripper, and people are gonna think she had it coming. God, just when I thought things were getting back to normal...or, you know, our weird version of normal."

"*Your* weird version." He tossed the lettuce in the air and caught it. "I'm completely normal."

"Yeah, I guess," I mumbled.

He cocked his head. "You okay?"

"Yeah. It's nothing."

"It's not nothing. I can tell."

"You can't tell," I countered, knowing I sounded like a petulant child.

"I think I know what it is." He grinned. "Stay here."

I flopped face down on his bed, my hand hitting his bedside table. I rubbed the sore spot as I sat up again and squinted at the partially open drawer. I tried to ignore it, but a growing curiosity made me hook my finger on the drawer and ease it open. Staring back from beneath the glass of the picture frame were two pairs of big, brown eyes belonging to two young boys. They had sandy brown hair and smiles people only sported in youth, before they knew better.

"What are you doing?" Josh asked from the doorway.

"I'm sorry, I—I—" I sighed. "I don't have a good excuse. I was being nosy."

"I guess it's all right," he said. "I looked through your medicine cabinet, too. You're using athlete's foot cream that expired in 2002."

"It's not mine, I swear!" He laughed, so I proceeded cautiously. "Is this a picture of you?"

"Yes, it is."

"And your brother?"

He cleared his throat. "Yeah."

"I know you don't like to talk about it, but are you ever going to tell me about him? Or about what happened between you and your parents?"

"It doesn't have anything to do with us, Birdie, with what we have."

"No, but it would give me some insight into who you are."

"Who I *was*," he corrected.

"Your parents weren't circus freaks, were they?"

"I wish they were." He expelled a sad hum. "Look, my brother had problems, and my parents couldn't deal."

"You said that before, but I don't really understand what that means."

"They weren't attentive. They didn't know or want to know anything about my brother and me, especially him. His mental issues made them uncomfortable, so instead of dealing with it, they wrote him off. He walked around that house like a ghost when I wasn't there. They didn't even want to look at him, let alone speak to him."

"If they really had that much of a problem, why didn't they just—God, I don't know how to say this without sounding like that Marion Crane chick in *Psycho*."

"You mean 'put him someplace?'" Josh asked.

Fuck, he really got me. It was hot as hell.

"They tried," he continued, "but I wouldn't let them. He didn't need to be ignored. He needed help."

"Did you help him?"

"For a while."

He cleared his throat, shaking his head as if the sad thoughts would simply fall out his ears. Both hands were behind his back, and he reasserted their presence with a chirp. "Pick a hand."

"Josh, I'm sorry."

He smiled, but I knew the subject was officially changed. "Please, just pick a hand."

"Left."

"Pick the other one."

"Okay, right," I chuckled as he merrily revealed a joint and a lighter.

"Ooo, thanks!"

Once I'd exhaled my first cloud, he showed his left hand: a plate balancing a triple-decker turkey sandwich.

My brain celebrated, but my hand hesitated.

"What's wrong?" he asked, the turkey hanging out to dry.

"I know it's weird, but I'm afraid you won't always be like this. You won't always be nice."

"What makes you think that?"

"My ex and I were happy for a long time. He was sweet in the beginning."

"I'm not your ex. I'm nothing like that tampon."

"He's not a tampon."

Josh looked at me curiously. "Do you still have feelings for him?"

"Josh..."

"You do."

"We were friends that became something more. Then something more became something not so friendly. He never broke my heart. We just grew apart. I mean, it was kinda bad in the very end, but I don't hate him for it."

"Birdie, he came into your job and basically called you and your coworkers sluts. I would never do that to you. I would make you eight turkey sandwiches a day." He waved the plate in front of my face.

"And you would watch me get super fat."

"I'd love it," he purred. An inch before the kiss, he halted and said firmly, "Please don't talk about him anymore. I don't like him, and I don't trust him."

"You hardly know him."

"I know he was there that night, the night Diamond was killed."

"A lot of people were there."

"Not staring at you the way he was. He looks like an angry guy."

"If I agree, can I get a bite of that sandwich?" I asked with a pout I hoped he'd find adorable.

With a pensive smile, he passed the plate into my hands. "I just worry about you. I care about you."

"I care about you too. And now that I've felt this air conditioning, I'm not going anywhere," I said, kissing him.

I forgot about the sandwich until the kiss ended fifteen minutes later. As Josh made use of the towel again, wiping my chest clean, I sunk my teeth into the moist turkey.

As July progressed and the heat wave escalated, I stayed true to my word. While I somehow kept "forgetting" to call maintenance about my broken AC, I camped out in Josh's igloo, dreading each time I had to leave. Why would I want to when I felt completely at home with him? He was great with Fidelio and me. When I got off work, the television was tuned to *Gargoyles*, a turkey sandwich was in the fridge, and a packed bowl was on the table. When Honey and James were over, I happily played the role of Josh's little housewife, entertaining the guests with games and snacks. Although I wasn't that close with James, the four of us spent a great deal of time doubled over in laughter...though the weed helped.

He wasn't terrible to be around, but I'd felt awkward around him after a recent group movie night at Josh's place.

The oven timer had gone off, so I went to the kitchen to fetch the pizza. In pure Birdie fashion, I'd burned it, along with the tray, but I tried to salvage what I could. James came out of the bathroom to see me struggling to force the knife through the charred crust, and he laughed.

"Here." He fetched a pizza cutter from a box on the counter.

"Thanks, but this knife is pretty sharp and it's not even getting through."

"This is sharper, trust me. I got it off the internet."

"Is that what you guys do when it's just the two of you? You buy kitchen supplies online?"

"It'll work. You just need the right amount of pressure."

I grabbed for the pizza cutter at the same time he thrusted it toward me, and the blade nicked my finger. I yelped and popped my finger in my mouth.

"Oh my god, I'm so sorry! Here, let me see it." I shook my head and he cracked a smile. "It can't be that bad. Just let me see it. Come on, Birdie, don't you trust me?"

"Yes," I creaked with my finger still clamped between my teeth.

With one last bite to dull the pain, I held up my finger. A drop of blood rolled from the tiny slice and I licked it away before holding my finger up again.

I don't know when he stopped looking at the wound and started looking at me; I just noticed he was closer than he should have been, and when I popped my finger back in my mouth, he got even closer. His leg brushed against me, and I looked down to see it hadn't been his leg at all. He was hard, and he was staring right at me. He must have seen the panic in my eyes because he abruptly backed away. He mumbled an apology, walked back into the bathroom, and we never mentioned it again. I was embarrassed enough for him that I didn't feel it necessary to involve Honey.

But since that day, James had been even more reserved. He still engaged in conversation as he always did, but more often, he smoked himself to sleep on the couch. I asked Honey if something was going on with them, but she swore he was livelier when they were alone.

"He just gets nervous around people he doesn't know that well."

"That's surprising for a guy who hangs out at Pins almost every weekend."

"He hangs out there for me."

I laughed. "I'm sure the other naked girls have nothing to do with it."

"What about Josh? He's there all the time too."

"I know he doesn't just come there for me, no matter what he says. They're straight men, Honey. They're going to look at other women."

"Maybe we should find some gay men," she said.

"I'm all for adding some to the mix, but I kinda like that my boyfriend digs my vagina. It's one of the reasons I spend time with him." She shrugged, and I narrowed my eyes at her. "You and James *are* getting along, right?"

"We're fine. I guess I'm—I don't know—he can be a little quiet sometimes, like I can't figure out what he's thinking. He wants to be alone a lot, which is strange considering how much he says he loves me. And he says it a lot, Birdie. Some of the things he says—" She looked down and nervously rubbed her hands over her thighs. "Some of the things he says are a little much. A little clingy."

"Considering who his girlfriend is, can you blame him?" I scrunched my nose at her.

"Maybe if we moved in together, it would be better," she said. "You and Josh seem closer than ever."

"We're not living together for real. It's just while my AC is out, which won't be much longer. The maintenance people came to my door the other day to tell me it's an apartment-wide issue and they'll be fixing them all soon. I'll have to go home after that."

"I bet if you asked nicely, he'd let you stay."

"Maybe. I do like playing house, but I'll be the first to admit we're going a little fast. It feels like Scott and I just broke up."

"You're probably right, but I'm still jealous."

I blushed. "Yeah, he's pretty great."

"Maybe *you're* not the one I'm jealous of," she said slyly, tugging one of my curls.

I giggled, my head drawing a little too close to hers. Accident or not, when I realized how close we were and saw her tongue slide over her lips, I backed away as smoothly as possible.

"Just as long as Josh doesn't get too clingy, I think we should be okay for a while."

"A while?"

"You never know."

"No, I guess you never do," Honey said. "After all, girls like us need our freedom."

"I don't think you and I are even the same breed, Honey."

"Oh shut up," she said and pinched another curl in my ponytail. "You're gorgeous and you know it. I just hope Josh knows it too."

"He tells me I'm beautiful all the time, but..."

"But?"

"It's hard to believe."

She sighed. "I know, I know. Your mom is a beauty queen and your sister calls you fat."

"It's not an easy thing to get past. You couldn't understand."

"Hey, I have my baggage too."

"Like what?"

"I don't mean to interrupt, but are either of you going to look at me during this private dance?" Petey said meekly, his back pressed so hard against the crushed velvet chair, he looked fearful one of us would smack him. "I did pay extra for the double."

Honey spun in front of me, than bent over for him. "You paid for tits and ass, Petey, and you're getting tits and ass."

"Eye contact would help."

Standing akimbo, Honey drummed her fingers against her hipbones before slipping her arm around my waist. She stared with dreamy passion into our customer's magnified eyes as her fingers slid over my body and made me forget we were dancing yet again. With our arms around each other, we dipped down and slid our bodies up his leg. I stayed closer to the knee, but Honey had no qualms about grinding herself nearer to his crotch. As his gaze slithered over our bodies, he exhaled a few words that sounded like grateful prayer to God, but when Honey leaned her head back and licked my neck, we became his God.

After the dance was done, he tucked extra money into our garters. Still under the spell of Honey's tongue, I didn't notice the bonus until we were backstage. It was a successful private dance, and I knew it was due solely to the double. If Honey hadn't been there, I probably wouldn't have gotten the extra cash and I definitely wouldn't have gotten as close to Petey. He might've been the nicest guy in the world, but he looked like the King of the Creepers. In a sex-related trade, it was always safer to judge a book by its cover. But you couldn't stop there. Covers could be misleading too. Just because Ramona Quimby was on the front didn't mean Patrick Bateman wasn't sneaking up behind, fantasizing about the tactile plunge of a blade into my back rolls.

I didn't have time to rest when the private dance was through. I was only able to take one toke before Brian announced Jade and I were on the main stage with Ginger and Destiny on the side stages. I exhaled smoke with a groan and Honey inhaled it with a chuckle. "Winds of Change" summoned me to the stage where Jade was already making good use of the pole and drawing in timid customers with her trademark toothy grin.

Once the Scorpions reached the chorus, most of the customers at Destiny's stage had wised up and moved to Ginger's side. But it was a short show. During the beginning of "Pussy Control," Ginger abruptly jumped off the side stage and started chasing a scruffy man dragging an unhappy child behind him. Ginger threw herself against the man in a burst of violence, scooped up the crying boy, and marched away from what I assumed to be her ex-husband. She stomped up the stairs, leaving a handful of disappointed men still at her stage. The music boomed, but I heard her scream "Get out!" when she entered the dressing room, causing Cookie and CJ to scramble down the stairs with their halter top strings undone.

It was difficult to keep dancing with such madness on parade, and the customers were so intrigued by the goings-on, it wasn't worth it anyway. When the song was over, Jade and I gathered our clothes and cash, and headed backstage. Ginger was crouched next to the kid, and Cecil actually appeared tender leaning over them with his hands on his knees.

"Don't worry. One of the other girls will watch him while you're onstage," he said and looked over his shoulder at us. "Birdie, Jade, could you—"

"No, no, no. Sorry, Ginger, but no." I quickly pulled

on my clothes while Jade just stood there, shaking her head.

"I'll call someone to pick him up, Cecil," Ginger said. "Just let me skip a couple of sets, okay?"

"Who's gonna take your place?"

Jade and I were trying to make a quiet exit when Cecil said our names again. When Jade bolted, I grabbed for one of her straps, but she slipped out the door.

Cecil said my name sternly. I turned, but he wasn't nearly as threatening face-on. His bald head revealed a full-cranial furrow, and the way he tapped his foot with his hands on his hips reminded me of an exasperated cartoon.

I mewled. "Come on, Cecil, no."

"You're always saying how you wish you made as much money as Honey."

"Because I want to be as hot as her, not because I want to work harder than her."

"It's just one set, maybe two, and the first song is almost over."

"Fine." I stomped back onto the stage.

Pantera was already naked, flicking her clit ring in the same rhythm as her tongue. "Highway to Hell" wasn't one of my usual songs, but by the time I did a few passes on the pole, it was over, and "Paradise City" began. From the floor beside Pantera, I saw Ginger lead her son around by the hand, pointing at different parts of Pins like it was a goddamn zoo. Then again, there were plenty of monkeys to be found, beating their chests and flinging shit in the form of pointless pickup lines. Ginger's kid didn't seem amused by the tour. Even with the glitter and flashing lights begging his eyes to bounce around the club, he focused on the floor. I felt bad for him. Knowing your mom being a stripper was one thing, but being smacked over the head with a T-and-A hammer was another. Eventually, he looked up, right into my gaze. He looked back down almost immediately, but in the few moments of eye contact, I felt akin to him. In my adolescence, my mother's status as a beauty queen always embarrassed me. The difference was, deep down, I wanted to be as beautiful as my mom. I doubted Ginger's son wanted to be anything like her.

When the set was over, I needed a serious break. Pantera hit a quick bowl of hash and headed back out, but not me. I flopped down onto the floor and savored my smoke. I didn't even bother with clothes as I puffed the pipe and blotted the sweat from my face. The door opened, but I didn't flinch. After a few weeks of working at Pins, I learned to stop frantically covering my body. However, once I realized that the eyes staring at my sweaty, smoky nudity were the baby blues of Ginger's son, I regressed back to day one. I clutched my clothes to my chest and crossed my legs with a squeak, even though he'd just seen me on stage.

"It's okay, Birdie. He's seen me naked plenty of times," Ginger said.

"I have little doubt," I said as I put on my clothes and waved away the smoke.

"What's the big deal? Strangers are always looking at our bodies."

"Those people choose to see us naked. They make the decision to come here. I doubt it was his choice."

"I guess you're right." She snarled. "Fucking Tom! I can't believe he brought him here." She lowered her head and whispered. "Thanks for taking my spot, by the way. My mom's going to be here to pick him up soon. Until then, I'm just going to stick him on the alley side. He'll be fine there."

"Why are you telling me?"

"I don't know. Just...thanks."

She smiled. It was the first time I'd seen it without a hint of malice, and I had no choice but to nod in reply. I just wished the kid would smile, if only to make me feel better about working in a place that could make someone look so miserable.

My double header struck the fancy of guys out celebrating their friend's birthday. One of the guys called me over with a stack of bills in his hand. He looked like a douchebag, but when he fanned out the money and wafted cool air over my sticky body, I didn't care. Plus, I knew my reaction to the cool air would increase my pay-off. With my head tilted back, lips parted, and arms unfurled to better embrace his breeze, he turned from a douchebag into an ATM.

"What's your name?" he asked.

"Birdie."

"What's your real name?"

"Why do you want to ruin the fantasy?" I asked, and he nodded as if I'd passed a test. "What can I do for you boys?"

"It's my buddy's twenty-first birthday. How much for a dance?"

"Five at the table. Fifty for a private," I said.

"The table will be fine. Do you take credit cards?" he asked, probably thinking he was the first genius to come up with that joke.

"Sorry baby, the only foreign object allowed in my slot is my dildo."

The guys howled like a pack of wild dogs on the trail of a wounded doe.

"This is the birthday boy over here!" one of the guys yelled, followed by a chorus of hollers.

I sauntered over to the grinning guy with a slew of empty shot glasses stacked beside his hand. His eyes fell to his lap when I stood in front of him, but they eventually made the slow climb from my thighs to my face. When I popped my hip and my leg slipped out of the slit in my dress, his eyes abruptly shot to my crotch. I leaned into him, admiring the beauty in his almond gaze.

"Hi, Sweetheart. I'm Birdie," I said over the drum solo of "Centerfold."

"Birdie?"

"You got it. Wanna fly?"

As I lowered onto his leg, the "Centerfold" music video entered my mind. When the drummer broke the milk's surface, I imagined it splashed over me, obstructing my vision. But from the ivory milk, chocolate eyes emerged, and all I could see was Josh. Eventually, my fantasy dissolved, and I saw the birthday boy's immense grin stretched up his blushing cheeks. He didn't have a dangerous vibe, so I scooted a bit closer, inches from his lap. When I pressed against his thigh and tossed my hair with a serpentine wave of my abdomen, his friends cheered. Once the music died away and Brian's voice oozed like cheddar from the speakers, I pressed myself against him and purred into his ear.

"Happy birthday, baby."

His friends slipped me some money, and he tucked an extra three bucks into my garter. All told, I walked away with eighteen dollars for two minutes of work. Brian finished his announcements and in the few seconds between his Velveeta voice and Foreigner's own brand of cheese, when the club was at its most silent, a bloodcurdling scream pierced the quiet.

Lou Gramm's voice began before the scream died out, quickly followed by guttural heaves of sickness and fright. Heaven stumbled out of the dressing room with a vomit-yellow top and crimson shoes, but she didn't make it down three stairs before her trembling knees gave out. The blood trickling from her nose as Stu lifted her up was all hers. But the blood leaking dark across the carpet as her stiletto tumbled across the floor was not. She tried to speak, but terror—a chomped tongue acquired in the fall—garbled her voice. Between terrified gasps, she spat red foam onto the floor.

Pantera ran up the steps, nudged the door open with her foot, then froze. When she looked over her shoulder at us, her face was drawn, and even from my distance I saw her lip trembling. I wasn't sure what propelled me forward, except needing to know what had scared a girl like Pantera. Cecil zoomed in front of me like he was cutting me off in Mario Kart, slashing through the amassing crowd. In the dressing room, Pantera was crouched beside a scarlet puddle in which lay a small, limp body. Cecil stopped in the doorway with a gasp.

"Don't come in here. You don't want to see this," he said, like I couldn't see clear over his head.

There were a few footprints in the blood, but the red-speckled prints looked like no shoe sole I've ever seen, and the growing ocean of blood covered them with every spurt from Ginger's slashed wrists. The cuts seemed like overkill considering her arms were no longer connected to her body. Her legs were crooked over one arm of the Crab Couch and her elbows over the other, but the rest of her sat up on the cushions between with a washcloth covering her face. Her son's face was covered too.

With a Wal-Mart bag. Seeing the makeup supplies scattered through the blood, I realized it was mine. My Wal-Mart bag. I killed Ginger's son with my cheap-ass lipstick-smeared Wal-Mart bag.

Pantera ripped it off, and the bag floated for a few seconds before sticking to the sopping rug. She held her fingers against his throat and her ear above his mouth. "He's alive. Barely. But he's alive."

But there'd be no "barely" for Ginger. With each second, the blanket covering her face flowered with more blood. Before I could wonder what mutilation caused those gory roses to bloom, I was pushed aside by the off-duty police officers that had been bowling on Lane Five. They passed me and the other bystanders through the room and down the stairs like an empty bucket of water in a fireman's chain, where the stench of Heaven's vomit grabbed me by the throat. I caught the burning bile at the last moment and gulped it back down, rushing through the thickening crowd to the bar on the alley side. I should've grabbed my duffle, my phone at the least. I needed to be rescued so badly, I briefly considered calling my mom and telling her every dirty truth I'd hidden behind "okays" and "fines" for the past few months. I wanted to call Josh, but I couldn't remember his number. Besides my mom, the only number I knew by heart was...

"Scott, it's me. Can you come get me?"

I immediately regretted it, but I couldn't take it back. I needed something safe, something familiar, something unaffiliated with Pins to remind me a sane world still existed beyond the neon and blood.

"Birdie? What's going on?"

"Something happened. Something bad."

"Are you okay? Did someone do something to you? Should I call the police?"

"The police are already here. Please, Scott, just come. I'm at Pins. And bring me some clothes, okay? I can't get to mine."

"I'm on my way."

"How soon?"

"Soon. I'm not far."

I hung up, my heart preemptively hurting for the moment when Josh found out what I'd done. I was still fretting over it, my stomach in spicy knots, when Stu let Scott through the barricade ten minutes later.

"What the hell? That was quick."

"I figured you'd appreciate the haste."

"Thanks, Shadowfax."

We smiled at the comfort of an old routine as he handed over a bag of clothes.

"What happened?"

"A girl was killed," I said, then amended it. *"Another*

girl was killed."

"I knew it. I told you. You don't belong here. It's too dangerous."

"Thanks for the clothes." I looked through the bag. "Hey, these are actually my clothes."

"It's the bag of stuff I kept telling you to take out of my trunk, from the rafting trip. I guess it's a good thing you never listen to me, huh?"

"Yeah, right. I'm going to change."

He said, "Promise?" and I groaned.

The old routine was tiresome again.

It only took a minute or so to slip out of my dress and into the t-shirt and jeans, but I stayed in the bathroom for much longer. I felt so nauseous, I was afraid to leave. I bent over the toilet, hoping for relief, but nothing came. It took three finger jabs to the back of my throat to induce vomiting, but I still felt sick. I thought maybe I'd feel that way forever. Maybe I'd just have to get used to it, like using a baby wipe after peeing, or remembering to shave my asshole.

When I walked back onto the floor, everyone was being ushered out of the club by the police, so I jumped into the stream. A hand grasped my wrist and I screamed as I thrashed against it. All eyes turned to me, but when I realized it was Honey, I waved an awkward apology to the onlookers.

"We have to wait until the customers are gone. Cops' orders," she said, handing over my bag. "This is all the stuff I could salvage." She eyed my outfit. "Hey, where'd you get those clothes?"

"Scott brought them. He's...well, I don't know where he went. I guess he's outside already."

Honey raised her eyebrows. "Your ex-boyfriend is outside with your current boyfriend?"

I screeched. What?"

"Josh. He's here with James. That's what his text message said anyway."

"Please tell me you're fucking with me."

I didn't stick around to hear her answer.

The processional out of the club had stopped, turning the line into more of a cluster. I wedged myself into it, hopping up and down to see if I could spot either Josh or Scott, but I was still too far from the outside. A jostle that rippled through the horde knocked a bulging bald man against me. When he apologized, he recognized me as one of the dancers and gave a grin full of teeth I pictured sitting next to bifocals on his bedside table.

Stu pushed past the customer and me.

"What's going on up there?" I asked, and he growled as he pointed back at the stage.

"Birdie, you're supposed to stay inside until everyone else is gone, especially during a fight."

"A fight?" I resumed hopping up and down. "Who's fighting?"

"Birdie! Over here!" Jade shouted, beckoning me to an alley-side window.

It wasn't the best angle, and the glass was frosted by smoke residue, but I could finally see the brawl.

"Hey, isn't that Josh?" Jade squinted through the crusty window. "Who's he fighting?"

I sighed heavily. "That would be my ex."

More police arrived, pushing through the crowds and trying to maintain order, but with their first priority still drenching the dressing room, a bar fight didn't seem so important. I winced as Josh rammed his fist into Scott's nose, knocking him backward into a car that promptly sounded its alarm. Scott sprang back up only to meet Josh's fist again. He got in one good punch before the bouncers pulled them apart, but while he'd given Josh a split lip, Josh had reduced Scott to a bloody mess that could barely stand.

Screaming into the parking lot, an ambulance lit up the night. Scott shielded his swollen eyes from the swirling light, mumbling. "I'm not that bad off. I can keep going."

Josh spat blood as a policeman rushed past them with Ginger's son in his arms. "It's not for you, jackass."

"Fuck you, man!"

With a growl, Josh broke free of the bouncers and scraped Scott off the ground. He slammed him against a car, shattering the headlight before cops dove on top of him.

"She'll never be yours!" Scott screamed as police pulled Josh away again, wrestled him to the ground and cuffed his hands behind his back.

The Ridgeley Police Department was having a busy night. They shoved Josh into the back of a car and slammed the door. His eyes scanned the crowd until they found my face in the window. He looked furious and devastated in one. His face was still there when I closed my eyes, like I'd been staring into a flame. They were loading Scott into a separate car when I wriggled my way back to the front door, where Stu and a policeman stopped me.

"Stay put," the bouncer said.

As usual, Brian inserted himself into the conversation. "Come on, she doesn't *need* to stay, does she? What do you guys think she knows?"

"Every employee is required to stay until we say so, son."

"That means you too, Honey," Stu said. "You're not sneaking off this time."

Honey dramatically batted her eyelashes. "What do you mean?"

"Just stay where I can see you."

She exhaled cigarette smoke in his face before taking a seat at the bar. Grabbing an abandoned bottle of whiskey, she poured a drink.

I sat beside her. "Can I have one?"

She pushed her glass into my hand, ripped the spout off of the bottle, and took a swig.

Like a problematic post from 2010, Brian appeared again. "I'm not sure the police want you drinking during their murder investigation."

"So let *them* tell us that," Honey said, refilling my empty glass.

"Birdie?" He tried to catch my gaze, but I kept it on my drink. "Are you okay?"

"No, Brian, I'm really not."

"You know, if either of those guys really cared about you, they wouldn't treat you like a prize. They would do something sweet to prove their feelings."

"Like what?"

He pushed one of the beer-bottle flower vases in front of me and tickled my nose with the pink carnation.

"Brian?"

"Yes, Birdie?"

"Your timing is seriously fucked."

"I'm just trying to cheer you up."

"Why don't you try to cheer *me* up?" Honey said.

"You have a boyfriend."

"So does she, you pinecone. She's dating Josh."

"Dating him, sure, but he's not really your boyfriend, is he?"

I didn't have an answer. I thought of Josh as my boyfriend, but calling Scott had been so automatic, some part of me still wanting to choose him. Instead of replying, I pushed the flower back to Brian and told him to fuck off.

The fight's damage was cleared first, followed by what was left of Ginger. The employees were questioned, but like we told the police again and again, we didn't see anything, we didn't know anything, and both facts had us terrified out of our wits. By the time the dancers were given the okay to leave, my stomach rumbled for a turkey sandwich; it disgusted me that I could be so hungry after what I'd just seen. Then I thought back to my grandfather's funeral. It was the saddest day I'd had up to that point in my life, but I only remembered two things clearly: how he looked like shiny clay in his coffin...and how much I ate after the burial. The buffet didn't stand a fighting chance. In my hastily-picked funeral pantsuit, I imagine I looked like a badly packed sausage that kept packing away the pork.

Unfortunately, the turkey sandwich would have to wait. First, I had to fix things with Josh; or at least try. When I pulled into the Ridgeley police station, James was in the parking lot.

"Hey."

He groaned as he slammed his door.

"Yeah, yeah, it's nice to see you too, James."

"Oh, I'm sorry, Birdie. Am I supposed to be nice to the girl who just broke my best friend's heart?"

"That's not what happened."

"That's his story, and I've known him longer."

"Three months longer. Big deal."

"I know him well enough to know when he's hurting. Josh isn't a physical guy. It takes a lot to get him that riled up. Me, not so much."

He lifted his chin, and I wondered if he meant it as a threat.

"So, what are you doing here?"

"I want to bail him out."

He snorted. "No need. That's why I'm here."

"Please, James. I want to apologize. I made a mistake."

"You really did. Josh is a great guy."

"I know that. Scott means nothing to me, I swear."

"I hope not. Because honestly, that Scott guy isn't right for you."

"You've never even met him."

"I can tell by the way he looks at you, by the way he hangs around the club. Maybe you haven't seen him, but Josh and I have. We've wanted to confront him, but we didn't because Josh didn't want to meddle in your life. When he saw him tonight and found out *you called* him there, he snapped, and I don't blame him." He lit a cigarette. "Besides, it's a $1000 fine for misdemeanor assault. Maybe more if Scott presses charges."

"I'll take care of it. And I'll drive him home."

"He may not let you," he said. "But for your sake, I hope he does. You deserve someone a lot better than that jackass. He couldn't even take a punch."

"Thanks, James. I really appreciate it."

"I'm glad." He jingled the car keys and exhaled a plume of smoke as he strode toward me. "I like hanging out with you. I like a lot of things about you."

I stepped back. "Um...thanks."

"Anyway, I should get to Honey's. I'm sure she needs me right now. I need her too." He winked at me, and I winced. "Good luck, Birdie."

He hopped in Josh's car, staring at me as he turned the key. The engine revved, and he grinned like he was auditioning for a toothpaste commercial before driving away.

I was starting to see why James had been getting on Honey's nerves. There was something weird about the way he reacted to my discomfort. I thought it was pretty obvious—I put distance between us, I didn't reciprocate his playful tone—but his smile indicated he didn't care how icky he was making me feel, which added an undercurrent of fear to the ick that made me glad to see him disappear into the dark.

I didn't feel any more comfortable standing opposite Josh. His eyes burned through the bars of his holding cell, but he didn't speak. After a few minutes of silent animosity, the policewoman popped in earbuds and turned her back to us.

"I'm sorry, Josh."

He didn't break his silence or eye contact.

"About everything."

Not a peep.

"I don't know what I was thinking."

Was he even breathing?

"I *wasn't* thinking. I was scared."

"So was I." It was so soft I barely heard him.

"I'm sorry."

"Honey called James," he continued, getting louder. "James called me. I expected you to be the next call, but there was nothing. *Nothing*. Do you realize how terrifying that was, Birdie? All I knew was that someone got killed, and for some reason, my girlfriend didn't call to let me know she was safe. I was so afraid something happened to you."

"I wasn't thinking," I said, my head hanging halfway to the floor.

"You said that already."

"So I'm *still* not thinking. I did see a dead body, you know. A coworker's mangled corpse, actually."

His expression softened. "I know. I'm sorry about that. No one should ever have to go through that. Especially twice."

Ginger invaded my mind. All her pieces, the roses on the blanket. I covered my mouth and burped up bile.

I pointed to the tissues on the policewoman's desk. "May I?"

Her answer didn't matter. I grabbed a tissue and pressed it to my lips. The nausea made me salivate profusely. I had to get home. The flicking florescent of the tiny precinct was making my head spin.

"How do I get him out of here?" I asked the policewoman, who plucked out an earbud and threw open Josh's file.

"Scott Davis called a little while ago. He said he would press charges unless a young woman named Eva Finch showed up to pay Mr. Parker's bail. I assume you're that young woman?"

I nodded.

"He also wanted to tell you he's sorry."

"You're kidding."

Through a scowl, she said, "Do I look like I'm kidding? The bail is set at $1000, and I'll need to see some identification."

I handed over my ID and debit card. As much as I wanted to bail him out, I was devastated to lose that cash. Thanks to my habit of almost instantly exchanging cash for weed, it had taken me almost two months to build up my account. I'd just passed the $1000 mark, the most I'd ever had in my account, and it was all about to disappear. But hoping that the gesture would repair the damage between Josh and me got me through processing the payment and the stacks of paperwork.

"You're free to go, Mr. Parker."

She opened the cell door, but he didn't budge. He glared suspiciously, like Scott was waiting around the corner to say it was all a goof, he and I were back together, and he was pressing charges against Josh. He looked at me like I paid $1000 just to humiliate him.

Once he crept out of the cell, he zoomed past me, out of the station, and to my car, where he cowered with his eyes directed to the distance. He didn't speak a word during the drive to his house. When I parked in his driveway, he snapped off his seatbelt, keeping his words, eyes, and everything else to himself. He started to open the door when I whispered his name. I didn't expect him to react, but the whisper actually stopped him. He didn't face me, but he sighed.

"I just want to get inside."

"I know, me too. I just want to go home, smoke a bowl, curl up with Fidelio, and cry." Josh finally looked at me. "But first, I have to know whether this is over or not."

"Which *this*?"

"Us."

He sighed again. I was sure it was the seal on the

story of us, but his eyes told a different tale. Even if he said it was over, there was hope in his expression.

"I don't want it to be over, Birdie, but I'm really pissed at you. If you hadn't called him—*him*—this whole thing never would've happened. I wouldn't have a black eye, I wouldn't have had to sit in that disgusting jail, and you wouldn't have to wonder if I'll ever forgive you."

"Josh, I'm really—"

"I'm tired of apologies. If you say you're sorry again, we really are done."

"—hungry," I said quickly. "I'm starving."

"You're way overdue for a turkey sandwich. Don't let me keep you."

"Will you call me?"

"Maybe. After I get back."

"Back from where?"

"I need some time to think. Maybe you do too. I think I'll take a road trip with James. It'll be good for us."

"Us as in you and me?"

"Right now, there is no you and me." He let his eyes slip to my face, but they didn't dwell there long.

He jumped out of the car, slammed the door, and started away quickly, but something stopped him. He ran back to my car and signaled for me to lower the window.

"Stay here a second."

My stomach flipped, hoping his decision had as well. When he didn't appear for nearly ten minutes, I began to wonder if he was fucking with me. When he emerged from his house, my heart sank at seeing the bulging bag in his hand.

"Here's your stuff. I guess it's a good thing you already took your cat home."

The exchange was cold, especially his use of the phrase "your cat." After weeks of Josh creating cute nicknames for Fidelio, he was suddenly "your cat." What happened to Fifi and Leo and Admiral Whiskerton? What happened to Josh and Birdie? My "goodbye" was lost somewhere in the sound of his front door slamming, just where he wanted it.

There was a line at Sheetz, if a loose configuration of wobbly drunkards could be called a line. Still sporting my glitter and high ponytail, I stuck out like a sore thumb that wanted to be sucked. After a few minutes of avoiding an unwelcome game of grab-ass, I decided to forgo the sub and settle for whatever I had at home—a scant selection to say the least. All I could scrounge up was one can of tuna and the sugary silt at the bottom of a box of Cinnamon Life. In the future, I'd have to spend more money on food than on marijuana.

For Fidelio too. He yowled as he circled my legs, so I gave him the tuna and I emptied the bag of Life dust into a bowl before filling another with a crystal-encrusted bud that looked far more appetizing. I smoked until I could feel the redness of my eyes and my imagination had astigmatism. I smoked until blood-soaked memories turned to glitter and the only gashes in my stripper friends were their vaginas. I smoked until sleep bestowed its mercy.

My dreams were unsettling, but they weren't the crimson swamps of spiked heels and corpses I'd feared. Instead, I saw greasy aprons and 6% tips. I heard the shrill beep of the incoming call and my weary voice responding, "Park reservations, how may I direct your knife to my brain?" The unemployment line stretched on for miles in a fluorescent-lit room with no bathrooms in sight, and as I waited, a shower of applications fell upon me, slicing my skin as they floated past.

I awoke to Fidelio gnawing on my drawstring, his ass discourteously planted two inches from my chin. Exhaling the horror of the dream gusted Fidelio's fluffy butt cheeks, and he turned with a chirp.

"Hell no. I can't go back to that shit."

The problem was I didn't know which shit I meant. I'd been so focused on the murder and Josh, I hadn't thought about my job. After the murder of two dancers, Pins wasn't likely to keep many customers, let alone employees. I sure as hell wasn't working there with a killer still at large, but I couldn't go back to telemarketing either, and waiting tables was much harder than dancing for way less money. Plus, I'd nearly emptied my bank account.

I pushed Fidelio off my chest, and he hissed like I was the jerk, stepping on my nipple to punctuate his annoyance. He looked back at me as he bounded away, trying to fetch me from my bed, but I had nothing to give him. I was still hungry too, and I didn't want to move an inch, especially at...oh, past noon. I guess I shouldn't have been surprised. I rarely saw the morning anymore.

Fidelio's cry snatched me from my cocoon, and I threw on shorts and one of Honey's tank tops I'd accidentally stuffed into my bag last week. It looked better on me than it would've a few months ago, but it still made me feel like my body shape was in open rebellion against me.

Discovering a pageant application in the mail didn't help my self-loathing. Even if the cartoon bee on the front of my mom's card did declare me "BEE-utiful," along with the additional handwritten pun, "So FLY the application my way!" I was tempted to call her and tell her to BUZZ off, but a knock at the door pulled me away from the bad idea. Based on the sounds of male desperation suddenly filling the stairwell, I could guess who my visitors were. Where Pins girls went, catcalls usually followed.

Honey and Jade were grinning when I opened the door, but Honey's nose crinkled when she saw me.

"Is that my shirt?"

"Yeah, sorry, come in."

Honey and Jade flew to the couch with musical sighs and thudded their fast food on the table. It was so blatantly casual. A little inappropriate, I thought.

"How are you guys holding up?"

Honey shushed me. "I don't want to talk about last night. I haven't been able to eat anything since, and I really want to keep this down."

"Okay." I gawked at what the trimmest girls in creation chose for food. "McDonald's? Really?

"You know you want it," Jade trilled.

True or not, once Honey's sparkly glass pipe made the rounds, I was cheek-deep in a bacon egg and cheese, much of which I shared with Fidelio.

"How did you know I needed this?" I asked, licking tater tot grease off my fingers.

Honey pouted. "James told me Josh dumped you."

"Oh shit, really? I thought we were just taking a break."

She winced. "I don't know. That's what James told me. Maybe it *is* just a break. Maybe—."

Jade stuffed a tot into Honey's mouth. "If you say he didn't dump you, he didn't dump you."

"He said he needed time, but I didn't think of it as breaking up."

"He is going on a trip though. James is going too," Honey said, staring at the smoldering bowl in her hand. "Just so you know he was telling the truth about that."

"I hadn't questioned it, but thanks." I pointed at the pipe. "Better bowl than a microphone, don't you think?"

She snorted, adorably of course, and passed it over.

"Truthfully, I'm more worried about money," I said.

"You're not alone there," said Jade. "We were discussing our options on the way over."

"I'm not going back to serving."

"What do you mean?" Honey squeezed my thigh and howled. "You serve it every night!"

"Thanks to you, boo," I said, giggling. "But not there. Not unless Cecil has a plan."

"No clue. Thankfully we have our own," Honey said.

Jade grinned when I raised my eyebrows. "We're doing the Oregon Trail." She hit the bowl and coughed when the ash pulled through.

"What?"

"Starting Friday, we're going to move through Martinsburg, from club to club, as many as we can knock out in a night, and rake in the cash on auditions alone," Honey proclaimed. "And hopefully none of us will die of dysentery."

"How am I going to eat until Friday?"

"Let Future Birdie worry about that."

"I can't believe you guys are so calm. I've been a wreck. How can you be so okay with all of this?"

"I'm trying to think of it as a well-deserved vacation," Jade said.

My chin dimpled. "It's not a vacation. Ginger is dead."

"Birdie, don't."

"Don't what? Feel fucked up after seeing a chopped-up body? Didn't you see the newest tweet?"

Honey dropped her gaze, and Jade poked the rest of her sandwich into her mouth.

Of course they had. They'd probably gotten the link to the tweet more than me. People knew they were strippers, people were rightfully scared for them. All I'd gotten was a beauty pageant application.

The language of the second tweet matched the first, the same sort of disrespectful pun, but the joke about "snapping Ginger" had come from a different username.

"It has to be the same person, right? Do either of those accounts sound familiar to you?"

"No, and I'm not digging into it," Honey said. "I'm

staying offline as much as possible."

Jade blotted grease from her chin. "Me too. Let's just try to enjoy our fattening breakfast."

"I don't know how I'm going to enjoy anything. I have fifty bucks to my name and my birth control costs thirty."

"Skip the birth control," Honey said. "You won't need it while Josh is away."

"If we're really broken up, why's it matter that he's away? I'm free to screw whoever I want."

"True. I guess you need the birth control more than ever."

"If you want, I have some Today Sponges left over from when I dressed as Elaine from Seinfeld for Halloween," Jade said.

"I don't think so."

"Didn't women used to stick lemons up their hoo-ha back in the day?" Honey drummed her chin. "Or was it onions?"

"I don't think you'll have to worry about getting knocked up if your cooch smells like onions," Jade said.

"Except by me," Honey bounced her eyebrows. "I *love* onions."

I leaned my head on her shoulder. "I would happily carry your baby, baby."

"Just in case smashing your onion cunts together doesn't help, you should have a back-up plan," Jade said.

I shrugged. "Well, you know what they say: abstinence makes the heart grow fonder."

"Who says that?"

"Junior High health class posters." Swallowing two tater tots at once, I moaned. "God, I'm depressed."

"Cheer up. You didn't think you were going to marry the guy, did you?"

"I guess not. He was a better candidate than Scott though."

Honey tilted her head. "Then why did you call him?"

"I...I don't know."

"Come on, Birdie..."

"I swear. He was the only number I could remember, and...I don't know...there was something comforting about that."

Fidelio propelled a rolling meow at me before jumping into my lap. I wrapped my arms around him and kissed his head. It smelled like cinnamon and spring, which is probably better than I smelled at that moment. But he didn't seem to mind. He bumped against my chin and buried his face in my armpit before curling up on my lap.

"Maybe I should just be single for a while," I said, petting his cheek. "Single and broke. What a year this is turning out to be."

"I don't know if I can help with the single part," Honey said, "but I can help out with money."

"And who's going to help me get the images of Ginger out of my head?"

Jade snarled. "We're not talking about that, remember?"

"I'm sorry, but it seems like it doesn't even bother you."

"Of course it bothers us. I just don't want to think about it."

"First Diamond, now Ginger—"

"I know!" Jade screeched. "Jesus Christ, Birdie. We know how close we came. We know it could've been any of us. Pins can stay shut down forever for all I care. I'll land on my feet."

"That's great for you, but I'm clumsy as hell. Landing on my feet isn't one of my talents."

"We're all going to be fine," Honey said. "I believe that with every annoyingly positive piece of my heart. And in the spirit of positive thinking, let's not talk about how close we came to death, rather how lucky we are to be alive."

"You want to continue testing that luck by dancing every stage in West Virginia?"

She twitched her nose like a bunny. "It doesn't hurt to be rich *and* lucky."

"Fuck," I whispered.

"What?"

"I wonder what's going to happen to her kid."

Jade stood up and threw a balled-up sandwich wrapper at me. It bounced off my chest and onto the floor, where Fidelio chased it to the kitchen.

"Listen, Birdie. I don't want to think about Diamond or Ginger. And I definitely don't want to think about some little kid having to explain why he doesn't have a mom for the rest of his life." Jade's voice wavered on the word "mom," and she grunted in tearful frustration.

"I'm sorry. You came over to cheer me up, and all I've done is bring you down."

"Actually, we came over hoping you'd cheer us up," Honey said, wrapping her arm around me. "Everything is going to be all right. You know that, don't you?"

I didn't, but at that moment, warmed by Honey's embrace I couldn't think of anything but the all-rightness of her arm around me.

"Are you really that light on cash?" Jade asked.

"After bailing out Josh, yeah, I'm pretty broke."

"Care to sell some of your weed?"

"From stripper to drug dealer. What a rise!" I threw my hands in the air triumphantly, then tilted my head. "Maybe I *should* apply for the pageant. Beauty queen does seem like the natural progression."

Honey rolled her eyes. "I'm not asking you to become a drug dealer. I'm just asking you to sell me some of your weed. Think of it as a trade if you want."

"I'll take some too if you're willing to part with it," Jade said.

"You're going to buy back the weed you sold me?"

"Why not? I'll probably end up selling it back to you after Friday."

"Not me." Honey lifted her chin. "Once money changes hands, it's mine. Of course, you can smoke some with me if you want."

"Thanks, guys." I embraced them both. "For everything."

I wanted nothing more than to cling to people who cared, and since Josh had decided I wasn't worth caring about, I didn't have many options left. I don't know what deity tossed the dice to decide what Josh and I would be, but whoever it was, I wanted to throw a drink in its face—or a Molotov cocktail. Our relationship was almost too short and bizarre to cry over, but I still did. The first time I saw a dead body, Josh and I became an item. The second time I saw a dead body, we became nothing. Whether Honey and Jade chose to mask their feelings about the situation or not, they made me feel like I had something real to hold onto.

CHAPTER NINE

Two ounces of weed lighter, with less than an eighth to spare, I was able to stock up my cupboards, and Fidelio was able to feast on fish packets to his heart's content. The days dissipated into the canopy of smoke hovering at the ceiling, and although I spent much of the week like a stony slug, wine consumption and music got me moving. I didn't want to get too rusty—or too pudgy—so I served as my own audience. I seduced the mirror to the sultry pain of Adele, causing Fidelio to meow at my bizarre air-humping.

Unfortunately, my dedication was gelatin when he started purring against my shins. Once he hopped onto the bed and flipped onto his back, I gave up on dancing and gave in to snuggling. It wasn't a stellar week for productivity, but I couldn't kick up the energy to hate myself for it.

When Honey and Jade picked me up for Oregon Trail Friday, it was clear the gruesome nights at Pins still had claws in our brains. Honey and Jade redirected their nerves into excitement better than I did, but I faked it well enough, just how I'd done my first nights at Pins. When Honey cranked the music, her car rattled enough for the both of us, so I allow my own interior rattling to disappear in dancing. It worked until Honey started dancing too. She didn't just groove in the driver's seat. She thrashed, tossing her hair and drumming the wheel, while I gripped the "Oh Shit" handle for dear life and stomped on imaginary brakes. It was an hour drive from my apartment in Cumberland to the first club on the list, and my nerves didn't make the journey any easier.

Glancing over, Honey laughed at me gnawing my nails to nubs. "You need to calm down, Birdie. What are you even so scared about? A new club? New people? The Twitter Stripper Killer?"

"Yes, yes, and uhh fuck yes?"

"Then let me assure you, the club will be fine, and the people will be as fine as people can be."

"And the killer?"

Jade leaned forward in the backseat, sticking her head between Honey and me. "Let's just hope he's not the 'have gun, will travel' type."

"Very funny. Maybe humor is the killer's kryptonite. Keep a few knock-knock jokes in your pocket just in case Martinsburg gets hit."

"What the hell does 'have gun, will travel' mean?" Honey said. "The dude, if it's a dude, hasn't shot anyone. Not yet anyway."

"It's an expression," I said. "And it's definitely a dude."

"Not one I've heard," she replied. "And no shit." Shaking out her hair, she refocused. "The point is, you can't let fear run your life. You were scared your first night at Pins, right? But you still got on stage. You still sacked up and dropped trou."

"There were so many incorrect things in that statement," Jade said, and Honey flicked her cheek.

"How about this? You can't let some homicidal nutbar make your decisions for you. You need to make the choice. Scared or not, do you *want* to do this?"

"We're nearly there, so..."

"Fuck that. I'll turn around right now if you want."

"No, you won't! I need money!" Jade said.

"If Birdie is uncomfortable, I won't force her to do it."

"I'm fine, really. I'm just being stupid."

"You know it's gonna be fun," Jade said, squeezing my shoulders. "Remember how much money you raked in for being new meat at Pins? That's what this'll be like. Shit, we might not even have to do more than one club a night if it's profitable enough."

"Where are we going first?"

"Velvet. It's a smaller place, but Cookie used to work there, and said she made bank."

"Cookie says she makes bank at Pins, and her electricity is always getting shut off," I said.

"That's..." Honey cringed. "...a fair point." Shaking her head and slapping on a smile, she added, "It'll be fine."

Jade retracted her head and spread out in the backseat. Honey stopped dancing, and I looked out the window at a stretch of brittle brown grass beside the road. It was ugly as hell but better to focus on than my bloody imagination...until it gave me the middle finger in the form of a roadside deer with a split skull and innards twinkling in the setting sun. I buried my face in my hands until we pulled to a stop.

From the look of it, Velvet was a few days from having its lights shut off too. It looked more like a pit beef joint from the outside, not usually something you wanted in mind as you walked into a strip club. The inside was better, if better meant looking like the tar-brown parts of the Eighties fucked the neon-migraine parts of the Nineties and gave birth to a driftless emo kid swathed in black pleather and student loans. And while every club had its own smokescape, unique as a fingerprint, in a place as small as Velvet, the stench tasted like the ghosts of tire fires, paper mills, and wig store arson having a blazing gangbang in the back of our throats. I gagged just as a biker with naked lady mudflap patches haphazardly sewn to his jean jacket strode past, licking his lips in sloppy hunger.

"You new?" he asked.

I hid my embarrassment in a twirl. "All over," I said. "The mother ship just dropped me off. How's human look on me?"

He either didn't understand me over the deranged Kenny Chesney techno mix, or he wasn't trying to listen in the first place. When a lanky cowboy nearby barked, "Back off, Bobby," the denim biker retreated.

The man in the crisp plaid shirt and ten-gallon hat was the cleanest-looking thing in the club, except for when he smiled. He was missing a few teeth, and some were facing imminent eviction.

"You ladies here to audition?" he asked, knowing the answer with one glance at our duffle bags.

"If you have the space," said Honey.

I could've sworn I saw a few of his teeth wave like weathered street signs when he grinned.

"Sure thing. Dressing room's through there. Let me know when you're ready and I'll announce you myself."

As we started toward the shiny black door, I realized I hadn't spotted the main stage yet. I thought I'd missed it when we entered, or maybe it was in a different area altogether, but as we neared the dressing room, I realized I'd been staring at it the whole time. Velvet's stage, if it could be called that, was nothing more than a three-foot wide ledge running around the perimeter of the club, the walls along which were mirrored, with the first and last panels bearing yellowed signs that read: "DON'T TOUCH MIRRORS." It seemed an impossible task until a dancer wearing nothing but sparkly red chaps spun along the ledge without touching the mirrors once. The crowd roared when she came to a stop; they whistled, threw money; I half expected a few to smack themselves with their shoes and howl like cartoon wolves as they slobbered over the stage.

They were disgusting, but no worse than the animals at Pins, and they clearly weren't concerned about hanging onto their money. Maybe Velvet wasn't such a bad place after all.

That thought hung in my mind for all of a minute before Honey pushed open the dressing room door. A cloud of smoke preceded a girl's yelp, and before we knew what was happening, the girl fell out of her chair. But not just any girl.

Ebony, or what was left of her, whose skin had reminded me of rich earth and volcanic stone, looked like an overcooked burger left out on the grill, stripped gray by the elements. Her eyes rolled up to us slowly, but our attention quickly jumped from her dull eyes to the needle protruding from her forearm, tugging at her skin as she floundered for her footing.

"Jesus, Ebony, what happened to you?" Honey helped her up, which Ebony allowed without a "thank you" or a "fuck you."

She didn't speak at all, intent on finishing the work we'd interrupted. I cringed as she pushed the plunger and the crimson junk charged back into her vein. She withdrew the needle and unwound her tourniquet, sighing as her eyes focused on us for the first time.

"Honey? Birdie? Jade?" She shook her head in puzzlement. "What the hell are you doing here?"

"*That's* the shocking thing about what's going on right now?" Honey rubbed her forehead in disappointment. "When the hell did you start shooting heroin?"

"It's not heroin. It's meth," she spat at me, even though I hadn't asked. "You guys working here now?"

"Auditioning."

"Figures," she hocked at Honey. "You couldn't let me have my own thing, could you?"

"It has nothing to do with you, actually. We didn't even know you worked here."

"Whatever." Ebony sucked on her cigarette and

coughed out a cloud with a gooey prize she swallowed with a grimace.

"Are you making good money tonight?" I asked.

"I was, but it's pretty much spent already." She flicked her tourniquet across the table. "That's most nights though. Ron's sweet like that," she said, only then noticing her smeared reflection. Leaning into the mirror, she took a baby wipe to her raccoon eyes.

"Please tell me Ron's not the manager," Jade said, and Ebony shrugged.

"Okay, I won't tell you that."

"Did he get you hooked on this stuff?" Honey asked.

"Nah, the stuff got me hooked on the stuff. He just happens to have the stuff."

Glimpsing the trashcan, I beheld a range of needles among the tissues and bottles, with dangerous peaks forming what looked like the AIDSppalachian Mountains. Only God could know how long they'd been there, and I doubted even He could survive that finger prick.

"I heard Ginger finally escaped her..." Ebony coughed. "...situation."

I scoffed. "Her situation? You mean life?"

"An escape is an escape."

"That's messed up," Honey said. "You know her kid almost died too, right?"

"He'll get over it. With a dad like that, I doubt it was the first time he had a bag over his head." Ebony's eyes settled on a line of coke on the dressing table and up her nose it went.

"I thought you didn't do coke," I said.

"Or meth," Honey added.

"I was too close-minded." She hocked into the trashcan and gave the mirror a grin. Standing and adjusting her halter top, she turned to us. "You ladies coming?"

When Honey looked over, I was desperately shaking

my head "no" while Jade clutched her duffle to her chest.

"I don't even want to put my bag down in here," she said.

"Thanks, Ebony, but I think we'll pass."

The dancer curled her lip in disgust. "Well, la-dee-da. The Pins girls are too good for Velvet, huh? You're getting a little full of yourselves now, aren't you? I guess it was a short trip for Honey, but the rest of you...I'm shocked."

"I'm shocked too." Honey pouted at me. "Are you shocked, Birdie?"

"I sure am. How about you, Jade?"

"I would be, but I'm afraid I might catch the plague if I breathe too deep," she said, now clutching her duffle to her face.

As we headed for the door, Ebony stomped after us. "You think you're better than me? You think you're hotter or better dancers?"

She burst out of the dressing room, climbed onto the narrow stage, and looked down on us icily.

"Ladies," she hissed, "you don't know shit."

Ebony's hips slammed left and right to Nine Inch Nails' "Closer" while the lights rode her curves like a tilt-o-whirl. The junkie was gone and the onyx sex goddess emerged as Ebony strutted across the tiny stage like it was an arena. Showers of green repping Washington to Jackson fluttered around her as she did a surprisingly graceful split. Bouncing on her haunches, stuffing money in her garter, she found us in the crowd again and blew a kiss. Her track marks were visible in the dramatic sweeps of white light, but she looked perfect in the charcoal dark. Then again, nearly everyone did.

"Fuck me," I said, stunned, and Honey laughed in spite of herself.

"She's always been a great dancer. A little meth

wasn't going to change that."

"Looks like more than a little," Jade said as we slipped past Cowboy Ron, into the damp parking lot.

Back in Honey's car, Jade sighed. "Not that I have room to talk about vices...or being a filthy bitch...I just wanted that whole getting dysentery on the Oregon Trail joke to stay a joke. Sorry for bailing, especially after making such a stink in the car about turning back."

"That was *you* who made a stink? I just assumed Birdie farted." Honey stuck out her tongue, and I crossed my arms over my chest in indignation.

"And I assumed when someone farts and no one says anything for the next hour, it's illegal to bring it up."

"Sorry," Honey said through a kissy pout. "On to the next one?"

"What is it?"

"The Golden Lariat. It's just down the block. It's much bigger, and they have a shower room in case you want to wash off the Velvet. A woman runs it, so it should be pretty safe."

"The key words there are *should be*," Jade said. "I've seen enough women who supposedly run shit bending over for douchebag men to develop a healthy fear of female bosses too. The more boss-bitch they are, the more I think there's some shitty man one rung higher."

"Sure, but the Christmas parties are way classier."

My eyes widened. "There's a Christmas party?"

Honey raked her lip with her bottom teeth. "Okay, the shitters are classier."

"The stabbings too," Jade added.

"I can see it now," I started dramatically. "Blood-soaked spats, broken monocles, gory diamonds—"

The word "diamonds" stuck hard in my throat, a fist-sized gem, all points and planes, but the image in my brain was mushier, blood-soaked, and moldering.

Dropping my head, I muttered, "I think I'm done

talking for a while."

CHAPTER TEN

The Golden Lariat was packed, and people were still filing in. When a group of men in their twenties or thirties, appropriately dressed for a night out, passed by the car with some female friends in tow, no one had to say, "This is more like it." The change in mood was palpable. We'd entered Velvet timidly, on the defense. Even Honey, with her typical, "I'm here to fuck or fight, and you don't get a say," attitude took more calculated strides. But we entered The Golden Lariat like sex on six legs, and it opened itself to us like a tulip drinking the sun.

The Lariat was nearly five times larger than Velvet and two times larger than the club side at Pins. With a main stage lined in gold fences, the rodeo motif also included a dozen saddles and strategically knotted ropes for the dancers to straddle—or hump, as a girl in spike-heeled boots displayed with gusto. The massive stage allowed for up to six dancers at once, and with two poles on either side and several rope slings for aerial work, it was serving Cirque du Soleil right up until I saw a bright purple speck of toilet paper gleaming in a dancer's asshole.

The manager was a lackluster lady named Pam. But I suppose I found her lackluster because I'd imagined her as a fiery brothel madam from *Deadwood* rather than a Duran Duran groupie subsisting on the glory of one backstage rub-and-tug. Her bangs were crusted into a high arc, the follicles probably knitted with some of her first spritzes of Aquanet in 1983, and she was wearing Mom Jeans with plastic bling on the pockets. If the manager was any indication of the club's success, I thought we might be in trouble.

Pam invited us into her office, a shrine to her horse-girl persona, but also to men with horse cocks. The pictures on the walls alternated between Clydesdales and Chippendales, making me wonder how this woman had gotten into the pussy trade. Then I noticed the autographed picture of Lynda Carter as Wonder Woman, her lips pursed and hands hooked on her shapely hips, and it made a little more sense. And surprisingly, it did make me feel safer.

Pam lit a cigarette and slapped the golden Zippo closed. "You girls serious about working here, or is this just a stunt to make cash?"

"Have you heard of Pins?" Honey asked, and Pam's expression softened in sympathy.

"I suspected some of you might show up here. It's a real shame what happened. Thank God you girls came through it all right."

"Have other Pins dancers been here?"

"No, but we've had an influx of clientele from that area. I guess Cecil didn't see that coming. Though, I suppose recouping your losses after two murders on-site is a pretty tall order."

I wondered two things at that point: one, if all the strip club managers in West Virginia knew each other, and two, if she was making a crack about his height.

"You," she said, pointing a pink acrylic at Honey. "You're first. Get ready."

She looked taken aback, but only momentarily. Shaking her hair over her shoulders, she said, "No problem. I'll get changed."

Pam responded with a slightly sinister smile. "We're

laid back here. It's 'come as you are' for now, girls. If you do well on your first dance, you're welcome to dig into your gear, but let's see how you do without your armor."

Honey was noticeably unnerved. I'd never asked her about her first dance, let alone her first audition, but her demeanor told me she'd always been prepared. She'd probably been a Girl Scout in her youth. A ritzy fuck-em-all Girl Scout, but a Girl Scout nonetheless.

"I'll go first," I said.

Pam looked at me like I was half bold and half stupid. I wasn't sure which one I was until I considered my clothing. It was Team Stupid for the win, because yet again, I was wearing jeans to a strip club audition. I just prayed my previous experience would grant me more grace this time around.

As I made my way to the stage, Honey and Jade hooted and sipped whiskey sours provided by a charitable drunk. When Gaga's contralto changed into Steve Perry's countertenor, Pam ordered the other dancers off the stage and cracked an imaginary whip at me to enter the arena.

"*I should've been gone!*" Steve Perry crooned, making a lot of silky-sounding sense.

Throwing Honey a nervous look, she laughed like I was a dumb kid scared to do a skateboard trick I'd already nailed ten times. She mouthed, "You got this," and she was right. I did, and deep-down, I knew it. With the first "Oh Sherrie," I stepped onstage. By the second "holds on," I was front and center with a trio of spotlights following my every move. Casting a wink at the faceless miasma of men around the fence, I popped my button and slid down my zipper. When I shimmied down my jeans, the crowd's exhilarated screams drowned out Honey and Jade's, boosting my confidence and reminding me that the only exhilaration that mattered was my own. I let my anxiety erupt like a piñata and belted the song from my belly as I dropped to the floor and drew my feet to a point. I tore off my pants and promptly spread my legs. Because of my new distaste for panties, I gave the goods straight away, which got the cash flying faster than expected. I was on fire, scissoring my legs with lusty grace. But when I stood and caught a glimpse of myself in a mirrored wall, I froze. With mussed hair and nothing but a white t-shirt covering my cooch and booty, I looked like Walk-of-Shame Winnie the Pooh.

This was a huge mistake. How could they want me? How could they throw their money away on someone like me?

Half naked and trembling under swirling spotlights, I felt a hand creep around my waist. The sick feeling that swamped my belly when customers got grabby struck hard, but through the smoke and cologne, I caught the sweet scent of safety when Honey planted her cheek against mine. My stomach switched from sickness to something else as she lifted my shirt, and the crowd howled in titillation. She tossed my shirt aside and pressed herself against my back. Wiggling up and down, she ran her fingernails over my thighs, across my stomach, and I rolled my head on my shoulders in ecstasy. As she nipped at my neck, I'd never admit I wasn't faking it.

My skin bristled, and she whispered, "Relax."

I obeyed gratefully, and she dropped my bra to the floor, followed by her own. She hugged me close before spinning away, but I could still feel her bare skin against mine. When she beckoned me to follow, and the crowd roared for more, my stripper instinct kicked in. I caressed Honey's face as I danced past her, and began working the crowd on a more intimate level. I moved from person to person pretending I was Sherrie, and I'd give them fever they'd never find nowhere else. As I spun past the bar, I called for Jade, who was locked in an emphatic conversation with a guy sporting a long, braided beard. When she saw me waving her over, she politely excused herself while removing her shirt. Swinging one leg over the fence, she gave it a wild ride before leaping onto the stage. The crowd roared with applause as she took a swing around the pole, then flipped upside down and pedaled her legs sensually through the air. The second song was "Lime in the Coconut" which was nigh impossible to dance to while looking sexy, but the tips argued otherwise. We split the money three ways with me getting the extra dollar for my initiative. For two songs, $42 was a damn good haul.

Pam was pleased with our act and invited us to stay for the rest of the shift. So, we changed into our armor and hit the floor, but before Honey and Jade could be thrown into the lineup for the stage, they were both approached with requests for private dances. If I thought the payoff for private dances was worth the panic attack, I would've been offended no one requested me. And I swore up and down I wasn't, but when Jade returned and confessed she hadn't actually done a private dance, I felt a twinge of relief.

"If you weren't dancing back there, what were you doing?"

She pointed at the bar. "See that guy with the braided beard?"

A hulking man with two full sleeves of vibrant tattoos waved at me enthusiastically, but he wasn't the only one. The other man flapping his hand drunkenly at me had three incomplete ropes of dull hair plastered over his otherwise bald head.

"Holy shit, it's Petey!"

"Who?"

"Petey from Pins."

Jade hummed. "Oh yeah, look at that. But you see the other guy, right?"

"He's kinda hard to miss. Wait, *what* were you doing in the back room?"

"Getting Mitsubishis," Jade said, withdrawing a tiny baggie from her bra.

When I saw the four ecru pills with little Mitsubishi logos stamped on them, I immediately got chills. The thought of rolling while stripping both intrigued and terrified me. Nevertheless, I nodded without hesitation when Jade proposed we go to the car to take them. Honey slid three crisp twenties into her garter as she emerged from the private dance quarters. Jade hooked her hand onto Honey's silver lamé chaps and threw her coat around her shoulders.

"Where are we going?"

"Heaven," Jade said.

"Huh? Heaven's here?"

"No, but Petey is," I said.

"Wait, we're going to see Petey?"

"I bought some E," Jade stated plainly.

"Oh, why didn't you say so?" she replied, her face a Cheshire grin.

Nestled in her dark car, we each popped a pill. Jade loaded bud into her pipe while Honey crushed the remaining pill in the bag with her high heel. I was like a little kid on my birthday, surrounded by friends in the dark, waiting for someone to carry in my glowing cake.

As Honey dumped the crushed pill onto a handheld mirror and separated it into lines, the bowl circulated and filled the car with skunky smoke.

Freshly frosted with candles ablaze, Honey handed me the mirror and a rolled-up fifty-dollar bill. "The higher the bill, the higher you get."

Already buzzing from the bowl, I snorted my share of the powder, and my eyes filled with tears as I fought the urge to sneeze. By the time we cleaned the mirror, I was in the thick of the drip: a side effect I loathed and loved for the same oogy-gooey reasons. Usually, the drip of mucus and MDMA tasted disgustingly bitter, but once in a while, you got a viscous deluge of something sweet. Maybe it was in my mind—it wasn't the first time I stitched birthday cake memories to my ritualistic vices—but the Mitsubishi drip had a smack of sweetness.

The powder went to my head immediately, and as we made our way back to the club, it found its way through the rest of me. I couldn't be sure how obvious we were, but I figured a few people knew the three walking grins glazed in cold sweat, enraptured by the swirling lights, and giggling at nothing were high as fuck. Kaleidoscopic colors traveled around and into me, picking up speed from town to town until the entire state of Birdie was aglow. Beneath the throbbing bass, the music begged me for a dance, and why would I refuse? It's why I came.

An hour in, I was deliciously off my rocker. My gown felt like second skin I peeled off to reveal a sleeker, sexier me. But after collecting my cash and donning the dress again, I didn't feel any less sleek or sexy. Shaking ass and faking names, I melted into the ecstasy of being a Golden Lariat girl, touching myself with boundless honesty as I writhed on the floor of the stage. The routine verged on masturbation, which no one protested, and I certainly wasn't about to stop during Billy Squier's "Stroke Me." Jade laughed as she danced past me, rolling just as hard but with a little coke kicker thanks to a dancer named Cherry. Caught up in her own giddy madness, Jade nearly toppled each time her sexy cyclone stopped, and she giggled as her brain caught up with the rest of her. Braidbeard held up some water from the sidelines, and Jade rushed over like Marilyn Monroe gushing over diamonds. She gulped gratefully but stopped at the halfway point. With a wink, she poured the remainder over her flushed skin and shook the water from her body like a dog. More punk rock than canine, she ran around the stage, sticking bills to her wet skin until the song faded. At the end of our set, she didn't even bother going backstage to change. She simply pulled on her thong, skirt, and top and jumped right into giving Braidbeard a table dance.

I, however, needed to chill out for a few minutes. Wanting a break from the stimuli, unaware of how much stimuli awaited me backstage, I fanned my face as I strutted into the dressing room. The first thing I saw upon entering was a bare bronze ass and light pink vulva. The dancer was on all fours with a crop of cocaine planted on the small of her back, right above a tattoo of a cartoon cherry dripping shiny red syrup. My mouth watered—from the coke, the cherry, or the chick, I wasn't sure--so I moved in the direction of the wiggling ass of the girl looking coyly over her shoulder. It looked like she was about to ask me if I wanted a line, but she didn't get the chance before a pink-haired girl named Lola shoved her tongue in Cherry's mouth. The Lariat definitely had a more intimate vibe than Pins, but I couldn't dissect it much before Honey sidled up next to me. Draping her arm around my waist, she coaxed me to my knees, handed me a straw, and gathered the loose curls from my face. The instant before I snorted, I wondered if I'd gotten in over my head. I didn't need the coke. I didn't even particularly want it, but how many times do you get the chance to snort coke off a stripper's ass?

I cleaned a line from Cherry's tramp stamp and my face immediately went numb. My snatch, however, felt like a cluster of falling stars granting every wish ever thrown at the sky. The coke kicked my roll into overdrive, making it feel like my skin was moving faster than my muscles and my muscles were moving faster than my bones, and slowest of all, my brain a tangle of simple pleasures as Honey wiped away tears I didn't feel streaming. Fixing my smudged makeup was difficult work the way I was swaying and twitching, but with her tongue cutely curled over her top lip, she swiped gloss on my goofy grin and declared me, "Perfect!" It was hard focusing on her face; hell, *standing* was hard, but when she held my hands, I felt gloriously in balance.

Lola coughed, "Dykes," as she walked by with Cherry's lipstick smeared across her face.

I wanted to kiss Honey like that. If my teeth weren't gnashing so badly, the drugs might've convinced me to shoot my shot, so thank fuck for my gnashing teeth.

Bursting into the dressing room, a dancer named Coco sang, "That guy is buying panties again!"

"Who is buying what?"

"A semi-regular," she replied, pulling a sweaty wad of bills out of her bra. "He comes in every so often to re-up on used panties."

I shivered. "That's disgusting."

A dancer named Kitty scoffed through uneven lip filler. "So is snorting coke from someone's pooper."

"*Off*, not from."

"Which one is he?" Honey peeked out the door to scan the crowd.

"The one in the Florida Marlins hat. With the brown coat."

Honey's face scrunched. "Yuck, you should never trust a Marlins fan."

"I think it's more important to distrust someone who buys used panties," I said.

He didn't look like a typical creep, but he was sitting next to Petey, who was falling asleep in his seat, so he might've looked normal by comparison.

I bounced my eyebrows at Honey. "Wanna sell your undies with me?"

"I'm booked in the shower room in five minutes, but good luck!" She squinted at me, then plucked an eyelash from my face. Holding it in front of my lips, she said, "Make a wish."

With all the stars and eyelashes falling over each other to hear my wishes, I really hoped at least one came true. I blew it off her finger, and she blew me a kiss before skipping out of the dressing room.

I searched for Jade. She was onstage with Tiara, bumping and grinding to Eazy E, so it looked like I was on my own. An independent businesswoman, I thought proudly, then snorted back the cocaine drip. With a deep breath, I gave the twins a quick adjustment and strode over to Mr. Marlins with every drug assuring me I'd come out on top.

"Hi," I purred, avoiding eye contact with Petey as I circled Mr. Marlins.

"Well, hello there." He smirked. "You're Birdie, right?"

"My first night and you already know my name? I don't know whether to be impressed by you, or by me."

He laughed. "You're pretty memorable. I like how you sing along with the songs while you're dancing."

"Do I?" I fanned my face. "I didn't realize I did it that often. That's a little embarrassing."

"No, it's cute! Lots of the other dancers keep their mouths shut and their eyes glued on the cash, but you look like you're having fun."

I touched his shoulder, but my crotch remained at a distance, even as I gyrated it in his direction. But he didn't seem to mind. For a profession a lot of men assumed dominated by easy girls, playing hard-to-get was incredibly effective.

"Are *you* having fun?" I purred.

He grinned as he shimmied up the bill of his cap. "A lot more now."

I suddenly noticed Petey staring at me, his face slack with lust like a dying basset hound. The longer I stared at him, the more his facial features melted into one another. His mouth disappeared into his greasy stubble, and his red nose was redistributed to his veiny cheeks. His eyes fused together, becoming one large bloodshot orb, white as spoiled eggnog.

"I gather you know why I'm here," he said.

I flinched, and refocused on Mr. Marlins, who cocked his head in intrigue.

Swiveling my hips, I deliberately pushed one of my legs through the slit in my dress, giving him a glimpse of my lucky thong. "Doing research for the Great American Novel?"

He chuckled. "I tell you what: I'll give you seventy dollars for the panties you're wearing right now."

"Seventy? That's a damn good price, but not for this pair. These are my favorites. I wear them all the time."

"I want them," he said hungrily.

"Nope."

I wasn't trying to up his price. I simply didn't want to part with the lucky thong I'd worn every night since my first dance at Pins. A slightly meshy material, sheer enough to reveal my thin strip of pubic hair while shielding my vulva, they'd already lost their original ivory. But no one could tell in the spinning rainbow lights, which also proved they were lucky, because "lost their original ivory" was a classier way of saying "my sweaty cooch turned my panties gray." Yet another reason I wasn't keen to sell.

"I have another pair you might like. How much would you pay for those?"

"It depends. How often do you wear them?"

"Pretty much whenever I'm not wearing these," I said, and he licked his lips.

I'd never worn them. They came with a red and white safari dress I bought from a sex shop, and much like the dress, they were uncomfortable as hell.

"I want to see them," he said, adding as I turned back to the dressing room, "On you."

Backstage, I snapped off my dingy luckies and

popped on the red and white thong that rubbed my skin raw. Hitting the floor again, I zeroed in on Mr. Marlins, moving with a sensuality the ecstasy tricked me into believing I owned. When I got closer, my hands drifted south and rubbed my pussy through the panties, raising the price with each wet thought rolling through my mind. Petey was watching too, but I didn't care. At present, it was just me and my intoxicants, and all of us were salespersons extraordinaire.

"I'll take them," Mr. Marlins breathed ravenously as I drummed my clit through the fabric. "How much do you want?"

I bent over and gave him the goods. Two fingers danced over the red and white safari under which a sweet little jungle cat waited for...

"$100."

I expected some sort of bartering battle, but by the time I faced him again, he had five twenties fanned for me.

"I'll give you another hundred for the other pair."

I bit my lip. "How about you give me another hundred for this one?"

"Nice try. But I will give you another fifty if..."

"If...?"

His nostrils flared, and he tilted his head. "Would you urinate in them?"

I could only venture a guess as to how my face reacted to the question, but I assumed it looked like I not only *smelled* garbage, it had been flung at me. My disgust toward the fetish aside, I'd experienced enough wild laughing fits to know that peeing in your pants, even a squirt, was extremely uncomfortable. Never mind the smell, it was the itchy wetness I couldn't imagine tolerating for more than a second, which was about how long I considered the proposal before shaking my head. He chuckled. I wasn't sure if he was trying to laugh off the request as a joke or if he was mocking me for being a prude. Either way, he still tucked an extra fifty in with the hundred and handed it to me.

"Thanks. I'm sure these will get the job done, just as they are," he said.

Trying not to show my revulsion, I gave my snatch a final pet and slid the panties down. Petey blatantly leaned forward to catch a glimpse at my money shot, which I hid from his thieving eyes, even though it gave other customers a view of the full wallet.

Once the transaction was through, I strode over to his table with a sneer. "See something you like, Petey?"

"I do," he said, nodding eagerly as he pushed back his chair so I had room to mount his lap. Instead, I grabbed his shot of Jameson and faced the stage where Honey, still wet from the shower room, danced to "Satisfaction."

Drinking up her beauty, I whispered, "So do I," and threw back his shot.

On my way backstage, a customer caught my eye. He blew past me before I could see his face, but I could have sworn it was Scott. I tried to catch up with him, but I lost him in the colorful swell of the crowd.

"You okay, hun?" Cherry asked when I returned to the dressing room, flushed.

"I thought I saw someone I know."

She shuddered in sympathy. "I saw my first-grade teacher here once. I almost died of embarrassment."

"That's awful."

"It was at first, but it turned out pretty well. Who would've thought the old man that taught you math would end up paying for your tit job?"

"They do look mathematically correct. Symmetrical, I mean."

"Thanks! Have you ever thought of having yours done?"

"Oh God, no."

She blinked in confusion, and I apologized.

"Yours are very nice, but it's not my thing."

"Looks like you're doing just fine without 'em anyway."

"I've done okay, I guess."

I'd done more than okay, but I didn't want to brag. It was obvious Jade, Honey, and I were stealing the other girls' money, but at least we weren't pulling a Cookie and stealing their clothes too. By the end of the night, I was nearly three hundred dollars richer, my buzz was still buzzing, and we had an offer of employment, provided we could start the following day.

"We're short-staffed for the first few hours tomorrow, so you'd be doing me a big favor," Pam said.

"No problem," said Honey. "We'll find a hotel nearby. Unless…" She touched my arm. "Will Fidelio be okay?"

The place she touched grew hot, and the places she didn't weren't far behind.

"I put out his self-feeder, yeah, but we'll probably be okay driving home and back, right? We don't need a hotel room."

"I know," she whispered. "But I *want* a hotel room." When she looked at me, I could've sworn I felt her smile between my legs.

"Do you mind if I tag along?" Braidbeard asked.

"Of course not. I mean, if it's okay with you all." Jade looked at us with an expression that would've been wide-eyed if her pupils weren't the size of bowling balls.

Honey laughed. "Why the hell not? It's a party, right?"

"And a job," I said as Honey wrapped her arms around my neck. "It is still a job, isn't it?"

No one had an answer, and once the car was flying down the road, I didn't need one. I didn't need the good sense that would've made us call a cab instead of driving either, or the logic that would've suggested we Google nearby hotels with vacancies instead of designating my stoned ass to be the lookout. But Jade was only interested in making out with Braidbeard, and Honey was doing her best to focus on the road without whipping her head from side to side—more than she already was to the music—so I was tasked with sounding the alarm when I saw a decent hotel. But too high for decency, I just kept an eye out for a vacancy.

Finally spotting one, I screamed, "Vacancy! Left!" and Honey turned sharply, throwing the slobbering conglomeration of Jade and Braidbeard against the window. Even that didn't stop their snogging.

Honey and I decided to share a room while Jade got her own. She didn't use it for a good while after we arrived, though. When I cracked the hotel window to exhale a hit, I caught the glint of moonlit skin to the right of our room. In the hotel's rundown gazebo, Jade and Braidbeard shed their clothes—a brief reprieve of separation before the lusty amalgamation resumed. I'd seen Jade naked a thousand times, but watching her in the gazebo was different. No matter how dirty the dance, onstage nudity never rivaled the raw vulnerability of one's nudity while making love. Yes, even fucking a stranger in a gazebo could be considered lovemaking compared to rubbing your cunt on a pole.

A prickling sensation danced up my arms and down my legs as Honey slipped her arm around my waist, just as she'd done earlier that night. The pulse in her wrist pounded against my belly and traveled to my quickening heart.

"Quite a night, huh?" Waves of hot breath rolled up and down my neck, and my skin bristled deliciously.

"Yeah...lucrative." I felt like a jackass even before it finished tripping off my tongue.

"I suppose you want to get to bed?"

A yes/no battle began in my mind. I wasn't sure how

to answer because I wasn't sure if she was referring to sleep or sex. If she meant the latter, I still wasn't convinced it's what I really wanted, despite my clit's thumping opinion.

She didn't allow me the time to decipher the question. With a tug, she twirled me to face her and gave me a few knee-quivering bats of her azure eyes. As much as they enraptured me, they also reminded me how easily I'd been enraptured by another person's eyes. Josh's rich brown irises entered my mind, followed by his face, his smile, his tongue, his hands gliding over every inch of me, pulling me into a cage of passion from which I never desired escape. His lust bloomed through my memory, but it was Honey who parted my lips and pulled me into her euphoric kiss. She tasted surprisingly similar to Josh, but her lips were sweeter, glossed in pear-flavored balm. They were softer too. And stronger. And her tongue moved the way she danced, graceful but powerful.

On second thought, I was lying to myself. She and Josh were nothing alike. Especially their hands. Hers were gentler, more empathetic, even anticipatory. It felt like she knew my body before the first touch, and I let her knowledge melt over me. At first, she did all the touching, but when her teeth grazed my neck, my own hunger awakened. It might've actually been the ecstasy's hunger, which made me nervous, but once I had her silky hair knotted in my fist, I was uncertainty melting into gratitude for all the world's mysteries. Her kiss quelled the need to gnash my teeth, but it redirected the agitation to my hands. I felt like I might explode if I didn't touch her, if I didn't rip off her clothes and plunge myself so deep inside I wouldn't have to answer all the questions starting to appear in the hotel room haze. I pushed them away and pulled down her bra, revealing the perfect breasts I saw all the time, but never like this, like the view belonged only to me. I kissed her hard, and she dragged her acrylics across my ass, making the denim sing, making me moan, making her purr in my ear as she unzipped my jeans.

Goddamn, ecstasy was a hell of a drug.

I pulled away from her, but not abruptly. I licked my lips, savoring the pear-Honey flavor as I touched her face. I glanced at the clock, and she did too. All the excitement suddenly drained from her, and as much as I hated being the cause, we both knew we had to stop. It was too late to open this can of clams, especially for someone who'd never eaten pussy before.

And I wasn't going to eat pussy at all! What the fuck was wrong with me?

It was the drugs, it had to be the drugs. I liked men. I liked Josh. His kiss was safe, uncomplicated. We were good together. We fit. We…

Honey kissed me again, and I didn't fight it. I leaned into her warmth, and all the danger of her embrace felt more like ominous shadows in the distance shifting into signs of safety.

Yes, I liked men. Yes, I liked Josh. But I wanted Honey. And like my relationship with Josh, if it was real, I had to believe I'd have another chance.

"I'm really tired."

I wasn't. My clit was a drum begging for a paradiddle, and she knew it. I was afraid she'd be embarrassed, maybe upset, but she just smiled and gave me a goodnight kiss. Unlike any other she'd given me, that kiss was like her hands: soft and perceptive, full of empathy and mercy.

"Sleep well," she said, and I said the same, but we both knew it was going to be a long night.

She lay on her bed, and I lay on mine, and as we spent the next few hours, grinding our separate bodies to sleep, we heard the prolonged cries of Jade and Braidbeard coming together.

CHAPTER ELEVEN

My mouth was a desert of ash and dread. I was starving and sick, and it both hurt and disgusted me to swallow my own saliva. My frenetic dreams were still knocking on my skull, or so I thought until Jade's screeching voice broke through the cacophonous pounding.

"Open the goddamn door! We're late!"

Honey was a nude blur to the door as I clumsily sat up in bed. Jade burst in with Braidbeard on her heels. While Jade didn't give Honey's nudity a second look, Braidbeard got stuck in the first.

"What time is it?" I croaked.

"It's one o'clock. We were supposed to be at the club an hour ago."

"Bullshit. If I just slept for eight hours, why am I so tired?"

"Because you were tweaked out, dummy."

I grumbled. "Pardon me, Miss Bright-Eyed and Bushy. We're not all lucky enough to have all the toxins fucked out of our systems."

She flipped on the lights, tore the covers off me, and grabbed my ankle to pull me to the foot of the bed.

"Jesus, Jade, let go! I'm up! I'm up!" I threw a pillow at her, which she squeezed, then dropped when she noticed a large stain on one side.

"Why'd they let us sleep through check-out?" asked

Honey.

"Take a look outside," Jade said. "Hell, take a look inside. This place might have a gazebo, but it's a shithole. We chose the first vacant hotel we saw and that's exactly what it is: vacant, except for us. They were probably eager to let us sleep in so they could charge us for an extra day. If we get moving soon, maybe we can argue them out of it." She clapped her hands. "Move your asses, ladies!"

The mirror was a bully. Clumped and hardened, my eyelashes were sparkling spears of mascara and glitter. Smoky eyeliner had allied with hot pink eyeshadow to colonize the wrinkles under my eyes. My fingernails were filthy, like I'd been rooting through ashtrays in my sleep. I looked like a raccoon raver having a Twiggy fashion moment. Or vice versa, I suppose.

Even Honey's industrial strength astringent and industrial strength compliments couldn't wash away the previous night. Tired and swollen, layered in primer, foundation, contour, concealer, powder, blush, highlighter, setting spray, and the motherfucking Serenity Prayer, I still couldn't make myself look like Birdie again. So the world, as always, would have to settle for the closest facsimile.

We were over two hours late once we pulled into the Golden Lariat. Seeing the number of cars already there, we knew Pam was going to be pissed. Cecil was easy to talk down from a tirade because he'd adopted a "you're late, your loss" philosophy, but Pam didn't seem the type. We decided it was safer to sneak in through the back. If we were lucky, and Pam was stupider than she seemed, she wouldn't notice how late we were. She hadn't set foot backstage all Friday night, so there was a chance she might think we were getting ready...for two hours...without coming out to set up music...or find out the dance order. It was slim, to be sure, but it was all we had. We snuck up to the back door, but before we could open it, a loud rustle made us shriek like little kids in haunted hayride. I thought it was a rat, and I wasn't far off, but this vermin was much larger. Petey-sized, in fact.

"What are you doing?" Honey said, but he just stumbled away with a plastic grocery bag in his hand.

Jade shivered. "What a weirdo."

Honey eased open the back door and it creaked in that ominous horror-movie way, but when she ducked inside and called "all-clear," we heaved a sigh of relief. Music pumped from the private dance rooms, and the sound of running water indicated someone was in the shower room. I figured some of the shower strobe lights were broken because red was the only color blasting through the glass, tinting the hallway. But as we neared, I saw Cherry pressed against the glass and figured the cherry-colored lighting was intentional. Girls frequently pressed themselves against the shower room walls to entice passing customers.

But she wasn't doing her usual come-hither body roll. She wasn't moving at all.

I waved to her, but she didn't respond. She didn't blink.

Drawing closer made the three of us fall back in fright. Cherry's eyes were agape and her tongue was hanging out of her slack mouth, which was missing several teeth. Her throat was a man-made valley, and her chest two crimson mountains smashed against the pane, which was scratched from the broken teeth still clinging to her gums. Her arms and legs were sporadically slashed, and blood pooled where the shower spray couldn't reach. It was everywhere. Even on the lights. Not cherry-colored. Cherry-*coated*.

Jade and Honey screamed, but I found myself muted by the thoughts pervading my mind. They transitioned from the memory of snorting coke off Cherry's ass to wondering if she'd ever had a cherry dessert pizza from

Pizza Hut. They had been my favorite part of working there in high school. Even when I made shitty tips, I could always cheer myself up with a cherry dessert pizza. But her face kinda looked like a cherry dessert pizza too, and it wasn't a cheery cherry. The thick crimson filling, the tooth crumbles sprinkled on top.

I slapped my hand over my mouth just in time to catch the vomit, but I had to drop to the floor to force it down. It wasn't an easy task when Cherry's face slid down the glass too, emitting a juddering squeal until her knees buckled and she fell to the floor with a sloshy crack.

"Birdie, come on!" Honey screeched as she tried to pull me away.

"Are we going home?" I asked woozily.

"Yes we're going home," she said, lifting me off my knees.

But home was a long way off. The police kept us in Martinsburg for hours. While the cops questioned Honey and me, Jade stared at the glittering horseshoe on the club's sign, catatonic. From what we described, the police were certain the murder happened within minutes of our arrival.

That's when we remembered Petey.

"He was by the back door. He had a bag or something, and he ran off when we got here," I said. "He looked really messed up. But he always does, I guess. Drunk. High. Who knows?"

"He was here last night too," Honey added. "And he was a regular at Pins. He was probably there during the other murders."

The steely officers nearly drooled at that information before dismissing us to pursue their new person of interest. The ride back to Cumberland was silent except for the occasional whimper. No one spoke. No one touched. I stared straight ahead at the road, trying to distract myself with the endless stretch of faded lines, but the only thing I could see was Cherry filling spiraling down the drain.

Honey dropped off Jade first. She was still so numb, we had to help her inside. Once on her bed, however, the ice of her catatonia melted, and she poured her sorrow into the pillow. When Jade whimpered "Jeff," Honey crinkled her brow.

"Braidbeard," I whispered, and she nodded. "Will you be okay by yourself, Jade?"

She squeaked "yes" before rolling onto her other side. We didn't know whether to believe her, but the click-clack of her texting fingers gave us an odd comfort.

I didn't need help getting to my door, but I appreciated the company. Fidelio also appreciated it. After a night alone, he was grateful for every pat and coo.

"Do you want to smoke?" I asked Honey.

"I think I'm good," she said. "I just want to get home and see James. I think he's back from the trip."

James. I felt the ghost of Honey's lips against mine and suddenly realized just how fucking much I hated James.

"I understand."

"I can put in a good word with Josh if you want. Maybe this will win you some sympathy."

I coughed. "I don't think that's the best way to fix things with him. I can't even come to terms with what the new *this* is yet."

"It was Petey, Birdie. The whole time. The police are going to find him, and this whole thing will be over before you know it. They'll reopen Pins, Josh will forgive you, and we'll go back to the way things used to be."

The way things used to be. Before the murders? Before Pins? Before I had the deep longing to slap this girl silly or fuck her brains out? Even with the darkness of these days, it was hard to recall the light from any of my befores. I was angry all the time then, mostly because I was sad. And I didn't realize it until that moment, standing opposite the person who'd introduced me to a new and truer happiness than I'd ever known. One that acknowledged my pleasure before anyone else's.

Before Petey ruined everything.

"I won't do it," I said. "I don't ever want to go back."

"What do you mean? To Pins? To dancing?"

"No, not that. It's funny, all my other jobs—waitressing, selling shit over the phone, faking a smile just so I can make a 10% tip—made me feel like a prostitute. But I don't feel that way at Pins. I don't feel that way when I'm dancing with you."

The smile looked somewhat odd breaking through the sorrow on her face, but that made it the most beautiful smile I'd ever seen.

"I only want to move forward."

"Then why do you look so scared?"

"Because as much as I hated those jobs, I'm not sure they're worse than being on a hit list."

"They'll catch him, Birdie. And we don't know we were ever targets."

"Honey, he killed two girls at Pins, and the day after three Pins girls showed up at the Golden Lariat, he killed again." My head felt like it was filled with broken glass when I shook it. "We were late. Maybe he got restless."

"You're not doing yourself any favors talking like that, and you're not doing me any favors acting like you might stop dancing. I need you there. You're my best friend, Birdie."

"Am I? I don't even know your real name. And you don't know mine."

I didn't know why I was so angry all of a sudden. Maybe it was the murder, or the fact that I'd recently snorted coke off the victim. I had no doubt the third beauty pageant application arriving in the mail that morning was a contributing factor, but the only one I chose to acknowledge was the one gnawing at my brain since the night in the motel: What the hell was going on between Honey and me?

"I have to know: am I just your little straight girl plaything? Do you actually like me, or are you going to get tired of me like you did with Ebony?"

She blanched and stumbled back a step. "What?"

"You haven't mentioned last night at all, and I assume it's because we're keeping it on the down low. You know, just hooking up when you get the urge to lez out."

"One, that's incredibly offensive, especially when you don't know what you're talking about. And two, fuck you."

"You wish."

At that point, I wanted to punch myself in the face, but I continued on like an idiot. I still wanted her, and for some reason, saying it aloud pissed me off.

"Come on, Honey. Do you have a third terrible defense?"

"Sure. Three, you're the first girl I've ever kissed." Her eyes glimmering with pain, she turned on her heel and stomped to the door. "Oh, and I *do* know your real name. It's Eva."

I broke my own heart, and it sounded like a stripper slamming my door. I'd seen her leap naked off a stage to tackle a girl. I'd seen her spit at customers for insulting her. I'd seen her slap, kick, and bite guys for getting grabby. But I'd never seen her so tearfully irate.

Fidelio mewed normally, but it sounded like, "Fuck you, Eva." And I deserved it. I didn't remember telling Honey my name, but I was probably too caught up in my own shit to notice. Now I was so caught up in my shit, I couldn't feel anything but shitty, and boy did it stink.

I flopped down in bed to pass out for as long as I

could—two hours or two days, it didn't matter as long as there was darkness. But the darkness that polluted my mind made it hard to find a peaceful void. Cherry's slack face against sweaty, blood-streaked glass, melting into anonymity, then into Petey's grotesque grin drawing closer to my front door, to my bedroom, my bed…

I awoke with a gasp, and Fidelio mewed. His claws were tangled in my hair, but for once, the pawing and tugging calmed me. With his fuzzy cheek calling me back to reality, it became a night like any other. There were no murderers baying for my blood, no memories of carnage to pollute my dreams, but once sleep claimed me again, I couldn't lie. I experienced sweet moments, but they were only *moments*. I saw Josh and yes, we ran into each other's arms in unsullied bliss, but he eventually pushed me away to harshly remind me that we weren't together. I'd hurt him, and now I deserved every ounce of my suffocating loneliness. It was the same with Honey, the same with my mom and that damn pageant. I let everyone down, and no matter how hard I tried to rectify things, I fucked them up even worse. I wasn't exactly surprised; I'd always been a fuck-up, but I'd recently started to feel like I had some positive control in my life. I guess I was wrong, and again, it was no surprise.

I dwelt in self-loathing for quite a while, sleeping the night and half the following day away. I woke a few times to groggily stumble to the bathroom and take large slurps from the faucet. I woke to the sound of birds and neighbors, but I always drifted back into the dark.

It was two days later when a furious knocking woke me for good. Having been roused the same way a couple days ago, I was disoriented as to my whereabouts and briefly wondered why I'd brought Fidelio to the motel. The voice on the other side of the door cleared my brain, and I ran to answer her pleas to be let inside.

Honey rushed in on a gale of tears. Although I continued to hold the door wide open, Fidelio was too intrigued by the wailing visitor to run out.

"What's wrong?"

Her response was incoherent, waterlogged by sorrow.

"If you're upset about us, I'm really sorry. I shouldn't have said all that stuff. I was just tired and scared and—"

"I'm not crying about us, you idiot! James cheated on me!"

She looked like she was about to punch me, but when I opened my arms, she fell into them like a wet feather. Though I was curious whether what we'd done in the hotel room counted as cheating, I just petted her hair and let her cry it out.

I hadn't realized how much it bothered me to see Honey brokenhearted. More than anything, more than I wished for a mind free of blood-soaked visions, I wished she would smile for me. When she was happy, when we joked and pretended like we hadn't seen three corpses in the span of a few months, it felt true, even temporarily. It was surprisingly easy to pretend we were okay; hell, it was our job as exotic dancers to crush our personal bullshit under spiked heels, slap on a grin, and pretend our pussies could rescue anyone from misery. If I could make her smile, I could forget about death for another few minutes.

"What happened?"

"He came home from his trip with Josh. I thought I'd be nice and unpack the car for them, but they beat me to it. They unpacked everything but—but—"

"Honey, what?"

She whimpered, then sobbed. "He had some slut's underwear in his car!"

"Oh my God! Wait, how do you know she was a

slut?"

"That's not important. The important thing is the underwear was there. Some slut left her nasty panties in my boyfriend's car!"

"Were they crispy with a bunch of different jizzes? Is that why you think she was a slut?"

Honey chuckled. "Shut up."

A smile. Mission accomplished.

"Just so you know, I'm not trying to argue with you. I'm sure she was a dirty, filthy slut who drugged his drink."

Honey batted her eyes hopefully. "Do you think?"

"Anything's possible, right?"

"Yeah. I appreciate that, even if you're a total bitch." Her voice was harsh, but her smile hung on.

"You're right, I am. I get into these states of superiority and think I'm better than the stupid mean girls I grew up with, and then I go and hurt the only person I care about."

Her spine straightened, and she sniffled.

"I'm really sorry, Honey. I don't know what I'm doing wrong." Fidelio bumped his head against my hand, then against Honey's. It felt like a Disney moment, like he was trying to coax us closer.

"You're not really a bitch, Birdie. You're just confused. Everyone has bad days. Everyone has problems. But right now, my problem is a little fucking worse than yours, okay?"

"I'm sorry. Did you confront him?"

"You bet your ass I did. In front of Josh and everything."

"What did he say?"

"What could he say? I caught him red-handed. He claimed he was innocent, of course, but he had to be lying. He was acting so weird."

"What did you do?"

"I dumped his ass." Then, with a snort, she pulled

something out of her pocket. "And I nabbed his unemployment check."

"Can you do that?"

She shrugged. "I did, so I guess I can. He owes me a bunch of money anyway. This should cover about half," she said, the sorrow draining away. "I'm pretty sure I deserve it."

With each phrase, her smile grew wider, and death retreated a little more. It may have been a sick way to deal with what we'd seen, but it was better than rocking back and forth in the corner in rambling terror.

"How are you going to spend it?"

"I want to go to the spa," Honey said. "And I want you to come with me."

"The spa? I don't know. It's not really my scene."

She jumped up, and her fists hit her hips with such an authoritative smack, she pounded my rejection to dust. "So you won't come with me?"

Part amusement, part adoration, part exhaustion, a sigh curled my lips. "Of course I will."

She hugged me giddily. "Thanks, *Eva!*"

"You're welcome."

"All things considered, it's the least you could do, *Eva.*"

"I know."

"I mean, after saying all those fucked up things, you really owe me, *Eva*," she said, snapping my tank top strap.

"Okay, I get it, you know my name." I chuckled. "But I'm really sorry because I still don't know yours."

"Just keep calling me Honey."

"Is it your real name? Honey Potter?"

"*Martha* Honey Potter, actually. Honey is my mom's maiden name."

"I thought you hated your mom."

"Not as much as I hate Grandma Martha." She held up her hand, noticing the impulse to pry commandeering my expression. "And no, I don't want to talk about it right now. But I appreciate that you care. You really are my best friend, Ev—Birdie."

"Then..." I pulled her back to the couch and sat cross-legged, facing her. "Can I ask you something else?"

"I guess it depends what it is."

"It's something you said the other night. About us. About the kiss."

Her cheeks warmed. "Okay...what?"

"Was I really the first girl you kissed."

The blush spread throughout her face, and she giggled as she lowered her head. "No. That was a lie. I just wanted to make you feel bad." Lifting her gaze, she raised one eyebrow. "Did it work?"

"It really fucking did. I can't apologize enough. I shouldn't have said any of that stuff."

"No, you shouldn't have, but it was a rough day for all of us." She gathered her hair, twisted it up on top of her head, and snapped a ponytail holder around the messy bun. "But just because you're not my first girl-crush doesn't mean you're not special."

The girl could read my mind like no other. So I wasn't the only chick who'd been kissed by Martha Honey Potter, but I didn't feel any less treasured by her. If anything, the feeling increased, because she could kiss any girl she wanted, she could bring them to their knees with the suggestion of her touch, and she had chosen me to kiss and touch and confuse in the most wonderful way possible.

"Look, I don't understand everything you're going through, Birdie, but I understand trauma. I understand the crazy things it can make us do, God knows I wish I didn't. You threw insults. I threw a lamp at James's head. The difference is that you care if I forgive you. I don't care if he forgives me."

"*Do* you forgive me?"

"I just invited you to the spa, didn't I?"

"Sure, but I don't know what's waiting for me there. This whole thing could be a trap, a twisted plot to get me relaxed so you can steal my kidneys."

"That's Petey's territory, not mine."

We laughed, but only for a few seconds. The faces of people who would never laugh again staunched it with belly-turning regret.

"A spa day will help, I promise. You, me, and Jade. How about it?"

"I suppose I owe you."

"I don't want you there because you owe me," she said. "I want you there so we can relax and cleanse ourselves of all this shit, maybe even have a little fun."

"You make it sound like we've been lacking in fun. I mean, the morning was terrible, but the night at the Lariat…that was a lot of fun."

"A night on ecstasy is borrowed joy. Just because you got satisfaction from eating cookie dough doesn't make you a baker. We need something real."

"If none of this has been real, I'm afraid of what *real* really feels like."

Holding my knees and leaning in, she said, "You don't ever have to be afraid when you're with me."

I chortled. "I've been afraid nearly every single time we've been together. But I've also been happy. So I'm in."

"Awesome!"

Pulling me off the couch, and into a powerful embrace, she lifted my feet off the ground as I yelped with laughter.

"I'm going to head over to Jade's and proposition her. I hope she'll be more excited about the notion of a spa day than you were." She grabbed her purse, then turned slowly. "Oh, about the other thing. The kiss."

"We don't have to talk about it."

"You freaked out because we didn't discuss it. Do

you want to discuss it?"

"I don't know what to say."

"Then I'll go first." She exhaled with a hum that lifted her chin. "I'm attracted to you, Birdie. I think you're hot and I want to fuck you. But if you have reservations, I'd rather keep this platonic than risk losing our friendship. Now you go."

I felt like my mouth hung open, silent, for far too long. But eventually a voice that barely sounded like my own creaked out.

"I'm attracted to you too, Honey. I think you're hot and I want to fuck you...I think. I liked kissing you and I could see myself enjoying...other things...but I've never—I thought I was just into guys—I don't know how—plus what you said about the friendship thing."

She shook her head as if my half-replies swirled around her like stars. Finding me through the twinkling idiocy, she gave a nod of approval. "Then I guess we're in agreement. We're just friends."

"Best friends," I said.

The dimple appeared so briefly that anyone else would've missed it. But I never missed it.

"Best friends," she replied warmly.

I wanted to ask her about Josh, but it was the absolute worst time, considering *his* best friend had just screwed her over. I tried to stop myself from asking, but before she opened the door, the question burst from my lips.

"Did you talk to Josh at all?"

Her expression confirmed what I already knew: it was a horrible time to ask that question, but she forced a tight-lipped smile and shook her head.

"No. Everything happened so fast. He misses you though."

"He said that?"

"No, but when I said you missed him, he made a face."

"What kind of face?"

"The kind of face that made me think he misses you. I don't know how to describe it, Birdie."

I grumbled. "Great. Now he has the upper hand."

"Who cares? You're the woman. If you get back together, the upper hand will naturally return to you. It's dating law," she said matter-of-factly. "I'll call you later and let you know the date for the spa."

"Okay. Oh, and if it means anything, I don't know what happened between you and your grandma, but I don't think Martha is that bad a name. My grandparents were from Martha's Vineyard."

"What's that?"

"It's an island off the coast of Massachusetts. But it's pretty expensive, so I doubt I would've ever gone if I didn't have relatives there."

"So when you hear the name 'Martha,' you think of an island most people can't visit? Isolated and distant?"

My answer stuck in my throat. I had to cough it up, regretful though it was. "Yeah, I guess I do."

She snorted. "Actually, that sounds right. But I think I'll stick with Honey." She blew me a kiss and shut the door behind her.

Fidelio invited me to the couch with a purr-meow that sounded like the word "marble." He curled up on my lap while I took bong hits, happy but still dissatisfied. I'd mended my rift with Honey, but I still had some messes to clean up.

A few taps and swipes were all it took to connect to Josh, but I couldn't bring myself to do it. Since the alpine stack of mail on the counter couldn't yell at me, I opted to deal with that instead. An aggressively pastel baby shower invitation sat on top, staring at me with disturbing pacifier eyes embedded in a cartoon baby's head. I had been expecting the invitation but hoped it would get lost in the mail.

My cousin Megan had gotten knocked up before her wedding. Before the proposal too, actually, but she didn't tell most people that part. Her version made the conception sound more romantic than the truth, but nearly everyone knew she conceived on a break between double shifts at Arby's. And even though she didn't fit the insult's typical definition, Megan had solidified her reputation as the cumdumpster of Carroll County by getting laid and impregnated against an actual dumpster. Ever since I heard the story, I smelled a mix of trash and Big Beef & Cheddars whenever she was around. Coincidentally, her best friend was a girl named Melody, who'd stunk of hotdogs to me since I first heard a rumor about her sticking one up her twat on a dare. Considering everything I was going through, I certainly didn't want to add a baby shower reeking of dumpster dogs to the list. An interesting twist to the story, however, was the fact that Arby's employee, Megan, and her husband lived in the biggest house on the block. My Aunt Linda and Uncle Mort were richer than God, and they'd bought their daughter the house as a wedding present. So, in addition to being a baby shower, it was also a housewarming party. I couldn't imagine anything worse until I realized it would probably be an unofficial high school reunion of sorts. I figured Megan opened the invitation to all genders so she could get a wider array of presents, but her greed had amplified my anxiety dramatically. Not only would I have to see a bunch of people from high school I was content never to see again, it's likely Scott would be there too. Ah, the flesh-rending joys of small-town life.

Attending the party was the last thing I wanted to do, but I knew my mom would give me eternal shit if I skipped such a big event, and all the pageant adjacent pestering was bad enough. With the invitation in one hand and the new pageant application in the other, I suddenly wished I had decided to call Josh instead of dealing with the mail. But when it came down to it,

I wasn't sure I could maintain my composure once I heard his voice. I could email my RSVP to Megan and be done with it until the date rolled around. If I called Josh, I'd have to deal immediately.

I jumped online, being sure to hit my obsession spots before getting to my actual task. No one had shared my picture of Fidelio in a pumpkin costume despite its obvious cuteness, and the only comment it received was from my sister Hollie. "Lots of time on your hands, huh?" I promptly deleted it.

The only other post that caught my attention was a link that led me to Twitter. I gulped hard as I read the tweet from @LustInMartinsburg, which stated: "I got her wet & popped that Cherry dry."

I screamed, and Fidelio ran in like a trained rescue dog, his nose in the air, his tail puffed and trembling. Moaning, I fell to the floor and wrapped my arms around him. He purred despite the occasional fall of teardrops.

I couldn't believe it. Petey had bragged about the murder under yet another username. How hadn't they caught him yet? A breadcrumb trail led me back to the timestamp: Three o'clock on Saturday, around the time we were on our way to the Golden Lariat. A bit of Googling led me to several news articles about Peter "Petey" Malusky's arrest for the murders of three exotic dancers, and I exhaled a sob. The police had picked him up at a motel only a few miles from the Lariat.

He was belligerent, unsure of how he'd gotten to the motel, swearing up and down he was innocent. His cellphone, however, told a different story. He was logged into the @LostInMartisburg account, and the previous tweets were saved as drafts in his notes app. He also had gloves in his bag, black nitrile, which he couldn't explain. Plus they found a strange pair of Styrofoam shoes. I remembered the weird, speckled footprints on the floor from the day Ginger died.

The blood soaked in the Styrofoam was confirmed as belonging to "Tiffany Hackett, an exotic dancer at the strip club 'Pins' in Ridgeley, West Virginia." So there was no doubt that Petey had murdered Ginger, and he had most likely murdered Diamond and Cherry. The police had the fucker by the balls, and I hoped to God they sliced the shriveled sack clean off. Actually, a rough removal wouldn't have bothered me either. As long as the bastard was locked away, I felt better. Safer. I felt like I could actually enjoy myself again. Maybe a spa day wasn't such a bad idea after all.

CHAPTER TWELVE

I was way too nervous about a day of relaxation, and the new weed didn't help. I preferred an indica for situations like this—something to slow down my brain too much to even attempt rattling off my litany of anxieties—but I'd actually gotten a sativa, which gave me jittery paranoia like I'd never felt before. Jade had run out before our audition trip, and though she was never dry for long, I didn't want to be pushy. I planned on being casual, asking how she'd been for the past—shit, two weeks? Had it been that long? After the profitable night at The Golden Lariat, there was no need for me to work, and I didn't want to. With Petey in jail, we could eventually return to Pins, but we hadn't discussed it. And I didn't want to. I didn't want to do anything but smoke and smile, so I tried to avoid anything that inhibited either. Including dealing with jobs and boys.

I hadn't intentionally avoided Jade. I was just with Honey most of the time, bathed in lightness and levity. Our talks were never heavier than deciding who'd make the sacrifice to go out for more beer. Time slipped through our fingers, and that's how we preferred it. Honey said she called Jade a few times, but she never picked up, so when I noticed my stash dwindling, I found a guy on campus with a medical card instead. But as delicious as his bud tasted, the buzz came with the unfortunate side effect of siccing my mind on itself like a junkyard dog. I'd realized it only two days before spa day, when the chick in the apartment across the hall threatened to jump off her balcony. I wasn't unnerved by her threat because I knew she wouldn't do it. I'd met the girl, and she had a shitty life for sure, but it wasn't because of any injustice against her. She was racist—and would've fought tooth and nail against that label while using a hard "r"—and she'd internalized her misogynistic upbringing so deeply, she said the word "feminist" like other people said the word "moist." And she loved herself and her hatred too much to end either.

I couldn't say any of that to the police officer at my door, though, not in my state, especially since it's exactly what the jittery little sativa demon that had seized control of my brain wanted.

Talk about her racism. Talk about her cruelty. Call her a cunt in front of this geriatric cop with dead eyes that'll probably light up in solidarity when you mention the hard "r."

The thing was, after I cashed my bowl and a horrible girl threatened to kill herself two minutes later, the knock on my door filled me with a stupid amount of hope. Honey had been the only one to knock on my door in weeks, so the first rap of the knock gave me a whiff of excitement. But the second, third, fourth, and fucking Five-Oh! rap twisted the butterfly-sick feeling Honey gave me into a millipede-nausea.

I crumpled to the floor, and Fidelio, cautious, approached with a squeak. He dashed away at the next knock, and as he meowed from a distance, I rolled to a standing position. I inhaled deeply. I found stillness. I let go of what didn't fucking serve me.

In a voice that was meant to sound confident but sounded more like Charlotte A. Cavatica wove a "Dumbass" web in my throat, I said, "I'll be right there!

Let me put my cat away!"

Nice, Birdie. Fucking nice.

I became a sweaty gazelle leaping around my apartment, stashing pipes and papers, while Fidelio followed in buoyant joy.

"Stop it," I whispered when he batted at my heel, and he galloped away on a carefree baritone chirrup that made me want to engage in a Freaky Friday deal with my little dude for the next fifteen minutes.

Maybe an hour. Or a week. Or…okay, Fidelio probably knew he was getting the better end of this deal. He wouldn't switch with me, because he knew I wouldn't switch back. How would he even handle this whole strippy murder situation? Or Honey? Would he even be into Honey?

Oh God, I was way too high to answer the door.

The knocking stopped before I could figure out the best non-stoned greeting, but I didn't move when I heard their footsteps disappear down the stairs.

"Pffrlp?" Fidelio suggested.

"No."

"RRrrrpmplf."

"That's even more suspicious."

Fidelio snuffled so hard a crusty booger shot out of his nose and pinged off my foot. He looked up, wide-eyed, sweet as pie, and huffle-mewfed in a way that let me know he had my back.

I knew the cops didn't care about me, but with the sativa magnifying my paranoia, I kept thinking they were lurking outside, waiting for me to slip up and open the door.

The memory of the incident was acid reflux as I waited for Honey to arrive for spa day. I was looking forward to her and Jade calming me down, but when Honey arrived, she looked like a chihuahua on ayahuasca.

"Is Jade meeting us at the spa?"

"I doubt it. She wasn't home when I went by, and she hasn't answered her phone all day. All week, actually."

"Are you worried?"

She nodded meekly. "I know Petey's behind bars, but I can't shake the thought that she's in trouble. After what happened at the Lariat, she's cut herself off completely."

"But she does that sometimes, right? Runs off? Disappears for a while?"

"I guess."

"I'm sure she's fine."

She expelled a heavy breath. "Famous last words," she said and directed her gaze out the window.

"Sorry." I held up my pipe. "Hit this bowl."

Her inhalation was tense, but her exhalation was like blowing a smoky kiss. I was tempted to shotgun her hit, if only for the closeness of her rosy lips, but I didn't need to generate any more anxiety before the spa.

Honey had signed us up for full body massages and light fare to be enjoyed during a pedicure. I'd never experienced either, but she assured me it would be just the thing to get us back to normal.

Alas, there was nothing normal about the spa. From the moment Honey gave our names to the receptionist, I felt more important than I actually was. The speedy elegance with which we were whisked down the many marble hallways led me to believe a choir of maids and butlers waited around every bend to sing a song of privilege. The ensemble in my mind warbled out the amenities, but my response definitely wasn't a cheerful, *"I think I'm gonna like it here!"* I felt incredibly awkward, especially next to Honey, who walked the halls like she'd inspired their immaculate construction. While I felt like an uptight, slave-owning southern belle, she was the kind of queen who ruled epic fantasy novels with a kickass warrior attitude and a sultry leading lady flair.

I felt like an impostor. I didn't deserve this luxury, so it had to be some kind of trap. Some kind of trick to expose me as the garbage person I really was.

Logically, I knew it was the weed talking, but logic wasn't helping me navigate the choppy waters intended to relax me, and it worsened as we proceeded through the garish halls. I'd been joking about Honey's desire to steal my kidneys, but it didn't seem so funny now. Every employee smiled as we passed, but in my periphery, their polite smiles fell to grimaces. I could've sworn I spotted a girl with tidy black hair point to me and then slit her throat with her finger. I turned quickly, and she giggled like her head was full of marshmallow fluff, not murder.

The glitzy receptionist led us to a waiting room that was a world in itself. "Candice will be along shortly for you, Miss Potter. And Miss Finch, you'll be with Greg. Help yourself to water or tea while you wait."

"Greg?" I squeaked as the receptionist pranced away, and Honey poured a glass of water.

"What's the problem?"

"I can't get a massage from a guy. It would be too weird."

"Why?" She smirked. "Don't you like guys more than girls?"

"I guess, but I'd rather have a woman for something like this. I don't really dig male gynecologists either."

"Don't worry, he won't go that low. This isn't that kind of place."

"So I see," I said, my gaze rolling across the wall-to-wall safari.

The room had a theme, for sure. It just wasn't clear what that theme was. It had an African vibe, but the plinky-plunky music and constant water trickle reminded me of a South American rainforest. Much of the room was adorned with giraffes, but there was also one brown zebra. The decorator must have figured it was close enough. I popped a mint in my mouth as I settled into the mushy couch and unchained my brain so it could run wild. Words careened through my mind unchecked, strung together without need or want of punctuation. However, certain thoughts were bolder than others. The most prominent was GREG, surrounded by every irky run-on thought:

I feel like I'm on a first date with GREG and he's super late, maybe because he ducked in to see me and ducked out so he wouldn't have to touch my fat pasty body he probably wants to touch Honey instead but who wouldn't? GREG is probably the type of guy who got into massage just to touch tits under the guise of therapy shit he could be a rapist for all I know he could be a real black market kidney thief God I could fall asleep during the massage and next thing I know I'm in a bathtub with blood pouring from my kidney hole and my cunt hole, knocked up with his demon masseuse seed. I bet he's hot as hell but I don't want him to be hot as hell I want him to have perfect hands and I couldn't care less about the rest. Honey isn't nervous at all cuz she gets a chick what's there to be nervous about when you're dealing with a chick—

"You're chewing your mint so loud," Honey whispered so as not to disturb the giraffes.

"It's a mint. Loudly is the only way to chew it."

"Just suck it," she said as a prim Asian woman sat down on the sofa opposite us.

The woman bristled, and I said, "Sorry."

"Why are you apologizing? I was just saying to suck on your mint. I wasn't implying anything dirty. Unless you *want* to be dirty..." She tiptoed her fingers up my thigh.

"Honey, shh."

"Are you a dirty Birdie?"

The more embarrassed I became, the thicker she laid it on. When the woman was called for her appointment, I thought she might cross herself in gratitude.

"I take it you haven't spoken to James," I said.

"Fuck him."

"So you haven't seen Josh either?"

"Birdie, you should really just get over that. It's been two weeks since you spoke. It's over."

"But I like him. I was really starting to…I don't know if *'love'* is right, but I really, really liked him," I said sappily. "Don't tell me there's not a part of you that misses James."

She groaned. "Maybe *one* part."

"Just one?"

She gave me a look that warned me to tread lightly, but I couldn't do anything but stomp. I was about to get a rubdown from a perfect stranger, and for some reason, it made my heart ache for Josh. I wanted to be his girlfriend again, and even though I still had feelings for Honey, I wanted her to be James's girlfriend again. I wanted things to really get back to the slight normality we had before. The four of us, hanging out in buoyant smoke.

"What if James didn't actually cheat?" I said. "What if he had a perfectly good reason for having that underwear in the car?"

"Give me one possible reason. Seriously. I'll consider calling him if you can think of one good reason."

"I suppose he couldn't have bought them for you?"

"And stuffed them under his seat for safe keeping?"

"Maybe he was doing some early Christmas stashing."

"Bullshit. I don't have the time or energy to teach myself to trust him again. He's always cranky and he's never even invited me to his house. We always hang out at mine."

"Yipes. Really?"

"He says his mom lives with him, but I have a feeling it's more like he lives with her."

"And you don't approve?"

"He's a little old for it. It's not creepy yet, but it made

his stock plummet, especially since he's constantly getting on my bad side. Plus," she said, scooting closer. "There's some weird sex stuff."

"What kind of weird sex stuff?"

"He likes to do it on my period."

"That's not weird. I've done that plenty of times."

"Out of necessity, sure, but he looks forward to it. I don't want to go into the gory details, but it really creeps me out. Plus, he wanted to watch *The Texas Chainsaw Massacre*."

"So?"

"While we were having sex," she said pointedly. "I mean, it was already on. I didn't want to watch it in the first place—you know, with everything that's been going on—but when we started to mess around, he didn't stop the movie. I actually caught him watching it while he was inside me."

"So he likes horror movies, and he still wants to have sex with you when you're ragging. Neither of those things are that strange."

"If you want me to make up with James so I'll talk to Josh, fat chance. If you want him back, you need to tell him yourself."

"I'm not sure I want him back *that* badly." When she stared at me doubtfully, I said, "Okay, I'll try."

"So will I, I guess." She sighed. "I have to admit, I do miss James sometimes. And even if we don't get back together, talking to him couldn't hurt. It'll help with closure."

"Then things really will get back to normal."

"I thought you didn't want to go back to the way things were."

I huffed. "It's all I have."

"That can't be true."

"I guess not completely, but living in denial is better than trying to figure out why it's easier for me to take off my clothes on stage than pile on sequins and makeup."

"You mean your mom's pageant?" She laughed. "Birdie, you're one hell of flighty chick. What's the difference between pageant sequins and strip club glitter?"

"Glitter is wild. Sequins are methodically applied."

"By Mommy Dearest, no doubt."

"She's not that bad. She just wants me to be someone I don't think I can be. She wants me to be pretty like her."

"Birdie, you're the prettiest girl I know. Plus, you're a good person. You have no idea how hard it is to find a real friend in our line of work. You never know who will disappear in a week, or worse, become career strippers. Most of that lot is rotten to the core. Too much glitter can blind you."

"For now, I'd rather be blind."

"That's not healthy, girl."

"I know. But I don't deal well with stuff like this," I replied. "Just look at us here. I used to Manic Panic and now I mani-pedi? It's too strange."

"Well, I used to not shave my asshole. People change. You have to adjust as necessary and grow whenever possible, or you'll never learn anything. Nothing lasts forever...except the song 'November Rain.'"

"Eva?" A silky but masculine voice chimed at me from the doorway.

I was afraid to look. In my mind, Greg was an oily Adonis in nature's garb. I had no doubt he was a tall, muscular fellow with hands made for pinning me to the headboard. Just thinking about it had my nerves doing a solo tango and my body begging for a partner. When I turned around, he gave me a massive toothy grin that crinkled his face into speckled folds. With ginger hair and freckles covering his lanky body, he looked like a wire sculpture of Clay Aiken.

"Are you ready?" he said through teeth like sun-bleached tombstones, and Honey chuckled.

"Go get 'em, Tiger!"

I threw a mint at her before gathering myself and following Aiken-Face to our room.

The giraffes were left behind, but the strange music stuck around, growing louder as we reached the private room. Closed inside the pale blue space, Aiken-Face spoke in soft, soothing tones, but I could barely hear him over the relaxing cacophony. I was baffled when he suddenly left the room, but I gathered I was meant to get undressed, cover myself with the provided sheet, and lie with my face in the hole at the end of the table.

I wasn't sure how to let him know I'd completed my tasks, though. Naked on the squishy table, I waited... and waited...and waited.

Was I supposed to call his name or say "I'm ready?" The bench felt increasingly damp with sweat as I pictured him standing outside the room, waiting for me to shout a codeword he'd provided during a particularly loud chorus of plink-plunks. I was just about to call out when he popped open the door and stuck his face into the room with a grin made ghastly by flickering candlelight.

"Ready?"

"As I'll ever be."

"So..." He oiled his hands and rubbed them together like a squelchy villain. "...are there any areas you'd like me to target?"

"I guess my legs and arms. I'm a dancer, so..."

"Oh yeah? I have a lot of dancers as clients. What kind of dancer are you?"

I wasn't ashamed of my profession, but I felt strange telling him I was a stripper, especially while I was currently stripped.

"Uh...ballet," I said shakily, and the squelching abruptly stopped.

It was obvious he didn't believe me. I didn't know what gave me away: my flab or the patches of glitter still clinging to my skin, but he was polite enough not to press the issue.

During the massage, I felt uncomfortable, physically and mentally. I believed everything he did was professional, but I also didn't have anything to compare it to. By the end, I felt good: looser and in less pain, but there wasn't a single minute that passed during the massage in which I didn't frantically wonder how many minutes were left. The pedicure was better. Honey and I sat next to each other, so we could chat, and I could snicker every time she accidentally kicked the pedicurist for tickling her feet.

All in all, it was a pretty good day. Feeling relaxed, perhaps even to the point of false confidence, I decided to call Josh. Honey wished me luck as she dropped me off, and I'm sure Fidelio would have done the same if he wasn't so preoccupied with the bottom of his food bowl. Once I covered the empty spot, he ate two pieces of kibble and turned his attention to me. He curled up on my lap as I stared at Josh's profile in my phone. My finger was hovering over the call button when Fidelio suddenly batted the hoodie string dangling overhead. His claw caught on the string, and when he tugged it in panic, the hood tightened around my neck. As I fumbled to hold onto my phone, I accidentally swiped the screen and initiated the call.

I desperately tried to cancel, but Fidelio flapped his trapped claw, and I couldn't get a good grip on the phone.

"Hello? Birdie? Is that you?"

I dropped the phone on the couch and leaned into it as I freed Fidelio's claw. "Yeah, hey. Hi," I said without a scrap of elegance.

"What's up?"

"Not much, you know, stuff."

"Did you call for a reason, or..."

"I'm sorry, Josh."

"It's okay. I know you're not great on the phone."

"No, I mean *I'm sorry*. I'm sorry about everything."

"Yeah, I know that too."

"Do you forgive me?"

He coughed. "Sure."

"Look, I know what I did was shitty, but it wasn't the worst thing in the world, was it? I understand if you don't want to be with me anymore, but can't we at least be friends?"

"I want to be with you, Birdie..."

I'd been waiting to hear those words for weeks. Unfortunately, I also had to hear the "but" that followed them.

"...*But* I don't know if I can trust you. And I don't know if you can trust me."

"Of course I trust you. Why wouldn't I?"

"Do you really want to know? It could change everything."

"Right now we don't have *anything*."

"It could stay that way forever after this."

"After what?"

Josh sighed, but it wasn't one of his deep, steady sighs with relief on the tail. It was shallow, and it shook.

"Birdie, I slept with someone else."

I couldn't believe it: one phrase that ignited my heart and another that pinched the flame within seconds of each other.

"While we were together?"

"It was after we broke up, but I feel guilty about it. And if I feel guilty, it must've been wrong."

His admission hurt me to the bone, but when it came down to screwing other people, he was free to hurt me as much as he wanted.

"Who was she?"

"A girl I met during the trip. She was no one. She meant nothing. After it happened, I could hardly believe I even did it. I didn't leave James's backseat for almost an hour, I was so ashamed. And then she left her underwear..."

The slutty girl! She'd fucked Josh, not James.

"So James was telling the truth. He didn't cheat on Honey."

"Nope. I cheated on you," Josh said. "I know we weren't together, but I still have feelings for you. To me, that's cheating. I screwed everything up."

"I'm the one who screwed things up. I'm the one who called my ex-boyfriend. I'm the one who let old habits speak louder than my heart."

His voice warmed. "Your heart?"

"Yes, Josh. I—I—"

"Yeah?"

"Umm...did you hear they caught the killer?" I said hastily, clumsily.

"Which killer?"

"Really, Josh? The Pins killer, of course. The Twitter Stripper killer, whatever the media's calling him now. The cops caught him while we were in Martinsburg. His phone was linked to the Twitter account; well, the LustInMartinsburg account anyway. He's denying it, but the trial's going ahead. Open and shut case," I said as I opened a drawer in my coffee table and slammed it closed, a little too loudly.

After a pause, Josh said, "You just acted out that statement, didn't you?"

"Kinda," I creaked.

"I fucking adore you, Birdie."

Unlike me, his affectionate declarations didn't sound like the vomitous sap of a teen trash novel. He was Michael from *The Mayfair Witches*. He was Henry from *The Time Traveler's Wife*. He was someone who used to be mine.

"I guess you'll be going back to Pins when it reopens?"

"I think so."

"I really hope it works out for you. I hope all of your plans work out. And I'm glad you called. It was nice to hear your voice."

"Yours too. I miss you, Josh."

"I'm sorry, Birdie, but I have to get back to work."

"Sure, sure. Maybe I'll talk to you later?"

"I hope so," he said.

He hung up, but I kept the phone glued to my ear for a full minute after the disconnect. I didn't want to let go. A dead line had never made me feel so alive.

CHAPTER THIRTEEN

Cecil scheduled the grand reopening of Pins for the following weekend. I wasn't sure if he didn't realize it was Friday the 13th , or if he'd realized it too late to change the date. Personally, I thought the coincidence blew over his head with plentiful clearance. The girls, however, were not so oblivious. Even though Petey was in prison awaiting trial, an unease hung over us as heavy as cigarette smog. I suspect it's why Cecil had four bouncers stationed at every entrance and exit. The illusion of security was just as comforting as the illusion of class, and we ate it up as readily as we hoped the customers would.

An hour before opening, we gathered in a circle around Cecil. Pantera had returned, thank God, but there were more new faces than old. We scanned the circle, taking stock of the new faces as well as the absent ones. Jade was the most obvious absentee, but Cookie and CJ were also missing from the line. I couldn't kick up too much sadness regarding the others, but I'd been hoping to see Jade.

Two weeks after the last time we saw her, Honey finally received a reply to her texts. The message read, "Fine." That's it. "Fine."

After an agitated discussion about what "fine" really meant, we did some sleuthing and found a Twitter account for her brother in Miami. He hadn't seen her either, but he assured us she was probably just pulling one off her famous disappearing acts. We asked if he knew what had been going on in the area, about the guy who'd been killing strippers.

"What does a stripper killer have to do with my sister?"

I quickly typed, "Nothing. Just asking," while giving Honey a "yeeshk" face.

No more texts came as the weeks passed, but we convinced ourselves to believe Jade was as fine as her message claimed. It was possible she didn't even know Pins was reopening. Cecil wasn't big on collecting contact info from his employees. I only knew about it because of an Instagram post, and Cecil was so grateful he said he'd give any returning dancer a $100 bonus. Considering I wasn't convinced customers would return, I accepted his offer. I was a little disheartened that it was happening on a weekend when I'd have my period, but as it turned out, Aunt Flo was still out of town come Friday. Of course, it didn't make precautions any less necessary. Normally, I'd just sacrifice the underwear to her mysterious arrival, but I'd be sacrificing my tips if she mysteriously arrived while I was dancing. Not wanting to wear a dry tampon for hours on end, I'd invested in a menstrual cup for such occasions. After all, the last thing Pins needed was more blood on the stage.

Several of the new Pins dancers weren't new to the profession. Shasta, in her sparkly sling-back stilettos, would've been a great candidate for Honey's rival if her personality wasn't hot garbage. Strip club souses probably wouldn't say a girl needed a good personality to be a good stripper, but those people never considered how deeply a girl's personality influenced her dancing style. Honey was rough-and-tumble, but she was also cute and coy. My girl-next-door persona also served me well, mostly because when I got down and dirty, customers thought they were the ones who'd corrupted me. A dirty girl-next-door was a huge draw, especially when teamed up with a rough-and-tumble cutie. Shasta was certainly the latter, but she lacked the sweet side. She was a West Virginia "fuck 'em and leave 'em" type like Ginger, but Shasta was more glamorous and more skilled—she knew what she was doing and looked good doing it—and had therefore earned the right to be a stuck-up bitch.

Another new girl who had acclimated fairly quickly was a Malaysian gymnast named Pearl was nice enough, but her stage name kept bringing "pussy pearls" to mind, and a few of the other girls teased her until she explained that her stage name was a play on words.

"I'm not just a clam," she announced, elegantly akimbo. "I'm a *Pearl*."

The declaration earned as many giggles as groans, and though it had a pretty gross connotation, I was impressed by Pearl's cleverness, so she won a place in my good graces.

Crystalline never quite got there. She was quiet and kept to herself. I initially thought she was a nervous first-time dancer, but she eventually disclosed she'd worked at the Golden Lariat, and she'd had a close friendship with Cherry. *Extremely* close. She was out of town during our Oregon Trail weekend and returned home to discover someone murdered her secret girlfriend. She never disclosed why she came to work at the place where the murders started, and none of us dared to ask.

A fistfuckful of bubbly chicks with artificial tits joined the ranks as well. With names like Radiance, Illusion, and Entice, the girls were useless beyond ass shaking, and even then, they needed a lesson or two. To the new girls, Honey and I ruled Pins. Actually, Honey ruled it, but as her faithful sidekick, I was just as important to befriend. You could see the endgame in every cordiality; they wanted to rule too. Who wouldn't? But for the time being, they knew their places.

Despite the new blood, a few old veins remained. Destiny was the most obvious. It wasn't because she took up a quarter of the circle or because she was chowing down on a candy bar while Cecil explained the "new, classier Pins." She stood out most because she was the last dancer I wanted to see again. She appeared to have gotten even heavier in the interim, not that I blamed her for stress-eating. I'd regained a few pounds in the last few weeks of rotting on the couch with Honey, but Destiny had slapped on a good twenty pounds more and squeezed it all into the same tiny stripper clothes. Unlike the healthy plus-sized dancers, she looked like she was two candy bars away from busting open her c-section scar, and I wasn't convinced the meat that spilled out wouldn't be as sugar-encrusted as Sour Patch Kids.

I hoped she'd be confined to the alley, but when Cecil called her name for both sides, several dancers groaned, some more blatantly than others. But Destiny didn't care, and it was hard not to respect that. She knew she was gross, and our disgust seemingly spurred her to become grosser still, perhaps the grossest stripper to ever hump the boards, because knowing you're the greatest at something, even if people gag at the stench of rotten teeth whenever you walk by, was sometimes the only thing you needed to ignore other horrors, like murder, assault, and early onset diabetes.

Contrary to my fears, customers started arriving an hour before opening. The line curled around the building, stretching nearly to the back door of the dressing room, so Cecil opened the doors thirty minutes early to appease the voracious crowd, despite the fact that the dancers weren't ready, and the bartenders had yet to arrive.

Cecil intended the opening number to include every Pins girl while highlighting the featured dancer, Roxi Rockets, but with our preparation time smashed to smithereens, it was less of an exquisitely-staged full-nude cabaret, and more of a sweaty jumble of big tittied-penguins arguing about who would be on the pole first, and whether Roxi was supposed to have any solo moments in the group number, or if we had to share tips if we didn't get moments of our own.

I was about to join the flock when the back door flew open. Shrieking, I grabbed the closest weapon: a Spencer's Gifts' cat-o-nine tails that probably tickled more than it could ever injure.

Josh laughed as he poked his head in the door. "With everything that's happened, they didn't fix the lock on the back door?"

His forgiving smile made me throw the whip to the floor and my body into his arms. He didn't kiss me, but he did touch my hair and run his fingers down to the small of my back. In some ways, more intimate than a kiss.

"You look really beautiful tonight," he said.

I scrunched my nose and shimmied my fringy top. "I look like a stripper."

"Well, you make *stripper* look damn good."

With the compliment, his eyes seemed richer, his stature greater, and his hands more insistent as they pulled my body to his. My yelp of surprise turned to a gasp when his fingers moved under my dress. I had missed those fingers, and it was obvious Josh had missed me too. Part of him, at the very least. His lust enraptured me so completely, I forgot where I was, that I was supposed to be onstage, and the fact that I had a menstrual cup in.

He said "Whooops!" when his fingers hit the silicone dam.

"It's okay. It's a preemptive strike. I haven't actually

gotten it yet."

His expression changed cartoonishly. He tore down my top and licked his way up my chest. Kissing me deeply, he hooked his arm under my leg and pressed me against the wall. His teeth nipped my neck, leaving a hot trail to my ear where he whispered wantonly.

His groin pressed into me so hard, I probably could've gotten off on the friction alone. I would've been dripping wet if not for the cup, and if I hadn't heard Cecil's voice boom over the collective stomps of the "Cupid Shuffle." I fixed my dress and shoved Josh behind a rack of clothes just before Cecil burst into the dressing room.

"Goddammit, Birdie, get on stage!" he barked.

Knowing how squeamish "lady business" made him, I said, "Sorry, I had to empty my menstrual cup."

Sure enough, it pushed him to retreat, but before he closed the door, he pointed at me. "By the way, your tit is out and I can see your man's feet. Make sure both are back where they belong before you hit the stage."

Cecil slammed the door and Josh poked his head through the clothes with a chuckle. I snapped my dress into place, but he promptly pulled it back down and dove at my chest.

"Does this mean we've made up?" I asked as he kissed his way to my lips.

"You mean, are we back together?"

"Yeah. I've really missed you."

"If you forgive me, if you want me, I'm yours."

As he kissed my neck, I hoped he wouldn't ask me why Honey entered my mind when I said, "Don't you think you owe Honey the truth? That James didn't cheat on her?"

"Sure, sure," he said, breathing heavily against my breasts. Then, he stopped and looked at me with his brain pumping palpably behind his eyes. "Unless it's better if they aren't together. James is weird when it comes to girls he really likes. If they don't automatically trust him, he tends to become the untrustworthy one. I could fix their relationship, but it might not stick. And one or both might end up getting hurt."

"It would suck having them apart now that we're back together. I like the four of us hanging out."

"Would you really mind if it was just the three of us?" He resumed kissing my neck.

"You want to cut out James?"

He chuckled. "That wasn't what I had in mind."

"Two girls, one guy?" I mused, and he squinted at me.

"You really like Honey, don't you?"

"You know I do."

"How much?"

"Josh, are you kidding?"

"Do you want to fuck her?" he asked.

I said "no" without a moment's hesitation, and he looked like he believed me even less. The truth was, I didn't know the answer to that question. I wasn't even sure *how* to fuck her, so I couldn't be sure it was what I really wanted. I was certain I'd enjoy exploring the mountains, but like most folks having gay thoughts, I was terrified to visit the deep south. I'd probably make a fool of myself and give baby bi's everywhere a bad name.

Though, I imagined Honey would be generous in bed. I bet she'd guide me gently and ride me hard, and we'd laugh a lot. I bet it wouldn't be as scary as I envisioned. But I wasn't big on betting, and the risk of losing her was too great.

"Honey and I are just friends, I swear."

The strength of his kiss told me he chose to believe it, and the way his hands moved over my body said he might not care either way.

"Will you stay and watch me dance?"

"I wouldn't miss it," he said, ravenous. "And I'll fix

James and Honey if it makes you happy."

I said "thank you" against his lips. His hands went for one more pass before he fixed my dress and I headed for the stage.

Josh's gaze was glued to me the entire time I was onstage, and Cecil's joined him when I left it, like he was looking for reasons to reprimand me. Since there'd be no sitting with Josh between sets, I propositioned customers seated near him so I could glance over and see his eyes locked on me. Every time I opened my legs, every time I got slick, every time I touched or grabbed or clawed my body, I thought of him.

"Something on your mind, Cupcake?"

I didn't hear the customer until he waved his hand in front of my face.

"Sorry," I said, dropping my gaze to his mouth and my crotch to his thigh.

I brushed myself against him, giving him a close-up of my tits as I pretended to lick the length of his body. Standing over him again, I realized he was wearing a backward Florida Marlins hat.

"Did I sell you my underwear?"

The man's belly shook when he laughed. My memory was hazy at best, but I was pretty sure it wasn't Mr. Marlins. With the jelly belly and white beard, he looked more like Santa Claus. I wondered how long I'd have to grind his lap for him to give me what I wanted for Christmas: to forgo the night's tips and grind Josh for free until sunrise.

"If you're selling, I'm buying," Santa said.

"Excuse me?"

"The underwear."

He and Mr. Marlins weren't the same person, but thanks to my mistake, Santa had new inklings about my spot on his naughty list.

"That was a joke."

"I don't get it."

"Sorry. I was distracted."

"Distracted, huh? That's not good for girls in your line of work," he said. "Distracted dancers end up dead."

I stepped back. "What did you say?"

"I said, if you're not careful, someone's gonna clip your wings...Birdie."

I backpedaled so fast I nearly fell onto another customer's lap. He didn't appear to mind, but Illusion accused me of horning in on her dance.

"Get your own guy," she snarled.

"He threatened to kill me," I said, pointing at Santa.

"What?" His belly jiggled when he hopped to his feet. "I never threatened you."

"You said 'distracted dancers end up dead'. If that's not a threat, I don't know what is."

Josh's hand on my back made me scream, but when I saw it was him, I collapsed into his arms.

"Whoa, Birdie, what's wrong?" He growled at Santa. "What the hell did you do to her?"

"I didn't do shit!"

Some of the other girls had gathered around to watch, still dancing slightly so as not to be accused of slacking off.

Santa pulled a ten-dollar bill from his wallet and held it up to my face. "Just take the money, you crazy bitch."

I was scared to reach out, so Josh plucked the bill for me and slid it into my garter. Santa waddled away, but I was too tense to move.

"Who was that guy? What did he do to you?"

"I don't know. He said—" I stammered, wiping my sweaty palms on nonabsorbent sequins. "I don't know what he said. I might have imagined it."

"Don't worry. No one is going to hurt you as long as I'm around, and I plan on always being around."

The crowd began to disperse, but Pearl hung back

and handed me a baby wipe to clean the mascara from under my eyes.

"That's a sweet guy you got there. Where'd you find him?"

"Here, actually," I said.

Her smile promptly fell.

"That's disgusting." She shoved the wipes back into her purse and marched away.

"Jesus. Do you think us meeting a strip club is disgusting?" I asked, and Josh bounced his head on his shoulders.

"I think being a human is pretty disgusting, so most aspects of love and relationships are disgusting. In and out of the bedroom, it's all one big sticky mess. Our meeting was just the catalyst for the other nasty parts of love. Nasty, and sexy as hell."

I chuckled. "You should write poetry."

"For you, my slippery strippery girl, I would do anything."

And he did.

After that night, we cloistered ourselves together as often as possible. He lavished me with gifts and compliments that lit me up like a Christmas tree for days on end. He fixed the rift between Honey and James—he even covered some of the money Honey had stolen and spent in vengeance—but Honey wasn't as enthused as me. She was glad James hadn't cheated, but she hated that I forgave Josh so quickly.

"Honey, we were broken up, and he regrets sleeping with that girl." We sat on my couch, preparing to roll a joint. While I stripped the bud off the stems, she broke them down to sticky dust. We made a damn good team.

"She wasn't a girl," she replied, hissing. "She was a *slut*. Make sure he gets tested before you let him back in the Birdhouse."

"He's clean."

"That's what they all say. Besides, what happened to

'taking a break?" You didn't even think you were really broken up. He just needed time, remember?"

"Did I say that?"

"You were pretty adamant about it." She sighed heavily, then licked the crystals off her fingers. "It's amazing the allowances we'll make for the perfect pecker. Or the one we want to be perfect. Maybe no pecker is perfect."

"I don't know. Josh's is pretty close."

"Wanna trade?"

"Not even for a night." I held up my hands in supplication. "No offense, but James really isn't my type."

"I'm not sure he's my type anymore either."

"So why'd you get back together with him?"

"He might not be perfect, but he still has a pecker. As long as he doesn't act like one, I'll stick around for a while longer. Besides, you wanted me to. At least now we can hang out as much as we did before you guys made up."

"You shouldn't stay with someone you're not into. You deserve way better than that," I said. "We'd still hang out all the time. If you don't like him, if all that period plowing grosses you out, you shouldn't waste your time."

"I appreciate you looking out for me, but I've been on my own long enough to learn how to handle myself, so you should probably let me decide what's a waste."

"Okay, I'm sorry."

She rolled her shoulders with a groan. "No, I am. I shouldn't have brought it up. James and I are fine. I'm sorry to rain on your parade."

"It was already a little soggy."

"In jizz, I'm sure."

"Now that you mention it, I am a little sticky." I wiped my hand on her shoulder and she wailed in disgust.

I flicked her in the nose and she snarled playfully as she pushed me down on the couch. Her hair fell into my eyes, onto my lips; her breath danced across my neck, covering me in her sexy coconut scent.

Maybe no pecker is perfect, I thought.

"Cut it out," I said, sliding out from under her. "You'll knock over the weed."

"So touchy," she said, sneering. "You sure *you* aren't the one doing the period plowing?"

"I fucking wish."

Her lip curled. "Are you sure James isn't your type?"

"Definitely. I just..." I resumed ripping the buds into small balls. "My period's a little late."

"How late?"

"I don't think it's worth worrying about yet."

"It sounds like you're already worried." She passed the papers. "Have you taken a pregnancy test?"

"No, and I don't want to. I have to go to my cousin's baby shower this weekend, and I don't think I could handle it being positive."

"It could be negative though. Instead of being all wound up and paranoid at the shower, you could be relieved and actually have a good time."

"That's not going to happen. Baby or barren, that party is going to suck," I said. "Distract me. What are you up to this weekend?"

"I'm working. God, I don't want to. I'm exhausted. But I need the money."

"For what?" When she bit her lip in response, I took it back. "I'm sorry, it's none of my business."

"You're my best friend, Birdie. You should know my business. The truth is, the money isn't for me." She exhaled heavily. "It's for my mom."

"I thought you hated your mom."

"I do...and I don't."

"I get it."

"I don't think you do."

"Hey, my mom isn't crazy supportive either. She's always on me to be beautiful."

"No, she's on you to *feel* beautiful. When your mom constantly makes you feel second to some asshole boyfriend, you'll get it. When she leaves you alone for weeks at a time with no money and an abusive grandmother, you'll get it. When she gets cancer and your bitch of a grandmother splits, you'll get it." Her voice remained strong through the entire speech, but in the silence following, she whimpered. The last barrier wall had fallen.

"How bad is she, your mom?"

"Pretty bad. And she's broke, so it's been tough getting any real answers. She'd rather ignore the problem until the cancer or the Jack Daniels kills her."

"Jack would never do something like that. He exists only to help people." I pouted my bottom lip, and she chuckled lightly.

"Then I wish he'd helped her faster. I'd love to keep my money."

My heart hurt for Honey. I couldn't imagine being in her situation: having a sick mother who, from what it sounded like, was doing all she could to make her daughter as miserable as possible, even to the grave. As much as my mom annoyed me, she wanted what was best for me. It wasn't all her fault she didn't know me very well, and maybe it was best she didn't, because I felt like a stranger to myself sometimes. The last thing I'd want to do is fool my mom into believing I was worthy of her love when I was actually a sack of shit.

"Maybe you should save your money," I said. "It sounds like she's determined to...pass away."

"Sweet people 'pass away,' Birdie. My mom is a bitch who deserves to die," she said fiercely, but it didn't hold. Her voice wavered and she sniffled as she blotted her eyes. "Goddamn, I hate this. I wish she was dead already, and I wish my grandmother would join her. I don't care how terrible it sounds."

"You're a good person, Honey. You wouldn't say something like that about someone unless they deserved it." I rubbed her arm. "By the way, thanks for telling me this stuff. You're right, I don't get it, but I want to be here for you as much as I can."

"Thank you. I don't want to hold it all inside anymore. Not like you're holding Josh's baby."

I smacked her arm, and she apologized through laughter. After sprinkling weed on the paper, she passed it over and watched intently as I rolled a near-perfect joint. Once it was rolled, I held it up for her to lick. She ran her tongue along the edge, eyes sparkling, and I finished the process by twisting the ends. Popping it in my mouth, I lit the tip and inhaled deeply.

"Ignoring it won't make it go away, you know."

"Stop being sensible." I passed her the joint, and she drew a massive hit. "What kind of friend are you anyway?"

She cupped her hands around my mouth, beckoned my lips to hers, and exhaled her smoke into me. It was strange how much sweeter it tasted coming from her. After I exhaled, she leaned over and wiped away a piece of leaf that clung to my lip. "I'm the kind that won't let you lie to yourself, Birdie. The best kind."

She hadn't exhaled enough. As she spoke, faint puffs of smoke escaped between her lips. I thought about breathing it in. I told myself it was because I didn't want to waste any weed, but the butterflies in my belly beat their wings in protest. The weed was already rocking my head and making my skin buzz. If Honey came any closer, I feared I wouldn't have the strength to stop her. I needed something to push her away.

"I'm sure I'll get my period soon," I said. It was an awkward transition, but it did the trick. She backed up to knock ash from the joint. "I'm sure it's no big deal. Stupid shit like this happens when I forget my pills."

"Stupid shit like pregnancy?"

"No, no. I still take them, just...later than I'm supposed to. Or I double up."

"If that's true, you only have yourself to blame."

"I'm not disputing that. I'm quite aware of how utterly intolerable I am." I crossed my arms over my chest, but she pulled them apart and wrapped them around her instead. "Just don't tell anyone, okay?"

"You have my word. And you'll text me if you need anything, right?"

"Thank you. And that goes both ways." I blew my hit in her face and she chomped at the cloud like a puppy chasing bubbles.

She was too cute. Why in the world was I leaving town?

"I gotta say, I don't envy you." Honey stubbed out the joint. "Stuck in a house with a pregnant skank and high school frenemies? I'd take a stripper killer any day."

I was inclined to agree, especially when the weekend arrived and my period still hadn't. I was sufficiently terrified, but I talked myself out of buying a pregnancy test as easily as I talked myself out of going to Megan's baby shower. A normal baby shower was bad enough. A cumdumpster's baby shower was worse. And the moldy cherry on top of the sucky sundae was that while everyone celebrated a new life, I'd be contemplating tossing myself down the stairs, just to cover my bases.

Unfortunately, my mom knew how my mind worked. Ten minutes before I was due to leave, she blew up my phone with calls and texts. My phone vibrated across the table so much, Fidelio thought it was a toy and pounced on it.

My mom chirped. "Birdie?"

Shit! Fidelio answered my phone. "Bad cat!"

"Birdie, are you there? Is this one of those 'butt-dials?'"

I snorted and swiped on the speakerphone. "Hi, Mom."

"You must have been getting ready to leave. Is that why you didn't pick up earlier?" she asked. I swore I could hear her smile.

"You know me so well."

"So, you are still coming."

With the phone gone, Fidelio had decided to start playing with a lighter. I switched the phone to my other ear and tried to shoo him from the table, but he started attacking my fingers.

"I don't know. I want to, but my car's been acting funny. I think it's the timing belt."

"What's it doing?"

"Shimmying and stuff."

"That sounds like an alignment problem. Megan's husband is a master at fixing alignment problems. Maybe he can take a look at it. He knows his way around a car."

"And a dumpster," I muttered.

"What's that?"

"Nothing. The truth is I'm not feeling too well. I've been having stomach issues."

"Stomach issues and a shaky car? That certainly isn't a good combination."

"Not really. I've been getting sick all morning."

"I'm sure you'll be fine as long as you don't drink during the shower," she said cheerfully.

Well, *that* certainly wasn't going to happen, whether I was faking sick or not. Otherwise, I wouldn't survive an hour.

"I don't think I'm going to go."

"Eva, if you don't go, I won't have anyone to talk to," she said, almost whining.

Fidelio caught hold of one of my fingers and nipped the knuckle. I yelped and nearly dropped the phone into my soda. I gently pushed him to the floor and he yowled as if I'd destroyed his hopes and dreams.

"Can't you just talk to Aunt Linda or Aunt Aggie?"

"Bores," she said. "I want to hear about what you've been up to: school, boys, everything."

"I haven't been up to boys, Mom."

"I want to see you, Eva. Why can't I see you? You haven't been hanging out at piercing places getting a hundred holes in your head, have you?"

"No, but if I have to listen much longer, I might put one really big one in it." Remembering the flush of appreciation for a mom who didn't delight in my devastation, I exhaled in defeat. "Okay, I'm on my way."

"Oh Sweet Pea, I'm so glad. Be careful in that shaky car and take some Pepto Bismol for your tummy, okay?"

"No problem."

"Love you, Birdie."

"You too. See you soon."

She was always able to change my mind, and I couldn't hate her for it. She was so sweet, and I guess I was a little resentful that I'd never be that sweet. Of course, I didn't even intend on trying during the baby shower, especially if Scott showed up, as I suspected he would, if only to throw a fresh scowl my way.

I stumbled around the apartment out of vexation, grunting with each childish grab of my essentials. I ripped my purse from the counter and kicked the baby shower present to the door; it was a good thing I had opted for a stuffed lion rather than the ostentatious stemware Megan had sprinkled throughout her registry.

It was going to be a long drive to Westminster. Thankfully, Josh had just curated a new playlist to distract me. With a giggle, I selected "Let's Flock, Birdie" from my library and pondered whether "flock" was supposed to be a play on "fuck" or "rock" as my phone connected to Bluetooth. Josh was so eloquent, so sensitive; I was certain he'd pick the perfect first song to helm the medley of our love. Turning up the volume, I waited for the music to reveal exactly how he felt about me.

"The world is a vampire..."

I flinched, accidentally tapping the gas and jolting my car. I waved an apology at the people around me, putting on my blinker and moving to the slowest lane so I could sit safely with the confusing feelings rushing through me.

It's not that I disliked The Smashing Pumpkins. I just didn't recall ever saying I was a fan. Had I ever even listened to "Bullet with Butterfly Wings" with him? Did he associate it with me in some way, and if so, why the fuck? Was I the rat in the cage, or was he? And was the cage our goddamn relationship?

I put a lot of hope on the second song. If it had been the Joni Mitchell version of "Big Yellow Taxi," a.k.a. the proper version, I would've forgiven the bumpy start, maybe even decided it was just a prank to make sure I was paying attention. But instead of Joni's complex musicality bringing the poem to life, the words tumbled dead from the clumsy lips of a whispering castrato too out of his depth to sound deep.

I knew it was silly to get upset, but I couldn't help it. It was sweet to make a mix for your girlfriend, but it would be much sweeter if it didn't nauseate her. I didn't think it would be that difficult to make a mix for me. It wasn't like I kept my musical likes and dislikes close to the chest. He heard my favorites every time he came to Pins. It didn't make any sense. Unless...he *wanted* me to like this music?

I was in an especially sour mood when I reached Megan and Bobby's McMansion. Trimmed in ribbons of saccharine pink, it had the same effect as the playlist. I must've looked like an angry toad on their doorbell cam because Megan opened the door before I could knock. I wondered why she was playing lookout for her own party, but I found out pretty quickly.

No one was there—except for caterers confused by the assignment to cater an empty house. Megan snatched the gift, threw it on the nearly-barren gift table, and slapped my hand against her massive belly.

"She's kicking. Feel."

"Is this how you greet people now?"

"Did you feel it?"

"I felt something, I guess."

She squealed. "It's amazing, isn't it?"

"So amazing. Where's the bar?"

"In the parlor with the other guests. You're a little early so there aren't many people here yet," she said cheerfully.

"I'm an hour late."

She waddled away, watching the doorbell cam feed on her phone. "It's okay. I won't judge you."

Scooting to the den, I turned the corner and immediately had to swallow the groan that rumbled up my throat. There weren't other guests. There was only Scott, already on his feet and unfolding his arms. I brushed past him and made a beeline for the bar.

"Predictable Birdie," he said as he sidled up to me.

I kept my eyes down, mixing a gin and ginger ale. "Thanks."

"Are you going to ask how I'm doing?"

"I can see how you're doing. You look fine."

"I am. Great, in fact."

"Awesome. Glad to hear it," I said, gagging when I hit a gin pocket in my gulp.

"Are you still with that guy?"

"Yes."

"Still working at the strip club?"

I slapped my hand over Scott's mouth and glared viciously. "Keep your voice down."

"Fffmmmtt," he mumbled and I pulled my hand away. "Why do I have to keep my voice down? You're not ashamed, are you?"

"No, I'm not ashamed, but most people are close-minded jerks. They'll assume things about me that aren't true," I said. "Look at me, explaining close-minded jerks to their goddamn president."

"I never judged you, Birdie. I was afraid for you."

I narrowed my eyes and sipped my drink. "Is that why you were at the Golden Lariat?"

"Huh?"

"The Golden Lariat. I saw you there a few weeks ago. Are you stalking me or something?"

"Don't flatter yourself."

"Do you swear you weren't there?"

"If I was, it would only be out of concern," he said.

"So it *was* you!" I lowered my voice and pulled him deeper into the room. "How did you even know I'd be there? Are you just hanging around my apartment waiting to see which strip club I go to?"

"Of course not. I didn't want you involved with stripping because I think it's gross, so I obviously don't want to be involved either."

"You didn't want me involved because you didn't want me flashing *your* pussy at other men."

"That too. Can you blame me?"

"If it *was* your pussy. But it's not, it's mine."

"Until the Strip Club Killer hacks it to bits," he said icily.

Petey was in custody, but Scott's words still made my entire body tense up. The only response I could manage was a lengthy gulp of my drink.

"I can see you're still worried, Birdie. Do you think I'd stop being able to read you just because we broke up?" He tilted his head. "Is it the murders, or something else?"

He touched my hand lightly, and a shiver shot

through my skin. It wasn't one of ecstasy, but it wasn't one of disgust either.

A high-pitched voice sang, "Hey, Sweetie," and a girl with a ponytail that bounced as much as her breasts skipped into the room. The girl looked familiar, but I couldn't place her. She was a basic beauty: thin and blonde with plump lips and shiny porcelain skin that only showed age when she saw me push away Scott's hand.

"What's going on?" she asked him like a lost child.

"Grace, this is Birdie," he said. "Birdie, this is my girlfriend, Grace."

I shot him a pointed look before shaking the girl's slender hand. "It's nice to meet you."

"You too...*Birdie*? Did I hear that right?"

"It's a nickname. My real name is Eva."

"Eva. Eva Finch!" she exclaimed. "I thought you looked familiar. I'm Grace Hartsock. I'm in the pageant."

I didn't realize I was sucking my stirrer so intensely until it slurped air. "Sorry? How do I look familiar? I haven't done a pageant since I was a baby."

"I work in your mom's office. She shows me pictures of you all the time. She said you were competing this year."

I nearly snorted gin out my nose. I coughed up a giggle and shook my head.

"What's so funny?"

"I'm not competing. I wouldn't be caught dead in a pageant."

"Oh?" She planted her hands on her hips. "Why not?"

"It's not my thing."

"So feeling pretty isn't your thing? Building confidence and making lifelong friendships isn't your thing?" she asked.

"I didn't mean it as an insult."

Her expression scrunched. "I think you did."

I looked around the room. I knew no one else had joined the party, but looking at an empty room was better than the pageant girl.

"I guess my mom isn't here yet?"

"We're the only ones so far," Scott said.

"I'm only asking because it sounded like my mom was feeding lines to your girlfriend through a hidden communication system."

I chuckled, but Grace was not amused.

"You don't think I can speak for myself?" she snapped.

"Settle down, Grace."

She threw Scott a glare that could've cracked glass. "Settle down? How do you expect me to settle down after walking in on you holding another girl's hand?"

"It's not what you think," I said.

"I think you two dated."

"Okay, it is what you think," I replied. "But we're way over. There's no reason to feel threatened."

"Threatened?" She laughed. "I don't feel threatened. Not by you. I've won more crowns than you can count."

"I don't know," I trilled, tapping my chin. "I can count pretty high."

Grace waved a manicured finger in my face. "You know what? I don't like you."

"Then it must suck knowing how much your boyfriend still does."

With a furious squeal, she stomped out of the room, and Scott grumbled, "Way to go, Birdie," before chasing after her.

I collapsed onto the couch and swallowed my surroundings with far less fervor than the gin. I had to admit the loveliness of Megan and Bobby's house. I was even jealous, which piqued my curiosity as to why. Was that the sort of life I wanted? A big house, a husband, and a baby on the way? Could I be that girl? If

I told Josh I was pregnant, would he be excited? Maybe he'd quit his Cumberland house painter job and move us to the suburbs where we'd get a couple of cats and drown in white picket debt.

Maybe.

Maybe he could tell me how his brother died first.

Or introduce me to his parents.

Shit, I didn't even know where his parents lived, or if they were still alive. All I knew was he didn't speak to them because they'd neglected his brother due to his condition. What condition? Was it hereditary? Could I be pregnant with some kind of Wolfboy? I knew so little about Josh, except that he liked me, and he might have strong swimmers.

"How's that Beefeater taste, Josh Junior?" I asked my belly in a simpering voice I immediately regretted.

When I looked up again, Megan was staring at me from the doorway, a tray of hors devours in her hand.

I coughed. "Hey, Megan."

"Hey," she said, her voice curling up into a question.

"Are those crab puffs?"

"Yeah, but I can't eat them. No shellfish, you know. Apparently, the caterers are a bit dim. I was going to offer them to you, but, umm..."

"I'd love some."

"Um...I don't think you should."

"Why not?"

She set down the tray and hippoed over to me. She groaned as she lowered herself to the couch, louder than intended based on the blush that pinched her cheeks.

"Birdie, is there anything you want to tell me?"

"Sure. Pass the crab puffs."

"I've been in your position. I was scared too, but guzzling gin and shellfish won't solve your problems."

"Are you sure about that?"

Looking down her nose, she grasped my hands.

"You can tell me, Birdie. Are you pregnant?"

I burst into laughter, surprising the both of us.

"Just because you're baby-crazy doesn't mean everyone else is," I said.

"So why were you talking to your stomach?"

"I talk to my stomach all the time. And when I eat too much cheese, it talks back."

"Everything's always a big joke to you. Can't you take anything seriously?"

"Suggest a topic with some merit and I'll be serious."

"Fine, I will. How's school?"

I downed my drink, popped a crab puff in my mouth, and tried to think of an answer that wouldn't make its way to my mom, but all I could scrounge up was, "Do you have any names picked out for the baby?"

She sat up slightly. "Bobby likes 'America.'"

"America?"

"It's a real name," she insisted.

"So is 'Zimbabwe.'"

"I don't like ethnic names," she said, scrunching her nose.

"You're right. Why be weird?"

A sing-songy greeting echoed down the hall, and Megan tried her damnedest to snap into action. It took her a few grunting attempts to get off the couch, but she eventually rolled to her feet and shuffled off to greet her guest. By the melodious hello, I knew it was my mom. As soon as she spotted me, she shrieked giddily and pulled me from the couch into her arms. She squealed as she shook me in her embrace while I tried my best not to barf the Beefeater.

"You've lost weight. And your arms look really toned. Have you been working out?"

"No, I spontaneously generated muscle. It's weird, but the doctors tell me it's fine as long as I don't start spontaneously Hulking out."

"Oh, Birdie," she sighed in equal parts exasperation

and entertainment. "So, tell me everything."

I wished "everything" wouldn't be a string of lies, but there was nothing to be done about that. Even though my mom was pretty open-minded, she would never have approved of her prospective pageant queen daughter taking off her clothes for money.

"Not much is happening. I'm just going to school and hanging out with friends," I said, trying to avoid eye contact.

"Are you still working at the park reservation place?"

"Yes."

"And you enjoy it?"

"It's okay," I said with a shrug.

"I thought you worked at Pizza Hut," Megan said.

"That was a while ago. Now I take park reservations."

"What does that mean?" she asked.

"You understand the concept of taking reservations, right?"

She said "duh" like it was stupid to assume a stupid girl like her was stupid. I could have fired back an obvious insult, but as I probably would've had to explain why it was an insult, I tried to answer her question as politely as possible.

"Well, like *you* would make a reservation for a fancy night at Bob's Big Boy, some people make reservations to visit national parks. People call and I answer. It's not difficult or glamorous. It just pays the bills."

My mom shot me a look, half for the Bob's Big Boy comment and half for my passionless reply about my job. "So you don't actually enjoy it," she said.

"It's fine for now. Can we talk about something else?"

"I have a question," Grace chirped as she entered the room with Scott dutifully on her heels.

"I'm sure you do," I muttered.

"I'm interested in visiting some parks," she continued. "Which ones do you take reservations for?"

She showed me every last tooth in her grin, and it got even wider when everyone looked to me for an answer. If I didn't know any better, I would've thought she knew exactly what she was doing. Then I saw the sheepish hang-dog look on Scott's face and realized I was right. That little worm told her I was a dancer.

"If it's a national park, it's on the list, but most people call for Yellowstone," I replied.

She folded her arms over her chest. "Name some others."

"It's my day off. I just want to relax and celebrate this blessed event," I said, and Megan rubbed her belly as if Jesus Christ himself were nestled inside.

"I take it you and Grace have met?" my mom asked. "They say she's the one to beat this year. Of course, once Birdie sends in her application, you'll have some stiff competition, Grace."

"I hear Birdie is well-acquainted with making things stiff," she said. "Anyway, she doesn't seem too keen on competing, so I'm not worried."

My mom waved away the response. "Pish posh, she'll be there with bells on. You did bring the application, didn't you Birdie?"

"Maybe. I was in a rush."

"Is the gin helping your stomach?"

"What's wrong with your stomach?" Megan pressed, and I stood up with a groan.

"I'm going to the bathroom. When I come back, I'd really like to discuss something besides me."

The bathroom seemed much too immaculate to piss in, but I gave it a whirl. In fact, I tried to blast a hole in the porcelain with the power of my stream. Petty, yes. Stupid, absolutely. Mood-boosting, you betcha.

I spent more time than needed fixing my hair and makeup and taking a dozen selfies I'd never post. There were a few knocks on the door, but I dismissed them with a grunt until my mom's voice followed one of the knocks.

"Are you okay, Birdie?"

"I'm fine. I'll be out in a minute."

"I'm sorry I dragged you all the way out here. I just really wanted to see you. You've been so distant lately."

"Mom, if I open the door and you're saying all this stuff in front of the bathroom line, I'm going to be really pissed."

I opened the door and saw only her, smiling sweetly. She pulled me into her arms and squeezed away the anger, as she was so adept at doing. But as much as she crushed with her embrace, she saw every lingering emotion written on my face.

"You seem sad, Eva."

"I'm not. I just feel a little uncomfortable here."

"Why? This is a family event. Plus, so many of your high school friends are coming."

"Megan's friends, not mine. And except for you, I don't really like any of the family."

"Are you upset about Scott? When Grace told me they were dating, I knew it was going to be a problem."

"It's not a problem, and it has nothing to do with him."

She squeezed my arm. It was like pushing my "sigh button." But when she shook me a little, the sigh became a light chuckle. I wished I had that same power over myself, but for some reason, it always took someone else to remind me that things weren't so bad, even if they had no idea how bad they really were.

"Eva, I'm your mother. You can't lie to me."

"I can, actually."

She shook her head. "A mother always knows."

"Then maybe your lie detector needs a tune-up, because I couldn't care less about him. There's some awkwardness, yes, but I'm perfectly happy with Josh."

She poked my side. "I knew if I pestered you long enough, you'd bring up your new boyfriend. He *is* your boyfriend, isn't he?"

I shrugged. "I think so."

Her smile fell. "That doesn't sound 'perfectly happy'."

"When I'm with him, I'm fine. Better than fine. It's when we're apart that I start to doubt things."

As she pressed, I tried to move away from the bathroom and back to the bar, but she kept stopping to admire the McMansion's objets d'art. Her observations didn't distract her from the interrogation, though. She fired bullet after bullet, getting increasingly annoyed by my terse answers.

"When do I get to meet him?"

"Soon."

"Does he go to school with you?"

"No, he works."

"Doing what?"

"Painting houses."

"How old is he?"

"My age...I think," I said, eyeing the bar.

"Where did he go to high school?"

"Somewhere in Ohio, I think. He said he moved to Maryland from Ohio, so I'm just assuming."

"You don't seem to know too much about this guy."

To that, I had no response because she'd taken the words right out of my trembling heart. Most of what I knew about Josh consisted of his ability to get me off and sidestep my questions about his past.

"So he paints houses," she continued. "What else does he do?"

Before a speculative answer could stumble out, Scott stuck his head around the corner and said, "He hangs out in strip clubs."

I whipped around and snarled, "Shut up!" like a rabid dog, more worried that his statement was a breadcrumb trail back to me than what they thought about Josh.

If my mom had been wearing pearls, she would've clutched them in shock. "That's not true, is it?"

"Of course not."

"She's lying," Scott said, and I smacked his arm.

"Birdie, what is going on?"

"Mrs. Finch, Eva's boyfriend is your worst nightmare. I know you and I didn't always get along, but this guy, Josh, is way worse than I ever was. Look what he did to my nose, for God's sake. It's crooked because he broke it."

She inspected his face in horror. "Eva, your new boyfriend did that?"

"It was in self-defense," I said.

"Self-defense, my ass. He kicked the shit out of me because you called me instead of him when that girl got killed."

"What girl? Who got killed?" my mother squealed.

"He's talking about a video game, Mom. No one got killed." I glared at him, and his crooked nose flared.

"The point is, he attacked me unprovoked. I would've pressed charges, but I figured I'd hurt Birdie enough." The way he looked at me was almost sweet, until he pouted his lip and whined, "I had to go to the hospital too. Did Birdie tell you that?"

"No, she didn't."

I pulled my mom away, and when Scott tried to follow us into the next room, I gave his chest a firm push. It wasn't as violent as I wanted to get, but it did stop him in his tracks. It did not, however, stop him from talking.

"I bet there's lots of stuff she hasn't told you, Ms. Finch!"

I was screwed. He was going to spill my secret, and my mom was going to hate me. Worse than that, she was going to be disappointed in me. She turned around to face him, and although I tried to stay between them, she marched past me and stared Scott directly in the eyes.

"I assume that's true," she said, "but if there's something my daughter wants me to know, she'll tell me herself."

"She'll never do that."

"Then I won't know," she said. "And if you think ratting her out is going to change my opinion of you, you're dead wrong. I've always thought you were a prick, and I'm glad she dumped your ass."

Scott was taken aback, but he wasn't humbled enough to stop scowling before he stomped away.

"Mom, that was awesome!" I threw my arms around her, and she patted my hand.

"Listen, Eva. If there's something you want to tell me, I'm here. If there's something you don't want to tell me, I'm still here. I just want you to be happy and safe."

She made me feel small in the best way possible. Like, no matter how old I was or how protective of my privacy, she would always defend me. Then she pulled a piece of paper out of her purse.

"Here. I figured you might forget the application. You can fill it out right now, and I'll deliver it this afternoon."

"Sure," I whispered, once again feeling too large for her to cradle.

Several other guests had arrived by the time I found my way back to the bar. It appeared as though most of them felt the same way about the shower as I did, proved by the long line waiting for whiskey. I knew several of the guests, and I didn't particularly like any of them. There were quite a few former classmates turned townies: jerks of jocks that had recently lifted more tallboys than weights, and ex-princesses thanking God for babysitters allowing them to escape domestic "bliss" for a couple hours. Odder than so many real-world rejects in one place, however, was how intently they were all staring at *me*.

"What's going on?" I whispered to Scott, but Grace pulled him away before he could answer.

I'd become accustomed to being nude around strangers, but the intrusive stares made me feel like the strangers were the ones stripping me naked. Each pair of eyes ripped away another piece of fabric, leaving me shivering in shame. I wanted to cover up, shrink, vanish into the nothingness where I'd always existed to these people.

And that's exactly what the old Birdie would've done. Now I thought, WWHD—What Would Honey Do—and nabbed the near empty bottle of gin and a can of ginger ale from the bar. No glass necessary. Perching on the couch, my intention was to drink the eyes away, but swigging from the bottle actually drew some closer.

Dylan Collings, one-time captain of the wrestling team and current Carroll County cad, purred as he scooted up to the couch. "Birdie Finch."

I groaned. "Dylan Collings."

"I didn't think you knew my name," he said, eyebrows lifted. "We didn't talk much in high school."

"Really? I didn't notice."

Melody Dreyfuss was next, filling the room with the stench of hotdogs. "Wow, Eva. I wouldn't have thought it."

My heart told me to let them walk on by, but the gin told me to press their buttons.

"What's that supposed to mean, *Harmony*?"

She sneered. "*Melody*. And I mean, look at you. You used to be so sweet."

"How would you know?"

"You certainly weren't drinking gin straight from the bottle in high school."

"I repeat: How would you know?"

"I guess I wouldn't. It's just the impression I got. You seemed sweet."

"It's easy to be sweet when you're shy as hell. And

fat."

"Wait, did you just call yourself fat?" Jeanie Miller scoffed. "You are not fat."

"Not now. Back then. Look, it doesn't matter. I'm not the sweet girl, and I'm not the gin-from-the-bottle girl either. I'm the girl who feels totally out of place here and would really like to go home."

"So why don't you?" Grace said with Scott cowering behind her.

"I came here for Megan."

"She has plenty of people to entertain her. I'm sure she wouldn't be into your kind of entertainment anyway."

"What's *my kind*?"

Like the words were a sour film on her lips, she spat, "The erotic kind."

"*Exotic*. She's an *exotic* dancer," Dylan said.

"She's a stripper!" Melody barked.

"What the hell? Who—" I looked past Grace to catch Scott dodging my gaze. "Scott, you son of a bitch."

"So it's true." Dylan chortled. "Birdie fucking Finch is a stripper."

"Keep your voice down," I said.

"Why? Are you ashamed?" Melody asked.

"I am so tired of having this conversation." I snarled as I set down the bottle and slung my purse over my shoulder.

"You're not leaving, are you? I was hoping we could catch up," Dylan said.

"I think you've already learned everything you need to know about me."

"Where do you work? I'd love to see you sometime."

"Pins," Scott said. "The strip club/bowling alley in West Virginia."

"You're an asshole," I growled at him. "I always thought you were a know-it-all and dickish at times, but I was wrong. You're a straight-up asshole."

"And you're a stripper. And according to Megan, a *pregnant* stripper...guzzling gin," he said. "I think I'd rather be an asshole."

The entire room was judging me, and I couldn't blame them. They didn't know the whole story, and they certainly didn't know the whole me. Whether or not they had proof of my stripper status or pregnancy, how could they not believe it after the show I'd given them? For the most part, I didn't care what they thought about me. But I cared how quickly and poisonously their thoughts might spread. My mom hadn't heard Scott's remark across the room, but she'd hear it soon enough from some ditz on the pageant circuit if not the moment I left the party. My heart raced and I found it difficult to walk without shaking. I wanted to cry. I wanted to scream. I wanted to finish up the bottle of gin and smash it over Scott's head.

"Are you leaving?" Megan asked as I stormed by. "We haven't opened presents yet."

"Did you tell people I was pregnant?"

"Oh, yeah, kinda," she said, unapologetic. "What's the big deal? Now we have two new lives to celebrate."

"I'm not pregnant, Megan, and I don't care about your new life. As far as I'm concerned, your dumpster baby is going to turn out as trashy as you are."

I'd crossed the line into cruel territory, but I couldn't muster up enough regret to care...until my mom jogged over.

"You're leaving?"

"Yeah, sorry."

"What about the application?"

"I'll get it to you later. I have to go," I said. "Oh, and don't believe anything these people tell you. Scott's been talking shit about me all day."

"I knew he would be petty if you broke up. I feel sorry for Grace."

"That makes one of us. I'll talk to you soon."

"Love you, Birdie."

"Okay. You too. Bye."

I hated not being able to say "I love you" back, but overanalyzing my shortcomings was what the three-hour drive home was for. I raced for the front door, but when I opened it, a beautiful boy standing in my way prevented me from running out.

"Eva Finch? I thought that was you. It's Tom. Tom Bowers."

He was even taller than Josh. I remembered his height making me fall in love at first sight in high school, and here he was, pretty as ever. With shiny shaggy hair that veiled his eyes and a crooked smile, he was the only jock I'd ever allowed to bewitch me. Granted, the basketball team was the least dickish group of jocks, but Tom stood out by becoming senior class treasurer and starring in the school's production of *Little Shop of Horrors*. All sorts of girls had crushes on Tom, but since he was one of the nicest and most interesting guys in town, he was perpetually involved. Even if he did experience a moment of unattachment, I wasn't even close to being on his radar. We ran in different circles, and while he didn't come off as a jerk, he certainly hung out with plenty.

"Hi, Tom. Sorry, I'm on my way out."

"That's too bad. I was hoping you'd be here," he said, walking inside.

I couldn't move. I could only squeak. "Why?"

"I heard you were doing well. I wanted to catch up."

I suddenly realized what was happening. His jerk friends knew he was on his way to the party and had obviously let him know that Birdie, stripper extraordinaire, was in attendance.

"No thanks. I'm not in the mood for your kind of catching up," I murmured and headed for the door again.

"What do you mean?"

"Look, I know what you heard about me, and it's not true."

"So, you're not going to Allegany College?"

"No—well, yes. Kind of."

"Do you like it?"

"It's all right, I guess. Honestly, I haven't been to class in a while."

"Why not?"

"You don't have to pretend you're interested. I know the game here."

"Could you fill me in on what the game is, because I'm a little confused." He pulled his phone out of his back pocket and swiped at the new message. "Sorry about that. Dylan just texted from inside. Apparently some chick named Grace is throwing a tantrum in the living room."

"I'm sure Dylan told you all kinds of things."

"I guess..." He cocked his head. "Am I supposed to know what you're talking about?"

"I know you know I'm a stripper. That's the only reason you're talking to me."

He blinked wildly. "I did not know that, actually. Is that true?"

"Oh." I snickered dryly. "No, it's not true. I was just kidding."

He laughed. "I hope you're a better dancer than a liar. I bet you are, though. I remember you being pretty good back in the day. You were in my sister's tap class, weren't you?"

"A million years ago. I can't believe you remember that," I said, blushing. I leaned against the door frame, forgetting a party I'd been very eager to leave was still happening down the hall. Looking at him, I even forgot I was in Megan's McMansion. At that moment, it was ours. I had so many of those little fantasies about him in high school. I never expected to have one again, let alone be so happy to get lost in it.

"You had that little pink leotard with green...trim? Stripes?"

I chirped, "Polka dots."

"That's right, polka dots. I guess you're making good use of those classes now."

"I don't do much tap dancing at Pins. But maybe I should start. I'd definitely stand out."

"I always thought you did," he said warmly.

I was going to say "that's sweet," but I was pretty sure my smile said it for me.

"This might be a bit forward, but are you seeing anyone?"

"That's not forward. Shocking, but not forward."

"Well, are you?"

Remembering the playlist made by my so-called boyfriend, my answer would have been a resounding "hell no," but Tom already knew I was a bad liar.

"Yeah, I am," I replied, and he gave an "aw shucks" snap. "You're not, I take it."

"Nope."

"Cool." I grumbled. "It was good seeing you, Tom, but I should go before I get into any more trouble."

"More?"

"I'm sure you'll hear all about it once you hit the actual party. If you can hear over Grace's tantrum."

"Maybe if—" he started and shook his head. "Never mind."

"No, what were you going to say?"

"Maybe if you come back to town, you know, permanently, you could call me."

I wanted to either curl up in a shy ball or explode like fireworks, but instead, I said, "Maybe..."

"Cool. See you around, Birdie."

"Maybe..."

I had to throw myself out the door to walk away from him, but my walk to the car was one of triumph. Someone had looked beyond the armor of gin and false bravado to see the ambivalent soldier. For a moment, the rear-view mirror reflected someone I didn't recognize, but she had some beauty about her. It was only a moment, but it was enough to keep me smiling through the rest of Josh's shitty playlist.

CHAPTER FOURTEEN

My bladder wasn't giving up the goods. It must've sensed my desperation and now refused to evacuate all the water, orange juice, and beer I'd ingested to take a second pregnancy test. When a thin stream finally splashed the stick, I set it beside the first, which had thankfully come up negative. Over the next few minutes, the liquid bled across the result window, forming one line, then crossing it with another.

Positive.

"What the hell?"

I scanned the instructions for an explanation as Fidelio hopped onto my lap and sniffed at the contradictory tests. I knocked them into the trash with a growl, just as my alarm chimed for the second time. I had to get moving, but there was no way I'd survive the night not knowing for sure. I was already going to be late for work, so I figured there was no harm in detouring to pick up another pack of tests. The same cashier rang me up at the store, but she was kind enough not to mention it. Tests in hand, I snuck in the dressing room door to find Shasta snorting a line off the back of her hand.

She coughed through the drip. "Hey." Eyeing up the transparent bag, she hocked up a caw of surprise.

"Holy shit, Birdie. Are those for you?"

"None of your business. Who's working tonight?"

"Pretty much everyone, but we're the only ones here

so far. I just got off the stage."

"No one's out there? Fuck. It's only a matter of time before—"

The door flew open, and Cecil stomped in. "Birdie, you're late."

"You have no idea," Shasta trilled as she marched out to the floor.

"I just need a few minutes."

"Sorry, you know the rules. Maybe next time you'll get here early enough to do what you need to do."

"Come on, man, have a heart."

Cecil strode over and tried to meet my eyes, but to make it level, he would've needed an apple box.

"Birdie, I got a business to run, a business that's been hurting big time. If I let you break the rules, everyone's gonna break the rules, and then my business becomes a playground."

"I thought this place was *supposed* to be like a playground."

"For the customers, not the employees. Now get your ass onstage."

He walked out and I stuffed the tests into my duffle bag. I dabbed glitter shadow on my eyelids, snapped my gown in place, tightened my ponytail, and with a grumble, I stomped to the stage.

Once the lights hit me and "Jessie's Girl" wrapped her arms around me, I was graceful again. I'd become adept at hiding my feelings within each twist and twirl. Every other word Rick Springfield sang sounded like "pregnant," but I kicked the delusions away as I rode the pole and spun the nagging thoughts out of my brain. I focused on the customers, which wasn't easy to do with the stage's current offerings. There was only one young, semi-attractive guy amidst snaggle-toothed geezers whose hands had disappeared under the stage. Although the woman hovering near the stage wasn't as young or buoyant as the female customers I usually targeted, her presence calmed me. I sat on my knees and tossed my head back as I pulled my dress aside and tapped my clit through my luckies. She blushed as she approached, then slid a dollar into my garter.

"Nice," the man next to her said. "Hey, you're not really into chicks, are you?"

I pretended not to hear him, which he noticed with a sour sneer. The expression revealed a dead tooth on the bottom row and a few past death on the top. Up close, I realized he wasn't that old, probably mid-to-late forties. He was just such an ugly son of a bitch that he looked older. He might've been a biker or a trucker. I imagined him sitting for great lengths of time, maybe shredding a plank of jerky with his rotten teeth.

"Don't be afraid," he said as gently as one could in Pins, where nearly everything gentle needed to have a jackhammer delivery to be heard over the thumping soundtrack. "I've been watching you."

"A lot of people watch me," I said with a forced giggle that made his fingers itch. "Have I danced for you before?"

"No, not me. A friend of mine on the alley side, but not me. I've never done those table dances before."

"You should get one. They're fun."

"Maybe you could give me one when you get off the stage."

Cecil jogged over and slapped the meaty guy on the back. "How ya doin', Marvin? Enjoyin' yourself?"

The man guffawed as he nodded. "You sure got some pretty girls working here, Cuz."

"I'm sure Birdie appreciates that. And you know, she'd be more than happy to give you a dance when she's off the stage. To celebrate your new start in life."

I spun my ass to them to avoid showing the annoyance crinkling my face.

"She gives a fantastic private dance," he continued. "You won't be disappointed."

"We were discussing a table dance."

"You want a private dance, believe me. It's more intimate."

Bent over, my head hanging between my legs, I narrowed my eyes at the plotters discussing my amenities like a washing machine. When they both focused on me again, I pouted my lips and tapped my pussy as I shimmied back to a wide-legged stance.

Cecil patted his cousin's back again. "Why don't you come to the bar now, Marv, and we'll get it all set up."

"Oh-kay." He stood, but Cecil didn't let him walk away.

"Tip her first," he said, and Marvin tucked a five into my garter.

I squeezed out a smile. "Thanks. I'll see you soon."

I despised all private dances, but this was the most irksome of all. I just wanted to duck into the bathroom for five minutes and pee on a stick, and now I had to hold my precious pee while waving my peehole in this man's face.

When "Raise Your Glass" faded out, I hurried backstage to dab the sweaty makeup from my face and readjust my dress. Honey and Pearl were making their own adjustments when I entered, panting.

"Sorry I'm late," Honey said.

"Can't talk, gotta hump a weirdo." I cinched my ponytail, pulled my halter straps tight, and gave the mirror a toothy grin. "Good enough?"

"Are you okay?"

"Yeah, why?"

"You're acting weird."

"I have to pee."

"Find me after the dance. I want to hear about the baby shower."

"Will do." We did a fist-bump explosion that made Shasta shake her head in secondhand embarrassment I chose to view as envy.

My customer was pounding a shot of Jack Daniels when I walked over, but the three empty shot glasses next to it unnerved me more.

"Want a drink?" he asked.

I didn't, but I let him buy me a whiskey sour for the payout. I took a sip and when I licked my lips, his body jerked. I couldn't tell if it was from a chuckle or a more perverse signal of his enthusiasm. Figuring it was best to get it over with, I curled my finger in a come-hither gesture, and he followed. When we reached the private dance rooms, I pulled the curtain aside and gave him the lead so I could ditch my drink.

"Room four," Stu said, and my mind groaned. Room four was the smallest. I'd be practically on top of him. Fortunately, the private room's music library contained two of the shortest songs I knew: Maurice Williams and the Zodiacs' "Stay" and The Pixie's "Allison," each of which were under two minutes. With any luck, I'd be out of there and pissing on a stick before I broke a sweat.

I shut the mirrored door and purred, "Take a seat."

He flopped down, overflowing the chair as I selected my obscenely short songs from the playlist. Then, focusing on my reflection in the wall behind him, I began to dance. Occasionally, I looked into his hungry eyes and saw everything he'd like to do to me, so I didn't look there often. I straddled his leg, my pussy as close as possible without actually touching his dirty jeans, but I backpedaled when he abruptly scooted forward.

"You're a nice girl," he said as I crouched between his legs.

"Thanks. You're pretty nice yourself."

"I bet you're not so nice in bed."

"Are you saying I'm bad in bed?" I giggled as I stood and planted one of my legs on his beefy shoulder.

He eyed my snatch, his hands clawing at his large thighs. "I bet you're a bad girl. I bet you like it rough.

Like that other girl. Ginger, was it?"

It had been a while since I'd heard her name. My stomach churned, and my leg fell from his shoulder. I covered the slip-up with a smile and a nipple pinch that made him smack his lips.

"Yes, there was a dancer named Ginger," I said, "but she doesn't work here anymore."

He wheezed. "I know."

At that moment, I felt like my bones might explode into dust and escape through my pores, reducing me to a pile of cringey flesh.

"Oh and that other one," he said. "What was her name?"

"Diamond?" I whispered.

He nodded emphatically, groping his legs as I backed away. "Hey, what's wrong? We're just talking."

"Well, it's freaking me out, dude."

"Sounds like your problem, not mine."

He stood from the seat, but he didn't walk forward. He continued to rub his pants, as if trying to dissolve them with friction. Beads of sweat clung to his forehead and ran through the tributaries in his jowls.

"You realize the bouncer is outside, right? All I have to do is scream."

His fingers stopped raking the fabric and he sat down, making the small chair creak. He folded his hands in front of him and looked dead at me with a cheesy grin that did his flabby face no favors.

"I'm sorry, okay? I didn't mean to freak you out. I figured people ask you about the murders all the time."

"Most people have more tact than that."

"Here." He held up a twenty-dollar bill. "Forgive me, Birdie. I had a few drinks."

I approached him cautiously and snatched the bill as soon as it was within reach.

"Ease up on the alcohol next time, okay?"

"I got nervous. Haven't you ever done anything

stupid when you were nervous?"

"More times than I can count."

"You really are beautiful," he said. "And you're nice. I was dumb not to do one of these dances sooner."

Cash was the only reason I forgave him, and the offer of more cash was the only reason I kept dancing, making me more than fifty dollars richer by the time "Stay" faded away.

"Thank you, Birdie. I appreciate your time and your understanding," he said as he stood. "Can I get a hug?"

I wondered if he realized how sweaty he was. By this point, glitter had become part of my DNA, but his shine rivaled mine, so I wasn't exactly sad to bring up the "no touching" rule, despite my dramatic pout.

"Sorry. Not allowed."

He stepped forward. "But you want to, don't you?"

I'd pretended to be hurt in hopes of another tip, but I was as serious as a UTI when I replied, "Not even a little."

"Just a small hug?"

"Your time's up, and I have to get back on the floor."

"I get it."

He clearly did not get it, because his next move was a massive step that put him nearly on top of me. I stumbled backward and smacked my back against the mirrored door. I shouted for Stu as Marvin's face drew closer.

The words "Such a pretty girl," landed wet on my face, but his hands concerned me more.

I screamed for Stu again, but Marvin got a hold of me first.

He moaned, "You have such nice fuckin' titties," as he ripped my top aside and dug his filthy nails into my flesh. He twisted the skin, and I shrieked in pain, but the feeling of my bare nipples against his palms was worse. Never before had I felt the sensation of wanting to puke out of my areolas, but there it was, in room four of my workplace.

I swiped and slapped at him, but I didn't do much damage until I caught ahold of his greasy hair. Clenching it as tight as I could, I yanked his head close enough to clamp my other hand into his scalp. Then I slammed his skull against the mirrored wall.

The sound of his face against the glass was like two eggs fighting to crack the loudest, and a flush of victory surged through me. But it only lasted as long as it took him to recover from the blow. I ran for the door, but he grabbed my wrist, and before I could contemplate my next move, his fist hooked under my ribcage and propelled me backward onto the floor. I gasped for air that wouldn't come, and pins and needles colonized every inch of flesh as I tried to scramble away from the man with shards of glass protruding from his left temple. When thin spurts of oxygen finally hit my lungs and the tingling subsided, I clambered for the door, narrowly avoiding Marvin's grasp.

The door flew open and Stu charged in, nearly knocking me off my feet, but I jumped aside in time for him and Marvin to collide. Grabbing his collar, Stu whipped him around and smashed him against the door frame, where he wobbled for a few moments before collapsing to the floor.

Wilting in the chair, I gripped my aching stomach and whimpered through shallow breath. It eventually deepened, but so did the feeling of Marvin's knuckles in my belly, his hand on my breast, his dead teeth everywhere, gnawing and shredding so much more than my body.

Stu ripped Marvin from the floor, but when he started to haul him out, Cecil appeared in the doorway.

"What did you do, Marv." He spoke slower and more methodically than I'd ever heard him, his question more of an accusation.

"I didn't--"

Cecil's fist cut him off. With a little hop that thankfully looked more superhero than bunny rabbit, he punched Marvin in the nose, spattering blood across the mirrored wall. As the man howled in pain, Cecil frowned at me, said, "I'm sorry," and smacked the man again, sending a dead tooth tumbling across the private dance floor.

Stu threw the man out, though I hoped he'd do more than that, and Cecil escorted me out of the private dance room. Curious dancers clogged the hallway, but once Honey spotted me gripping my stomach as I used Cecil like a cane, she pushed through them and wrapped herself around me.

"Take her home," he said, passing me into Honey's arms.

"What the fuck happened?"

My breath was back, but I couldn't use it to form words. It felt like my throat was clotted, worse than any cocaine drip, but not with drugs or mucus or blood. I just...couldn't speak...yet my mind whirred so madly I could barely finish one horrible thought before it spun into another. I didn't even recognize how far Honey had walked me, or that someone had gotten my bag, or that she'd sat me in the front seat of her car until she buckled me in and adjusted the shoulder strap.

I lifted my head, and she touched my cheek.

"Are you okay? Do you want to go to the hospital?"

"I'm fine," I squeaked, and lightning struck my belly.

"You don't look fine, Birdie. Please just tell me what to do."

I told her to take me home. I'd be fine. I just got the wind knocked out of me, that's all.

She drove fast but much smoother than usual. Then I felt it. Warm, oozing, soaking through my thong, soaking into her seat, cooling quickly as my cup runneth over.

"Honey—"

"We're almost there, Eva."

"Honey, your seat."

I scooped my hand under my legs and when I withdrew it, my fingers were slick with russet blood.

"Jesus Christ, Eva..."

I felt woozy. "Do you know anything about false positives? Does it happen?"

Brown gore collected beneath my fingernails and clung to my knuckles. I almost passed out from looking at it, but Honey wrapped her hand around mine, clutching the horror and vanquishing it, even as our fingers stuck together.

"Let me take you to the ER."

"I'm fine. I'll be fine. Just get me home." Staring at her with tear-filled eyes, I added, "But stay with me, okay?"

"Of course I will. I'm not leaving you, Birdie."

Her voice, those words, rang through my mind the entire ride home. I faded in and out, the shock of the incident wearing off like a sleepy-time gummy kicking in, and though I knew I climbed stairs, changed my clothes, and curled up in bed, all I felt was the honeyed warmth of her care.

I awoke to Fidelio's face pressed against mine. His steady purr made me feel safe through and through, but there was still one more friend I wanted to see.

I squeaked, "Honey?"

"I'm here!" Josh scuttled into the room and sat on the bed.

"Honey?"

"Oh, you want *Honey* Honey." He frowned. "She's not here."

"Where is she?"

"I told her to go home. I'm here now. I'll take care of you." He stroked my hair and gazed upon me lovingly, but I kept searching the room, hoping she was still there, and he was just joking about doing something as dumb as sending her away. "It's okay that I'm here, isn't it?"

"Why did you tell her to go?"

"Don't you want me here?"

I sniffled. "Yes, but I wanted her, too."

Josh stood up from the bed, grumbling. "Yeah, I'm starting to see that."

"What?"

He paced the room, nearly stepping on Fidelio's tail.

"Hey, watch it!" I cried.

He apologized, then sat beside me again and held my hand.

"I'm your boyfriend, right?"

"Last time I checked, yeah."

"Okay, I just wanted to get that straight. I'm your boyfriend." He squeezed my hand...a little too hard. "There's no room for a girlfriend."

"There's room for plenty of friends. Why are you trying to start a fight within a minute of me waking up, especially after what happened? If you were a good boyfriend, you wouldn't give me shit right now. You'd give me comfort and care."

"That's what I wanted to do, until I realized you wanted Honey more than me."

"Goddammit, Josh, please just shut up and lie next to me while I watch *Gargoyles*, okay?"

He did, and he didn't say another word about it. But he was right. I did want Honey there more than him.

I couldn't talk to Josh about the pregnancy scare. Or more accurately, I didn't want to. I also didn't want to be mad at him for sending Honey away, but the more he clung to me, the more I resented his presence. When I was feeling better the next day, I told him he could go, but he insisted on sticking around just in case.

"We don't know what kind of internal injuries you might have."

I snorted. "I think I'm okay. He was a big guy, but he wasn't *that* strong. I'm just made of pudding skin."

"And I want to make sure my little pudding skin sweetie stays as safe as possible," he said, bopping my nose. "Besides, your car is still at the club. You'll need me to drive you the next time you go."

The first chance I got, I used both pregnancy tests to confirm what my period purported. Both negative. I would never know if I was pregnant—in all likelihood, I'd begun filling my cup long before Marvin attacked me—and if Marvin's fist had caused me to miscarry, I was lucky, wasn't I? I wouldn't have to pay for an abortion or suffer further mental anguish over a stupid accident. But I felt guilty anyway, for so many things, including calling a potential fetus a stupid accident. I knew how ridiculous it sounded, but shame clung to me like a nightmare, preventing me from celebrating the bullet I'd dodged. It also gave me a new aversion to Josh I just couldn't shake. Every clinging gaze and needy embrace felt so desperate, they also felt fake.

Two days later, I was still sore from my injuries, but it was nothing compared to my cramps. Learning what happened to Marvin was a nice balm for the pain, though. I got the story from Pantera, who'd watched every second of the guy's beat-down in the parking lot. After Stu threw Marvin out, Cecil had followed him to his car and slammed the bastard's hand in the door, shattering two of his fingers. Pantera described it in gory detail, being sure to include the exact degree at which the shafts of bone protruded from his flesh. I thanked her for the bedtime story and asked her to thank Cecil for me. It was mighty big of him.

CHAPTER FIFTEEN

I was hardly the first stripper to get assaulted. At some point, every Pins girl had. Some still trembled when they told their stories. They crossed their arms over their bodies and tugged on their lips like they were trying to unmake certain parts of themselves. Others talked about assault like they'd gotten sneezed on. Disgusting, yes. Unwanted, for sure. But as Faith used to say, "When you work in a pepper factory, can you really be surprised if you leave covered in snot?"

They unmade those parts of themselves long ago.

But they all said the same thing about returning to the stage after the first time, and I understood what they meant now. The club looked different. Bigger somehow, with sharper edges and more twisted shadows, more masked monsters with malicious intent, and more dark corners where intentions could become actions. I thought the club couldn't look more sinister after seeing two of my colleagues obliterated a few hundred feet from me, but it appeared anamorphic in that way. Each new horror showed me a side I hadn't seen before, and I kept wondering what the next scale to fall from my eyes would be.

Honey had my back most of the time, but even the world's most perfect girl had rough days. The following Saturday night, she was extraordinarily late, and it took her even longer to get backstage due to a lengthy scolding from Cecil. She relayed the scene to me from her chair at the dressing table, barely pausing for breath as she waved her hands wildly; it was a fantastic Cecil impression. When the argument was out of her system, she collapsed face-first on the table and groaned.

"I really don't need this shit today."

"I'm sure you had a good reason," I said, leaning on her back. "But this is late even for you."

"I had a very good reason."

"You're not cheating on me, are you?" I tousled her auburn hair, and she spun off the chair to start undressing.

"Never," she said, dropping her bra to the floor. "I'm all yours."

"So why were you late?"

For the first time that night, Honey acknowledged Entice, who'd been sitting at the other end of the makeup table, redrawing an eyebrow that had gotten smudged off.

"It's probably not the best time to talk about it. It's kinda involved."

She rubbed coconut oil over her body, and as her faded angel tattoo brightened, I forgot what we were talking about.

"I wouldn't have asked if I wasn't down for getting 'involved'," I eventually said. "If you're upset, I want to help."

Once Entice had doused her brows in setting spray and left the room, Honey exhaled a gigantic sigh.

"It's my mom."

"Oh no. What did she do now?"

"She died."

I sucked in my lips. "That *bitch*."

Honey snorted. "Right? But also...thank you?"

I slapped my hand over my mouth to stifle the laughter, but she didn't hide hers. It did disappear though, slowly twisting into sorrow that dimpled her chin. I held open my arms, and she flung herself into them with a whimper.

"I'm sorry, Honey. I know you didn't like her, but I'm still sorry."

I thought she thanked me, but her voice got lost in my neck, my hair, my inappropriate lust. Tears hit my shoulders, tickling me as they rolled down my back, but I didn't dare break our embrace before her.

"Is there a funeral? Do you want me to come with you?"

"No funeral, no wake," she said, disconnecting to wipe her face. "I finished making all of the arrangements today, which is why I was late." She snapped the last word at the door like Cecil was listening on the other side. "I didn't want to give my grandmother the opportunity to swoop in and further fuck up this fucked-up situation."

"Does she know yet?"

"I don't care."

"Damn. What did your grandma do to you?"

When Honey tensed up, I withdrew the question.

"No, it's fine. But real quick, and I don't want to talk about it again, okay? I'm over it." When I nodded, she glanced out at the floor to make sure Cecil wasn't coming, then took a deep breath. "My mom was a drunk and a serial monogamist. Most of her suitors weren't in it for monogamy though. I had to fight off a lot of shit back then, but it made me strong, so I've chosen not to be angry about it anymore." She cleared her throat. "*Most* of the time. My mom would marry and inevitably divorce, and all the while, my grandmother laughed at her. At me too. Even when she got sick. She put us down constantly, but my mom wouldn't send her away or even defend herself. She wouldn't defend me."

"What about your dad? Your real dad?"

"He was just another meal ticket for my mom. His

name was Barry—until I was twelve—then, it was Harry. The last time I saw her, I think she called him Henry, but who knows? She was really out of it by that point. And my grandma was still laughing. She'll probably laugh when she finds out her daughter is dead too."

I pulled her close. "We should laugh at *her*."

"Yeah right."

"I'm serious. We go over to her house one day, stand outside her window, and just laugh. Maybe we point at her too. Let her see how it feels to be mocked all the time."

She chuckled as she shook her head. "Thanks, but I don't get off on laughing at sadness like my grandma does."

"Fair enough." I bopped her nose. "We'll do whatever *does* get you off."

I regretted it the moment the words left my lips, especially when Honey's eyebrows jumped up to her hairline and she exploded with chuckles.

"You know what I mean," I breathed into her. "Whatever you think will cheer you up, I'm down."

She hummed as she tightened her heel strap, then headed for the door. Tossing her hair over her shoulder as she looked back at me, she said, "It's a date."

Her secret dimple was my reward many times that night. She was the only thing about Pins that didn't agitate me these days. One of the only things that didn't agitate me outside the club too.

After we finished humping the planks at the night's end, I wished I was going home with her instead of Josh.

Things had changed between Josh and me, and they worsened with each day he refused to unstitch himself from my hip. Heading into the second week of sleepovers, I was desperate for privacy, and I didn't think I was being subtle about it.

Did he not notice, or did he not care?

I wasn't sure which pissed me off more, but it became more evident by the hour that I was, indeed, extremely pissed off. Unfortunately, the bathroom was the only place I had the time and privacy to contemplate my anger. So, I worked through a lot of shit over the next few days and came to the conclusion that 1) I needed to eat more fiber, and 2) why was I giving Josh full access to the light of my life when he was keeping me in the dark about so much of his?

It was clear his past caused him pain, but so did Honey's, and she'd opened up about everything. Yes, she was my best friend, not my lover—the dynamics were different, the intimacy, the trust—but should they be?

The toilet tank was still refilling when I stood before him, hands on hips. "When are you going to tell me about your brother?"

"Huh?" he replied, lost in his game of Skyrim.

"Your brother. When are you going to tell me what happened, how he died? I think we've been dating long enough, don't you?"

"Sure. Whenever you want," he said, focus unbroken.

"Unless you don't think I can handle it."

"No, it's not that." He grumbled and shook the controller. "Fuck, I died." Facing me, he squinted. "What's this about, Birdie?"

"What about your parents?"

"You know I don't speak to them."

"But I don't know why. All I know is that it has something to do with your brother."

"It's complicated."

He grabbed the controller again, but I pulled it out of his hands. "So I don't get to know anything about you?"

"You know I love you. What else do you need?"

He leaned in to kiss me, and I nearly allowed him,

but when a felt a twinge of pain in my abdomen, I stood abruptly.

"Wouldn't you think it's weird if I didn't tell you about my past?"

"Not really. If I could forget everything you've told me about your overbearing mom pushing you into pageants or how your asshole sister makes you feel fat, I would."

"What the fuck does that mean?"

He groaned. "It means all I need to know about you is that you love me. Our pasts are behind us. That shit can disappear for all I care."

"I don't want it to disappear. My past made me what I am, the same as you."

"You mean a spineless stoner with the self-esteem of an obese preteen?"

He wasn't even looking at me when he spoke, but I felt the brutal chill of every word. My eyes filled with tears, and pain knitted itself into a knot that blocked my throat. If he didn't want to know everything about me, he didn't want to know the real me. He wanted the exact Eva Finch he met, the new Pins girl, the one who feigned confidence to hide her struggle for flight, not the one who soared without fear. He wanted the day we met to be both of our beginnings. But it wasn't. It never would be.

Our ending, however, could be arranged.

"I want you to leave."

"Birdie, you're being irrational."

"You have to give a little to get a little, and you've gotten a lot from me."

"I've also given a lot."

"Not what I've asked for. I don't need or want a shitty playlist. I need to know you."

"Hey, I worked hard on that playlist. You don't have to call it shitty."

"If I could think of a word that means worse than

shitty, I would, but I'm not sure one exists yet."

He whined. "Hey!"

"I'm not sorry. That playlist sucked."

He leapt to his feet and began to storm out, but he stopped at the bedroom door, keeping his back to me. I didn't think he'd ever face me again, but when he did, there were tears in his eyes.

"They left us," he said. "My parents left my brother and me because they couldn't handle his problems. They wanted me to go with them, but I wouldn't leave him behind. Someone had to protect him. I thought I could, but..." His voice trembled. "He killed himself a month later." He smacked his thigh and shook his head and grunted in pain. "I hate this. I hate talking about the past. And believe it or not, my parents are just a small part of what made my childhood hell."

"I'm sorry."

"I wish you didn't have to be. I wish you could love me without all these stupid stipulations. I've tried so many times to start over, Birdie, and I thought you'd understand. I thought you'd let me start over the way you did."

"I didn't start over. I'm the same person I've always been."

"If that were true, would you be in a relationship with someone you met at a strip club? Would you have done any of the scary things you did this year if you hadn't made a choice somewhere along the line to change? Maybe not consciously, but in your heart, in your soul, you wanted a new life, just like me."

"That's bullshit. A pantydropper of a line, maybe, but bullshit."

He threw his hands in the air. "Jesus Christ! What do you want from me?"

"I just want to know you. The good stuff, the horrible stuff. As long as it's true, that's all I want from you."

He advanced on me, his chin in the air. "I am Joshua

Parker, and I love Eva Finch. That's the truth."

"Not the only truth."

"But it's all I feel like giving, so I hope you can accept it." He held my hands. "Can you, Birdie? Please, can you accept my love?"

His height was more imposing than sexy now, and his devotion was utterly annoying. His refusal to let me see behind the curtain while talking like a dashing, put-upon fae prince from a twelve-year-old girl's dream journal only amped my vexation. No matter how sweetly he explained his reasons, they still soured my heart against him.

I smiled anyway, exhausted. It felt even faker than the smiles I wore at Pins, but he embraced me gratefully, and again, I had to question: did he not notice, or did he not care?

I supposed it did not matter. His love wasn't enough for me, not ultimately. And even though I wasn't looking for anything ultimate, I also didn't want to be with someone who was so incredibly wrong about who I was. I wasn't the kind of girl he'd sway with grand declarations of love and speeches about the choices my soul made. If I'd made any choice, it was to go on vacation. And yes, I could learn life lessons on this getaway, the experience could change me, for good or bad, and forever, but eventually the vacation would end. The girl who stripped for money wasn't the real me, and I felt sad for anyone who thought she was.

His eyes begged for my surrender, and I tilted my head in pity.

My surrender did come, but only my pussy meant it. Shutting off my brain to enjoy fucking someone with whom I'd fallen out of love was sadly not a new practice, but it was still difficult. I filled my mind with colors, with music. I saw dancing flames, and molten rainbows twisting with the rising heat. With his smooth face between my thighs, I filled my mind with honeyed tongues that spoke the truth I needed. But all the amorphous shapes and light eventually found form. And form found me, past the glitter and vice, past the vacation disguise, where best friend and lover were one in the same, and I melted into the pleasure and dazzling beauty of knowing exactly what I needed to do.

"We need to break up with them," I said to Honey as we peered out from backstage at Josh and James doing shots of Goldschlager.

"Oh thank God. I didn't think I could stand it much longer. James has slept over every night for the past three weeks." She sat on the floor and began packing a bowl.

"I'm sorry it's taken so long." I sighed as I sat beside her. "But of course his birthday is coming up, and it seems so mean to drop someone around their birthday."

"You're too nice."

"Obviously not, breaking up with one of the nicest guys I've ever met."

"If he told you about his past, every detail, would things be hunky dory?"

She handed me the bowl, and I took a hit, considering her question as deeply as I inhaled.

"Probably not," I said through a cloud of smoke. "But I'd be willing to give it a shot."

"Not me. I'm done with James. The mood swings, the weird sex stuff, everything." She took a long hit, then nodded definitively as she exhaled. "I'm breaking up with him tonight."

"No, not tonight."

"Why not?"

"Because I'm not ready yet, and if you dump James, he's going to spend all his time with Josh, and Josh spends all his time with me. I'll get stuck with both of them!"

"Okay, I see your point." She took another hit. "How much longer?"

"A day. Two, tops. I just have to build some courage."

Shasta tapped me on the shoulder and held up a vial of cocaine. "You wanted some courage?"

"Thanks, but it's probably best if I do it when my heart isn't beating a million miles a minute."

"Suit yourself." She was cutting up the cocaine on a mirror when Honey piped up.

"Well, we already decided we're not doing it tonight. I don't see the harm in a line or two."

"God, make up your mind," Shasta said as she passed over the mirror.

Honey snorted, then gave her gums a quick rub. As I was taking my turn, she gasped, then slapped me on the back and smashed my nose into the mirror.

"Whoops! I'm sorry!" She giggled as I wiggled my powdered nose. "But I just got the best idea. We could break up with them together."

"Didn't we already decide that?" I asked, transferring the nose powder to my gums.

"Yes, but we should tell them we're breaking up with them *because* we're together. We can tell them we fell in love."

"You're kidding."

"You know Josh won't take 'I'm not into you' as a reason. He'll try to talk you out of it."

"But you think he'll let it go because I'm into *you*? I've already told him a bunch of times that I'm not."

She pouted. "You're not?"

"I mean…" I winced. "That's what I *told* him…"

Delight played upon her lips. "So we might have to fake it for a while. Would you mind pretending to be my girlfriend? It certainly wouldn't hurt our tips."

The cutest smile in history gave rise to an even cuter dimple, and just when I was about to shout, "Yes, yes, a million times, yes!" Pantera burst into the dressing room.

"Come out front! You guys have to see this!"

I shuddered. Even with the Strip Club Killer locked away, I couldn't help thinking, "Oh God, who's dead now?" Had Pearl been impaled on the pole? Did someone find Illusion's head in the ball return? Destiny hadn't shown up for work that night; was she stacked up like a pancake breakfast on the side stage?

A jaw-dropping scene greeted us when we hit the floor, trimmed in taffeta rather than blood. A vision in wedding white, Jade opened her arms, and Honey and I crashed into her, shrieking with joy. It took me a minute to notice Braidbeard, but it was hard to see anything but the lithe girl with jet-black hair in the sheer white gown.

Jade spun, her hands in the air. "Aren't you going to tell me you like my dress?"

"Not until you tell us why you took off without a word. We were worried about you." I smacked her embellished sleeve, then carefully re-poofed it.

"Oh I'm sorry," she said, batting her eyes. "Were you expecting to be bridesmaids?"

"No, we were expecting to know whether you were dead or alive."

She linked her arm with Braidbeard's. "Very much alive. And very proud to announce that you are now looking at Mrs. Jeffrey Briar."

"Congratulations!" Honey hugged Jade again. "I'm so happy for both of you!"

"Me too." Braidbeard pulled his wife close and kissed her rosy cheek.

"We should celebrate," I said. "How about my place after work?"

"How about this place right now?" Jade smirked in a way I recognized well. She had something up her poofy taffeta sleeve. And in her purse. She unwrapped the folded cellophane, and my ears perked like Fidelio's when I grabbed his food bag.

"Blue Dolphins," Jade said as she tipped a pill onto

each of our palms.

"Smacky or speedy?" Honey asked.

Jade shrugged. "I guess we'll find out."

I tossed it in my mouth, but a hand on my back made me jump, and the pill became lodged in my throat. I swallowed repeatedly until it was gone and only then acknowledged Josh standing behind me.

He crinkled his brow. "What are you doing?"

"Nothing, Just saying hi to Jade. She got married. This is Jeffrey."

"Nice to meet you," Josh said curtly, then turned back to me. "Did you just take a pill?"

"Yeah."

"Of what?"

"E."

"Are you sure that's a good idea? You know, *here*?"

Honey rolled her eyes. "Chill out, Josh. We've done it before."

"This is between me and my girlfriend, okay?"

Honey grumbled, "She's *my* girlfriend," and I elbowed her side.

Seeing Josh's agitation as he joined the group, James crooked an eyebrow. "What's going on?"

"I think our girlfriends are conspiring against us," Josh replied, and Honey scoffed in amusement.

"No, that's not it," I said, but he clearly didn't believe me.

"Look, I know you've been in a shitty mood lately," he said, "but do you think dropping Ecstasy and rubbing against strip club customers is the way to solve anything?"

"I'd be rubbing against them sober too."

He grunted. "You've never been sober."

Jade took a massive step forward, but the size of the gown made it look like she floated toward him. "What the fuck is your problem, Josh?"

"What the fuck business is it of yours?" he thundered,

causing Braidbeard to plant himself between Josh and his bride.

Braidbeard wasn't quite as tall, but his glare made up for the extra inch Josh had on him. "If you speak to my wife or any of these ladies like that again," he said calmly, "I will hurt you."

"I wouldn't threaten him if I were you," James said.

"Yeah? What happens if I do?"

"Look, you don't know me, so let me give you a quick lesson." James cracked his knuckles. "I don't much consider the consequences of my actions when it comes to violence, but maybe that's because I'm so damn good at it. Consequences rarely come back around if there's no one to complain. Are you good at it, kid?"

Braidbeard sputtered. "Kid?"

"What the hell is going on over here?" Cecil barked as he inserted himself into our cluster. "Jade, where have you been? Are you in a play or something?"

She twirled with a playful flourish. "No, I'm in a marriage."

He tilted his head. "You realize that's not a wife's uniform, right? You can take the wedding dress off."

She grinned. "Exactly what I was thinking. So it's cool if I work tonight?"

"No, you can't work tonight. You quit."

Her jaw dropped. "I did not quit!"

"You didn't show up for nearly a dozen shifts. In my book, that's quitting."

Crossing her arms over her chest, she pouted. "Your book sucks."

"And you're not helping your case."

"Fuck the book and the case," she said as she gathered up her dress and pushed past Cecil.

There wasn't an eye in Pins that didn't latch onto Jade's unique bridal march. She stepped on an empty chair, and a trucker clad in green plaid offered his hand to help her onstage. She pointed at Brian who quickly cut the music and began a new song. As Billy Idol began, Jade loosened her laces and kicked her shoes to the edge. Cecil was furious, but he couldn't argue with the ecstatic roar of the crowd. She'd been nude beneath her dress except for sheer white thigh-highs and a sparkly ivory garter belt.

I could have watched her rock out to "White Wedding" forever, but Josh yanked me away in the middle of the performance.

"What the hell is going on with you?"

Stealing glances at the stage, I said, "That's a loaded question. Would you be more specific?"

"Fine. Why are you being such a bitch?" My gaze shot back to him, and he added, "Specific enough for you?"

"Yes, that's very helpful." I shook my head, confounded. "Unfortunately, I don't feel like I'm being a bitch, so I can't answer that for you. If you perceive me as a bitch, that's your problem."

"You're right, and the last thing I need is another problem. Until you find a way to apologize, consider this over." Grabbing James by the arm, Josh towed his friend out of the club.

Honey jogged over to me. "What did he say?"

"I think he broke up with me."

"Really? Score!" She held her hand in the air until I gave her a high five. "Does that mean I can break up with James?"

My voice trembled. "I guess so."

"What's wrong? This is what you wanted."

"Not like this."

"It's okay. Just try to stay calm. You're going to ruin your roll," she said, putting her arm around me. "Look at Jade. How can you watch that goofy girl using a wedding dress like a matador's cape and be depressed about some guy you don't even like?"

"I did like him. I just didn't love him yet."

"If you don't love him by now, I doubt it's ever going to happen."

"You don't know that."

"Birdie, stop being an idiot. You're making *me* want to break up with you too." She frowned, then winked, and when I smiled, she grabbed hold of my shoulders and shook me as she proclaimed operatically: "There she is! She's a pretty bird! Who's my pretty bird?"

I said, "Cut it out," but I didn't push her away.

"Hey, I have a good idea."

"Your ideas always get me into trouble."

"That's a weird way of pronouncing *fun*."

Over the din of the cheering crowd, Brian said, "Let's give it up for Jade," as she plucked her wedding presents from the stage. "Next up on the main stage, we have Honey and Birdie."

"It looks like the fun will have to wait," I said as we headed up the stairs.

"Don't even pretend we're not going to have fun up there."

I scowled, but it couldn't cling to my face for long. Not with Honey twirling around me, caressing me, blowing me kisses, and cheering me on as we worked the stage. Our Joan Jett set was one of my favorites. While I took the lead during "I Love Rock-N-Roll," doing my best pole and floorwork to stoke the crowd, all Honey had to do was work her lava lamp silhouette while mouthing, "Do you want to touch me there?" to set the audience aflame.

By the time we left the stage, our rolls had arrived in force. As I pointed every box fan in our direction and toweled the sweat from our bodies, Honey unwrapped a few sticks of gum to counter the dreaded grind. We moaned in delight at the gust of icy freshness, powdered our shiny spots, and with Jade by our sides again, our T and A troika traversed Pins like we were the only T and A in the joint.

"Three waters," Honey said to the bowling alley bartender.

Leaning against the bar with her gold bikini on display, she scanned the crowd. I was doing the same when a renegade drop of sweat rolling down Honey's chest captured my attention. I had an overwhelming urge to catch it on my fingertip and hold it aloft like a bead of starlight. Though, a quick lick would have sufficed too. I was gradually drifting toward Honey's chest when she pointed at a group of guys bowling on lane six.

Cracking her neck, she smiled at the flush of relief, then fluffed up her hair. We didn't make a group decision to follow her. We were just suddenly in step, a chimerical three-headed creature with the same set of enviable dancer's legs.

Approaching a guy wearing dark black sunglasses, she purred, "May we join you?"

"We don't want a dance," he said snidely, and she collapsed beside him with a musical sigh.

"Thank goodness. I'm not in the mood to dance anyway. I just want to play with some balls."

Jade and I groaned, but the boys ate it up, just like Honey knew they would.

"You can be on my team," said a guy with a white-blond crew cut, and Honey giggled as she toyed with his popped collar.

"Really?" she replied, bouncing on her toes. "You sure you don't want to go head-to-head with me and see who comes out on top?"

I wasn't nearly as cute or clever, especially not on Ecstasy, and I didn't want to be. I wanted to run my hands over the marbled skin of the bowling balls, so shiny they looked wet. I wanted to watch the lasers swoop and jump and sprinkle fluorescent freckles across the lanes. I wanted to dissolve into the bench, turn just as squishy and orange, and disappear into the neon-dappled floor. I wanted the noise. I wanted the color, bragging the vastness of its spectrum across every surface in the club.

Except the Diamond Lane. Whenever the multicolored lights passed over lane five, only the red spots showed. In spatters, and puddles, leaking into gutters, overflowing with thick crimson blood.

"Are you okay?"

A guy with long brown hair sat next to me, but I had no idea how much time passed between his question and my disconnection from lane five.

"Huh?"

"Are you okay?"

I cleared the stiffness from my throat. "Yeah, I'm fine. Why?"

"You're doing a number on that cup."

Looking down, I realized I'd torn huge pieces from my Styrofoam water cup, littering my lap in chunky snow. I brushed it away with a goofy laugh I was sure would frighten him away, but he surprised me by smiling back. He was a pretty boy, with tresses sparkling in the swirling light like he'd sewn in golden tinsel. Through the stale smoke, I caught a vanilla aroma wafting from him and scooted closer, my eyes closed like I was smelling fresh baked cookies.

My nose was planted against his shoulder when I opened my eyes, and he giggled.

"What are you on?"

I wanted my reply to be as cute as Honey's, but there were too many choices buzzing through my brain to discern which worked best. I tried buying time by asking him to repeat the question, but it didn't help in the slightest. I still fumbled the response, adding a few more "ums" and "uhs" before stating: "Ecstasy.

He puckered his lips in interest. "Yeah? What's it like?"

"It's like having a horny four-year-old in your head."

His face scrunched in disgust, and I winced.

"Sorry. I think that came out wrong."

"God I hope so."

"Maybe it's best if I don't talk.

I scooted away from him, taking note of how smooth the bench was on my bare skin. I'd felt it before, of course, but not on E. It felt like a surfboard, although I couldn't recall if I'd ever touched a real one. I thought, then, of touching surfer boys covered in Sex Wax, even though I was fairly sure it wasn't wax for sex, and it made me want to keep on sliding myself across the bench until I tumbled into the sea. There was no sea, of course, but the pretty boy had moved to the other side of the bench and caught me like a fisherman's net.

"You don't have to go that far," he said. "Maybe just *think* before you talk."

My tongue felt like a dried-up sprig of mint. I swished it around, trying to generate spit. "That sounds like something my ex would've said."

"I'd hate to remind you of an ex. Feel free not to think at all!"

I snorted, knocking more Styrofoam bits to the floor.

"Is that why you two broke up?" he asked.

"Among other things."

"Like what?"

"It's really not that interesting." I lit a cigarette, pausing to savor the menthol sting.

"Then why did I ask?"

I twitched my lips. "I guess I wasn't the kind of girl he wanted me to be."

"So what kind of girl are you?"

On the lane, Honey was bent over at the waist with her legs spread. She swung a blue ball between them, but before hurling it down the lane, she winked at me between her thighs.

"I think I'm still figuring that out," I said, beaming

like a proud parent when she released the ball. "Not who I was at the beginning of all this, that's for sure."

Honey knocked down two pins, but she jumped up and down like she'd conquered every pin in the alley. I clapped for her, hoping she'd come sit beside me, but she stayed at the line while her customer waited for the pins to reset for his turn. There was some commotion over a malfunction—one of the pins didn't descend—so they cleared the lane and started over.

"What's changed?" the pretty boy asked, causing me to flinch.

I coughed up a smoky chuckle. "Are you a therapist or something?"

"Maybe I'm just looking for a distraction." He ran his hand through his silky hair. "I'll be honest, this isn't my scene. Which is why I begged my friends to grab a spot in the bowling alley rather than in the...you know..."

"*Back* alley?" I scrunched my nose.

"It's not that I don't like naked girls—"

"The naked girls thank you, sir."

"I'm just not the kind of guy who frequents these types of places."

"I never did either." I stubbed out my cigarette and immediately withdrew another from my pack. I needed something to suck on. I squirmed on the bench until the pretty boy held a lighter to my cigarette. I whispered "thanks" and sucked hard.

"I imagine your boyfriend wasn't happy about you working here."

"Scott didn't approve, but Josh was fine with it."

"Josh is your current boyfriend?"

"He was until—" I checked a watch I wasn't wearing, "—about an hour ago."

"Hence the mood-boosting Ecstasy," he said.

"I actually took it before we broke up."

"Oh. Now I'm really confused."

"You're not the only one."

What was happening? Why was I talking to a stranger about my ex-boyfriends? Honey was hanging on her guy like she'd never seen anyone so cute, and although the flirty looks she threw my way betrayed the act, her customer swallowed it hook, line, and sinker.

"Birdie, you're up," she warbled, and I trudged over. "Having fun?" She handed over a sparkly purple ball.

"Not really."

"The guy you're talking to is pretty cute."

"I have a feeling I'm not his type."

"What makes you say that?"

"Because no one's type is..." I framed the words with my hands. "Stoner Stripper Dropout with Low Self-Esteem, Questionable Sexuality, and Abhorrence for Underwear."

Honey squinted one eye. "I feel like that's *everyone's* type."

"Yeah, right."

She took the ball out of my hands and set it in the rack. "Excuse us," she said to the group, then led me away. "What's going on, Birdie? You know you're a lot more than that."

"I love you, Honey, but maybe you don't know me any better than these idiots."

She snorted. "If I don't, neither do you. But that's okay," she said, rubbing my arm. "You don't need to have everything figured out yet."

"Maybe it's okay for you, but I don't like floating around aimlessly."

"You've liked it just fine the last few months."

"I know...but something feels weird. I guess these days I drown my pain too quickly to ever feel it—and I shouldn't be able to feel it now—but it's all coming back." I belched into my fist. "I think my lunch is coming back too."

Honey wrinkled her nose. "That's the E messing with you."

"Maybe."

"Birdie, you were fine an hour ago. You're just a little loopy right now."

"What if I wasn't fine?"

"Are you going to take your turn or not?" one of the guys whined at us.

With a grunt, I marched back, grabbed a bowling ball, and heaved it down the lane. It sped down the center, primed for a strike, but when it made contact, it only punched out the center pin, leaving a hole in the formation.

I grumbled. "Perfect."

"You get another turn," Jade said.

"You can take it. I'm out."

When I turned, the alley's neon gleam swept me up in its cyclonic grasp, and I teetered on the edge of my heel. I yelped, and the pretty boy jumped up to catch me, but I caught myself just fine. I thanked him, though—I thanked Honey too—and after a stabilizing breath, I started away.

Destructive thoughts filled my mind, fueled by drug-addled despair that told me I was crazy, I was possessed, I was the subject of a psychological experiment to see how much it would take to push a stoner stripper dropout over the edge. The more I panicked, the more I perspired. I was certain the state of my makeup appropriately represented my meltdown, but I couldn't see my reflection clearly in any mirror; even the one over the sink made my face look like a gigantic smudge. I splashed water on my face and whispered, "You're just rolling" at the gooey girl in the glass, but it didn't help.

When a woman in a red sparkly dress emerged from one of stalls and asked if I was okay, I thought I said "I'm fine," but she gave me such a strange, pinched look, I might've just grunted at her as I stumbled out.

My lungs felt like they were shrinking, and my vision

crossed with every step. I threw myself up the stairs to the dressing room, but my sweaty hands slipped on the banister, and I crashed to my knees.

Pantera ran to the stage's edge. "Hey, you okay?"

My kaleidoscopic vision quadrupled the piercings in her face. Dozens of titanium studs pitched light at me like ninja stars that stabbed my eyes. I scrambled up the stairs, pushed through the dressing room door, and collapsed inward. But I didn't land on the matted carpet. I fell through it, getting an intimate view of how disgusting the carpet actually was. Infested with microscopic mites feeding on our feminine rot, it was much grosser than the Crab Couch, yet we planted our bare asses on it every day. I didn't know whether it was fortunate or not that the fever dream sucked me from the carpet like a hairy clog from a drain, because it did flush the thought from my mind, but it flushed every other thought too.

Everything went black, yet I sensed I was not alone.

In the dark wet heat that enveloped me, a faceless man fingerbanged me like an earthquake. I was frightened, but it also turned me on in spite of myself. I didn't fight him; I must've asked for it, or at least given some sign of interest. An invisible rug burned my back as he slammed me over and over, but when he laid his cheek on my chest, he was as cold as marble. I caught glimpses of his alabaster face in the darkness, expressionless, his eyes like blank ivory stones, as cold and hard as the palm slamming against my pelvis. I moaned pain with an afterburn of pleasure, hating myself for liking how he hurt me. Each thrust shoved the hate a little deeper until it became nausea like a hornet's nest solidifying in my belly. I had to get away from him.

I kicked and flailed, but despite the increasing strength of his fingerfucking, my fists and feet passed through him like mist. Only when I cried a name into the dark did my hand make contact with his face. Pain rang through my bones like I'd punched a brick wall, and his body immediately froze. Like moonlight shining through an icicle, he gradually appeared on top of me, but his white eyes had absorbed all the darkness, now glossy onyx in his translucent skull. At the point of impact, a crack splintered in every direction, deepening, then opening to ravines that caused his hard gelid skin to snap and flake and rain cold upon my burning body, filling the space with steam. I could no longer see the stranger, only his body falling to pieces on top—and inside—of me.

Then I heard a voice in the distance, soft at first but crescendoing to an operatic "Eva...Eva..." that became so loud I couldn't hear my own voice. With a blood-curdling scream that broke through the warbling and shattered the man into a million frozen shards, I saw safety at last, in chestnut waves and sparkling blue eyes.

"Eva, can you hear me?"

I hummed a tune from "Yentl," and Jade laughed, "She's good."

I shivered, suddenly aware I was on the floor, my dress soaked from the bags of ice melting on my chest. When I rolled over, they flopped to the floor, giving rise to a din of parental voices urging me to stay still. I pushed them away and sat up, my roll reduced to a soggy sickness as Honey helped me into a chair at the dressing table. Looking in the mirror made me dizzy— and depressed—so I stared at the table, specifically a kiss print that covered two planes, like someone had closed their mouth on the edge.

Cecil tried to catch my gaze, but despite focusing on one spot, my eyes bobbed and weaved too much to nail down. "What happened?" he asked.

"I got overheated. It's not a big deal."

"What did you take?"

"Nothing. I got overheated. It's not—"

"A big deal, right," he said mockingly. "I won't put up with this shit, Birdie. I've dealt with enough junkies for a lifetime, and I'm not going to deal with you."

"I'm not a fucking junkie."

"Well, it's not fucking Halloween." He pointed at the mirror. "Take a good hard look. You can lie to yourself as much as you want, but that bitch won't."

"Ease up," Honey said, and he glowered at her.

"Ease up? Like dancing here isn't the easiest job in the world already?"

"It's not that easy," Jade said. "And it's not just dancing."

Cecil rolled his eyes. "You've all gotten too comfortable. With everything that's happened, it makes me sick. You have no idea what I've gone through these past few months. Dealing with police, with cleanup crews, closing and reopening, scrambling for employees. Do you know the kind of stress it put on my family?"

My chin quivered. I hadn't even considered Cecil's family. His tiny bald-headed family, sitting around the dinner table waiting for the pater familias to bring home leftover bar food contaminated with clit-glitter. I should've just apologized—I wanted to—but my teeth sunk into my bottom lip, harder and harder, staring at my reflection, allowing only bloody dribbles of "fuck you" to spill from my mouth.

He shook his head. "I thought you were better than this, Birdie."

"Why? You don't know anything about me." I took a makeup wipe to my melted mascara, only then realizing how many other people were in the room. "None of you do."

Honey's face crumpled, and Jade's head tilted like a scolded puppy. I wanted to apologize to them too, but the monster inside wouldn't permit it. She could only wound now; it's all she was now. All the little scrapes and boils had burst and bled in into each other, leaving a wet, red, roaring thing that stripped me barer than I'd ever been.

Hiding my tears, I packed up my clothes and headed for the door.

"If you walk out, you're done," Cecil said.

"Like Jade was?" I scoffed. "You're too desperate to turn any willing dancer away."

"Try me." He shook his finger at me. "But I'm warning you: if you try to come back, not only will I turn you away, I'll make it so no one in West Virginia will hire you."

"Is that supposed to scare me? Your only business is strip clubs. I don't have to be a stripper."

Icily, he countered. "You sure about that?"

"Fuck you," I snarled.

"You said that already. What's wrong, Birdie? Struggling to find the right words to describe your anger? I think I can help." Leaning into me, he whispered, "You fucked up. And you know it."

Grief stabbed my throat like a sideways potato chip. Cecil was right, and I knew I was being stupid by denying it, but I'd sure as hell wasn't going to admit it.

"I'm done," I said.

"You're too high to know what you're saying."

"No, you're too low to understand me," I replied, grasping for whatever clarity I could find in the returning haze of sickness. "Even if you're right."

I slammed the door and jogged down the stairs, glancing only once behind me to see if Honey was following. She wasn't. No one was. And I wasn't surprised. I was given every opportunity to walk back my attack and promise to do better, but my weeping sore of a soul had grown to love its agony too much to let me see how my apologies would fix anything. Even if Cecil forgave me in words, I would always be tainted in his mind. Like I was to my family, to Scott and Josh. Probably to Honey now too.

That one hurt the most, and the monster inside shivered with delight, another injury to treasure.

"Birdie, where are you going?"

I glanced over at Brian, whose face was a question mark as I sped by. Stu was much the same, and Pearl, but I didn't want them to know where I was going. Or that I'd never be back. I just wanted to disappear from their minds.

Most of them.

Honey was standing beside my car when I stumbled out, searching my bag for my keys. Tears filled my eyes as I stomped past her and unlocked the door. As much as I'd wanted her to follow me, I didn't want to talk to her. I didn't want her to see me like this, with the monster exposed, raw and raging. I locked my car as soon as I was behind the wheel, but she'd already opened the passenger side door and slipped into the seat.

"Honey, please...I just want to leave."

"Why? What happened back there?"

"I feel sick."

"Okay, so you go home, you get better--"

"My thoughts exactly."

"Cecil would understand you needing to leave early. You didn't need to quit."

"Well, it would've been a hell of a commute if I didn't."

"What do you mean?" Her brow crinkled, and she crossed her arms over her body like she just realized she was scantily clad. I'd never seen her so sheepish about her body, especially with me.

"I'm going home, Honey. *Home* home. Tonight."

"To Westminster?" She batted her eyes in disbelief. "Why? To do what? Work at Pizza Hut with your shitty cousin?"

"She works at Arby's," I muttered. "And I don't know. I just can't be here anymore. I thought sex and drugs would make my life rock-n-roll, but it feels like a goddamn requiem now. I don't know why."

"Because you're overdramatic," she said.

"You're right." I buckled my seatbelt. "I'm sorry, Honey. I need to leave."

"Look, I understand if you want to move away, and I know you feel like no one knows you, but you don't want to leave like this, so sudden, like you've hated every moment. I know you don't want to forget this. I know you don't want to forget *us*."

She was more beautiful than ever. Through the sparkly spandex, false eyelashes, and iridescent highlighter, she was just a girl slouched beside me on the couch with a pimple patch on her chin and a weed-cough tickling her throat.

I could never forget her. I'd never want to. And for that gift, I owed her more than a vanishing act.

"I won't leave tonight." When light leapt back into her expression, I touched her hand. "But I am leaving. I'm sorry, but I can't do this anymore. Moving to Cumberland for school was supposed to be a fresh start after too much slacking, and I ended up falling into a different version of my old pattern. I lost two guys in less than a year, and much worse than that, I lost any grasp I had on who I'm supposed to be."

"You gained stuff too."

"I know, and I am grateful."

She frowned. "But it's not enough. Our friendship isn't enough."

"You're the only person in this world who could make me stay."

"And the only person who won't pester you to change your mind."

The pain in my throat returned, and it was in my chest now too. I'd never had a best friend, and I certainly didn't expect to find one at Pins.

"You could come with me. Nothing's holding you here."

"I like it here."

"You could like it somewhere else."

"I know." She smiled and looked over her shoulder at Stu standing in the doorway of the club. Brian was probably summoning her to the stage, but she didn't seem concerned. It was all reserved for me.

"I don't want to lose you," she said, and I threw my clammy body against her.

"I don't want that either," I whimpered. "But I'm afraid of losing myself even more."

"Soooo overdramatic." She released me and wiped a tear from my cheek. "But I get it. It sucks, but I get it. Are you going to tell Josh?"

I winced. He'd dumped me, that was clear, but it also felt like he was waiting for an apology, waiting for me to fix what I'd so carelessly broken, and I felt like I owed him the courtesy of telling him face-to-face there were no fixes this time.

"I probably should." I glanced at myself in the mirror and shook my head. "Maybe he'll take pity on me and let me end it quickly."

"Sure, that sounds like something he'd do," she said, rolling her eyes. "At this point, I don't think anyone would blame you for ghosting him. Even Josh."

"You seemed pretty upset about me trying to cut and run a few minutes ago."

She sat up in the seat and gave a little flourish with her acrylics. "I'm not Josh."

I didn't want to let go when she hugged me again. We'd established we were just friends, but I wanted to kiss her so badly at that moment. And it wasn't just the ghost of my roll talking. I wanted to kiss her as a goodbye, as an apology, as a thank you. I wanted to be closer than ever before we were a hundred miles apart.

"Good luck," Honey said, relaying one of my damp renegade curls. "And don't forget the story: we're madly in love."

"Like I could ever forget."

CHAPTER SIXTEEN

Josh didn't answer his phone, so after giving myself a quick fix-up in the rear-view mirror, I drove to his house. I knocked several times to no avail, but the door was unlocked, so I walked in. The house was quiet until I called Josh's name. Then, the quiet turned to clamor beneath my feet. Swift stomps pounded the basement stairs, and James gawked at me from the doorway.

"What are you doing here?" He downed the rest of his beer.

"I need to talk to Josh. Is he here?"

He belched. "He went out for more beer."

"Are you sure you need it?"

"I can't believe you're lecturing me after all the drugs you've ingested tonight."

"You're right. And I regret it."

"The lecture or the drugs?"

"Fucking all of it." My head spun and my stomach burbled with acidic waves. "I actually feel pretty sick."

"Me too," he said, twirling the empty bottle in his fingers. They were red. Like he had a rash. Or…was he bleeding? "I guess you heard Honey broke up with me."

"No, I didn't. When?"

"A little while ago." He grunted. "Over text."

"She didn't tell me."

"Yeah right. Look me in the eyes and say that."

"I'm pretty sure I just did."

"No, you didn't." He threw his bottle to the floor, and I jumped back when it smashed at my feet. It was a shock, but not as much as when he grabbed my face and pulled me closer. "Tell me you didn't know."

"I didn't know! Get the fuck off!" I pushed him away, and he laughed.

"Don't play." He wheezed hungrily. "Josh told me you liked it rough."

"Excuse me?"

"We'd get along, you and I."

"No thanks."

"It wasn't an offer. It was a fact."

"If you say so. Just tell Josh to call me, okay?"

"No."

"Fine, don't. I don't care." I turned to retreat, but James caught me back the arm. I shook him off, and he snickered at me. "Look, I've had a really bad night—"

"Me too. I got dumped by text message."

"That sucks, but it has nothing to do with me."

"It does, actually. I've had my eye on you for a while. I think you know. You remind me of her."

"Of Honey? That's pretty weird. Then again, she said you like weird sex stuff."

"What did she tell you?" he asked, advancing on me again.

"Does it really matter? It's over."

"That's right. I don't have to hide the way I feel about you anymore."

He breathed the words across my neck, and my stomach sloshed with nausea, dwarfing the E sickness when he desperately pawed at my waist.

"Stop!"

I tried to shake him away, but he pinned his body against mine. His groin forcibly rubbed against my hip while his teeth dug into my shoulder. I tried to kick him away, but he slammed my head against the door, causing me to hit the bulbous peephole and chomp down on my lip.

He grunted. "You don't know how hard it's been, seeing you. Seeing her and seeing you. I did what I could because I didn't want to hurt her."

"Let me go," I cried, blood spilling down my chin. "Let me go and I'll talk to Honey for you. Maybe I can get her to take you back."

He shook his head. "No need. I don't have to protect her anymore, and Josh doesn't have to protect you. I can do it instead."

He licked my chin, scraping the skin with his teeth. I shuddered and my stomach turned so violently, bile shot up my throat. My body jerked, and he stepped back in shock, just in time for the next spurt of sickness. That time, I didn't try to catch it.

Watery vomit clung to James's shirt as the chunks dripped onto his feet. He froze in disgust, trying to hold his own sickness down, and I didn't wait around to see if he did. I tore the door open and took off like a shot.

With the porch lights off, the night was a cloak of choking darkness, and I sped blind into it. I only made it a dozen feet before I crashed into something that groaned upon collision. My mouth was acid and blood, my mind fight or flight. I stood, dazed, and began to retreat when a cellphone screen illuminated the other person's face.

"Scott?" I scrambled to my feet. "What are you doing here?"

"What are you running from?"

I grabbed his phone and pointed the screen at Josh's house. Nothing. James wasn't chasing me. I spotted my car just down the street, but I didn't see my purse on the ground anywhere. I must've dropped it inside.

"Where's your car?" I asked.

"Down there. What's going on?"

"Let's just get out of here. I'll explain later."

He wrapped his arm around me as we walked to the car. I shrugged him away for a lot of reasons, but when he opened the door and lightly touched my back, a memory was softly kindled. It was only a flash in my mind, but it echoed in my body.

"Your dome light's out."

"No, I—I like to keep it off." He cleared his throat. "Just tell me what happened."

I forced myself to breathe slowly, deeply. I wasn't sure how to reply, because I wasn't sure what the fuck had happened. Just that he'd attacked me.

"James was drunk, and he tried to..." I stammered through welling tears. "I don't even know. It came out of nowhere."

"James? The guy dating your friend Honey? Why the hell were you alone with him?"

"It's Josh's house. I went there to break up with him, but he wasn't there." My mouth, still coated in a film of vomit, suddenly tasted even worse. Dryer, stickier, and I struggled to swallow. "Wait. How do you know about James and Honey?" I looked around the dark car. "What are you even doing here, Scott?"

Moonlight poured through his windshield, dramatizing the angles of his face. His gaze dropped and his nostrils flared, as if he was searching for the gentlest way to admit he was a motherfucking stalker.

"I care about you."

"Oh, Jesus Christ, Scott."

"What? What's so wrong with caring about you?"

"What about Grace?"

"Grace isn't you."

"Thank fucking God."

"You don't get it. I want you back."

"I'm sure you do, and I feel sorry for you. I imagine it must be incredibly difficult for you to feel superior now. Grace is better looking than you, she makes more money than you, she's more respected in the community than you, and she sure as fuck doesn't need you. She's too good for you, and you can't stand it. You need someone to fix, to save—"

"I love you, Birdie."

"Yes, that used to do the trick. You pulled this relationship out of the fire so many times with those words. Because I wanted to feel real love so badly, I'd ignore every other wretched feeling gnawing up my insides, every doubt about us, every dream you said I'd fuck up. Because old movies and epic poetry told me love was enough. But I don't believe that anymore. 'I love you' is Fix-A-Flat at best. And your 'I love you' isn't even that anymore. It's poison."

His jaw clenched. "Poison. I just saved your ass back there."

"Which is fucking terrifying, Scott, because I just escaped one evil man and ran into the dark, locked car of another."

His lips parted in shock, and he hit the button to unlock the car. "I didn't mean to do that. Yes, I've been watching you. But I'm not…" He shuddered. "…evil."

I hummed dubiously. "So why are you here?"

"It's been difficult watching you all this time, and I guess I overcompensated. I've done things I'm not proud of."

"What are you talking about?"

"I've been worried. About you. About your baby."

"There's no baby, Scott. If there was, it wouldn't be yours anyway. I don't need your concern. I'm fine."

"Working in a strip club, snorting coke, selling your underwear? Yeah, you're really fine, Birdie."

"Underwear? How—" I dropped my face into my hands. "Holy shit. You *were* at the Lariat that night. I knew I saw you. I *knew* it."

"Of course I was there. I've always been there." When he reached out, I flinched, and he held up his hands in supplication. "If you knew it, why didn't you follow me to make sure?"

"I figured my eyes were playing tricks on me. I was high."

"I'd be lying if I said I didn't use that to my advantage. Lots of people do, I'm sure. And you just accept the drug haze as this sort of safety because you couldn't know for sure. Just like you all think you're safe because that Petey guy got arrested."

"Well, he's the killer, so I'm certainly saf*er*."

"You really think a guy like that could've done all those horrible things? He's a weakling."

"They found his phone, the Twitter account—"

"Easily faked. Easily cloned and hacked and covered with burner phones. Someone could've framed him as effortlessly as I've followed you all these months."

"You're psychotic, Scott. You're—"

The nights of danger and death flashed through my mind, layering it in so many grisly scenes, it would be impossible to fully clean. There would always be a brown sticky grime in the corners, collecting fuzz and dirt and memories of my childhood sweetheart watching me from the sidelines during every murder.

"Oh my God." I shrank in the seat. "It's you. *You're* the killer."

I grabbed for the door, but he flipped the automatic locks.

"Birdie, don't be ridiculous. I was just joking around." He laughed and craned to look at the stars. "Of course Petey is the killer."

"Why the fuck would you joke about that? You understand I saw those girls, right? I saw three of my coworkers torn apart by a madman, someone who's allegedly in prison, someone who I've tried to erase from my mind because he's allegedly in prison," I said. "Does the possibility that the madman who killed your coworkers isn't behind bars sound funny to you?"

"No," he replied. "Then again, you got yourself

into this situation. You knew the risks, and now you're paying the price. So did those other girls."

A knock on the passenger side window made me shriek and crumple into a ball.

"Birdie? Is that you?" Josh peered into the dark car. "Whose car is this? Who's in there with you?"

"Open the fucking door," I said to Scott, and he flipped the switch with a grunt.

Josh backpedaled when I flew out of the car, but he reclaimed the lost ground when he saw Scott pop out of the driver's side. He slammed the door behind me, and I flinched in the futile search for my purse in the now-illuminated porch light.

"I guess you're not here to apologize," Josh said, "since you and your ex are obviously back together."

"We are not back together, and I'm frankly scared out of my goddamn mind, so please…" I looked into his eyes, even richer under the wooded shroud of night. "Josh, I *am* sorry about so much shit, but right now, I just need you to get my purse from your house."

"Your purse? Why's it in my house? And what the hell is that asshole doing here?"

I was fucking done. I exploded at Josh with shrieks and frantic slaps. Men were so fucking stupid. You don't need answers for every fucking thing to help someone out. Just do what I fucking ask, or say 'fuck no' so I can devise a plan to get my shit back without your drunk friend trying to fuck me. After smacking his chest, his face, his arms, I fell wearily into weeping. Pulling me into his embrace, he overwhelmed me with the smell of cannabis and chocolate. I clutched his shirt, dazed by the frantic rhythm of his heart. I still felt so sick, but fuck if there wasn't a little E left in the very tip of my clit. I wanted to scold it, tell it these men had terrified me in their own ways too much for the fantasies spilling into my mind, but I thought my clit might like the shame a little too much.

"Why can't you get it yourself? Why can't your *boyfriend* get it for you?" Josh spat.

Scott shook his head. "Not her boyfriend, dude. Not her anything. She's made it perfectly clear you're the one she wants."

Josh inhaled sharply. "Is that true?"

"No. Well, yes... I don't want to be with Scott, but I don't..." I grunted. "Can we please stay on topic here? If you won't get my purse, can I please use your phone to call the cops?"

"The cops? Why?"

"I think he might be the killer, okay? Phone. Please."

Josh squinted at Scott. "Him?"

"He was there," I said. "He admitted he's been following me, and I saw him at the scene of every crime. Even in Martinsburg."

Scott ran to me, his hands crumpled against his chest like dead crops once intended as a dowry. "Birdie, I'm not a killer. You know me. You loved me. We've been friends since we were thirteen. Do you really think I could kill someone?" When I didn't answer, everything he'd minimized to make me feel safe exploded in massive blood-red blooms, and he lunged for my arm.

I darted away, and Josh opened his arms to collect me, but I dodged him too. I didn't need comfort. I didn't need men. I needed a goddamn phone. With Josh and Scott flanking me on either side of the car, I shook my head and whimpered. "Please don't touch me. I just want my purse so I can get out of here."

"Fine, I'll do that for you," Josh said. "But first, I need to hear you say what you came to say. I need to hear why you keep pushing me away."

"Fucking hell, Josh, I just told you I think Scott killed a bunch of girls, and you want to talk about our relationship?"

"I'm not afraid of him, and you shouldn't be either. If he tries to hurt you, I'll slit his goddamn throat."

"I don't want to hurt anyone!" Scott screamed.

Josh pointed at Scott sternly, causing him to shrink back. "Just stay where I can see you. Birdie and I need to hash this out."

"I just want my purse. Hell, I don't care about the purse—I don't even like it—but if I could get my phone and keys—"

"I want to hear you say it."

He felt closer than he was. The way he stared at me allowed his hands full rein of my body, on me, inside me. His tongue turned me into a puddle of submissive glee, and I wanted so badly to splash around in his lust. Josh needed the apology like I needed the "I love you," but neither would fix anything at this point.

"Okay. I'll say it." I cracked my neck and resettled my gaze on him." Goodbye, Josh."

He shook his head, baffled. "Wait, what? Goodbye?"

"I'm moving back to Westminster." When Scott perked up, I pointed at him. "And it has nothing to do with you. Because you'll be in jail, you psycho." I blinked at Josh, truly apologetic. "I'm sorry, but I need to get away."

He scoffed. "You mean *run* away."

"Sure. However you want to frame it. I'm a coward. I'm a fickle bitch. You deserve someone so much better than me, and I'll happily get out of your way so you can find her, but I can't do anything without my keys, which are in my purse, which is in your goddamn house, within spitting distance of your rapist friend."

All emotion dropped from his face. "What? Did James do something to you?" He reached out to my split lip. "Did he do that?"

"I don't want to talk about it. I could rattle off a hundred reasons why I'm leaving, but I've already wasted enough of your time. I just want you to know I really liked you, and I wanted us to work."

"Yeah, well, wanting it and working at it are very

different things, and let's face it, Birdie: all you care about is play."

"Not anymore. In fact, to show you how serious I am, if you don't at least run interference while I go in there for my purse, I'll report James to the police too."

Josh's eyes widened. "For what?"

"For assaulting me in your goddamn house. If I hadn't gotten away...God, I don't want to think about it."

"He's drunk. Honey broke his heart."

"So that's an excuse for trying to rape me?"

"He didn't try to rape you." He rolled his eyes, mumbling, "He wouldn't have to *try*."

"What the fuck does that mean?"

"Forget it." He looked me up and down, his face drooping into sorrow by the second. "I can't believe I wasted so much energy on you. I gave you my entire fucking heart, and you shit all over it."

"I never meant to hurt you."

"Hurt me?! You haven't hurt me, don't you dare worry about that. You're not near hot enough for that."

Tears filled my eyes, and he chuckled cruelly.

"Now who's hurt?" He advanced, backing me against a tree. "Good. You deserve it for lying to me about how you felt. Shit, you probably deserve it for lying to Scott too."

Scott said, "Thanks, man," and Josh and I both barked, "Shut up!"

"Look," I continued gently, "I know I didn't handle this well, but I never lied about how I felt. I wanted to love you, Josh. I wanted to know you. You wouldn't let me."

"But I'm sure your little fuckbuddy Honey did, right?"

Scott blinked in shock. "You fucked Honey?"

"No!"

"But you wanted to," Josh said. Anger was the most

obvious emotion powering his voice, but I felt his lust too, like he couldn't figure out if he wanted to wring my neck or screw my brains out. When his breath pelted my neck, I forgot about his cruelty, I forgot about Scott's stalking, about James's attack, about everything but the delicious tickle of his words. "I could always tell, you know. Every time she was there, I knew you'd rather be playing house with her than me."

He edged up my chin with one finger so I would meet his eyes.

"Be honest with me. With yourself."

"Josh," I said softly, but when he raised his eyebrows, I snarled. "Both of you sad little boys can go straight to hell."

As I marched away, Josh tried to grab my arm. He only got a taste of my sleeve, but when I instinctively swung around to smack him away, my nails took a substantial bite out of him. Slashing two red tracks in his cheek, I whimpered an apology before dashing toward his house while he remained frozen in shock.

I didn't see James when I leapt into the house—I hoped he was still washing puke out of his clothes—but my purse and its contents were on the floor next to the broken bottle. I quickly shoved my stuff back inside, but by the time I turned to leave, my exit was blocked.

Josh's anger was clear enough, but there was a shine in his eyes I'd never seen before. It stole all familiarity from his face, making him look like a complete stranger, and a dangerous one at that. I brandished my cell phone like a weapon as I typed in 9-1-1.

"Please get out of my way. I'll leave. You'll never have to see me again. Just like you want."

His shoulders rolled forward and his lips peeled back. "You think that's what I want? I wanted *you*, you dumb bitch!" His offended gasp was louder than mine. His hand flew to his mouth, and his head wobbled in shame. The rage subsided for a few moments, allowing everything else to bleed through. He was the man I knew again: soft yet powerful, and trembling with pain when he whispered, "I thought you were different."

"Nope," I said, my thumb hovering over the call button. "Just another dumb bitch."

His eyes glimmered with sorrow, and his hand moved from his lips to the weeping welts I'd ripped into his beautiful face. For a moment, I considered taking everything back. Even with the insults and anger still scorching the air between us, I envisioned leaping into his arms and begging him to forgive me, if only for a half-hour or so. Just until all the emotion had burned off like alcohol in a flambe, then we'd be right back here again, swollen and broken with blood under our fingernails.

"It's because of her, isn't it? Because Honey broke up with James. So you and her can be together."

I sighed heavily, lowering the phone. "Fine. Yes. We're madly in love. Can I go now?"

"That's what we thought."

He bellowed for James, who appeared around the corner, mumbling something about "that fucking bitch" when he spotted me.

"This fucking bitch?" Josh asked, pointing at me, and James nodded. "We sure can pick 'em. bro. It turns out our inside joke is an actual fact. Birdie and Honey are fucking."

"I knew it. I *told* you." James grunted at me. "How long?"

"This is pointless. You guys can work this out on your own. I'm out." I veered to the left, but Josh stepped into my path, and James closed the distance behind me.

"No. We working this out now," he said, glaring down at me like a gargoyle from a gothic spire. "I don't want any loose ends."

Staring up at him like an aerosol can at the ozone, I said, "Get out of my way, or I'll report you to the cops right after Scott."

"Yeah? How are you going to do that without a phone?"

Before I could process his question, James wrenched the phone out of my hand and threw it down the hall. They laughed as they craned their heads around me like cartoonish ostriches.

"Where's your big threat now, huh?"

I pointed down the hall at my phone glowing on the kitchen floor. "Probably on its way here right now. I connected to 911 a couple minutes ago."

James's eyes widened while Josh's shrank to a glower, but they both stepped back from me at the same time.

Opening the door, Josh chuckled in a sort of bitter delight. "It's been fun, Birdie. Not tonight, but..." He looked like a stranger again, older, more nervous than I'd ever seen him, knuckles ash white as he wrung his hand on the knob. "We had some good times, didn't we?"

I didn't answer him, but I did glance at him sadly, which his nod indicated was answer enough. I imagine James didn't expect one either when he whispered, "Are you really sleeping with Honey?"

I walked out, silent, strong, remembering only when I hit the front porch that Scott was still out there somewhere. I armed myself with my keys and hurried to my car, feeling a little silly through my fear. The truth was, I found it hard to believe Scott was the real killer. His violent tendencies capped at "major nuisance." He'd been weirded out when I told him to spank me during sex. He approached games of whack-a-mole with cautious consideration for the game itself. "I don't want to go full-out and rip off the mallet. Do you have money to pay for a busted mallet, Birdie?" He was all talk, and it was pusillanimous bluster at best.

But lots of killers flew under the radar due to their

unassuming appearance and reserved personality, didn't they? "He seemed so nice," had gone so wrong so many times it should qualify alongside heart disease and breast cancer as a major cause of death for women.

As I headed for my car, I spotted him in the shadows. He looked menacing in the dark, but he kept a good distance. It was his first smart move in months, but he fell back into his typical idiocy when he asked, "When are you coming home?"

"Like I'm telling *you*."

Locked inside, I started the car and put it in drive, but Scott didn't move. He clutched his chest like I'd torn out his heart. He looked like he was about to die, not kill.

I lowered my window an inch and said, "The police are on their way, so you should probably start thinking of what you're going to tell them. I suggest the truth."

"I didn't do anything! Dammit, Birdie, why don't you believe me?"

Again, I didn't answer. And my reason for it was the same as my reason for not believing him: What was the fucking point? What benefit to anyone but them would come from giving the egos of badly-behaved boys even the faintest stroke? They certainly didn't intend to repay the favor, and seeing as I didn't intend on seeing any of them again, I chose for the last word on the matter to be no word at all.

I sped away thinking of every mistake I'd made from self-awareness to that moment. None of this would have happened if I'd been a pageant girl like my mom wanted. Or maybe things would've been worse. I thought of myself in an alternate universe, where I grew to love the taste of petroleum jelly and bile. After being so pretty for so long, would aging terrify me? Instead of hiding in seedy clubs and clouds of drugs, would I hide behind boob jobs and lip filler? I tongued my plump lip in the visor mirror and pouted so dramatically I reopened the wound. When a drop of blood bloomed, I smeared it across my mouth and, for a moment, across the cosmos, I connected with beauty queen Birdie, and she with me. Both envious. Both unsatisfied. Both disappearing into the dark.

CHAPTER SEVENTEEN

I would've liked to write off the previous night as a bad dream, except I could still taste it. Upon arriving home, I'd filled Fidelio's bowl and collapsed right into bed. Through the night, vomit and blood thickened on my tongue, making the organ sit heavy in the dry bowl of my mouth. My hair was somehow both knotted tight and limp, and dislodged bobby pins hung from my tangled bun like discount Christmas ornaments. Fidelio noticed them before I did. As I sat up, he bounded onto my pillow for a better chance at batting the dangling things. He hooked one before I was able to fully grasp what was happening, and he was soon tangled up in my hair too. My head pounded like a jackhammer as I freed him, and because of it, I didn't interpret the knocking on my door as real for several minutes as I poured lukewarm tap water down my blistered throat. Once it permeated my hangover haze, I glanced out the peephole, rested my forehead on the door as I took a deep breath, then opened it for the whirling dervish comprised of Honey and Jade.

Jade flew past me to the couch and immediately started packing a bowl, but my haggard appearance stopped Honey with a start. She frowned as she inspected my face.

"Jeez, Birdie. You okay?"

"Yeah." I snorted, lifting my dirty claws. "You

should see the other guy…sss."

"You didn't answer your phone."

I sighed heavily. "Yeah, I'm going to need a new one of those."

"What happened?"

"For one, you broke up with James over text."

Jade stuffed a bud into her bowl. "Honey, you didn't."

"Can you blame me? Look what happens when you dump a guy in person." She gasped. "Wait, that's not what happened, is it?"

"Not exactly."

"How'd you even know about the text?"

"James was there. Super upset, super drunk."

Jade released her hit, then pulled a heroic pose in the resulting smoke as she proclaimed, "Here I am: SUPER DRUNK!" She knocked the smoldering pipe to the floor, and Honey moved to clean it up before it singed the carpet.

"Whoops, sorry!"

I crinkled my nose. "It's so easy to be a joker when you don't have a fat lip."

She beckoned me to join her on the couch, and though I was still sore, I allowed her to enfold me in a hug. "Don't hate me, I had to squeeze in one last burst of idiocy before you leave our lives forever."

"I could never leave you guys forever."

"Don't call yourself 'Blondie' if you're a fire-crotch," Honey said, and Jade chuckled through a wistful sigh.

"It feels like a lifetime since I heard a Faith-ism. I miss Faith-isms."

"Me too," I said. "I'm going to miss a lot."

Honey whined as she landed next to us on the couch. "Then don't go."

"I'll admit, even while I was headed there to tell him I was leaving, I had second thoughts. Not about dumping his ass, but—"

Honey batted her eyes. "You want to stay."

"I *did*. Not anymore. Not after last night."

"Let me guess," she said, brushing a tangle of hair out of my face. "Josh didn't take the news well."

"No, no, he was just peachy about it." I punctuated the sarcastic response with a prolonged hit from the bowl.

"Did he do that to you?"

"No, but..." Feeling James's reeking tongue skirt across my bristled skin, I cringed. "...I'm glad we broke up with them. Even by text. He—they—all of them are bitter dicksplatters."

"I bet they weren't too happy to hear about our relationship." Honey pinched my thigh, and Jade jumped to her feet on the couch, her mouth agape.

"Nuh-uh! Are you bitches finally doing it?"

I collapsed into my hands, my hair flopping sloppily like a turkey shot from the sky. "No, we're not doing it."

"We only made out once," Honey said, and I whipped my head up, smacking her with my knotty tresses.

"Are you sure you don't want to stick around to see if you can get to second base?" Jade asked.

"We're just friends." Knowing I looked like wet garbage, I still added slyly, "And I know I can get to second base."

Honey yawned theatrically. "Maybe you *could*. Not anymore. Not after you leave me."

"I'm moving to Westminster, not Mars."

"Thank God for that," she said coyly. "I'm a Venus girl."

She smiled before taking a hit from the bowl. Then, she leaned into me, her hands cupped around her lips, and exhaled the smoke into my mouth.

Jade snorted. "You guys are so weird."

Honey flicked her fingers at my hair again. "At least

we know one thing won't change when you move away."

"I guess we'll find out."

"Yes, I guess we will."

"When are you leaving?" Jade asked.

"It shouldn't take me long to pack. Tomorrow maybe."

Honey gripped my arm with a squeal. "In time for the pageant!"

"You're right. Maybe I should leave late tomorrow, just to play it safe. That way my mom isn't tempted to rush me in before the sign-up deadline that afternoon."

"Tomorrow's cool." Jade nodded. "We can work with that."

"What do you mean?"

Honey leapt to her feet and whipped open her arms. "We're throwing you a going-away party! After Pins closes tonight, you, me, Jade, and some of the other girls are sending you off in style!"

"After Pins closes? So...at 2 am?"

Jade winced. "Probably closer to 2:30."

"Where?"

"Pantera's working on it, but we'll let you know as soon as we do."

"I don't know." My head was aching again, and I massaged my temples. "Maybe this isn't the best time."

"It's the only time!" Jade mewled.

"I don't need a party."

"Yes, you do, and so do we. With everything we've endured this year, with everything we've survived, we need a night to let loose and celebrate."

I pouted. "You want to celebrate me leaving?"

"That you *can* leave."

I didn't know if she meant I could leave because I hadn't been killed, or because I had a place to run away to, but most of all, I didn't know why she couldn't just run away with me. Without me owning up to my actual feelings and asking her seriously, of course. I launched into a protest that Honey stopped by picking up Fidelio.

An adorable version of my protest commenced, but when she scratched his neck and sang a little nonsense song, his wriggle squeaks gave way to deep, contented purrs.

Jade leaned into me. "Is that how the make-out sesh went?"

"Pretty much."

"We're having a party," Honey said, her voice still pouring sappily into Fidelio's fluff. "Don't you dare try to fight it."

"Okay, okay. We're having a party." I sighed. "A 2:30 AM party." I wrenched the ponytail holder out of my hair and shook out the tangled mess. Smoothing it best I could, I coiled it on top of my head and snapped the elastic. "Since you're here, do you want to help me pack?"

"Want to? No." Honey tossed a smirk at Jade, who shrugged.

"But we'll help you anyway."

Part of me wished packing was more difficult. I wished I had mementos that made me procrastinate in remembrance, to look back on the things of worth I'd accumulated during my time in Cumberland: a seashell from my vacation to that Bermuda Triangle beach called Life. But there weren't many tokens at all, let alone that made me feel worthy of the vacation. My acquisitions were intangible, and therefore, vulnerable to memory's artistic flair. Even they couldn't promise to give me that joy forever. With distance, I might come to realize I would've been better off working at the park reservation place at that time. The only parts of those days I wanted to cling to, the only ones that made me feel like my life had an ounce of value, that I had reason to think things would get better, were at my side, loading meaningless trinkets into beer boxes.

We'd finished packing the living room and kitchen by the time Honey and Jade had to leave for work. I took one more hit, then set the weed aside to start on my bedroom. If I kept smoking, there was no way I'd make it to party time. I was able to resist my vices for a while, but after sunset, I started craving wine. I repeatedly visited the refrigerator in the hopes of finding something I wanted as much as Chablis, but nothing healthy appealed to me. The darker the evening, the darker my mood. I wanted so badly to drink and smoke my remaining hours in Cumberland away, but the last thing I wanted to do was show up to my going away party already partied out. Once I deemed the packing "done enough," I still had five hours to go, so I slept to avoid intoxication.

It was a bad idea. Honey emailed at 1 AM and told me where the celebration would be: an abandoned house that Pantera's friend used for his more rambunctious parties. Groggy and achy, I did my best to make myself presentable. After the third time re-doing my hair, I contemplated scrapping the whole thing. I didn't want a party. I didn't even want to drink anymore. I just wanted to sleep. On my dusty laptop, I Googled the address Honey gave me and found the house plunked in the middle of nowhere, like it had sprouted up with the surrounding woods. From Honey's description, the place sounded seedy, which also meant it was the only appropriate place for our particular brand of merry making.

The party was in full swing when I arrived. Music rumbled the path leading to the house, and paired with the exuberance inside, shook its flimsy foundation. It was even more rundown than I'd imagined, but the raging bonfire in the yard gave the slanting shack a touch of life, filling in the peeled gray paint with licks of red and orange, and magnifying the shadows of spiders who'd long ago built their homes in the smashed light fixtures barely clinging to the house.

"Hey Birdie, you got a light?"

Jade and Braidbeard were barely sharing one of the blanketed logs around the fire, both with matching unlit cigarettes dangling from their mouths. I was too tired to question why they didn't just lean forward. I lit their cigarettes and figured I might as well light one for myself. It tasted terrible without intoxicant-induced hunger.

"Beer's inside," Jade said, reading my expression. "Pantera got a keg."

"A keg of what?"

"Milwaukee's Best."

"*Beast*?" I groaned, eying her red cup like an old enemy.

"You better develop a taste for it unless you brought your own. Though, I think Crystalline is drinking rum and Coke."

"Nope, just Coke." Braidbeard grumbled. "I already asked. No one brought liquor."

I kicked a rock. "Well, damn. I didn't know I had to bring anything. This is supposed to be my party."

"Nah, nah, it's everyone's party now," Brian said as he walked by. Stopping on the edge of the woods, he unzipped his pants, and looked over his shoulder as his stream painted the brambles. "You just gave us an excuse to throw it. Thanks, I guess."

"Forget him. Just grab a beer and chill," Jade said.

"I think I'm going to stick with water. I'm exhausted. It's not even nighttime anymore."

"But it is the witching hour," Pantera said as she strode over, which provided the perfect opportunity for Jade and Braidbeard to resume making out. She held her cup aloft. "To Birdie, someone who dared to teach us that even shy girls can be rotten girls, and rotten girls can still have a sweet core."

"Thanks for that, I think. The last part anyway."

"I'm going to miss you. You were a pretty cool chick. Now that you're leaving this life behind, you're going to be a boring little nerd again, but whatever. Your vacation on the Dark Side is over."

"I like the Dark Side."

She opened her arms. "We do throw the best parties."

"I'll be the judge of that. Anyway, you make it sound like you'll never see me again. I'll be back to visit, you know."

"No, you won't." She flicked her cigarette at Jade and Braidbeard, but neither noticed it hit Jeff's shoulder.

"Come on, don't be like that."

"Then don't be a liar. Some people take root, some people tumble," she said, leading me inside.

It didn't take long to absorb my surroundings. Wet and wilting, the house's soul soaked into me before I could get the full tour. Not that I needed it. The living room was a serviceable example for every other room. With warped walls hardly enclosing the occupants, the rooms allowed the wind to enter through innumerable cracks. Bugs too, and woodland creatures, I assumed, when I heard a strange hissing coming from behind the moldy shower curtain. They also allowed their past to play tricks on the increasingly intoxicated partygoers. The more fucked-up we got, the more we tried to guess about the children whose heights had been documented over decades on the kitchen wall.

"Different children," Jade surmised. "They'd have to be, considering the years."

But every marking had been made in the same color, the same marker, the same handwriting. It was intriguing, for sure, but I had to walk away when a gaggle of girls insisted the children were trying to communicate.

While I didn't give in to the suggestion of a séance, I'd succumb to peer suggestion—pressure wasn't necessary—to drink the Beast. After guzzling one beer quickly so the second wouldn't taste as horrendous, I toddled off to the keg for a refill. Honey was pumping it, her bicep like smooth butterscotch candy, solid, sculpted, but begging for its melting point. When she noticed me staring, she gave a little hop, putting all of her weight into the final pump, then reached for my cup.

"Thanks." As she filled it with bland beer, the peeled wallpaper and I regarded each other with similar feelings of having outstayed our welcome. As if trying to make us both feel better, I said, "This is a neat place. Dilapidated but cool."

"Sometimes, that's the best we can hope for," she said, handing back my cup. "Just avoid the basement. It's a disaster area, apparently."

"Uh…" I looked around. "If the basement's a disaster area, this must be the goddamn Biltmore."

"Well, thank you," Pantera said, her head bobbling on her shoulders as she sashayed up to us. "It was pretty gross when I first showed up. But once I added curtains…" The woman with barely an inch of untouched flesh between metallic facial modifications flicked her fingers through the air as if casting the daintiest of magic spells.

"You added curtains?"

"That's what I said." She tilted up her chin. "Plus, I brought Annabel Lee."

"Who?"

With a crooked smirk that couldn't find a foothold in either cheek, she beckoned me to follow her. The house buzzed with people I didn't know encircling people I did know, two stranger dangers for each defending friend, and in Shasta's case, eight burly bikers. I didn't expect Shasta, as fiercely feminine as Glinda the Good Witch, to hang around with that sort, but I also didn't expect Pantera to gesture to a slender towel covered object in the corner of the kitchen and pronounce:

"Neither the angels in heaven above, nor the demons in the sea..." She removed the towel with an expert flick of the wrist *"...can ever dissever my soul from the soul of the beautiful Annabel Lee."*

The five-foot-tall glass bong glistening turquoise and gold instantly made me wet. It deserved my gasp, but it also demanded the gasps of others, gathering as if summoned to exalt the bong like Excalibur waiting a legendary pull.

In awe, I whispered, "Please tell me this is a going away present."

She cackled. "You wish!" Then she shook her jar of weed.

People from various rooms appeared like cats to tuna treats, following Pantera as she carried Annabel Lee reverently to the living room. Honey's nose was freshly powdered when she grabbed a spot next to me on the sofa, and Jade and Braidbeard took a hiatus from their make-out session to cuddle up next to us on the wraparound couch. As Pantera packed her bud into Annabel Lee's party-sized hitter piece, Honey nervously played with the string on my hoodie.

"Something on your mind?" I asked her.

"Nah."

She was an expert liar at Pins, but she was as transparent as a kid who'd un-and-re-wrapped her Christmas presents when she twirled my string around her finger.

Leaning against me, her eyes to the burnt popcorn ceiling, she emitted a musical exhalation. "Do you think you'll be happier in Westminster?"

"I think it's a better place to start over."

"That isn't what I asked."

"I know. But I can't say how happy I'll be. I probably won't be at first. Back in my mom's house. Back in the heart of the bullshit. But maybe I can start to shovel it away there. Maybe even bury it." When she deflated,

I clapped my hands over hers. "Hey, I'm the bad guy here, not you."

"But I've always been the bad guy; whether it was my mom's inability to keep a husband or my grandmother's inability to control her children, it's my fault. If it's mom's cancer or grandma's hate, it's on me for being so…" She snapped her nails. "Her."

"It's not you."

"It's always me."

"Welcome to the fucking club, my love."

I said it with a playful pop of the lips, but Honey's mouth opened with less rancor.

'You weren't happy here," she whispered.

"I never said that."

"So say it."

"I can't. I *was* happy."

In hearing it aloud, I felt honest for the first time in ages.

"I was happy," I repeated, and she dug her hip a little closer into the sofa with me. Unfortunately, the exuberant jostle released a sour scent from the ungoliant bacteria colonizing its Ethan Allen innards, so we relied on the celebratory exhalations of Pantera's cumbersome bong to cover the stink.

Another smoky substance traveled the party too. While the mammoth biker named Max hungrily sucked on one blunt, he passed the second to Pantera with a sloppy wink. The nearer it came, the more it reeked. With a stench like one of those jumbo permanent markers, the mysterious blunt devoured the delicate blueberry aroma of the weed, reaching my end of the couch with a burst of noxious acidity.

Pantera laughed when she saw my twisted expression. "It's boat."

It twisted even more when Honey said, "Oh fuck that," and shooed it away, right into my hand.

I inspected the blunt like it would include a list of

ingredients and potential side effects. Barring that, I wasn't about to stick something so unappealing in my mouth. But at least it had the decency to be blatantly abhorrent before I wrapped my lips around it, which was more than I could say about some things I'd swallowed over the last year. Wincing, I said, "Thanks but no," and offered it to Jade.

"No thanks. Jeff and I are actually taking off for a bit. We'll be back though."

"Where are you going?"

"Sideling Hill Overpass."

"Make-Out Point, you mean."

She snorted. "No one calls it that."

"They will once they see you two up there."

"More like Bang-Out Point," Honey said, and Jade shrugged in agreement.

"We'll see you once we've given them a good reason to rename the mountain. Try to have fun without us."

"It'd be easier to have fun if Birdie ever passed the boat," Shasta said, plucking the malodorous blunt from my hand.

"What even is that shit?"

"PCP and weed," Pantera said.

"I don't smell any weed."

"That's because it's soaked in embalming fluid," Shasta replied. She sucked the blunt so hard a squeak accompanied the long drag, then coughed violently, gripping her chest and leaking ashy drool as she struggled for breath.

"That can't be healthy."

"And you think all of that E y'all been eating *is*?" she rasped. "You know they cut that shit with heroin, right?"

"No shit, Shasta. By the way, I think you can take off those heels now. You're not on stage."

"Oh yes I am. And so are you." She pushed the blunt at me again. "Go on, Birdie, treat yourself before you leave the real world behind."

"*This* is the real world?" I held out the blunt, and Entice skittered over enthusiastically while Max the Biker snickered in the corner.

"You're goddamn right it is. The life you're going back to, the one at Mommy's suburban estate--"

I started to protest, but Honey waved for me to drop it.

"--that world chock-full of safety nets and second chances is faker than Illusion's boobs and riddled with just as many tough spots. The real world is hard. It's mean. You think you're headed back to motherfucking Care-A-Lot, and I'm sure it looks real as hell right now, but it'll dissolve, Birdie, like the silly little dream it always was. And you'll be there again, in hard places with mean people. And the only ones left to turn to will be the ones you left behind. In the dark." She twirled her shiny slingback. "Hence the glitz. You gotta be shiny to stand out from the rest of the shadows."

I jiggled my head in confusion. "First off, was all that supposed to convince me to stay here?"

"I don't care what you do." Shasta's gaze slowly rolled toward the ceiling. "I just hope you know the life you're going back to is as big a lie as this one."

"Like the *Matrix*..." Entice said with ribbons of reeking smoke pouring down her chin.

Honey rubbed her forehead, eyes peeled. "Can someone please tell me why we're smoking PCP and talking about the *Matrix*?"

"Seriously," I said. "If I start looking like I have plugs in my arms, please tell me so we can ditch you tripped-out bitches."

"It's not like tripping," Pantera said. "It's deeper than that. But also..." Her tongue protruded slightly. "... lighter. Like a boat. You float like a boat. Sometimes you float so high you leave yourself behind completely."

I winced. "That sounds awful."

"It's not," Biker Max said before swallowing a cloud of nostril-searing smoke.

I bounced my eyebrows to acknowledge him, but I was more interested in what was causing Crystalline's uncharacteristic animation across the room. Holding a phone to her ear, she shouted, "It's me, Mrs. Cherrywood. I got your text," then waved for the people around her to quiet down. "What do you mean they let him out?"

Her boyfriend tugged on her arm. "What is she saying, Crys?"

"I can't hear her. She keeps cutting out."

"What did the text say?"

"That Petey guy. The one who killed Madeline. They're saying he didn't do it."

I leapt to my feet, hoping I'd misheard her when I rushed over. "What did you just say?"

Crystalline was shaking. "If you can hear me, I'll try again later." She hung up and gazed at me, eyes bloodshot. "They let him out. They let Petey out."

"But he killed Ginger and Diamond--"

"And Cherry," she added softly, shaking her head. "But I guess he didn't. They say he didn't."

"What about the Twitter stuff on his phone?"

"Faked. Or…set up? The police think someone framed him."

"No, that can't be true."

Honey joined my side, immediately sensing my panic. I grasped her hand and pulled her closer.

"Crys, tell her what you said."

"I said the boat's not awful," Max growled from his perch in the corner.

"Uh…okay, we believe you. We're just trying to figure out something over here." I turned back to Crystalline. "Go ahead."

"Anchor's away!" Max shouted, and we nodded civilly.

"Petey's out of jail," she said. "At least that's what Madeli—Cherry's mom said."

"It's a trip! From the slip!" Max continued loudly. "It's a boat! Time to float! You have to float the boat!"

I urged Crystalline to continue, but Max prevented her from replying. Shoving himself in my face, he snarled, stinking of Sharpies and Beast. "Are you listening to me?"

"Yes, I'm listening. Float the boat. Whatever."

He held up the stunted remains of the blunt he'd been smoking alone, and I declined. "Can I see the message?"

"The signal is really spotty here. Her last text message was from three hours ago." Crystalline handed over her phone, but Max intercepted it and threw it at the wall.

"No! Not *whatever*! You have to float the boat! You have to float!"

His face reddened, and his fists balled so tight they looked like chunks of white marble. Shaking madly at his sides, he smacked himself in the legs, accidentally at first, but with increasing intention. We returned to the couch as Shasta tried to corral him to the kitchen.

"It's cool, Max. Just chill out."

She touched his shoulder, and without turning his head, or any clue as to his response, a wet crack echoed through the room, and Shasta sank to the floor, screaming. He was still holding her hand, her fingers protruding at unnatural angles from his fist as he crouched to roar in her graying face.

"It's not cool! It's time to float the motherfucking boat!"

He released her like a kid throwing whippersnappers, slamming her against the ground before charging at us on the couch. Honey and I were tiny balls of fear tucked under the tent of his massive body as his fists pummeled the wall. Chunks of plaster and earth spewed onto the partiers' heads, sending them running. Max's friends tried to pull him from the couch, but he smacked them away like gnats.

Brian picked up the nearest thing he could find to subdue the biker, and when he lifted it over his head, Pantera finally joined us all in fearful sobbing.

Annabel Lee crested the mountain named Max, briefly catching the firelight before cutting through the air and crashing against the biker's head. Glass and bongwater sprayed through the room, and the partygoers struggled to get their bearings as they navigated the blue shards on every surface.

Max, however, didn't struggle at all. The blow made him stumble, and he cut his fingers pulling a chunk of the hitter piece out of his gnarled beard, but he was undaunted. Even motivated now. Brian was still holding the hilt when Max latched onto his arm, but it spun out of his grasp when the biker whipped him across the room like throwing an Olympic hammer.

Brian hit the wall like a wet noodle, and Max lunged at the couch again. Pantera ripped Honey and me from our seats and pushed us toward the exit, but Max caught hold of Pantera's jacket on the muddy threshold of the house. She fell backwards, her head slamming against the floor. Max, Honey, and I dove for Pantera at the same time, and there's no doubt in my mind he would've gotten her first if his friends hadn't wrapped themselves around his body.

Pulling her from the house, we helped her limp behind a cluster of cars. Crouched behind an SUV, we tried to quiet our panicked breaths.

"Are you okay?" I asked Pantera as she patted the back of her head.

There wasn't enough blood on her palm to freak her out, but it had me freaked out enough for the both of us. "We need an ambulance. We need the police."

"Find a phone with a signal, and I'll call the bacon brigade myself," Pantera said. "Did either of you see a landline? He's gotta have one."

A series of shrieks and snaps resounded from the house, and Max roared in what we could only assume was triumph when we heard a thud on the front porch, followed by a giggle, then the familiar tune of a childhood rhyme I would never find charming again.

"Float, float, float the boat, gently out to sea..."

He lumbered clumsily, scraping through the gravel as we crept around the other side of the car.

"Merrily, merrily, merrily, merrily..."

However, we didn't consider the length of his stride. Once he spotted us peeking around the back bumper, he bounded from the front of the SUV and smacked the window a half second before I darted away. We ran for the woods, but his meaty claw caught my arm before I broke through the tree line. Jerking me backward, lashing my shoulder with blaring pain, he pulled me to his whirling red face and whispered musically, "The devil is inside of me." He turned his eyes to the stars and howled, "Everybody now! Float, float, float the boat..."

I wailed in agony as he towed me back to the house, certain he'd dislocated my arm, but when he pushed me up against one of the cars, I felt a pop that decreased the pain, and my fingers tingled in a way I could only describe as "comparatively good."

"Merrily, merrily, merrily, merrily..." He hissed, and I tasted his madness. "Would you like to meet the devil, Birdie?"

I choked on my words. "No, I don't want to meet the devil."

A burst of firelight caught both our attention, and Pantera appeared beside us with her jacket aflame, wrapped around her fist. "The devil's a pussy, Max. I'm not."

When Pantera's fiery fist sailed at Max's face, Honey yanked me out of his grip. The explosion of cinders and burning leather pelted us all, but it clung to the biker as Honey and I scrambled back to the house. He wailed and clawed desperately at the leather melting into his flesh, trying to free himself from the growing fire.

We ran back inside, over several bikers whose slack bodies made it impossible to fully close the door. We shouted for Pantera, who smacked out the small fires on her shirt and bolted for the house. Once inside, we overlapped as many corpses as we could, then joined the search already in progress amongst remaining partygoers to find car keys and phones among the glass-littered rubble. Honey mewled as she recovered the pieces of her broken phone, which had landed beside a smashed internet router.

"Fucking hell."

Honey stared at me. Every time she blinked, her wet eyelashes printed another row of mascara tallies under her eyes. I held up a piece of the router, and one more layer of strokes appeared.

She whispered, "Fucking hell."

A loud bang made everyone jump. There were several more, and we all huddled in fear while simultaneously looking for barricades, feeling like kids again, hoping the teacher would tell us what to do, but knowing she was probably even more terrified than we were.

Max appeared in the doorway, glistening with sweat and delirium. The only twinge of relief came from seeing he didn't have a gun.

"Float, float, float the boat…" His face was raw melting meat as his pointer finger skated around the room. "…gently out to sea. Merrily, merrily, merrily, merrily." He spotted Honey, Pantera, and I huddled by the router. "I'm going to fucking kill you three."

Pantera's devil of a punch had robbed him of one eye and all depth perception. When we scurried from the room, he followed, but he hit nearly everything in his path. Delaying him, but also wounding him along the way. When we cleared the kitchen and back hall and found a door to close ourselves behind, it was almost a relief to hear his ragged breath smack the door long after we'd latched it. When he pounded on the door, I jumped and nearly tilted backward on the top step of the staircase where we clung to each other.

He fumbled with the lock, grunting, and then we heard what sounded like a large wet flag folding on pavement. Silence followed, and we tasked ourselves with finding a light.

We smacked the empty air for pull strings and pawed the walls for switches, but the only light came from a small blue glow in the basement below.

"There's gotta be a light down there. Just be careful," she said as we began our precarious descent. "He said the basement was a mess."

"He who?" I asked.

On the bottom step, Honey shrieked, and I instantly imagined the worst. She'd stepped on a rusty nail—or a bear trap made of rusty nails—or a man named Rusty Nails who lies on the floor with his mouth open pretending to be a bear trap.

Honey pulled a tangled string dangling from the ceiling, and a bulb dimmer than she deserved illuminated above her head. I threw myself against her in gratitude, then gasped in time with my friends as we beheld our surroundings.

The basement wasn't a disaster. It didn't even qualify as a mess. It was carpeted. Furnished. It had a perimeter of shelving neatly holding boxes and other cumbersome items. It had a wraparound desk with flatscreens, laptops, and gaming consoles. It also had framed pictures. So many, propped like shining stars on the evergreen of each surface, and leaning against every wall as if waiting to be hung.

The multi-level gallery was like one of those optical illusions you couldn't unsee once the hidden image appeared. The moment I recognized one of the pictures as an enlarged version of the photo I'd found in Josh's bedroom drawer, I recognized him in nearly every photo in the basement.

"What the fuck is going on? Why is Josh in these pictures?"

"Oh my God," Honey said, gazing around the room. "Who's the other kid?"

"He said it was his brother..."

The boys aged around us.

"...who died..."

They grew taller, stronger.

"Holy shit, Birdie..."

They grew more familiar.

"It's James."

Somone pounded on the basement door, and Pantera slammed against us. "What the fuck are you two doing? You're supposed to be looking for a way out."

"This basement is filled with pictures of Josh and James," I said, shoving the picture at her.

"Probably because it's James's party house. Now help me look for a fucking door before he breaks through." She tossed the photo aside, and it landed on the keyboard, waking the computer from its slumber.

"His *what*?" Honey squealed.

"His party house. I ran into him at Sheetz and mentioned the going-away party, so he offered the house. What's the problem?"

The curved screen illuminated the room in soft blue light, and the Twitter account for a user named "TheLastDance666" appeared. There was no internet connection, but the "What's Happening" box contained a tweet in draft. In stiff Helvetica, it read: "My Birdie flew away, so I took Destiny into my own hands."

As I read, I couldn't tell which pounded louder: my heart or the crazed biker at the door.

"We need to get out of here," Honey mewled.

"No shit. That guy will kill us if he gets through."

"He's not the only one." I pointed to the screen, and cold realization bled across their faces.

"You've gotta be fucking kidding me." Pantera grunted as she peered at a childhood picture of Honey's ex-boyfriend beside the monitor. "Does this mean James is the killer?"

"Or Josh." Honey tugged open a desk drawer and dug through its contents.

Setting aside a few blocks of Styrofoam, she withdrew a handful of condoms, followed by a sandwich bag stained with brown sludge. She squeezed the small object inside, and it flexed, disgorging a glop of rotten menstrual blood from its stiff cotton petals. She shrieked at the used tampon and dropped it to the floor. But we all shrieked when something else hit the floor with a loud wooden whack we recognized as well as the boys in the photos. From the shadowy stacks of boxes along the wall, a bowling pin rolled into the dim blue light, revealing a new patch of dried blood with each rotation. Grabbing a flashlight from the desk, Pantera shone it on the shelving, and we all recoiled in horror.

Even from behind, curled into a ball—or perhaps crushed—we knew the bulgy broken thing on the second tallest shelf was Destiny. We couldn't see her face, just her bare back, mottled with stretch marks that had always been there and massive contusions that hadn't. She didn't respond when we called her name. I didn't expect she would, but I hoped for it—the smallest noise, the tiniest jiggle—because as we approached the shelves, I remembered every instance of wishing her ill. Nothing serious: just indigestion, run-of-the-mill shits, something to keep her out of the doubles rotation for the night. My stomach turned, and tears pinched my eyes as we looked up at her misshapen body and Pantera gently poked her with the flashlight.

Her body shuddered, then began to slip. Swelling

out of storage like the shelf was blowing a bubble, Destiny's head unwedged from the upper rack and tilted backward, too far to be natural. The wound in her throat gaped nearly as wide as her propped mouth, and both were clogged with candy wrappers. From Snickers to Chuckles, bouquets of colorful plastic encrusted in various fluids sprouted from Destiny's body, so horrifyingly spellbinding we didn't notice how much she'd slipped until her bloodless eyes were level with ours.

Honey shouted, "Look out!" and we scampered backward as Destiny plummeted off the shelf and hit the floor with a sloppy smack that answered the question no one wanted to ask. Where had all the candy gone?

The corpse exploded like a pinata. From the cavernous gash in her abdomen, chocolate bars and lollipops sprung from her tangled innards. But some clung to her organs, Twizzlers and Skittles secured to her twisted meat as methodically as holly on a wreath.

Honey took one look and vomited in the corner, where the carpet turned to cold concrete. And once the stench hit me, far worse than any Destiny ever emitted, I was doubled over with her. Pantera held strong until she noticed millions of tiny ants picnicking on Destiny's sugary corpse, then she belched up a night's worth of Beast beside us.

Max stopped pounding the door. We froze, wiping our mouths, waiting for the next slam. It didn't come, but we did hear a soft fluttering. A curtain in a breeze. A soft gurgling, like something lapping at our vomit. Crouched, Honey looked under the shelving unit. The wall behind it was covered with a drape, but it wasn't quite big enough to cover it all, or the inch-wide opening exhaling night air behind the curtain.

"A door!" Honey stomped through our puke and started tugging the racks away from the wall. The first moment I could, I slipped behind the shelves and yanked down the curtain.

With a triumphant howl, Pantera turned the deadbolt, flipped the lock on the knob, and said, "Let's get the hell out of here." Throwing open the door, she dashed out and turned back to us grinning.

She got two good breaths of freedom before Max the Biker charged through her like a bull, launching her through the air. As she landed in a disjointed heap, someone in the distance screamed, and Max whirled around, sniffing at the air as we ran to help Pantera. Her ankle looked broken, her arm too, but she was able to move. We were trying to help her up when a rock suddenly smashed again Honey's leg. She wilted beside Pantera in pain, and Max giggled in delight, another rock at the ready. He galloped at us, foaming, snorting, his eyes whirling like cartoon madness. I tried to get them both, but I was only able to pull Honey away in time before Max reached us.

Grabbing Pantera by the shoulders, the biker lifted her into the air.

"Let her go!" I screamed, and Honey's arm shook as she pointed at a shadowy figure behind them.

When the figure lifted a gun, I only had time to gasp before two shots rang out. Max's body jerked, but he didn't fall. With the third bang, a chunk of flesh exploded out of the biker's cheek. He dropped Pantera, who landed in a motionless heap as Max swayed over her body.

We called out from the basement, begging her to crawl to us, but the biker fell on top of her like a sack of wet cement before she could move. She wailed and struggled beneath him, and we inched from the basement to help her, but another gunshot sent us hurtling back inside.

"Leave her," said the gunman, and when we peeked around the door again, Honey sobbed.

Stepping into the moonlight, James smirked as

he reloaded his gun. Stashing it in his waistband, he crouched beside Pantera.

"How do you like the house?" he asked. "Didn't I tell you it was great for parties?"

She sputtered blood, and James fished her arm out from the messy pile. Pushing on Max's body with his foot, he was able to wriggle her loose and drag her free of the biker's dead weight. Gratitude dripped crimson from her lips, but it quickly turned to burbling fear.

He dragged her over rocks and broken bottles, and her pain filled the night even after he tossed her in the clearing ahead of us and stood over her shivering wet body.

"James, stop! She's hurt!"

Staring at us in dramatic shock, he gasped. "*Is she*?" With a contemplative "hmmph," he sat on her stomach forcefully, and she screeched in agony. He sighed like he could taste it, and gazed down on her with a satisfied smile. "I always liked you, Pantera. I honestly never thought we'd be in this position, but..." His hand moved up her arm, over her shoulder, around her neck.

"James...don't do this..."

"What? Admire you? Your spunk? Your beauty?" When his thumb smeared a spot of blood across her throat, he licked his lips in delight. "You really are beautiful. Just a little...monochrome..." He wiped his bloody thumb across her lips, but it quickly ran out of juice, and her lip jewelry interrupted his attempt at artistry. With an epiphanic tilt of the head, he crinkled his nose. "You need more color."

We couldn't quite see what he was doing until we heard Pantera's plea, followed by blood spurting into the air and a silver hoop sparkling in flight across the night sky. My hands flew to my mouth in horror as he continued ripping out her lip rings. Little spurts followed each violent removal, one by one, each silver hoop went flying until her lips were natural enough for him to paint in all her new color. But he didn't stop there. He wrenched the large black CZ out of her philtrum and yanked the spiky ring out of her septum. The nostril rings connected by a black chain he plucked out simultaneously, the trauma of which finally caused her to pass out. She didn't even flinch when he ripped the curved barbell out of her eyebrow.

He frowned, then smeared the scarlet lip gloss across the rest of her face until he was smiling. With a little nod of accomplishment, he stood up and swung his gaze to us. We gasped, and his smile spread to a toothy grin as he aimed his gun at Pantera.

"Close the door," I whispered, and Honey pulled it shut with a moan that became a yelp at the gunshot. She locked the door, and I searched the room for weapons. I gave her a shovel and found a pair of rusted gardening shears for myself, but I felt woefully unprepared when James knocked lightly on the door and trilled.

"Lllladies? Can you hear me?"

"Why are you doing this?" Honey bawled, the shovel pointed at the door as if he'd burst through it like the Kool-Aid Man. "Why did you pretend to love me?"

His voice deepened as it neared, even reverberated, like he was speaking against the door and delivering his words through every bone of the house.

"I didn't pretend. I loved you. I still love you. I never wanted to hurt—well, no…" He cleared his throat and tapped the door. "That's not true. I *did* want to hurt you, but I was trying very, very hard not to."

"You're a murderer."

"Yes, but you still loved me. The most beautiful girl in the world loved me. And for a while, it was enough. You made me feel…" He sighed, and the gun barrel screeched as he dragged it across the door. "…like I didn't need all the horrible things I usually need. You gave me joy without having to inflict pain. But you also tempted me more than anyone. It was torture. Did you know that? When you looked at me from across the club, your legs spread, teasing your pussy for me, did you know how much I wanted to split your body in half?"

"Shut up!"

He moaned in amusement. "I guess not. So you probably didn't know about my favorite fantasy of you, either. The one where you quit dancing. To be with me, yes, but also because I've cut off your legs. And no pole tricks either because your arms, they're gone too. In fact, there's not much left of your body at all, which is a shame because you're a fucking smokeshow, but it's nothing compared to that beautiful face. That perfect head. Your eyes rolled back, or missing sometimes, mouth open and empty, or sometimes filled with blood, or meat, or my cum..."

"You're fucking crazy!" I screeched at the door.

"Some would say."

"*Everyone* would say!"

"I don't think so. Not the people who count."

"Who? Josh?" Honey cried. "Do you really think even your best friend will understand all this?"

"Maybe not." The stairs creaked, and Josh stepped into the dim light. Aiming a gun at Honey, he said, "But his brother would."

He fired, and the bullet spun her before dropping her like a rock. I fell beside her, holding my sleeve to her hemorrhaging wound as my ears rang and I tried to call her panicked gaze to mine.

James pounded on the door. "Where's she hit?"

Flipping the lock and letting him in, Josh gestured flatly at us. "It's just a shoulder wound. She'll be fine."

I grabbed the shovel and swung it at the boys. I missed by a mile but quickly swung again, clipping Josh's elbow as he stumbled backward, in a mix of surprise and fascination. Swinging again, I hit his hand and knocked the gun free, darkening his expression.

Aiming for the darkness, I swung again and sliced his chin as he fell against the door. I was about to bring the shovel down on his head when I heard a whimper.

"Eva..."

Honey's face was slimy white in James's hands. His fingers tightened around her skull, crushing her, trying to smash her flat like a triple-decker sandwich he wanted to taste entirely in one bite.

"Get your hands off her!" I wheeled around to smack James with the shovel, but fingers suddenly clamped the back of my neck, and hard, hot metal pressed against my cheek.

Josh's breath flared against my neck and he took the shovel. "Let him have his fun."

Honey wept as James kissed the gunshot wound, then her cheek, her forehead, her chin, leaving bloody lip-prints on her face.

"You call this fun?" I growled, and his fingers twitched on my neck.

"It doesn't matter what I think. I'm just here to make sure he's safe, one last time."

James sucked a drop of blood from Honey's ear. "That's right, baby. This is the big finale. Our last dance. Then big bro and me are off to see the world and suck the marrow outta life. Maybe outta some French chicks too."

"You sick fucks, you're out of your minds," I spat, and James released Honey to gaze up at Josh in wide-eyed reverence.

"No, not him. My brother is a saint. He's a goddamn superhero."

"A superhero that kills people?"

"No!" James smacked the floor beside Honey's head, and she curled into a ball. "Josh has never killed anyone! He protects me. He loves me. Even when he doesn't like me."

Josh's grip loosened. "James—"

"Don't deny it. I know how hard it is for you to stomach this stuff. I know you wish you had a normal life. No secrets."

"You're my little brother. No life would be normal without you," he said. "Or without secrets."

"Most people would have turned me away, turned me in, but you stuck with me through everything. I don't say it enough, but I love you, Josh. I appreciate every sacrifice, and I'm sorry I can't be a superhero like you."

"You don't have to be anyone other than yourself, Jay. You didn't deserve this curse. You didn't deserve what that bastard did to you."

When he noticed me silently urging Honey to crawl away, James smacked her across the face, pinned her to the floor by the throat, and said, "Neither did you."

Josh shuddered and readjusted his grip on the gun.

I whispered, "What happened to you?" and he whirled me around to face him, pressing the gun against my chest.

He gave me an irate look that melted into one of sorrow. His eyes searched my face, perhaps looking for something in me that would give him the courage to speak, to finally tell me the truth about his past.

"Mr. Reavers." James spat the name like it tasted bitter. "He was our neighbor."

"Shut up, Jay. You always do this. Why do we have to relive it every fucking time you get your hands on a girl?"

"It's the blood." He squeezed Honey's shoulder, the wound oozed, and her tears streamed. "It's like any other intoxicant; it makes me introspective."

"You don't owe them an explanation."

"But the more she empathizes with me," James said, inhaling her screams, "the more she'll want to give me what I need. She'll beg for it. Like Marlene did."

"You're disgusting," Honey burbled.

"Amongst other things. Gifts from the next-door neighbor," he said. "I wasn't the same after that. Neither of us were. And our parents couldn't handle it. It was hard for Josh to handle it too, but he did. He *does*. Over and over, he accepts me for who I am." He pulled out his gun and released Honey's neck. "I wanted you to be the same way. I thought you would be. But that's not who you are, and I can't fault you for that. Especially since you gave me so much. You made me feel capable of being loved, and capable of loving you without needing to hurt you. But your love made me realize I still need to get that aggression out *somewhere*." He hissed in her face. "Or maybe I don't need it. Maybe I just like it."

She sobbed, but he muffled it with a kiss.

"Josh, please, stop this. You can leave like you planned. We won't tell anyone."

"We..." He hummed. "You mean you and your girlfriend?"

"What do you want me to say?"

"There's nothing you can say, Birdie. And frankly, if you don't like this situation, you have no one to blame but yourself. I tried to spare you the pain. I planted that underwear in his car so he and Honey would break up. Then, his feelings for her wouldn't have tortured him so much. He would've killed her quick and clean like he wanted—"

"Not that clean," he muttered.

"—fine, but it would've been over. He would've found his peace. And with her out of way, you and I could've been happy. But you had to have her around all the time, so you insisted they stay together. You refused to accept what *we* had was the best thing for you. *I* was the best thing for you. Well, look at us now, Birdie, because I'm about to be the worst fucking thing that's ever happened to you."

I whimpered, the gun barrel grinding against my

breastbone. "I was leaving."

"You should've. You could've. But no, you had to throw a fucking party. Now everyone here is going to die because of you."

He was right. I thought my one good decision to move away would somehow derail the future bad decisions, for a while at least, but it seemed making mistakes was my default state, and my errant life had dragged down everyone in my orbit too. People I cared about. People I loved.

Honey wailed as James plunged his finger into her bullet wound, and I begged him to stop.

"You wouldn't say that if you knew how it felt. It's not like sex. It's always fucking spectacular. The first time, the fifteenth time, every goddamn time." He sucked the blood off his finger noisily, then dipped it back inside for another taste.

"You won't get away with this" I said. "The police are probably on their way. Someone called the cops when that biker dude started going off. I know it."

Josh pushed me to the floor beside Honey, where James trained his weapon on both of us. "Maybe," he said. "But the reception's kinda intentionally shitty out here, so I doubt it. Besides…" At the computer, Josh pulled up a few windows, typed in a few passwords, then clicked a button to reformat the hard drive. "We've been getting away with it since he was thirteen."

"Thanks to you, bro."

The shared devotion and esteem between the siblings froze my blood. It wouldn't matter how hard we pleaded, James was going to kill us, and Josh was going to let it happen. The epitome of brotherly love.

"There has to be something we can do to change your mind," Honey said, her voice weak and grasping. "James, please, anything."

"You couldn't handle it. You didn't even like having sex on your period, which, I have to admit, is pretty uptight for a chick who flexes her asshole to the beat of "Country Roads" onstage."

"I'll do anything you want." She clutched at his shirt. "Whatever makes you happy, I'll do it. I want to do it."

"You do?"

"Yes," she purred as evenly as possible. "I wish you'd told me about these...desires. I would have behaved differently. I would have been more open. More...fluid. I can be everything you want me to be now."

"That makes me so happy, Honey. Thank you for saying that." He danced his fingertips down her chest. "But it makes me much happier thinking about wearing your ribcage as a vest."

She sobbed as he clawed at her blood-soaked breasts, and Josh pulled me to my feet. I wanted to cover my ears, but I couldn't move. I couldn't speak. All I could do was imagine how I'd die. Or more accurately, how long I'd live until James let me die. How long did it take him to find his peace with Diamond or Cherry? Did Destiny watch every moment as he split her open and sweetened her offal?

In contemplating what time remained, I also thought of the life unlived. So much left undone. So many things done improperly. I'd had some fun, but as Honey had once said, it was borrowed joy. I'd made a mess of my life, and I'd run out of chances to clean up my act. The show was over. The curtain was falling.

Somewhere else, somewhere safer, someone with a long life ahead started an episode of *Gargoyles*. Just before Josh's gun bashed against my head, I heard a deep, resounding voice.

"It was a time of darkness. It was a world of fear..."

CHAPTER EIGHTEEN

I woke up alone on the dirty kitchen floor. The bandana in my mouth tasted like miso soup with a bloody bone broth, and my tongue was so dry, crunched into the back of my throat, I felt like I might choke every time I swallowed. Blood stiffened the corners of my mouth, but any tiny movement of the gag reopened the cuts, stabbing my cheeks with pain that echoed under the cord shredding my bound wrists and ankles. And beneath it all, running throughout my body, a persistent, agonizing, pounding: the rhythm of every wound uniting against me, within me.

When I heard laughter, followed by a *slam!slam!siiigh*, I realized the pounding existed without me too. Scrunching up against the oven, I cowered at the soundscape in the next room. Whimpering, gurgling, then feet hitting the floor, coming to find me.

"Look who's awake," James sang at me when he strode into the kitchen, his hard naked body glazed in blood. It coated his face so thickly, his goatee looked like an internal organ, soaked through, thick and dripping. And though he whistled as he searched for the perfect knife, his lips were too sticky to hold the tune.

I screamed as loud as I could, and James chuckled. With a knife selected, he bent over me and patted my head.

"Be patient. I'll get to you soon."

Less than a minute after he returned to the bedroom, I heard her dying. *Honey. Martha.* She didn't deserve this. She deserved to be on that posh little island with a fruity drink in her freshly manicured hand. Or in a spa. Or smoking weed on a sofa. With me.

The house vibrated with gut-wrenching noises that sounded like James ripping apart carpets and tenderizing steaks. The whirring sound of an electric carving knife got me fighting harder against my bindings as I tried to wriggle across the kitchen floor. The cord was no looser, only bloodier, and I'd only crossed half the kitchen when James returned, his scarlet feet squelching on the linoleum.

"Time to play, Birdie." He crouched by me, holding the dripping knife to my face. "My brother told me you like to play hard. He told me you like that sick Hentai shit." He stroked my thigh with the knife. "This should be right up your alley."

I tried to say, "fuck you," but it sounded like "farfegnugen." He pulled down the bandana and asked me to repeat myself.

"Fuck you." I stretched my jaw. "Where's Honey?"

"Oh…here and there.."

My heart ached so intensely my stomach cramped. "You fucking monster."

"*I'm* the monster? You just confirmed you never even cared for my brother by asking where your lezzie lover is instead of him. He's the one who needs concern and love. Honey had all she wanted and more. But Josh… he's given up everything for me, and he never asks for anything in return. When you two met, I thought he'd finally found someone who could give up something for *him*."

"*You* could," I said wearily.

"What?"

"Give up something." I tried to lick my lips, but my tongue was still too dry, so I summoned what spit I could and said raspily, "You could do your big brother the biggest favor ever. You could kill yourself."

His lips quivered into a snarl, and he howled like a mad chimp in my face. Grabbing me by the ponytail, he dragged me across the kitchen floor and hurled me onto the bed. I'd screamed the entire way, but it was nothing compared to the guttural sounds of revulsion that escaped me when I beheld my bedmate.

Her mangled hands were still attached to the headboard, but her arms were not. And the rest of her was so jumbled up, with panels of skin removed from her legs and belly, she didn't even look human. Just piles of meat. The way he'd always seen us Pins girls.

I tried to verify it was Honey, but the girl's face was across the room, drying on a dresser. It wasn't until I took stock of the shoes on the floor that I realized who this woman was. Her foot was severed but still strapped in, still onstage somewhere. Shasta, in her shiny sling-back stilettos.

James cleared her off the bed with a couple clumsy slaps and kicks, then pulled out his phone. "I can't post this right now, of course, but it's going to be a good one." He brayed. "A good tweet, *Birdie*."

No one wanted to die on social media, but the thought of James spraying my guts across Twitter in 280 characters or fewer was more revolting than any alternative, and nearly as nauseating as watching Shasta's face slowly slip off the dresser.

When he finished, he climbed on the bed and tried to roll me over. I screamed and thrashed as hard as I could, but it only took him one jab to my face to stop my struggling. My eyes filled with tears, my nose filled with blood.

He rolled me over and secured my hands next to one of Shasta's. He yanked my shirt up to my armpits, then scooped his hand under my hips to unzip my pants. I cried into the pillow when he cut the cord on my ankles and tugged my pants down.

"Don't sound so sad. You'll enjoy yourself." James purred against my back. "Come on, Birdie, trust me."

I shuddered violently when his fingers moved between my legs, then froze when the cold blade pressed into the small of my back.

"On second thought, maybe you don't deserve to enjoy yourself. If I cut your spinal cord, you won't feel a thing. And you won't fight. You'll let me do whatever I want."

He carved into my back, and I wailed.

"No…if I do that, you won't scream, and I like it when you scream. It's so sexy." He sighed. "The rest of you isn't bad either, but it's just so…I don't know… bare. Have you ever thought about getting a tattoo?"

I craned to look at him, but my vision went bleary.

"How about a tramp stamp? A girl like you really needs a tramp stamp. What do you want? A butterfly? A heart? How about the word 'bitch?' You Pins girls call each other 'bitch' and 'whore' as terms of endearment, don't you? That would be the perfect tramp stamp, don't you think? A badge of honor *and* a red flag."

With a chuckle, he pierced my skin. It was like no pain I'd ever felt, the worst, the most terrifying and degrading—or so I thought before the knife started moving.

"I don't usually devote this much time to someone I've never fucked, but you're different, Birdie. You remind me of her. Chastity. The prettiest girl in school."

I sobbed as he curved the blade through my flesh.

"She was the one who made me realize how much pleasure this gave me. Not at first, of course. We did normal kid stuff, covered a few bases. But I wanted more. She wanted it too, I could tell, but we were still so young, and she was scared. I was honestly shocked she liked me. She liked the strong silent type, she said, and we got along great. I really loved her, you know? But she didn't know what I was staying silent about. And she didn't know how strong I was. Honestly, neither did I until—" He twisted the knife into my back in way that felt like dotting the "I". "Her love taught me so many lessons."

I panted. "Like your neighbor?"

His thighs squeezed me hard. "No. There was no love in what he did. Plus, he only liked his own blood. He liked to be watched while he bled. He liked to be touched while he bled. It was all about him. This," he said, drawing closer, "is a shared experience."

"Sounds like you've had lots of shared experiences. Maybe you're the one who needs a tramp stamp."

He chuckled. "What can I say? I've never been satisfied with just one gash."

"I'm sorry that happened to you. I'm sorry it turned you into this."

The room was so silent I heard him gulp. Just when I thought I might've found a weak spot, he resumed carving into me, and I wailed under the searing weight of his trauma.

"Josh is the one to feel sorry for. He carries around so much guilt for not protecting me from Mr. Reavers. That asshole hurt him too, but he didn't bleed himself in front of Josh. He spared him that part of the curse, and I think it's because Reavers must've seen a hint of it already in me somewhere. Like a vampire smelling out a nest of its own kind. Not Josh, though. He was too good." He crossed the "T" and dragged the first line of an "H." "Sometimes I think he'd be happier if Reavers hadn't spared him. Sometimes I think he wishes we were the same. But there's still plenty of time for that."

He flicked the knife one more time, and as the bed shifted, something wet slid across my wounds, and I heard James smacking his lips.

"You taste like her."

"Who?" I whimpered.

"It doesn't matter."

His nails dug into my ribs and he lowered his body to mine. One hand moved into my hair, gripping it tight while the other moved between my legs. Then he stopped.

"Are you sure you don't want a go? For old times' sake?"

I swiveled to see Josh standing in the doorway, eyes averted.

"No, thanks."

"She won't be any good when I'm done with her."

"I figured," he said, finally bringing himself to meet my gaze.

"How's Honey?"

My heart raced, and I wriggled until James pressed my face into the pillow.

"She's trying to chew through the ropes. How much longer are you going to be?"

"Did you see?" James sat up to show off his handiwork. "Appropriate, don't you think?"

"Very," Josh said dryly. "How much longer?"

"She needs more work. She's not wet enough."

"Don't tell me that shit. Just do what you need to do as fast as you can so we can get out of here."

"It's not about doing it fast."

"Believe me, I know."

"Josh…" He looked at me again. I knew he wouldn't help me, but he seemed sad about it. "Will you tell Honey I said goodbye? Will you tell her I said she was my best friend? Will you do that for me."

"Yeah, sure," he said shakily and cleared his throat. "You're right. She needs more work."

When I moaned in fear, James chirped. "I have the perfect idea. My new pizza cutter!"

"I wish you wouldn't call it that. We both know it's

not for pizza," Josh said.

"But it looks like one. What else am I supposed to call it?" He leapt up and threw on a robe. "Is it in the kitchen?"

"No, because it's not for pizza." Spotting the other instruments of torture around the room, he groaned. "Jesus, James, we have a safe full of tools for this shit, and you're using whatever you find in the kitchen? Are you going to use a fucking whisk next?"

"Who knows? I'm resourceful."

"And I'm nauseous. I need some air." He glanced at me again, then pointed at his brother. "Hurry the fuck up."

I tugged at my cords, but I stopped when the knife stabbed the pillow beside my face. One quivering eye stared back at me in the blade's reflection; the rest was too russet to reflect.

"Stay, little bird." He withdrew the knife out of the bed, then leaned it against my ear. "And listen."

The blade moved so quickly I didn't know he'd cut me until the basin of my ear filled with fluid. Once I was alone, I shook my head and blood emptied across the pillow, but it had pooled long enough to clog my right ear. Hollow sounds from behind me made my mind whir with thoughts of what James had in store next. I closed my eyes, tilted my head to the left, allowed my blood to deafen me.

My hands jerked suddenly and fell loose of the bindings. I barely had time to question it before I felt someone's arms around me, pulling me from the bed. I could barely hear, barely see, and the pain that charged through every molecule made me want to cry out, but everything about the way my rescuer guided me to the window instructed me to be quiet. There, the moonlight illuminated his scowl.

"I'm going to get you out of here," said Scott.

I nodded, and he quickly locked the bedroom door

as I winced through pulling up my pants. He opened the window and helped me climb out.

"Scott, what are you doing here?"

He shut the window behind us. "Following you as usual." Holding out a hammer and wrench, he said, "It's all I could find. Which one?"

I took the hammer. "Thanks."

"Bet you're glad I was following you now."

My waistband brushed against the fresh tattoo, and I grunted. "We'll talk about that later. Much later. If we get the chance…"

"The police are on their way. I had to go miles away to get a signal, but I got them. We're going to be okay." Scott said, letting me lean on him as we rushed from the house. "They told me to wait in my car, but I couldn't. I didn't know what was happening to you. After I saw the house—the bodies—and what he was doing to you—" He squeezed my hand, and pain surged throughout my arm, but it was worth it. "Come on, my car's on the other side of the house."

I stopped abruptly. "We can't leave Honey."

"Eva, it's a miracle I got you out."

"I don't care. I am not leaving without her." I started back to the house, and he rushed after.

"Goddammit. Okay. I think I might've seen her in the living room."

We ran around the house, creeping past the blood-spattered windows. When we reached the living room, I instantly regretted peering inside. Clamping my hand over my mouth, I sank to the earth beneath the window and choked back the burning vomit.

"I see her," Scott said. "I can get her." He fished out his car keys and shoved them into my palm. Grabbing me by the wrist, he tugged me from the house, past the bonfire, and to his car. "Get in, lock up, and start the car. If one of those bastards comes out, you drive, do you hear me? Whether Honey and I are with you or not, drive."

Scott opened the door, and the dark interior whispered, "That's good advice."

Josh was in the passenger seat with a cigarette and a gun, one of which he flicked at me, the other, he fired at Scott.

The bullet propelled him backward onto the rocks, where he lay motionless as I smacked away the cigarette burning a hole in my shirt. I ran to him, started to check if he was still alive, but Josh fired again, and grabbing the wrench, I took off into the woods. My wounds seared, and my breath thinned, and when a patch of brambles snagged my shirt and wouldn't let go, I thought I might pass out.

Then I heard her. She called my name. We were both still here.

"Honey."

I tore myself free of the thorns and crept back through the woods. Peering out from behind a tree, I saw Scott on the ground. He was moving now, gripping the gunshot wound in his belly. James was by the bonfire. He had Honey by the hair with the scariest damn pizza cutter I'd ever seen hovering an inch from her throat.

"Come back to us, Birdie," James cooed. "Or I'll do things to your girlfriend that disturb even me."

Josh stood on the other side of the bonfire, scanning the perimeter of the woods. "Come on, Birdie. We know you're out there. We know you wouldn't abandon your best friend."

James tugged Honey's hair, twisting her neck to the left as he pressed the cutter just under her ear. The smallest amount of pressure caused a spurt of blood that instantly made Honey droop. But James wiggling his tongue over the wound revived her, and she screeched in disgust.

I felt like I was going to puke out of every wound. My guts told me to run—I should've been halfway to the highway already—or hide—just wait it out, the cops would be there soon—but peering toward the house at Honey and Scott, my guts couldn't convince my heart to agree. Maybe I was making yet another gigantic mistake, but I could live with it, even if I didn't.

With a stabilizing breath, I lifted the hammer and wrench and crept closer to the tree line beside the bonfire.

"I hear something." James pushed Honey into Josh's arms. "Give me the gun."

"It's out of ammo."

"She doesn't know that. Take the cutter. If Martha gives you any trouble, feel free to spill the Honey."

"I'm not doing that, James."

He took Josh's gun and shoved the people-cutter into his hand. "Yes, you goddamn will."

James entered the woods closer to me than I expected. I didn't want to prolong him singing my name and making kissy noises like he was calling a cat, but I would've preferred a longer pursuit so I could summon more courage. When only a few trees separated us, I held my breath and tried to keep my toes as still as possible. After a few more steps, I glanced from behind the tree, and seeing the firelight upon his face, saw my opportunity to shine.

I flew out of hiding with the wrench and hammer swinging wildly. I don't think he even got a good look at me before the hammer nailed him between the eyes, but I was damn sure he wouldn't be able to look at anything else afterward. He dropped the gun to grab his face, and the wrench got there first, snapping a few of his fingers like celery and bashing in his nose. He roared as my tools took bites out of him, pushing him out of the woods and stumbling backwards onto the loose stone lining of the fire pit.

Then gravity took over.

As James toppled backwards onto the fire, I dashed

to the bottles of lighter fluid on the edge of the clearing. Josh screamed as he ran toward us, dragging Honey behind him. I lunged at him with the hammer, but he swung the people-cutter first, ripping a jagged gash in my arm. He raised it to strike again when an inhuman screeching erupted around us. As Honey squeezed all the lighter fluid into the fire, she howled in furious vindication at her ex-boyfriend's face melting off his skull.

Josh shoved her aside and wrapped himself around James's burning body. Pulling him free, he dropped him on the driveway and thrashed against him: one brother on fire trying to extinguish the other. He first covered James with the blankets lining the log benches and worked to suffocate the flames, then removed his own smoldering clothes. When he was certain the fire was out, Josh pulled off the blanket. He cringed, a sob caught in his throat like a lump of chicken gristle. He leaned over the smoking corpse and kissed him. Pieces of melted flesh clung to his lips when he pulled back, still sizzling when he turned his gaze to Honey and me.

"You're fucking dead," he said. "Both of you."

He'd never been so fast, so strong. It was his grief that chased us, not him, and it caught us without trying because our grief had been reaching out just as desperately. We ran, but Josh caught hold of my arm and whipped me against a car. My face hit the window with a wet crack, and I spat out a wad of grainy blood before wilting to the ground.

Jumping on top of me, he pinned my arms under his knees. "You killed him, you bitch! My little brother. My poor little brother." He closed his hands around my throat. "You ruined everything. You ruined my life!"

"Josh, please—" I squeaked.

"Say 'please' again, bitch. Say you're sorry. Say you loved me. Say everything you can for as long as you can. Keep pleading and I'll keep squeezing."

"Josh!" Honey screamed, and when he turned his head, she swung the hammer at his face.

It crushed his cheek with a squelchy snap that made her cringe but didn't stop her. She swung again, hitting his temple and knocking him off me. He crumpled to the ground, his head caved in and the whites of his eyes quickly turning crimson. I wasn't sure if he could see us when we leaned over him, but his eyes managed to fix on mine. They were so dark with blood that there was no trace of the rich brown irises I'd loved so.

"You killed him. You killed my brother." Then he smiled. "I fucking adore you, Birdie."

The words rode his last exhalation, and when his face went slack, Honey began to sob. But I was too tired to join her. I took the hammer out of her hand, and with my last ounce of strength, I brought it down one more time and took out one of Josh's scarlet eyes.

"I've seen enough movies."

I tossed the hammer aside, but my hand wasn't empty for long. Honey slipped her hand into mine and pressed her lips against it. She whispered "thank you" against my skin, and the resulting shiver summoned tears I didn't know I had left. She held me and didn't let go even when I told her I was okay. I was grateful for that. If she'd let go, I might've crumbled into a thousand pieces.

CHAPTER NINETEEN

I'd never been so happy to see cops. As much as I wanted to chide them for being late, I couldn't help thanking them with every other breath. EMTs tended to Scott and Honey first, and I was glad to let them while I explained the night's events to the police. I'd reached the part about my impromptu tattoo when it began feeling like someone was whipping me across the back. My body had been pumped full of so much pain and adrenaline, I'd forgotten just how bad my wounds were. The "bitch" on my back brought me to my knees, and Honey abandoned the ambulance to run to my side. She held my hand as a whirling darkness claimed every sense but that which let me feel her.

When I regained consciousness, there was an oxygen mask on my face, and an EMT was cleaning and dressing my various wounds while a policewoman told Honey they'd found some other survivors. She said some names, but I didn't recognize them. I only knew their stage names.

When someone screamed, I thought maybe I wasn't sucking fresh oxygen, surrounded by cops. Maybe I was still on that bed, waiting for James to return with the people-cutter. Maybe I was already dead, and the only heaven I'd ever know was in the glance Honey

Potter tossed my way.

But then I heard the struggle between a woman and the police, and I recognized the scream. I sat up, removed the oxygen mask, and gawked at Jade shoving the barrier of officers.

"What happened? Honey, Birdie, are you okay? Let me through!"

She didn't break through them as effectively as through Cecil while in her wedding dress, but when Honey explained that Jade and Braidbeard had been at the party, they allowed the couple to cross the line. As I embraced Jade, I saw my reflection in the police cruiser window and inhaled sharply.

"I can follow you all to the hospital," Braidbeard said.

"Thanks, Jeff." Honey bopped her head at me. "Birdie, why don't you ride with Scott, and Jade can come with me?"

I tongued my chipped teeth. "There's something I have to do first. But I'll meet you there."

"What are you talking about? You need medical attention."

"I'll be okay."

"At least ask one of the EMTs for a painkiller or something," Jade said, and I shook my head.

"No. I'm done with all that. Pills, powder, everything."

"What about weed?" Honey asked.

"What?"

"Are you done with weed? When you move back to Westminster, I mean."

"Well…" I crinkled my nose. "Probably not."

"Good. I just know it's hard when one person in the house smokes and the other one doesn't, and I'd like to keep smoking."

"What are you talking about?"

She wiped a rosy tear from her blood-stained face.

"I want to go with you. To Westminster, to Mars… wherever you go, I want to go with you."

She was in too much pain to smile, but her shooting star of a dimple appeared anyway.

"You mean it?"

She nodded, and I started to throw myself into her embrace, but I stopped. I didn't want to hurt her. Luckily for us both, she didn't have the same worry. Crying in gratitude, she pulled me into her arms, and all the hurt that rang through me rang through her just as loudly until we felt nothing but each other: two weeping women drowning each other's pain.

"Where are you going?"

"I need to check on Fidelio. Then I'm going to Westminster."

"Now?"

"I'll be back as soon as possible, I promise. There's just not much time left to sign up."

Honey released me from her embrace. I thought she was angry at first, but then she cupped my face and pressed her lips against my forehead. As the EMTs escorted her away, Jade and Braidbeard wrapped their arms around me.

"I can check on Fidelio," Braidbeard said. "You have a spare key?"

I nodded, tearfully. "You'd do that?"

"Of course I would."

"He's a good 'un." Jade pinched her husband's cheek and bopped his nose.

"Yes, he is. I don't know how you did it, Jade. All of this horror, and you got something genuinely good out of it. You found someone to love."

She tilted her head. "Didn't you do the same thing?"

Honey waved at me from the ambulance, and a trembling smile bloomed on my face. I tried to answer, but she patted my shoulder like it wasn't necessary.

"I'll see you later, Eva."

"See you later, Jes."

The best part was knowing "see you later" didn't just mean at the hospital or the time leading up to moving day. For the first time ever, I knew I'd been seeing Jade later for a long time to come.

My car keys had gotten lost in the shuffle, but I found Scott in a blood-speckled mud puddle next to his car. With the key in the ignition and my aching ass in the driver's seat, I stared ahead at the house, at the crime scene. It seemed every minute another body appeared on a gurney. Some moved, most didn't. But I was glad the rescue team was tending to the partygoers before the hosts. I couldn't see Josh from Scott's car, but I knew he was close. If I craned to the side a bit, I could see—

The emergency lights shifted, and the ambulance carrying Honey reversed out of the driveway. As if in a trance, I followed it, thinking maybe she'd peer out the back like a mischievous kid in a school bus. But I only saw her in my imagination, and when the woods opened up to the highway, I saw the morning sun for the first time in what felt like ages.

The drive gave me plenty of time to talk myself out of my newfound confidence, as I'd done countless times before. Hundreds of nagging voices pervaded my mind. They called me fat, ugly, stupid, weak: all the judgments I was afraid I'd never shake, no matter how many enemies I defeated. When the Westminster Community Center came into view, I squirmed in my seat, and the bitch on my back joined the chorus.

But I didn't listen to any of them. Maybe they were right, but it didn't matter anymore, because when I looked in the mirror, I didn't see any of the things they called me. Sure, my clothes were filthy, and I was still caked in blood, some of which cracked when I moved and caused my scrapes to weep again. Yes, my matted muddy hair fell in my face, and clods of dead grass occasionally fell out. And of course my entire backside was soaked through with blood when I got out of the car. But despite my ghastly appearance, I marched into that building like I was taking the stage at Pins. Everything else fell away. It was just me and the droves of suckers eager to empty their wallets.

With the pageant only a week away, the Community Center bustled with preparations, but everyone stilled as I stomped through the room and approached the signup table.

I barely recognized the woman behind it. Her hair had grayed since the last time I saw her, but it looked good. A perfect bouquet of silver swooping just so across her forehead.

She didn't recognize me either, though I could hardly blame her.

"Birdie? Is that you?"

"Yeah. Hi, Hollie."

Grace approached from behind my sister, red-faced, teeth clenched. "What are *you* doing here?"

I answered by snatching the pen from her hand and an application from the table.

"Is that blood?" Hollie asked. "Jesus, what happened to you?"

"Save the questions for the onstage interview," I said, scrawling down my information.

"She's not a judge," Grace said. "And I'm competing, remember? County Queen, three years running."

Signing my name, I slammed down the bloody application. "You can say goodbye to year four."

As I walked out the door, a young girl strode in carrying a red velvet cushion on which the winner's prized crown sparkled exquisitely, even under the cheap community center lights.

"That's a nice crown," I said to her. "Sequins?"

She shook her head. "Glitter."

"Wild."

She crinkled her nose. "Are you okay?"

"Yeah," I replied and looked over my shoulder at my sister gawking at me from the table. "Nothing a little glitter won't fix."

Scott's phone was ringing in the glove compartment when I returned to the car. I didn't recognize the number, but I answered it, and I was so fucking happy I did.

"Hey, it's me," Honey said. "I just wanted to make sure you got there okay."

I exhaled happily when I heard her voice, and tears nipped my eyes.

"Yes, I'm fine. I'm heading back now."

"Good. Scott's in surgery, but they cleared me." She whispered shakily. "I'm all alone."

"Not for long. I'll be there soon."

There was silence then, but somehow, I knew it was the good kind. The "I love you so much, I can't speak" kind.

"Honey, can I tell you something?"

"Of course."

"Here's the thing," I started. "Over the past few months, I've made a lot of money and had a lot of fun—well, except for all of the murders...and the past few hours..."

"Yeah, I was going to say..."

"But of the parts that were good, there was only one genuinely good thing," I said. "It was you. You were the best thing about my time at Pins, and you still are. I think we're going to be happy in Westminster. Because—" My smile stretched the cuts on my face, but I couldn't feel the pain. "I want to see if I can do it."

"Do what?"

"What you offered before. I wanna try to get to second base."

Her voice broke. "Really?"

"Hang in there. We'll be together before you know it." I ended the call with a soft "goodbye" my mind left against her lips.

Eager drives tended to drag, but as if sensing my need to be in her arms, the universe granted me one note of good luck. I was one of few cars on the road, making the ride a breeze. And I wasn't even wearing my luckies. I probably wouldn't wear them again, but I doubted I'd throw them away. They would be tucked away in a drawer, a dingy reminder of the best and worst time in my life, while the most important mementos would be displayed and held and loved proudly.

Honey was the most obvious.

But there was also me.

I didn't know what would happen when Honey and I moved to Westminster, or when I made the monumental journey from her mountains to her deep south, but I wasn't afraid. For the first time, I felt genuinely powerful— and sexy as hell. Gazing into the rear-view mirror, I didn't see my bloody face, chipped teeth, or my disfigured ear.

I saw a beauty queen.

Who Is
Jessica McHugh?

Jessica McHugh is a 3x Bram Stoker Award-nominated poet, a multi-genre novelist, & an internationally-produced playwright. She's had thirty books published in fifteen years, including her Elgin Award-nominated blackout poetry collection, "A Complex Accident of Life," her sci-fi bizarro romp, "The Green Kangaroos," and her cross-generational horror series, "The Gardening Guidebooks Trilogy." Explore the growing worlds of Jessica McHugh at McHughniverse.com.